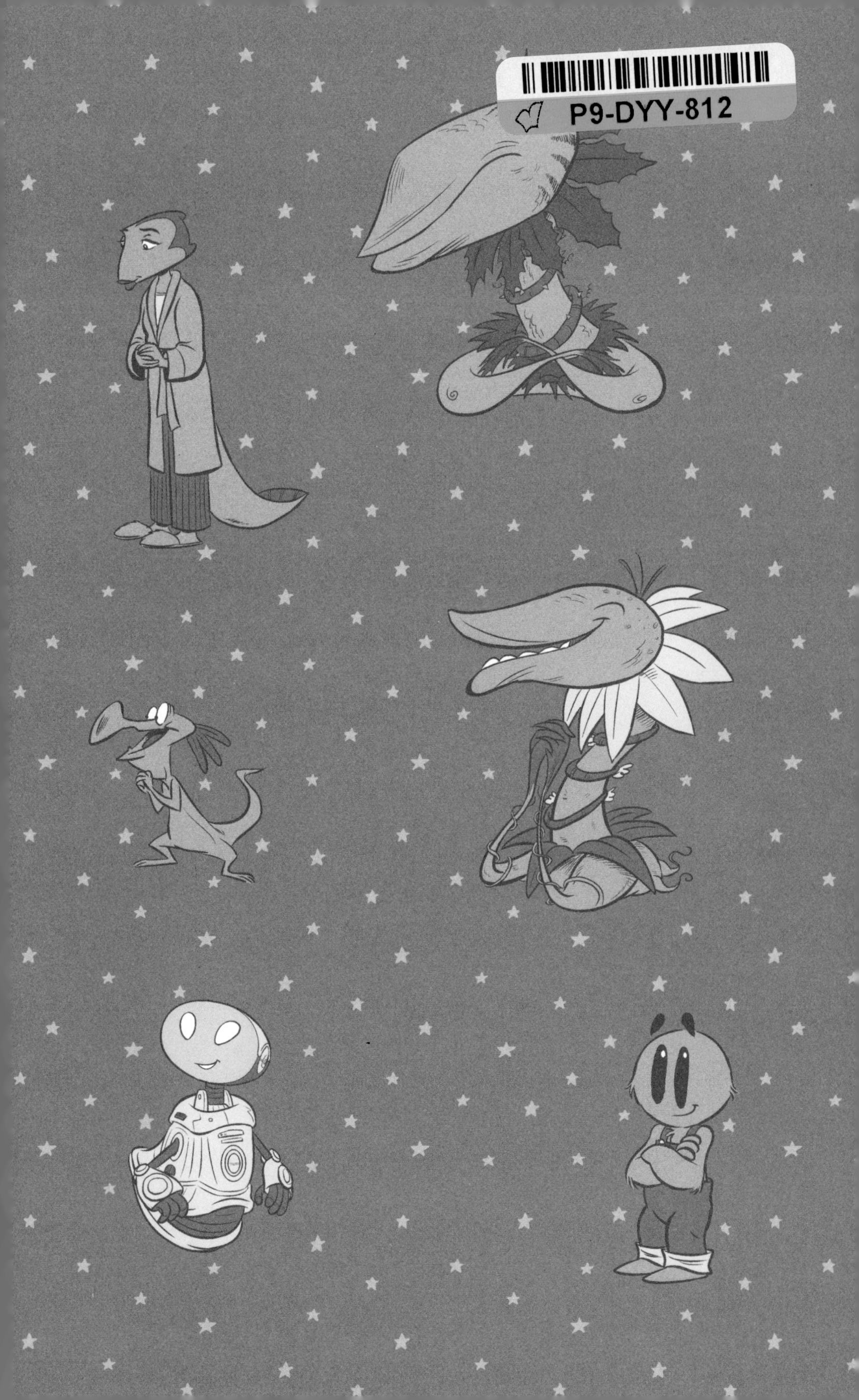

Eddie Pittman

Red's Planet

2

FRIENDS AND FOES™

AMULET BOOKS
NEW YORK

Cataloging-in-Publication Data has been applied for and may
be obtained from the Library of Congress.

ISBN 978-1-4197-2314-8 (hardback)
ISBN 978-1-4197-2315-5 (paperback)

Book design by Eddie Pittman and Chad W. Beckerman

Published in 2017 by Amulet Books, an imprint of ABRAMS.

Printed and bound in China
10 9 8 7 6 5 4 3 2 1

ABRAMS The Art of Books
115 West 18th Street, New York, NY 10011
abramsbooks.com

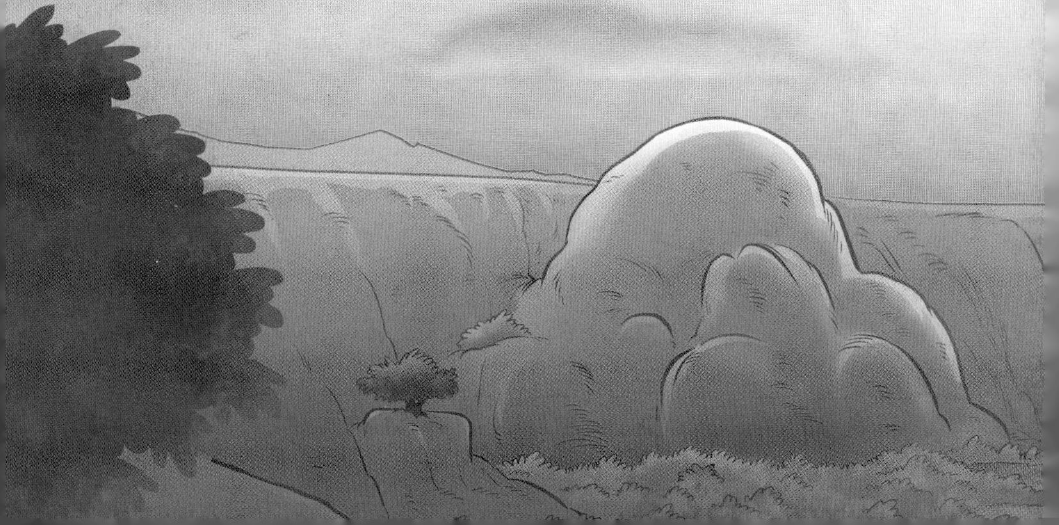

To Ginny and Teagan—
my first and most important audience

Thanks to:

Beth Pittman, for her support, encouragement, and help along the journey.

Ginny Pittman, Jose Mari Flores, Rachel Polk, John Steventon, and Scott Ball for their production assistance.

Charlie Kochman, Andrew Smith, Jody Mosley, Amy Vreeland, Chad W. Beckerman, Maya Bradford, Trish McNamara, and the whole amazing team at Abrams for their continued support.

My wonderful agent, Judy Hansen.

And all the librarians, booksellers, and Red's Planet fans whom I've had the chance to meet over the past year; your enthusiasm keeps me going.

Made on a Wacom Cintiq.

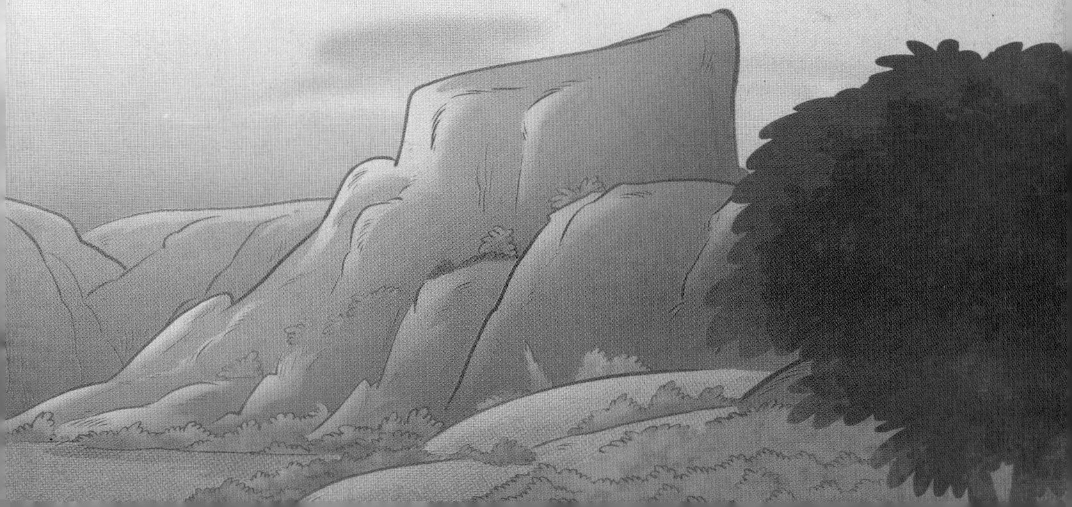

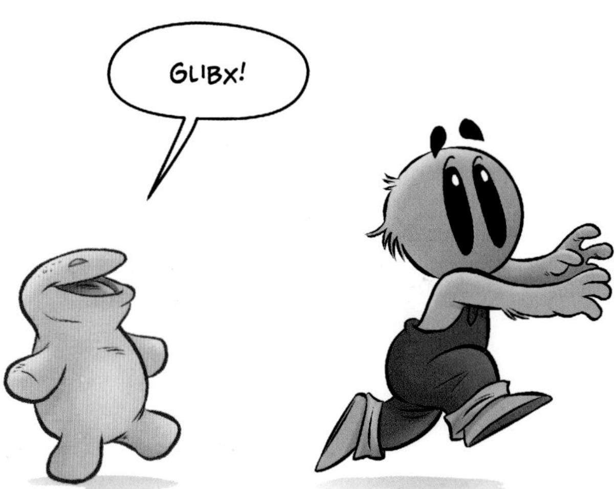
GLIBX!

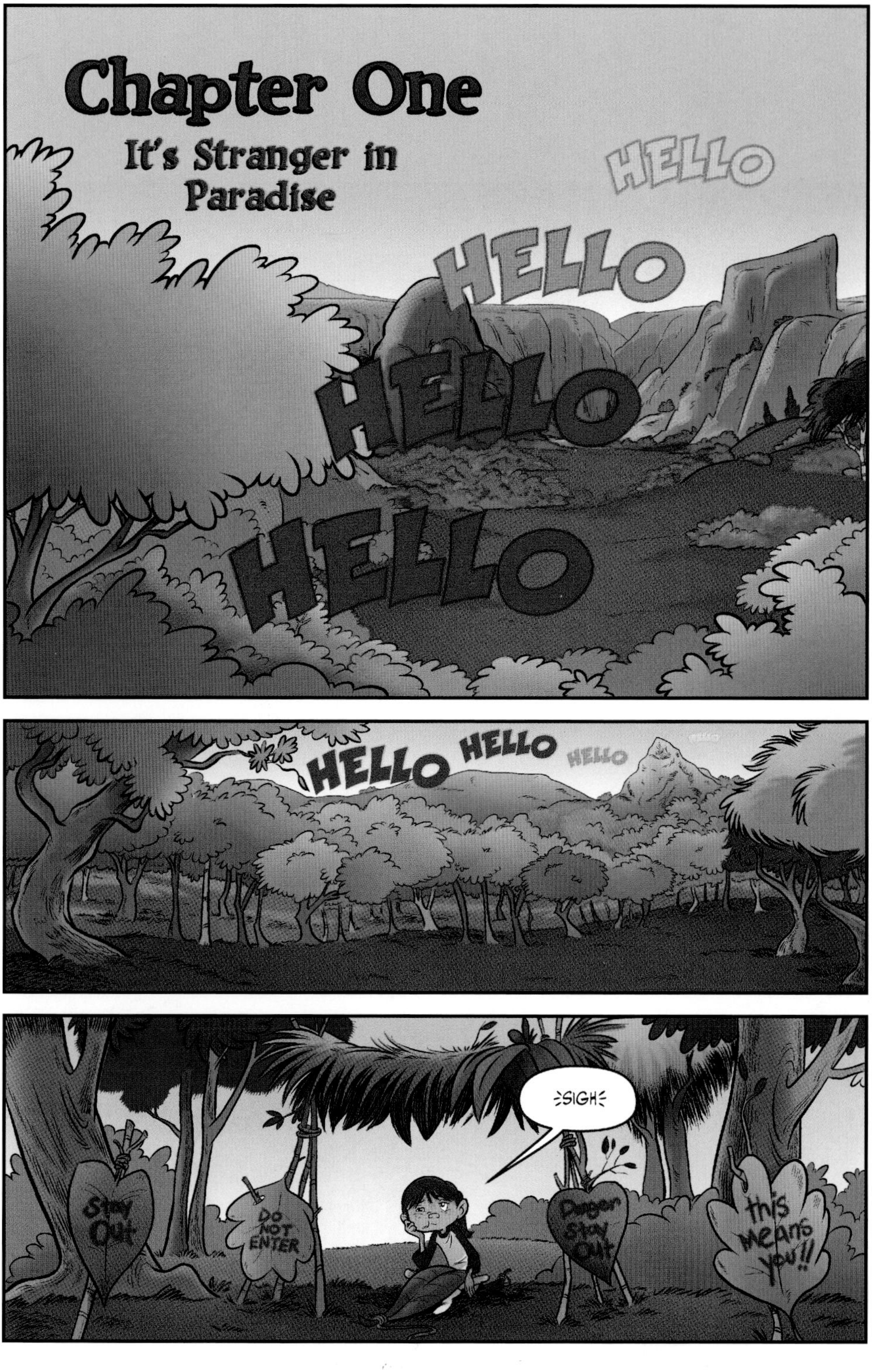
Chapter One
It's Stranger in Paradise
HELLO
HELLO
HELLO
HELLO
HELLO HELLO HELLO
Stay Out
DO NOT ENTER
SIGH
Danger Stay Out
this means you!!

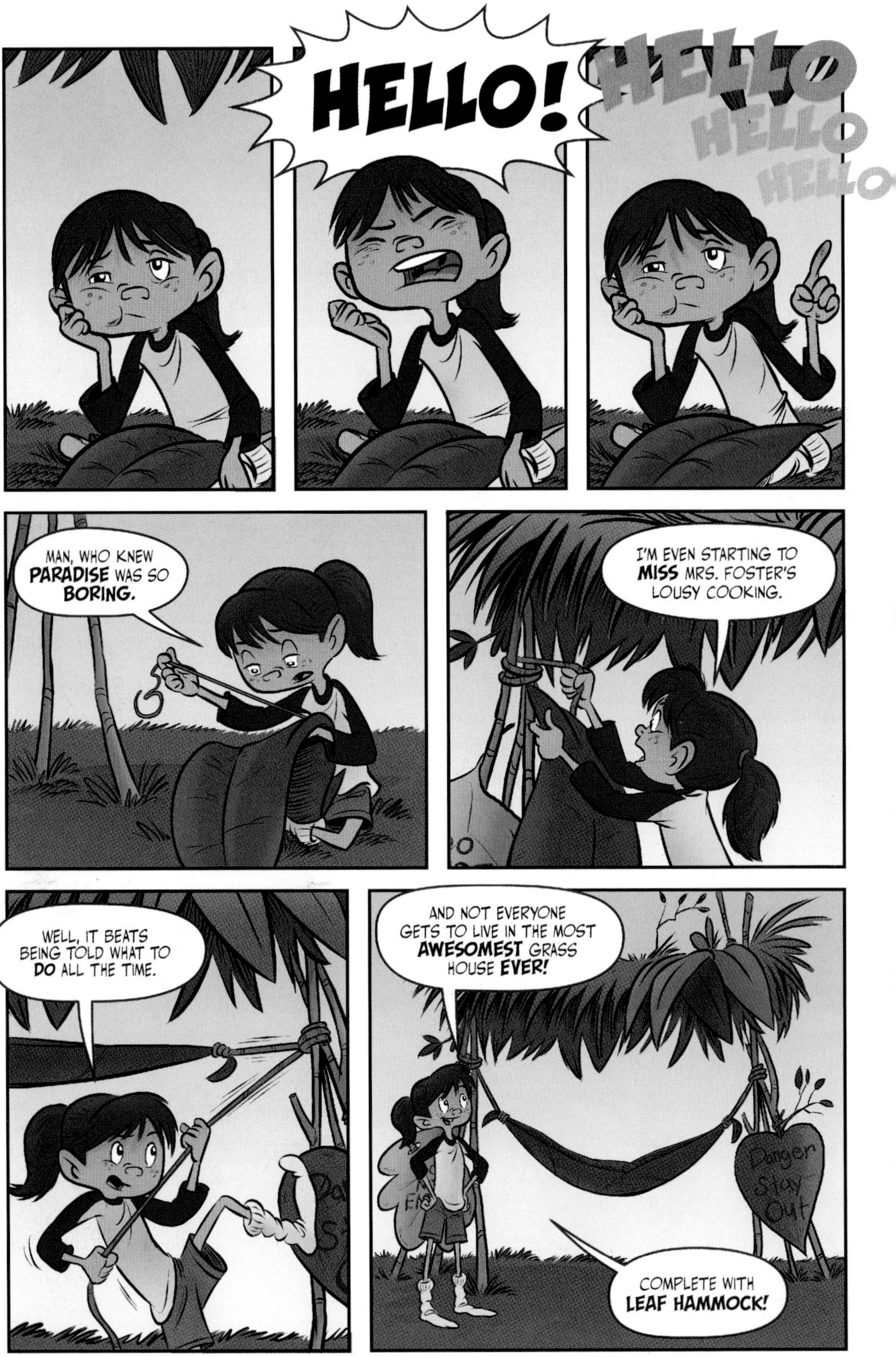
HELLO!
HELLO
HELLO
HELLO
MAN, WHO KNEW PARADISE WAS SO BORING.
I'M EVEN STARTING TO MISS MRS. FOSTER'S LOUSY COOKING.
WELL, IT BEATS BEING TOLD WHAT TO DO ALL THE TIME.
AND NOT EVERYONE GETS TO LIVE IN THE MOST AWESOMEST GRASS HOUSE EVER!
Danger Stay Out
COMPLETE WITH LEAF HAMMOCK!

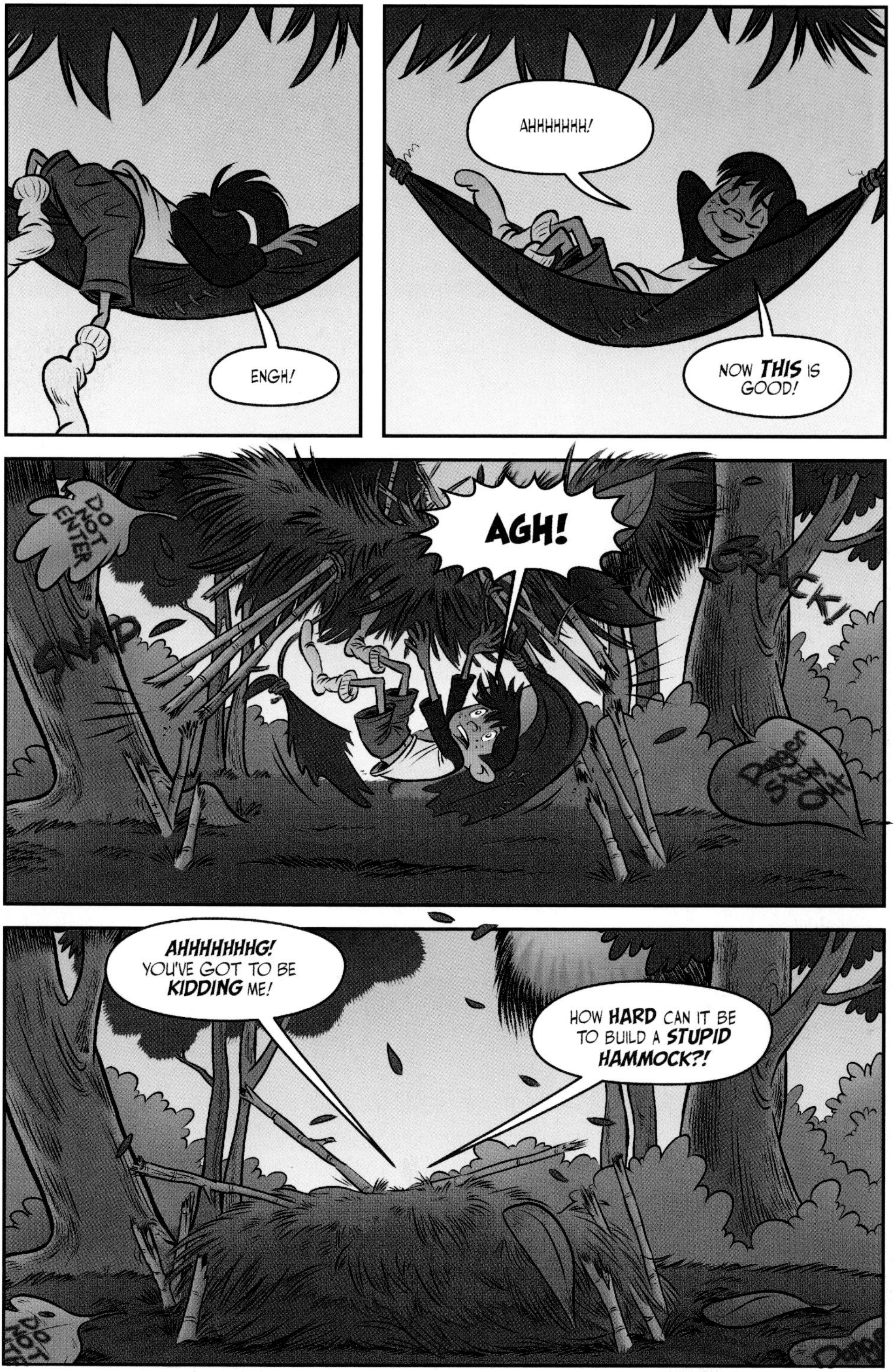
ENGH!
AHHHHHHH!
NOW **THIS** IS GOOD!
DO NOT ENTER
SNAP
AGH!
CRACK!
Danger Stay Out
AHHHHHHHG! YOU'VE GOT TO BE **KIDDING** ME!
HOW **HARD** CAN IT BE TO BUILD A **STUPID HAMMOCK?!**

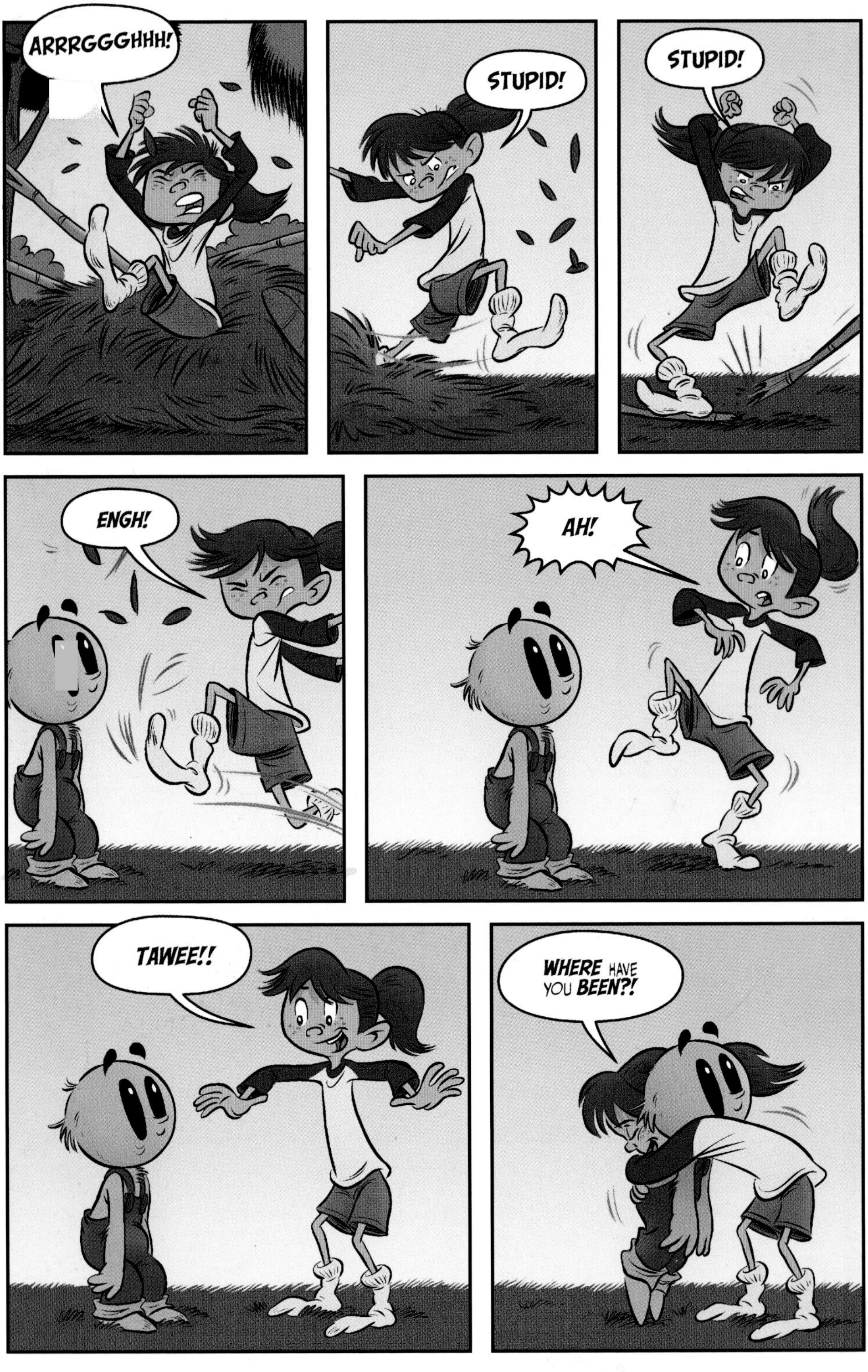
ARRRGGGHHH!
STUPID!
STUPID!
ENGH!
AH!
TAWEE!!
WHERE HAVE YOU BEEN?!

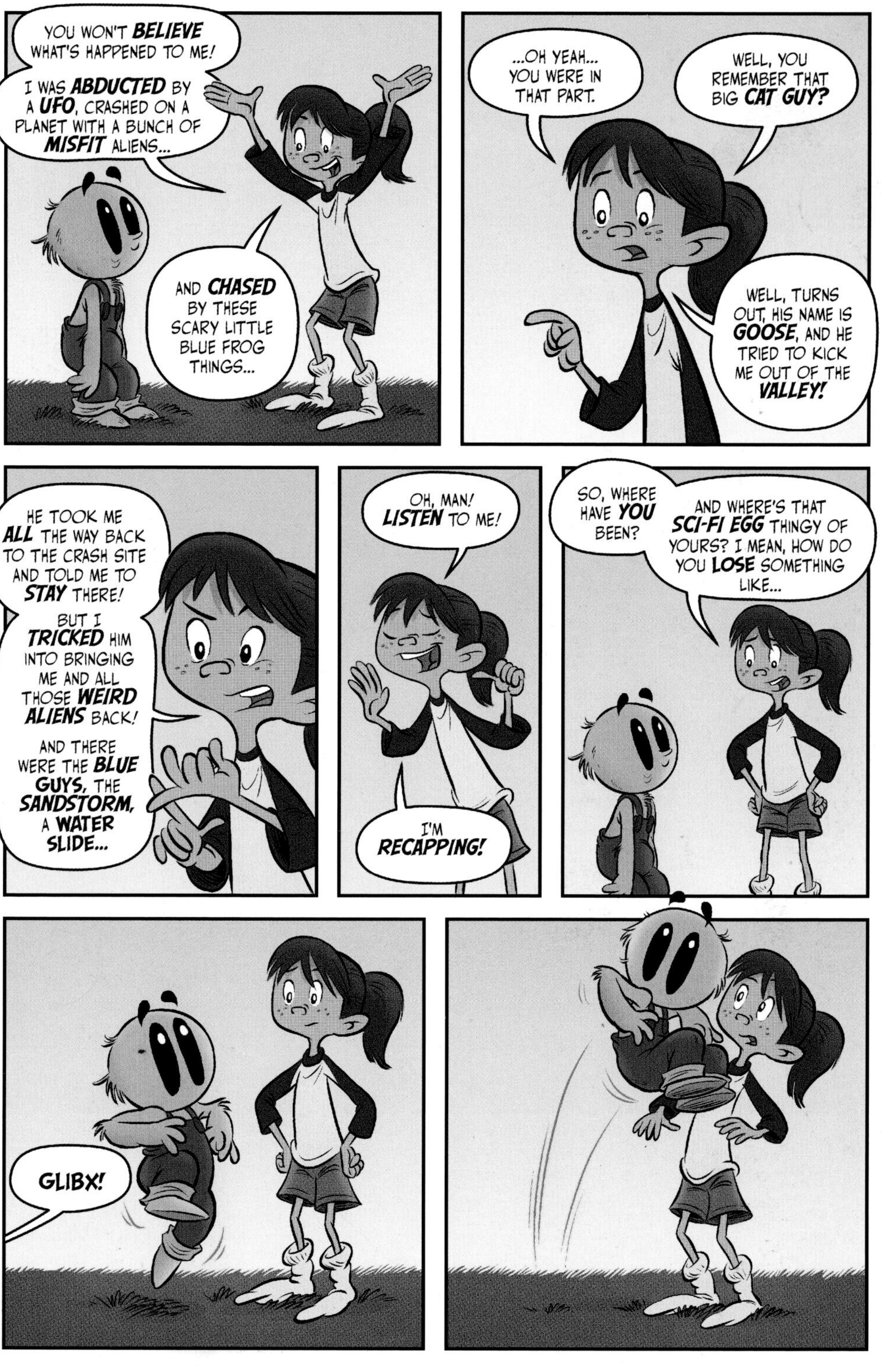
YOU WON'T BELIEVE WHAT'S HAPPENED TO ME!
I WAS ABDUCTED BY A UFO, CRASHED ON A PLANET WITH A BUNCH OF MISFIT ALIENS...
AND CHASED BY THESE SCARY LITTLE BLUE FROG THINGS...
...OH YEAH... YOU WERE IN THAT PART.
WELL, YOU REMEMBER THAT BIG CAT GUY?
WELL, TURNS OUT, HIS NAME IS GOOSE, AND HE TRIED TO KICK ME OUT OF THE VALLEY!
HE TOOK ME ALL THE WAY BACK TO THE CRASH SITE AND TOLD ME TO STAY THERE!
BUT I TRICKED HIM INTO BRINGING ME AND ALL THOSE WEIRD ALIENS BACK!
AND THERE WERE THE BLUE GUYS, THE SANDSTORM, A WATER SLIDE...
OH, MAN! LISTEN TO ME!
I'M RECAPPING!
SO, WHERE HAVE YOU BEEN?
AND WHERE'S THAT SCI-FI EGG THINGY OF YOURS? I MEAN, HOW DO YOU LOSE SOMETHING LIKE...
GLIBX!

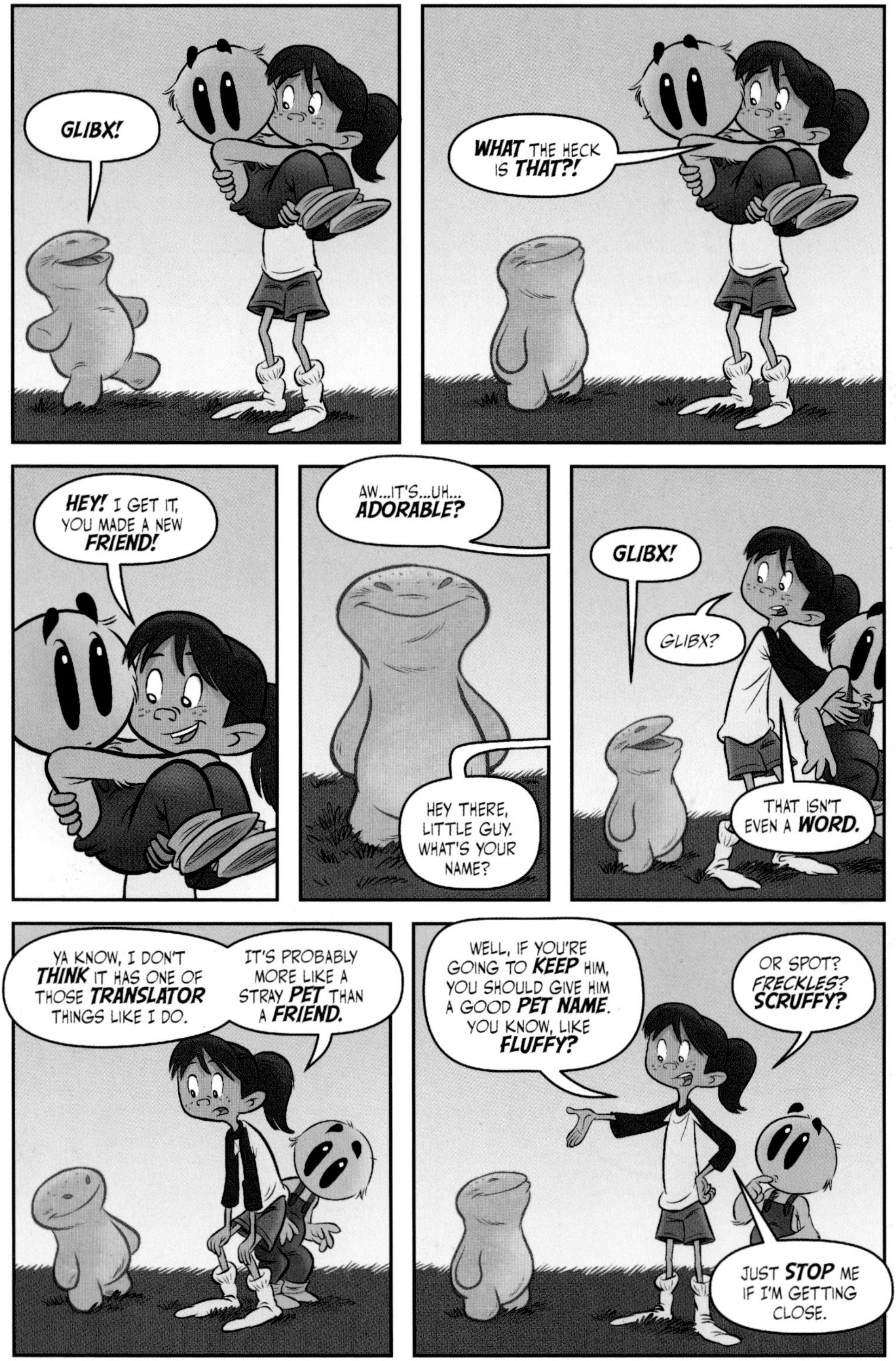
GLIBX!
WHAT THE HECK IS THAT?!
HEY! I GET IT, YOU MADE A NEW FRIEND!
AW...IT'S...UH... ADORABLE?
HEY THERE, LITTLE GUY. WHAT'S YOUR NAME?
GLIBX!
GLIBX?
THAT ISN'T EVEN A WORD.
YA KNOW, I DON'T THINK IT HAS ONE OF THOSE TRANSLATOR THINGS LIKE I DO.
IT'S PROBABLY MORE LIKE A STRAY PET THAN A FRIEND.
WELL, IF YOU'RE GOING TO KEEP HIM, YOU SHOULD GIVE HIM A GOOD PET NAME. YOU KNOW, LIKE FLUFFY?
OR SPOT? FRECKLES? SCRUFFY?
JUST STOP ME IF I'M GETTING CLOSE.

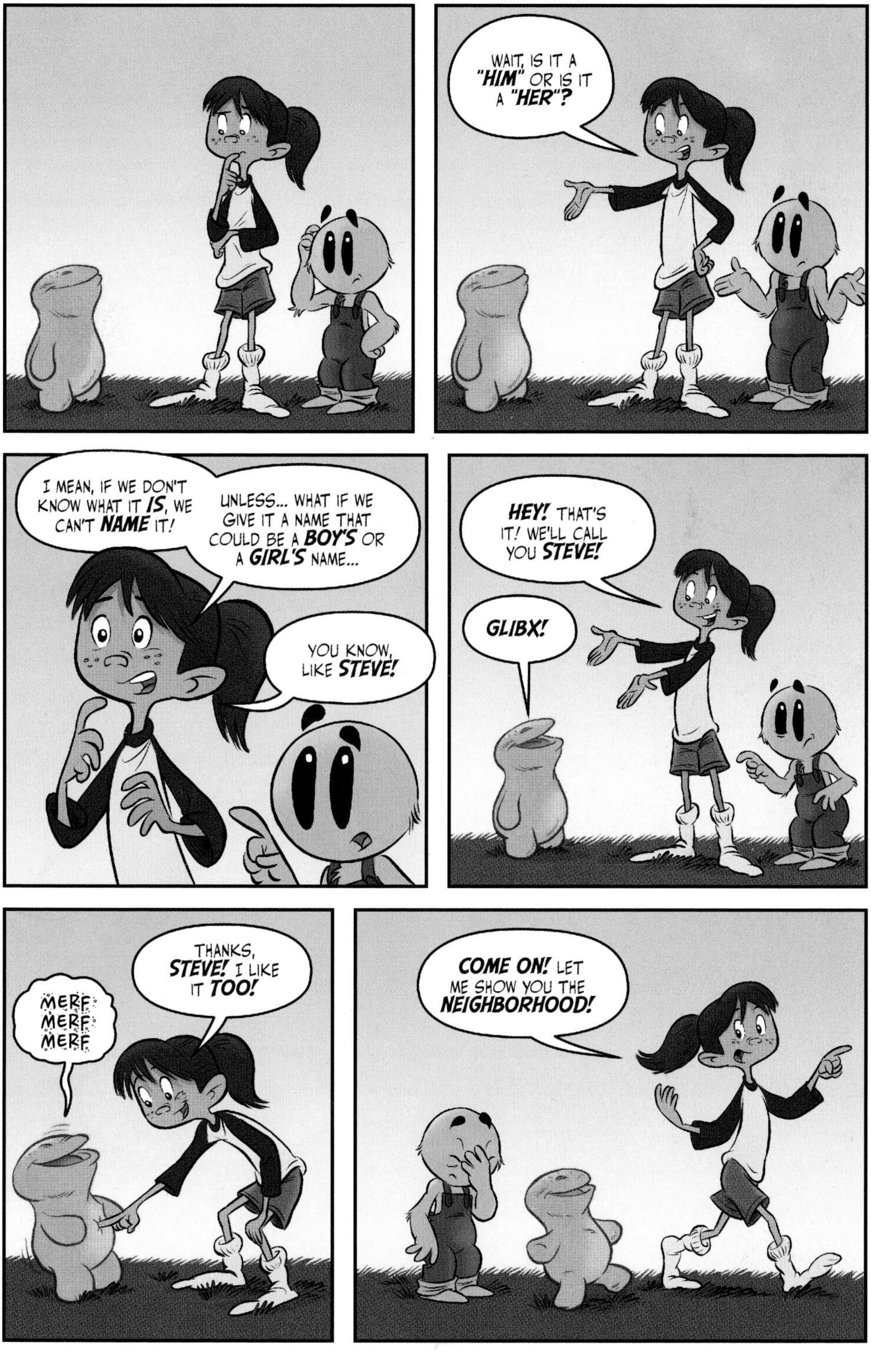
WAIT, IS IT A "HIM" OR IS IT A "HER"?
I MEAN, IF WE DON'T KNOW WHAT IT IS, WE CAN'T NAME IT!
UNLESS... WHAT IF WE GIVE IT A NAME THAT COULD BE A BOY'S OR A GIRL'S NAME...
YOU KNOW, LIKE STEVE!
HEY! THAT'S IT! WE'LL CALL YOU STEVE!
GLIBX!
MERF MERF MERF
THANKS, STEVE! I LIKE IT TOO!
COME ON! LET ME SHOW YOU THE NEIGHBORHOOD!

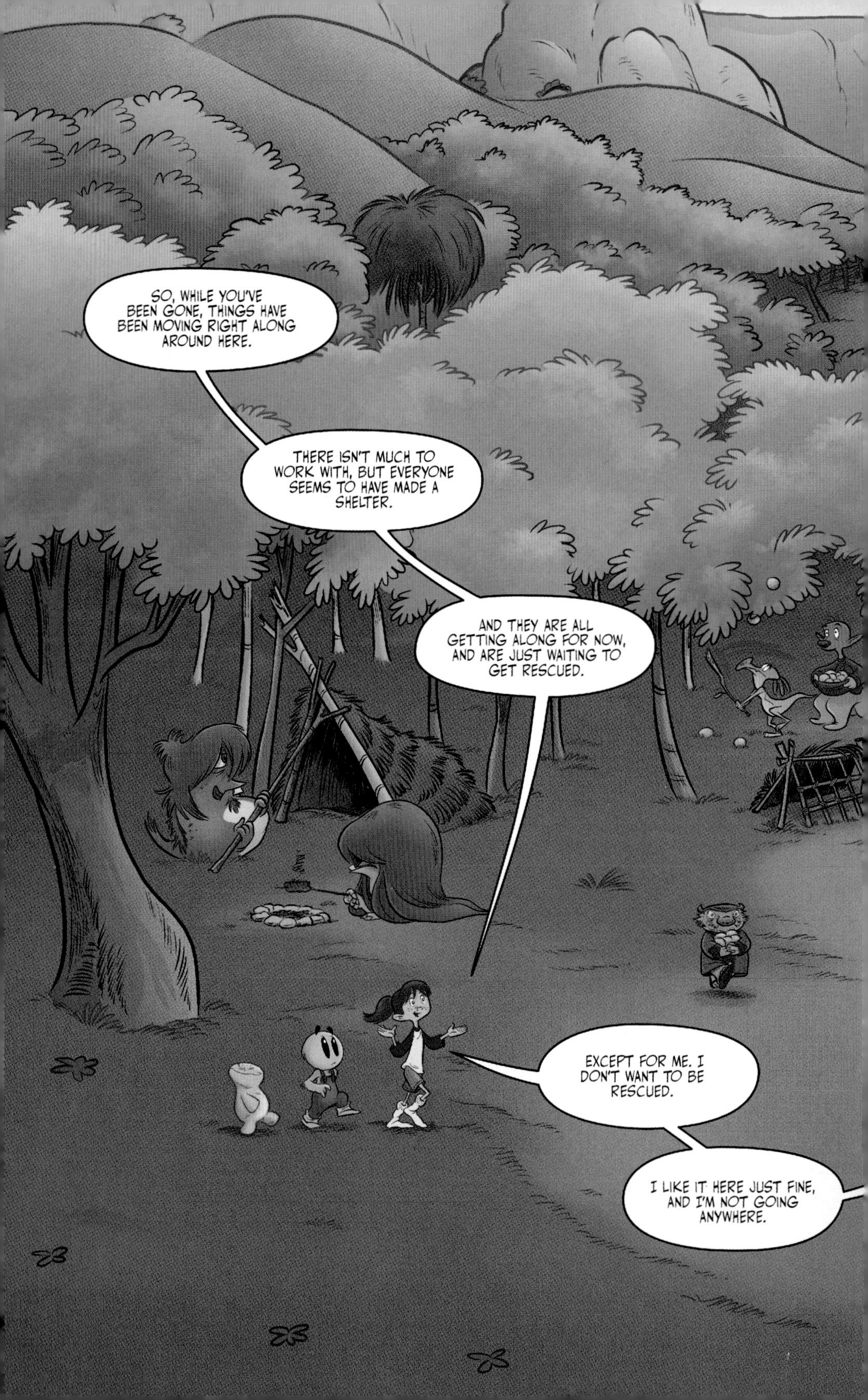
SO, WHILE YOU'VE BEEN GONE, THINGS HAVE BEEN MOVING RIGHT ALONG AROUND HERE.
THERE ISN'T MUCH TO WORK WITH, BUT EVERYONE SEEMS TO HAVE MADE A SHELTER.
AND THEY ARE ALL GETTING ALONG FOR NOW, AND ARE JUST WAITING TO GET RESCUED.
EXCEPT FOR ME. I DON'T WANT TO BE RESCUED.
I LIKE IT HERE JUST FINE, AND I'M NOT GOING ANYWHERE.

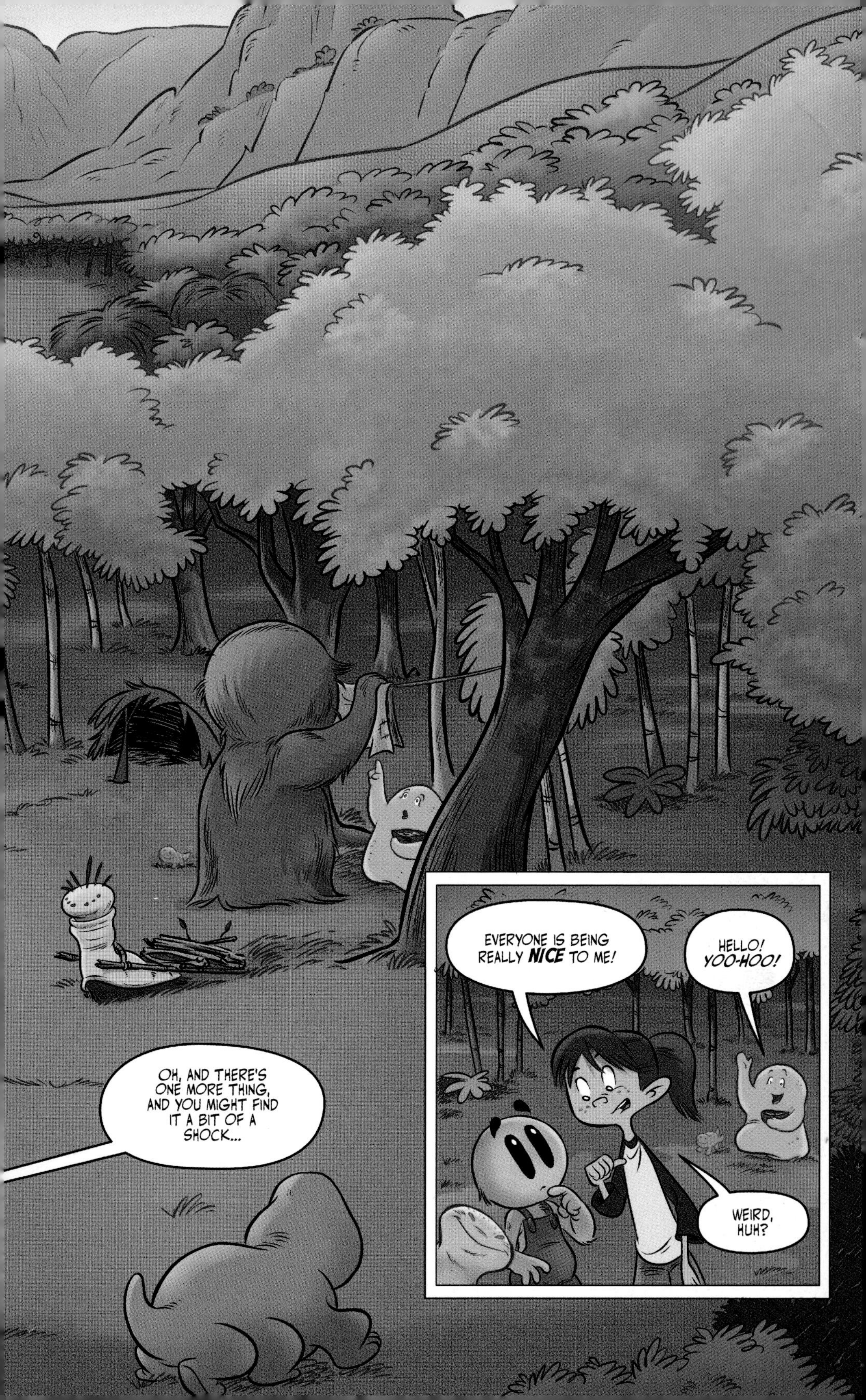
OH, AND THERE'S ONE MORE THING, AND YOU MIGHT FIND IT A BIT OF A SHOCK...
EVERYONE IS BEING REALLY NICE TO ME!
HELLO! YOO-HOO!
WEIRD, HUH?

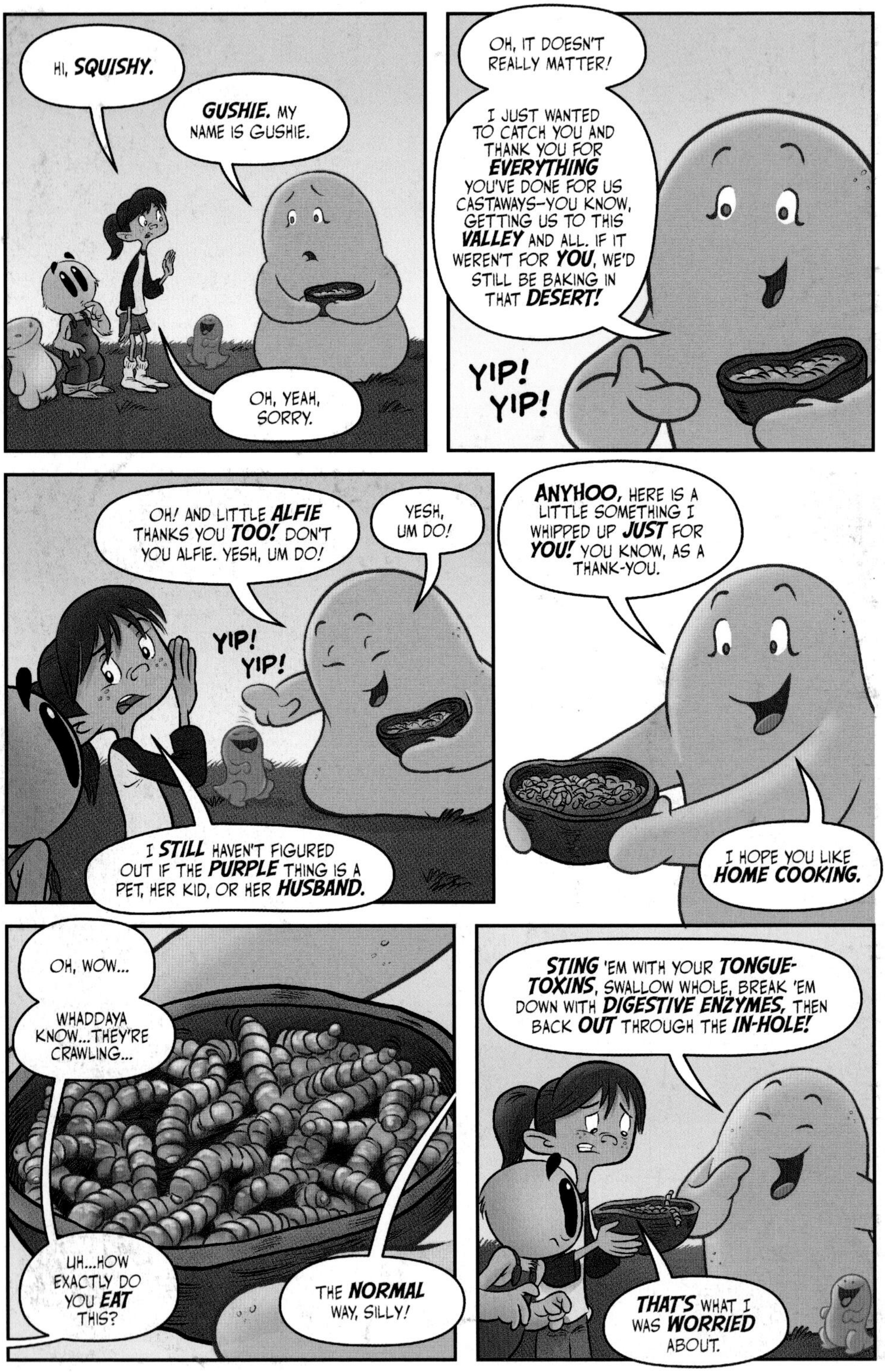
HI, SQUISHY.
GUSHIE. MY NAME IS GUSHIE.
OH, YEAH, SORRY.
OH, IT DOESN'T REALLY MATTER!
I JUST WANTED TO CATCH YOU AND THANK YOU FOR EVERYTHING YOU'VE DONE FOR US CASTAWAYS—YOU KNOW, GETTING US TO THIS VALLEY AND ALL. IF IT WEREN'T FOR YOU, WE'D STILL BE BAKING IN THAT DESERT!
YIP! YIP!
OH! AND LITTLE ALFIE THANKS YOU TOO! DON'T YOU ALFIE. YESH, UM DO!
YESH, UM DO!
YIP! YIP!
I STILL HAVEN'T FIGURED OUT IF THE PURPLE THING IS A PET, HER KID, OR HER HUSBAND.
ANYHOO, HERE IS A LITTLE SOMETHING I WHIPPED UP JUST FOR YOU! YOU KNOW, AS A THANK-YOU.
I HOPE YOU LIKE HOME COOKING.
OH, WOW...
WHADDAYA KNOW...THEY'RE CRAWLING...
UH...HOW EXACTLY DO YOU EAT THIS?
THE NORMAL WAY, SILLY!
STING 'EM WITH YOUR TONGUE-TOXINS, SWALLOW WHOLE, BREAK 'EM DOWN WITH DIGESTIVE ENZYMES, THEN BACK OUT THROUGH THE IN-HOLE!
THAT'S WHAT I WAS WORRIED ABOUT.

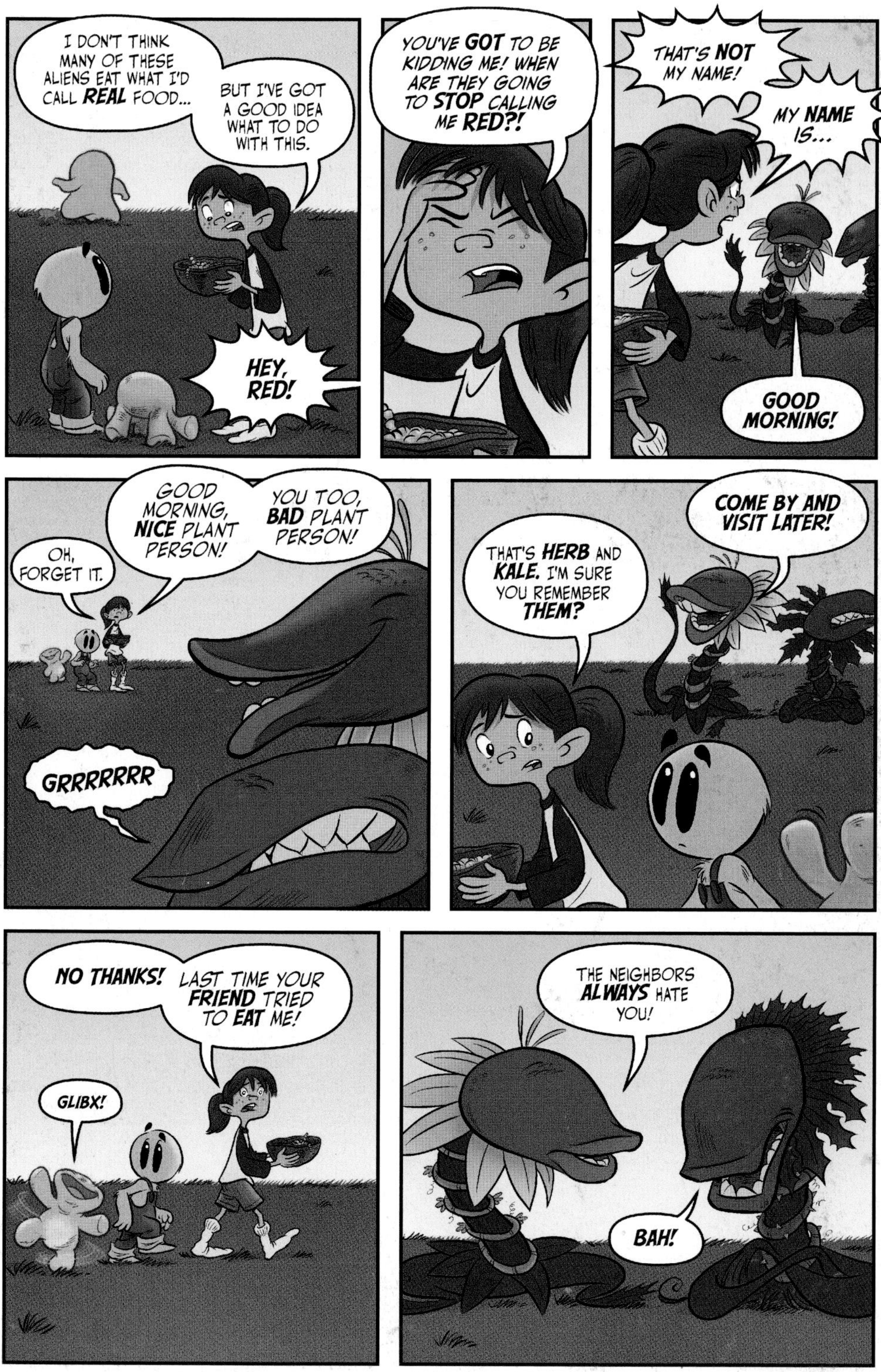
I DON'T THINK MANY OF THESE ALIENS EAT WHAT I'D CALL **REAL** FOOD...
BUT I'VE GOT A GOOD IDEA WHAT TO DO WITH THIS.
HEY, RED!
YOU'VE **GOT** TO BE KIDDING ME! WHEN ARE THEY GOING TO **STOP** CALLING ME **RED?!**
THAT'S **NOT** MY NAME!
MY **NAME** IS...
GOOD MORNING!
OH, FORGET IT.
GOOD MORNING, **NICE** PLANT PERSON!
YOU TOO, **BAD** PLANT PERSON!
GRRRRRRR
THAT'S **HERB** AND **KALE.** I'M SURE YOU REMEMBER **THEM?**
COME BY AND VISIT LATER!
NO THANKS!
LAST TIME YOUR **FRIEND** TRIED TO **EAT** ME!
GLIBX!
THE NEIGHBORS **ALWAYS** HATE YOU!
BAH!

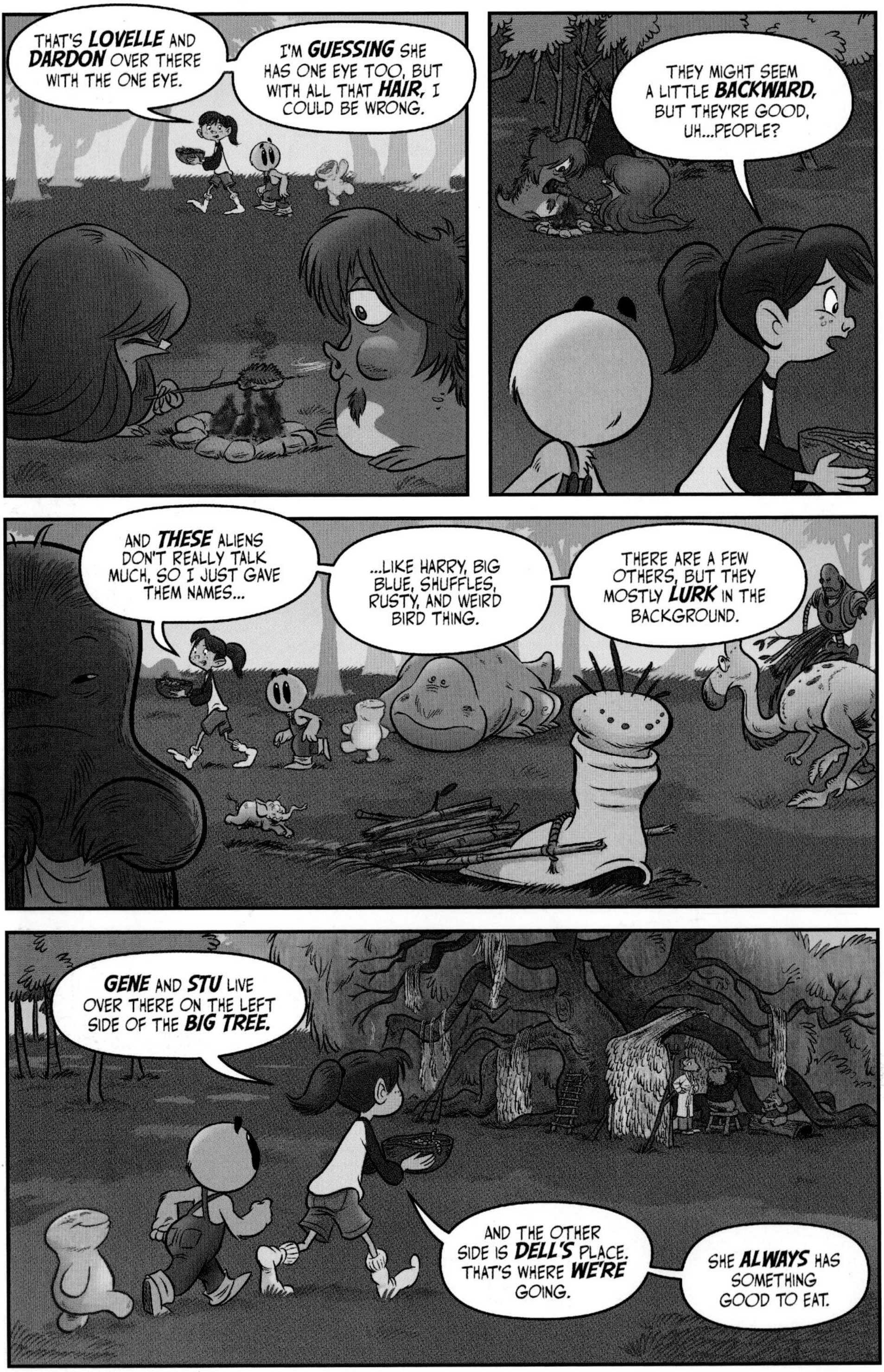
THAT'S LOVELLE AND DARDON OVER THERE WITH THE ONE EYE.
I'M GUESSING SHE HAS ONE EYE TOO, BUT WITH ALL THAT HAIR, I COULD BE WRONG.
THEY MIGHT SEEM A LITTLE BACKWARD, BUT THEY'RE GOOD, UH...PEOPLE?
AND THESE ALIENS DON'T REALLY TALK MUCH, SO I JUST GAVE THEM NAMES...
...LIKE HARRY, BIG BLUE, SHUFFLES, RUSTY, AND WEIRD BIRD THING.
THERE ARE A FEW OTHERS, BUT THEY MOSTLY LURK IN THE BACKGROUND.
GENE AND STU LIVE OVER THERE ON THE LEFT SIDE OF THE BIG TREE.
AND THE OTHER SIDE IS DELL'S PLACE. THAT'S WHERE WE'RE GOING.
SHE ALWAYS HAS SOMETHING GOOD TO EAT.

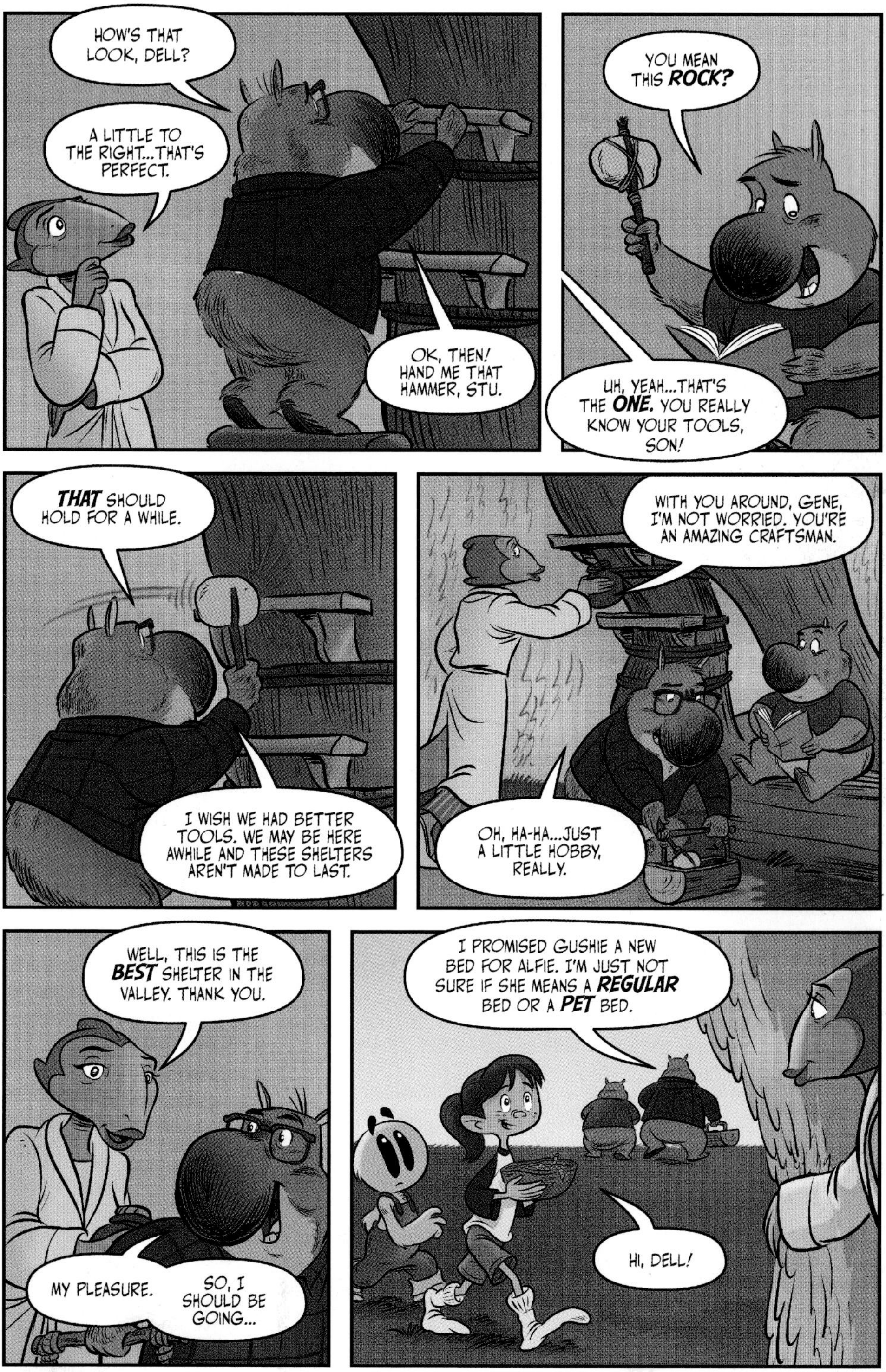
HOW'S THAT LOOK, DELL?
A LITTLE TO THE RIGHT...THAT'S PERFECT.
OK, THEN! HAND ME THAT HAMMER, STU.
YOU MEAN THIS ROCK?
UH, YEAH...THAT'S THE ONE. YOU REALLY KNOW YOUR TOOLS, SON!
THAT SHOULD HOLD FOR A WHILE.
I WISH WE HAD BETTER TOOLS. WE MAY BE HERE AWHILE AND THESE SHELTERS AREN'T MADE TO LAST.
WITH YOU AROUND, GENE, I'M NOT WORRIED. YOU'RE AN AMAZING CRAFTSMAN.
OH, HA-HA...JUST A LITTLE HOBBY, REALLY.
WELL, THIS IS THE BEST SHELTER IN THE VALLEY. THANK YOU.
MY PLEASURE.
SO, I SHOULD BE GOING...
I PROMISED GUSHIE A NEW BED FOR ALFIE. I'M JUST NOT SURE IF SHE MEANS A REGULAR BED OR A PET BED.
HI, DELL!

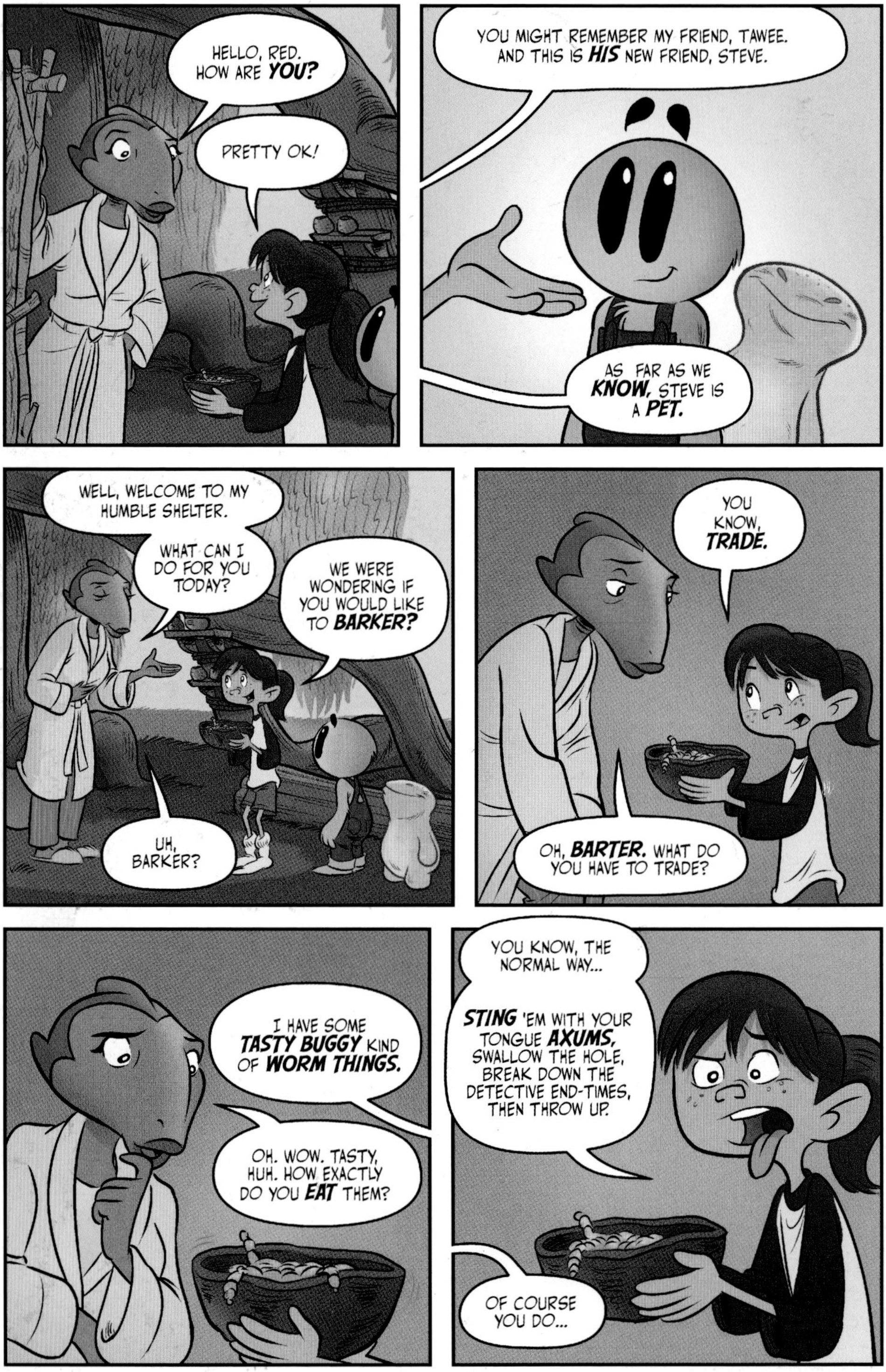
HELLO, RED. HOW ARE YOU?
PRETTY OK!
YOU MIGHT REMEMBER MY FRIEND, TAWEE. AND THIS IS HIS NEW FRIEND, STEVE.
AS FAR AS WE KNOW, STEVE IS A PET.
WELL, WELCOME TO MY HUMBLE SHELTER.
WHAT CAN I DO FOR YOU TODAY?
WE WERE WONDERING IF YOU WOULD LIKE TO BARKER?
UH, BARKER?
YOU KNOW, TRADE.
OH, BARTER. WHAT DO YOU HAVE TO TRADE?
I HAVE SOME TASTY BUGGY KIND OF WORM THINGS.
OH. WOW. TASTY, HUH. HOW EXACTLY DO YOU EAT THEM?
YOU KNOW, THE NORMAL WAY...
STING 'EM WITH YOUR TONGUE AXUMS, SWALLOW THE HOLE, BREAK DOWN THE DETECTIVE END-TIMES, THEN THROW UP.
OF COURSE YOU DO...

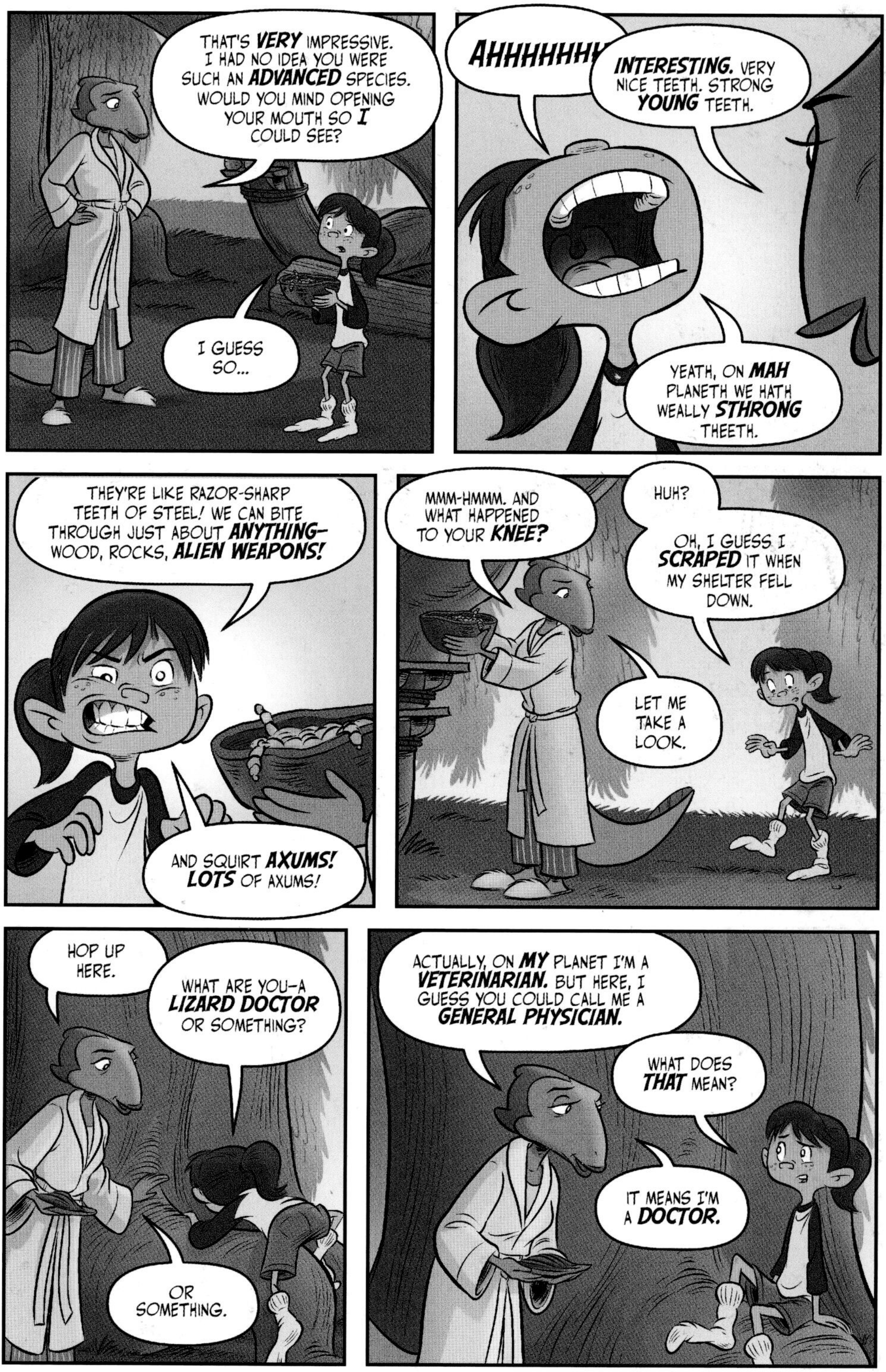
THAT'S VERY IMPRESSIVE. I HAD NO IDEA YOU WERE SUCH AN ADVANCED SPECIES. WOULD YOU MIND OPENING YOUR MOUTH SO I COULD SEE?
I GUESS SO...
AHHHHHHH
INTERESTING. VERY NICE TEETH. STRONG YOUNG TEETH.
YEATH, ON MAH PLANETH WE HATH WEALLY STHRONG THEETH.
THEY'RE LIKE RAZOR-SHARP TEETH OF STEEL! WE CAN BITE THROUGH JUST ABOUT ANYTHING-WOOD, ROCKS, ALIEN WEAPONS!
AND SQUIRT AXUMS! LOTS OF AXUMS!
MMM-HMMM. AND WHAT HAPPENED TO YOUR KNEE?
HUH?
OH, I GUESS I SCRAPED IT WHEN MY SHELTER FELL DOWN.
LET ME TAKE A LOOK.
HOP UP HERE.
WHAT ARE YOU—A LIZARD DOCTOR OR SOMETHING?
OR SOMETHING.
ACTUALLY, ON MY PLANET I'M A VETERINARIAN. BUT HERE, I GUESS YOU COULD CALL ME A GENERAL PHYSICIAN.
WHAT DOES THAT MEAN?
IT MEANS I'M A DOCTOR.

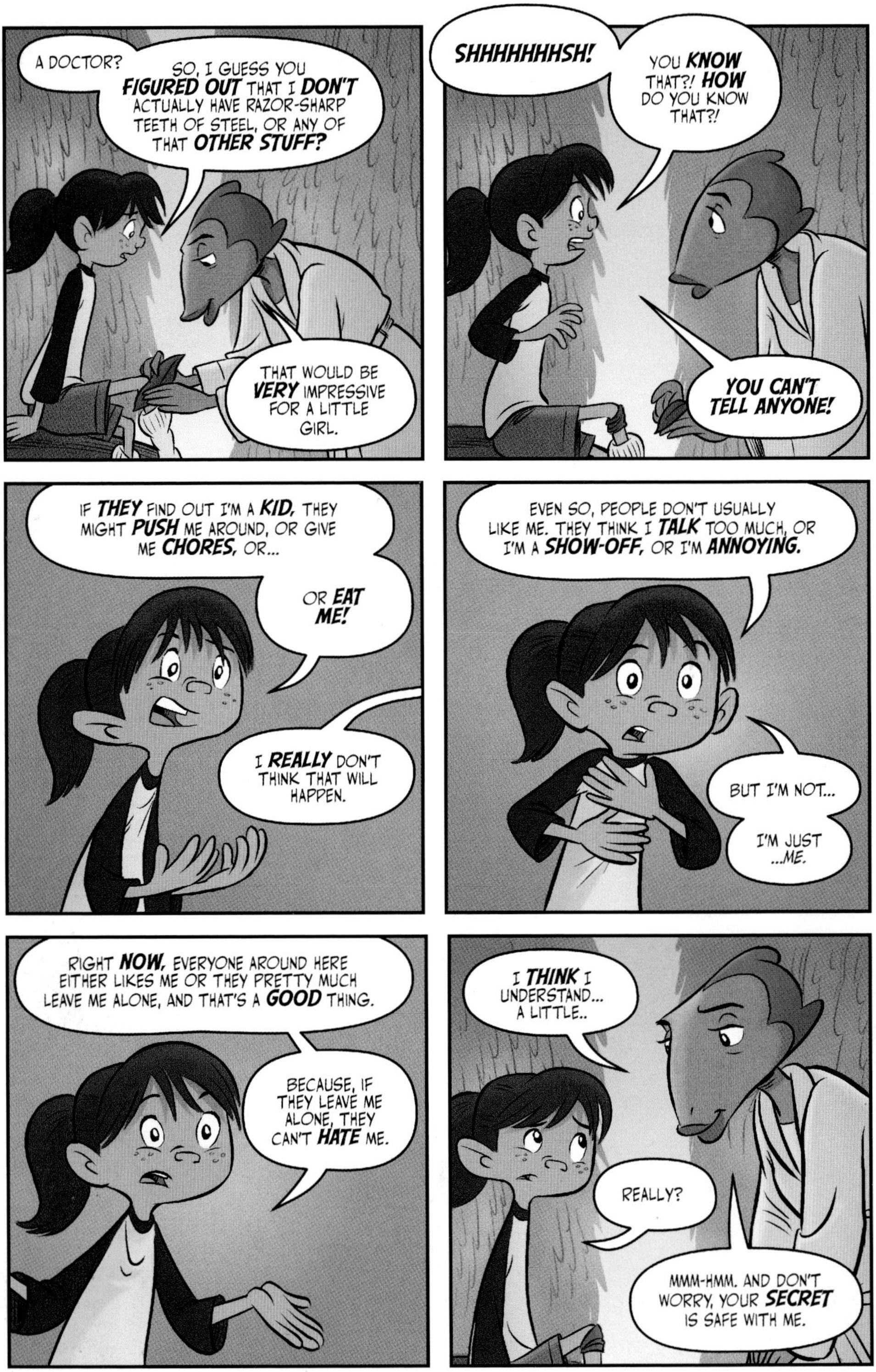
A DOCTOR?
SO, I GUESS YOU FIGURED OUT THAT I DON'T ACTUALLY HAVE RAZOR-SHARP TEETH OF STEEL, OR ANY OF THAT OTHER STUFF?
THAT WOULD BE VERY IMPRESSIVE FOR A LITTLE GIRL.
SHHHHHHHSH!
YOU KNOW THAT?! HOW DO YOU KNOW THAT?!
YOU CAN'T TELL ANYONE!
IF THEY FIND OUT I'M A KID, THEY MIGHT PUSH ME AROUND, OR GIVE ME CHORES, OR...
OR EAT ME!
I REALLY DON'T THINK THAT WILL HAPPEN.
EVEN SO, PEOPLE DON'T USUALLY LIKE ME. THEY THINK I TALK TOO MUCH, OR I'M A SHOW-OFF, OR I'M ANNOYING.
BUT I'M NOT...
I'M JUST ...ME.
RIGHT NOW, EVERYONE AROUND HERE EITHER LIKES ME OR THEY PRETTY MUCH LEAVE ME ALONE, AND THAT'S A GOOD THING.
BECAUSE, IF THEY LEAVE ME ALONE, THEY CAN'T HATE ME.
I THINK I UNDERSTAND... A LITTLE..
REALLY?
MMM-HMM. AND DON'T WORRY, YOUR SECRET IS SAFE WITH ME.

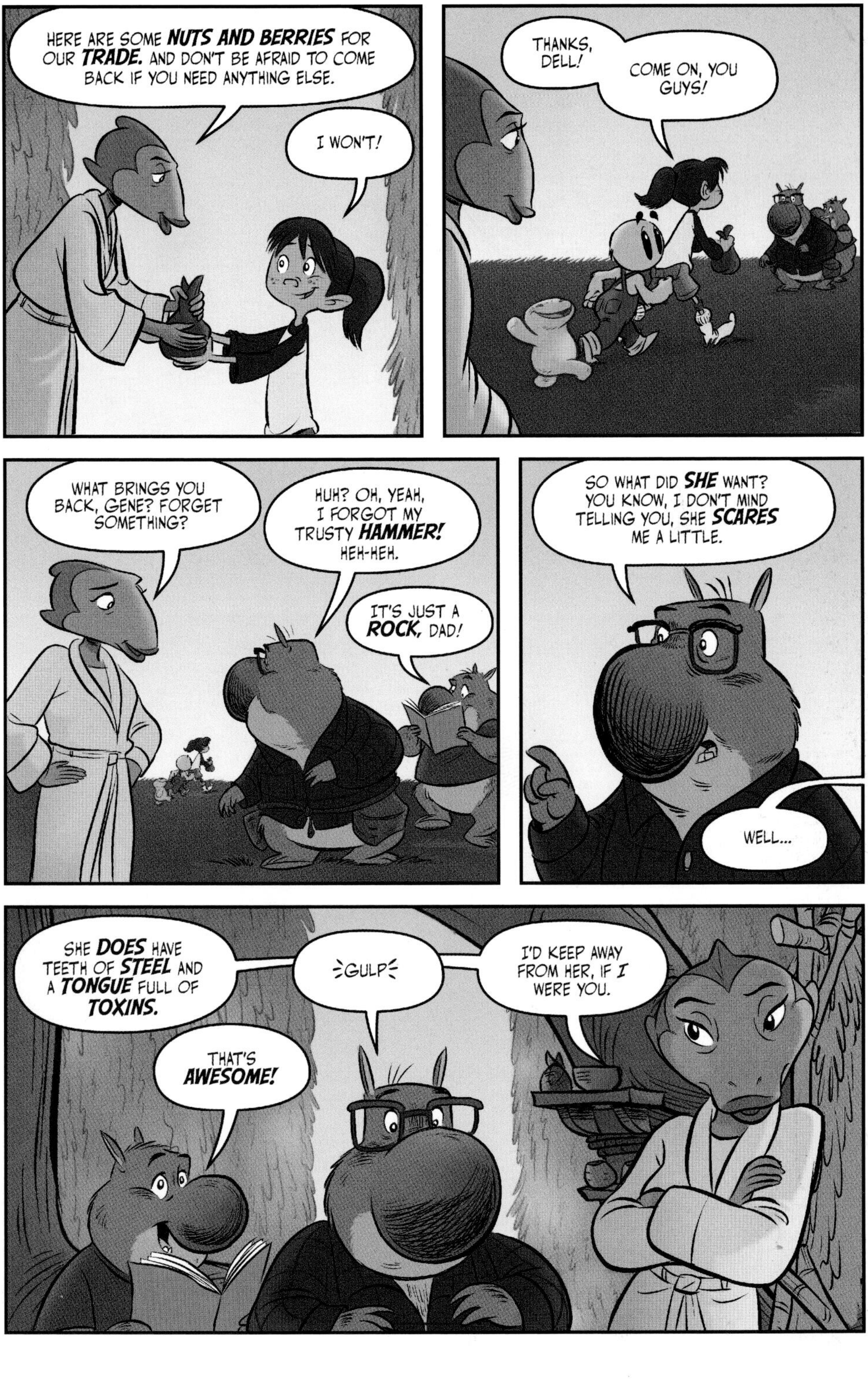
HERE ARE SOME NUTS AND BERRIES FOR OUR TRADE. AND DON'T BE AFRAID TO COME BACK IF YOU NEED ANYTHING ELSE.
I WON'T!
THANKS, DELL!
COME ON, YOU GUYS!
WHAT BRINGS YOU BACK, GENE? FORGET SOMETHING?
HUH? OH, YEAH, I FORGOT MY TRUSTY HAMMER! HEH-HEH.
IT'S JUST A ROCK, DAD!
SO WHAT DID SHE WANT? YOU KNOW, I DON'T MIND TELLING YOU, SHE SCARES ME A LITTLE.
WELL...
SHE DOES HAVE TEETH OF STEEL AND A TONGUE FULL OF TOXINS.
GULP
I'D KEEP AWAY FROM HER, IF I WERE YOU.
THAT'S AWESOME!

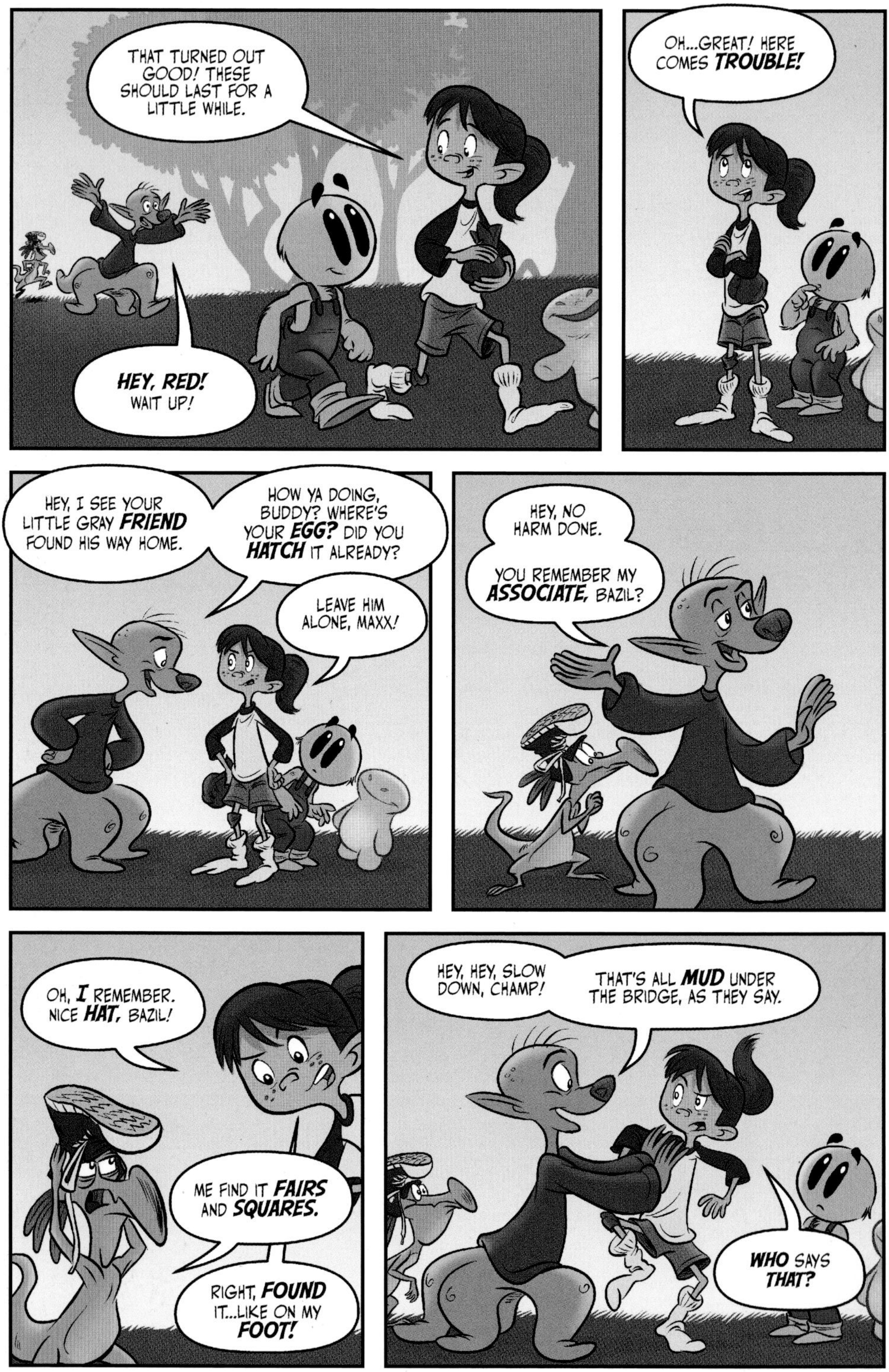
THAT TURNED OUT GOOD! THESE SHOULD LAST FOR A LITTLE WHILE.
HEY, RED! WAIT UP!
OH...GREAT! HERE COMES TROUBLE!
HEY, I SEE YOUR LITTLE GRAY FRIEND FOUND HIS WAY HOME.
HOW YA DOING, BUDDY? WHERE'S YOUR EGG? DID YOU HATCH IT ALREADY?
LEAVE HIM ALONE, MAXX!
HEY, NO HARM DONE.
YOU REMEMBER MY ASSOCIATE, BAZIL?
OH, I REMEMBER. NICE HAT, BAZIL!
ME FIND IT FAIRS AND SQUARES.
RIGHT, FOUND IT...LIKE ON MY FOOT!
HEY, HEY, SLOW DOWN, CHAMP!
THAT'S ALL MUD UNDER THE BRIDGE, AS THEY SAY.
WHO SAYS THAT?

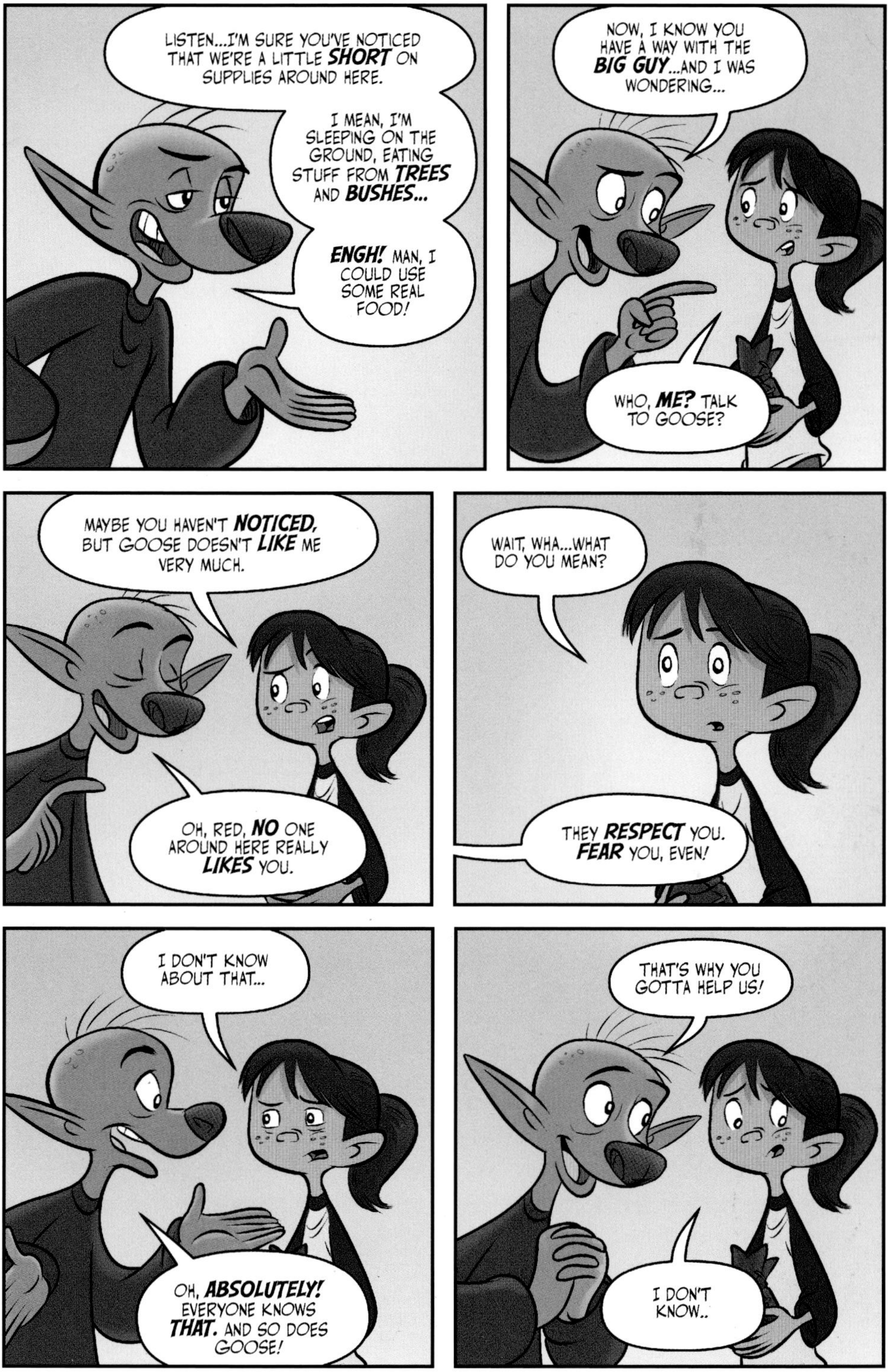
LISTEN...I'M SURE YOU'VE NOTICED THAT WE'RE A LITTLE SHORT ON SUPPLIES AROUND HERE.
I MEAN, I'M SLEEPING ON THE GROUND, EATING STUFF FROM TREES AND BUSHES...
ENGH! MAN, I COULD USE SOME REAL FOOD!
NOW, I KNOW YOU HAVE A WAY WITH THE BIG GUY...AND I WAS WONDERING...
WHO, ME? TALK TO GOOSE?
MAYBE YOU HAVEN'T NOTICED, BUT GOOSE DOESN'T LIKE ME VERY MUCH.
OH, RED, NO ONE AROUND HERE REALLY LIKES YOU.
WAIT, WHA...WHAT DO YOU MEAN?
THEY RESPECT YOU. FEAR YOU, EVEN!
I DON'T KNOW ABOUT THAT...
OH, ABSOLUTELY! EVERYONE KNOWS THAT. AND SO DOES GOOSE!
THAT'S WHY YOU GOTTA HELP US!
I DON'T KNOW..

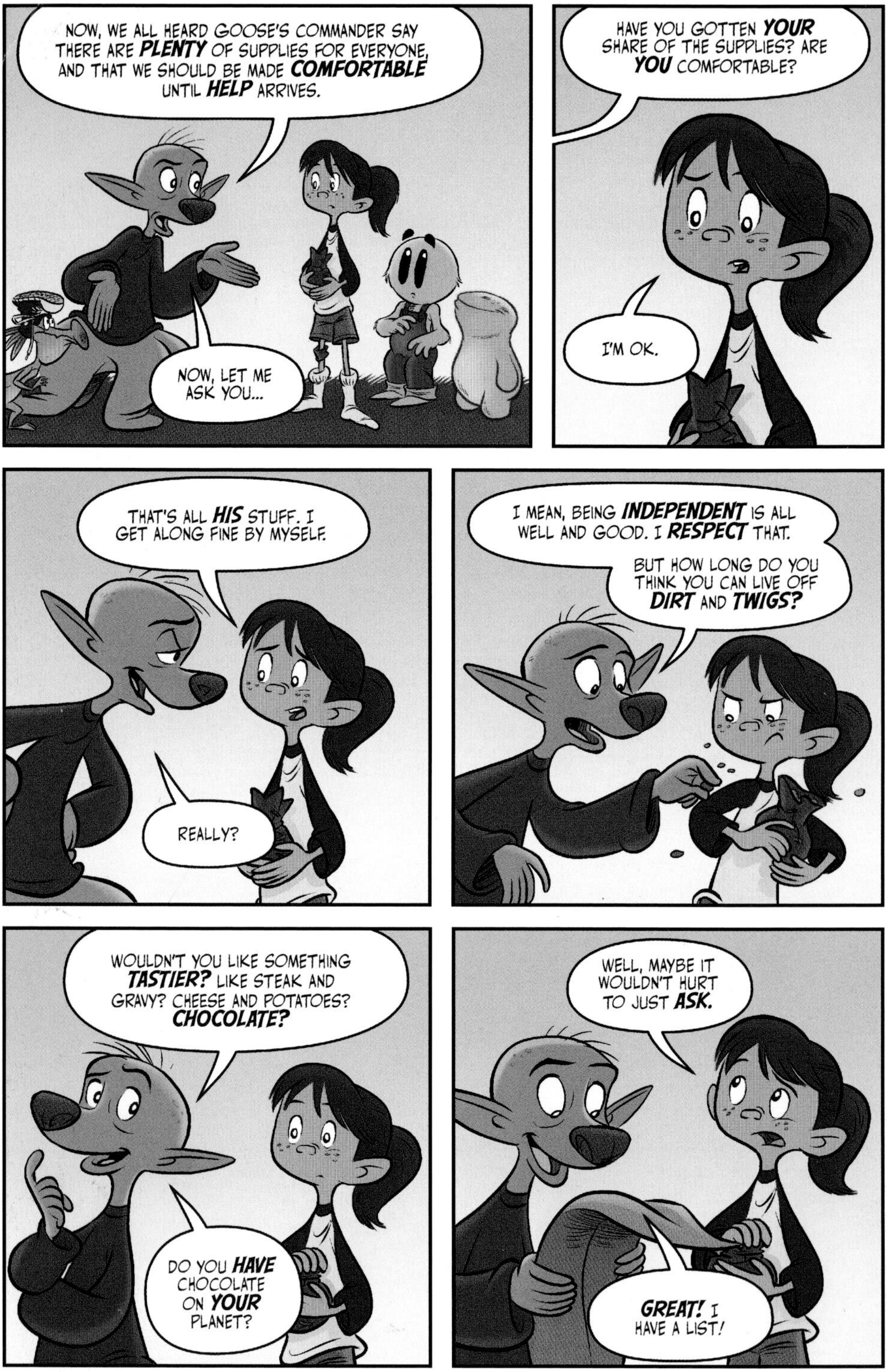
NOW, WE ALL HEARD GOOSE'S COMMANDER SAY THERE ARE **PLENTY** OF SUPPLIES FOR EVERYONE, AND THAT WE SHOULD BE MADE **COMFORTABLE** UNTIL **HELP** ARRIVES.
NOW, LET ME ASK YOU...
HAVE YOU GOTTEN **YOUR** SHARE OF THE SUPPLIES? ARE **YOU** COMFORTABLE?
I'M OK.
THAT'S ALL **HIS** STUFF. I GET ALONG FINE BY MYSELF.
REALLY?
I MEAN, BEING **INDEPENDENT** IS ALL WELL AND GOOD. I **RESPECT** THAT.
BUT HOW LONG DO YOU THINK YOU CAN LIVE OFF **DIRT** AND **TWIGS?**
WOULDN'T YOU LIKE SOMETHING **TASTIER?** LIKE STEAK AND GRAVY? CHEESE AND POTATOES? **CHOCOLATE?**
DO YOU **HAVE** CHOCOLATE ON **YOUR** PLANET?
WELL, MAYBE IT WOULDN'T HURT TO JUST **ASK.**
GREAT! I HAVE A LIST!

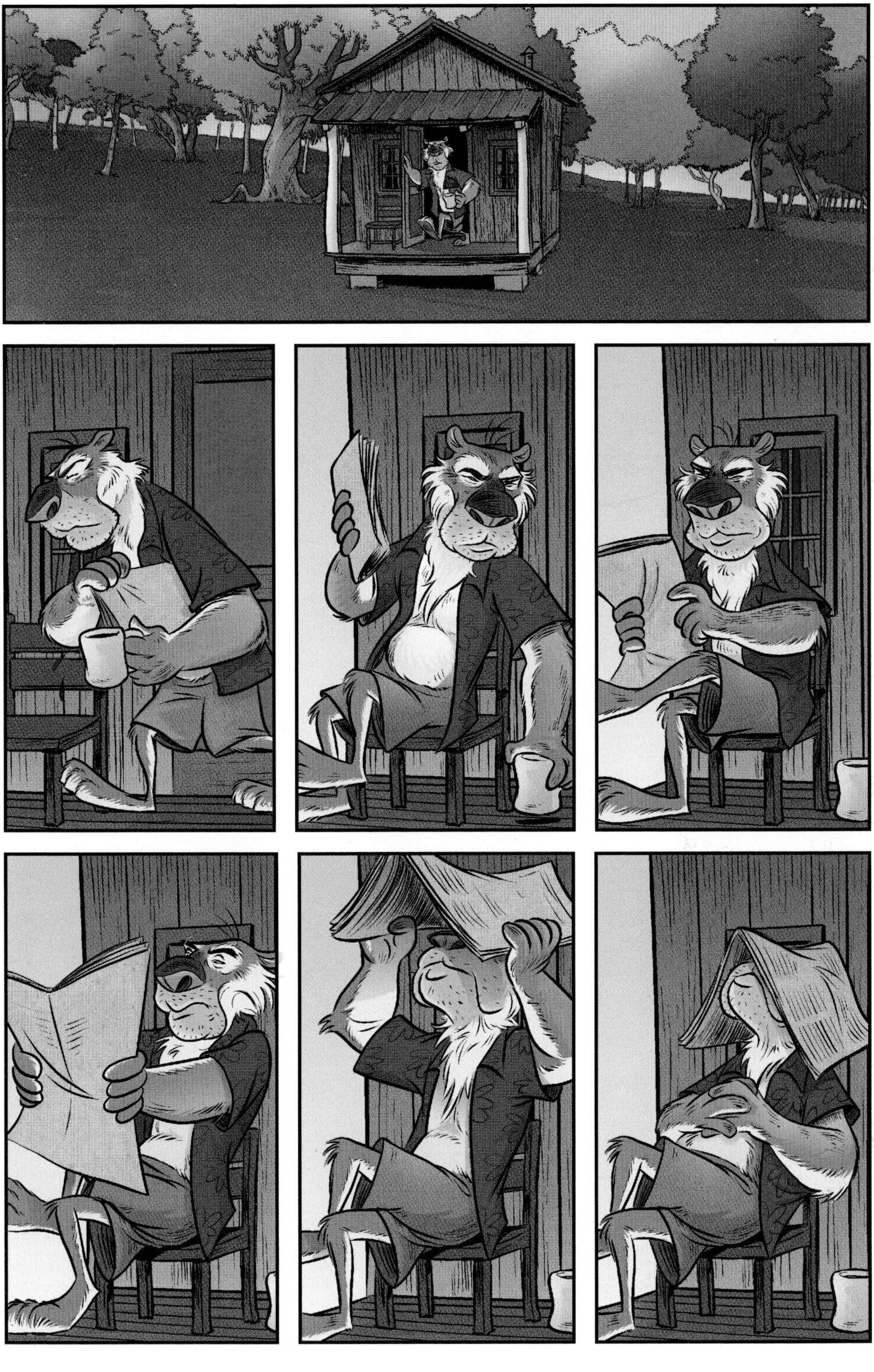

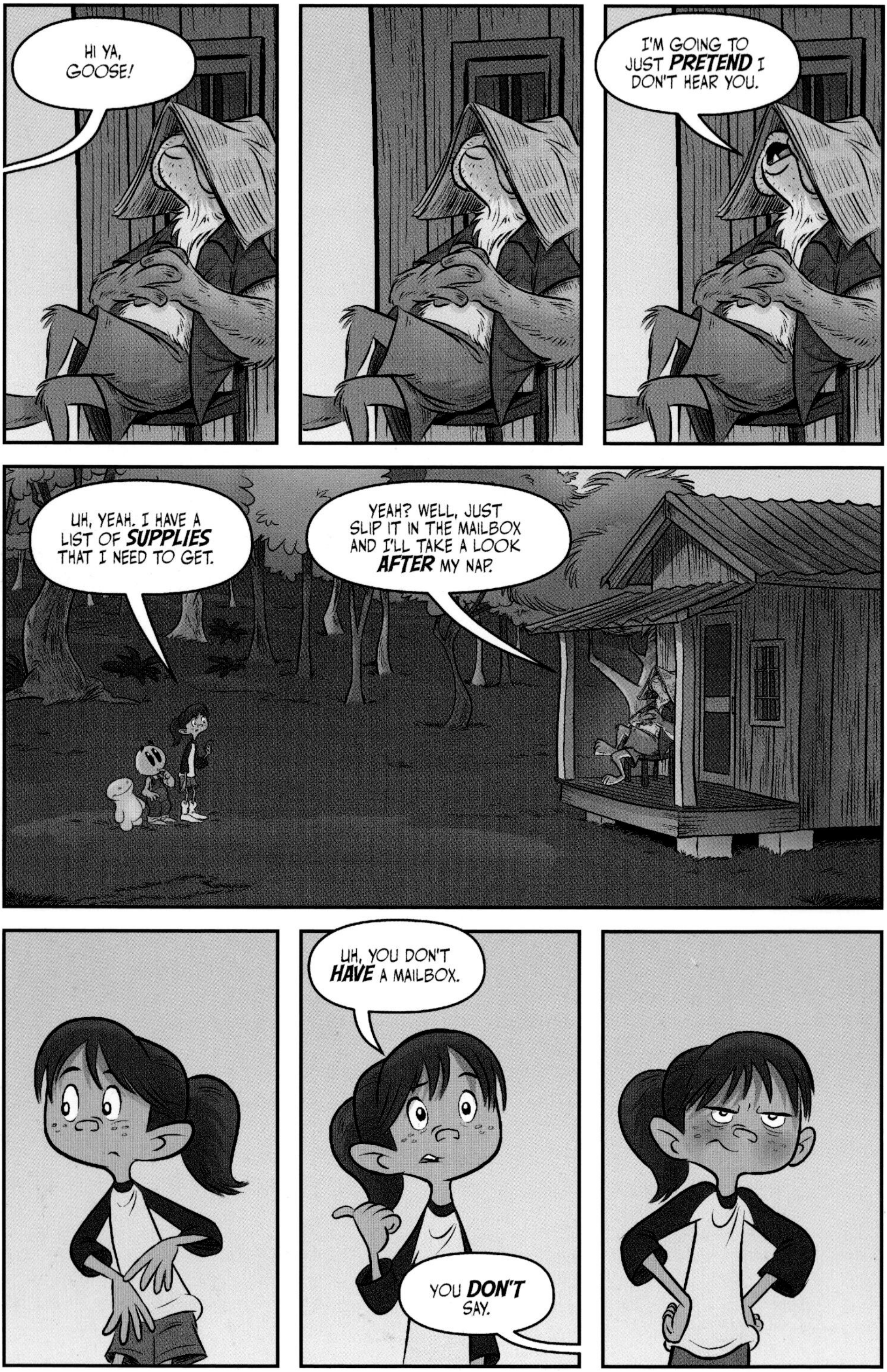
HI YA, GOOSE!
I'M GOING TO JUST PRETEND I DON'T HEAR YOU.
UH, YEAH. I HAVE A LIST OF SUPPLIES THAT I NEED TO GET.
YEAH? WELL, JUST SLIP IT IN THE MAILBOX AND I'LL TAKE A LOOK AFTER MY NAP.
UH, YOU DON'T HAVE A MAILBOX.
YOU DON'T SAY.

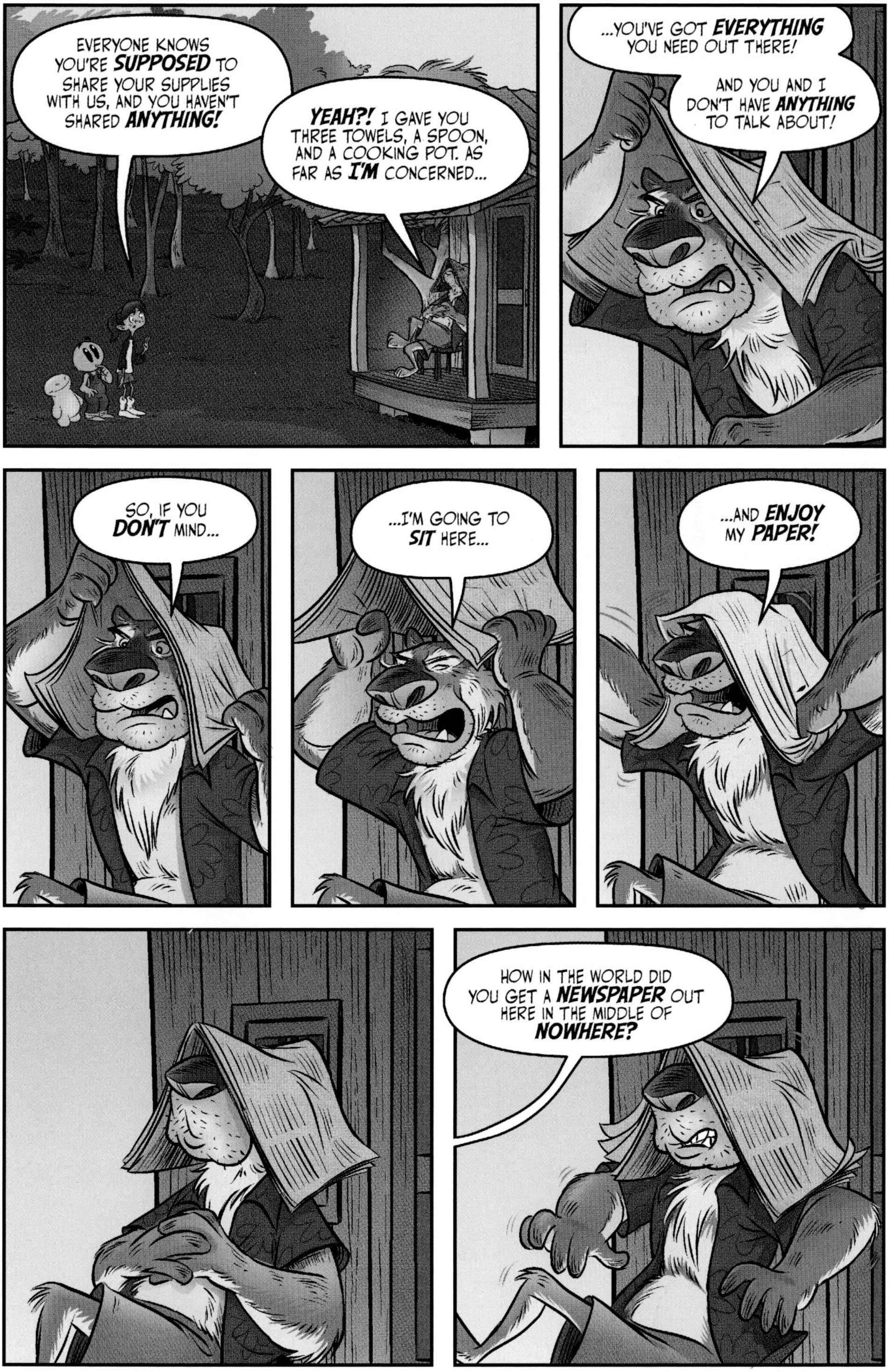

EVERYONE KNOWS YOU'RE SUPPOSED TO SHARE YOUR SUPPLIES WITH US, AND YOU HAVEN'T SHARED ANYTHING!
YEAH?! I GAVE YOU THREE TOWELS, A SPOON, AND A COOKING POT. AS FAR AS I'M CONCERNED...
...YOU'VE GOT EVERYTHING YOU NEED OUT THERE!
AND YOU AND I DON'T HAVE ANYTHING TO TALK ABOUT!
SO, IF YOU DON'T MIND...
...I'M GOING TO SIT HERE...
...AND ENJOY MY PAPER!
HOW IN THE WORLD DID YOU GET A NEWSPAPER OUT HERE IN THE MIDDLE OF NOWHERE?

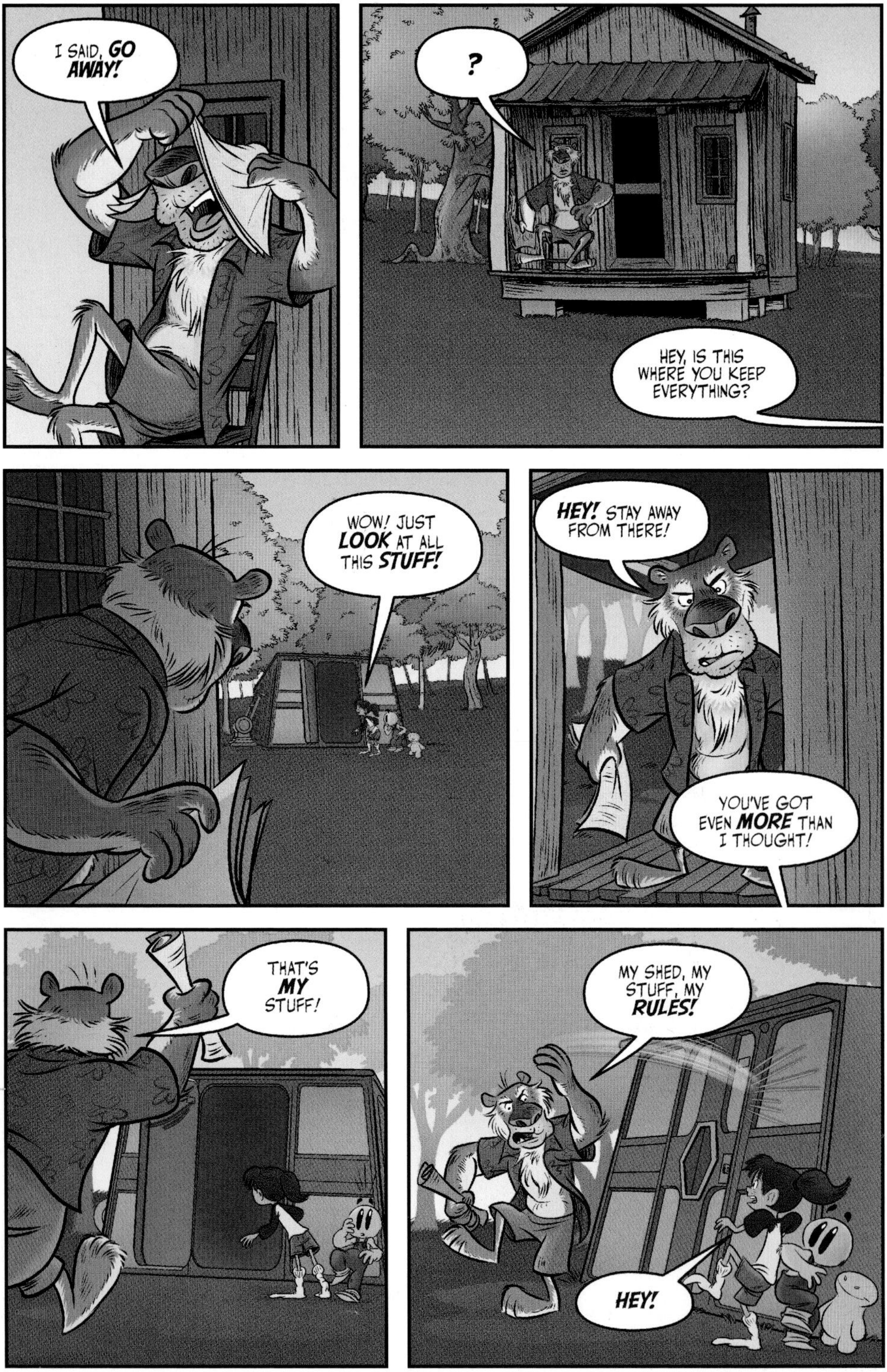
I SAID, **GO AWAY!**
?
HEY, IS THIS WHERE YOU KEEP EVERYTHING?
WOW! JUST **LOOK** AT ALL THIS **STUFF!**
HEY! STAY AWAY FROM THERE!
YOU'VE GOT EVEN **MORE** THAN I THOUGHT!
THAT'S **MY** STUFF!
MY SHED, MY STUFF, MY **RULES!**
HEY!

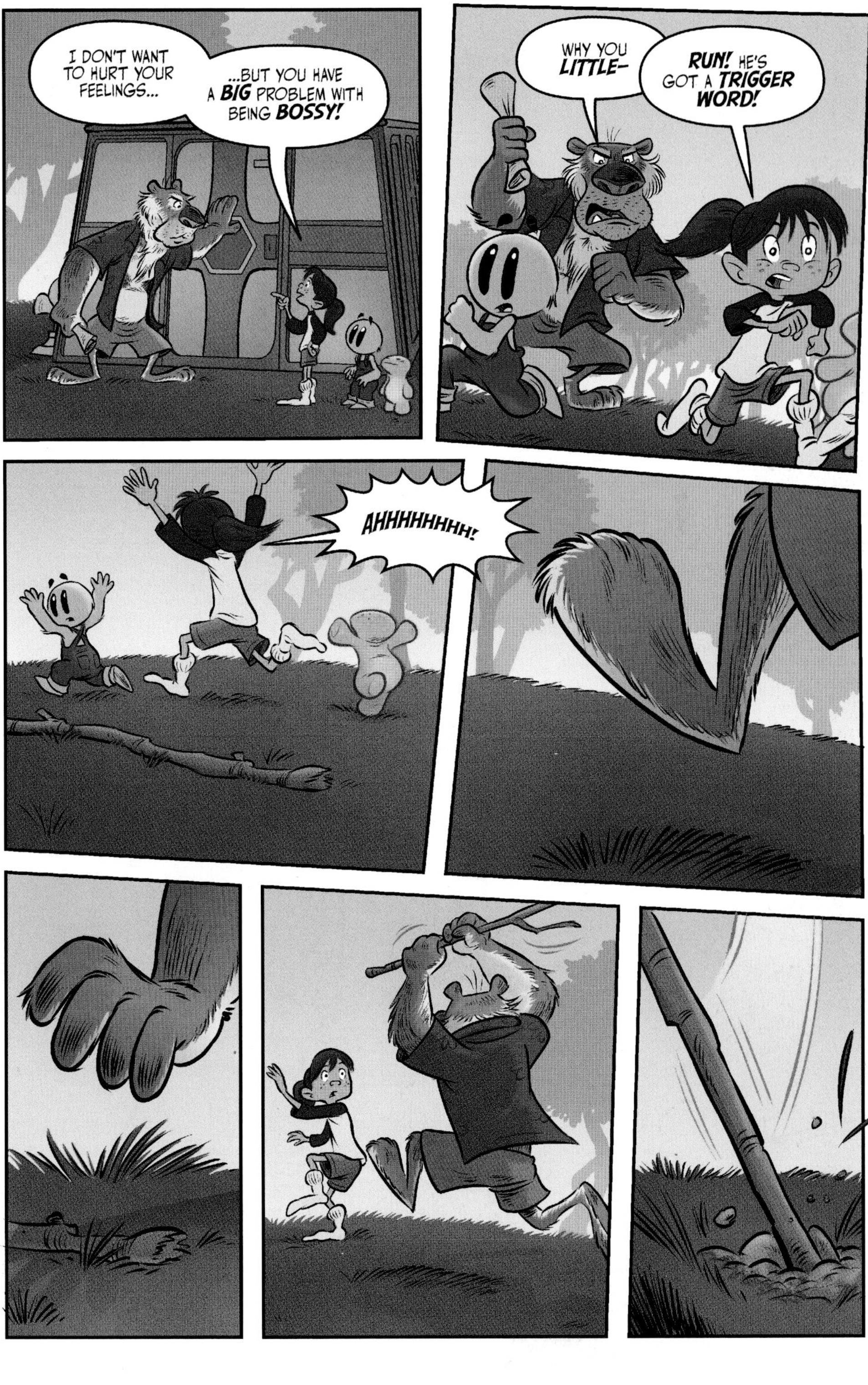
I DON'T WANT TO HURT YOUR FEELINGS...
...BUT YOU HAVE A **BIG** PROBLEM WITH BEING **BOSSY!**
WHY YOU **LITTLE-**
RUN! HE'S GOT A **TRIGGER WORD!**
AHHHHHHHH!

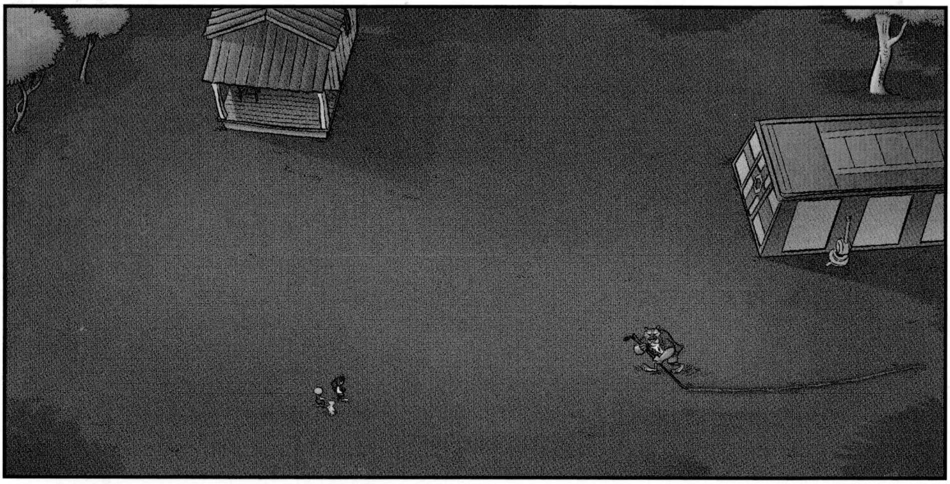

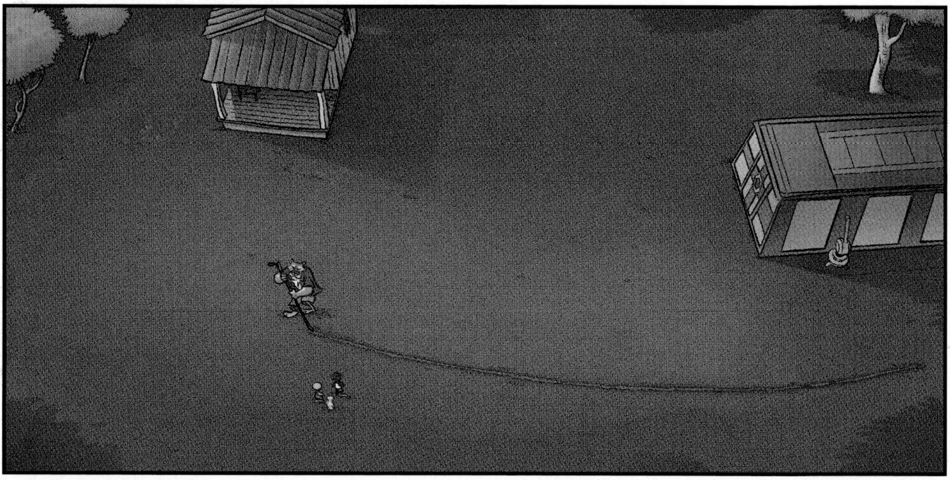

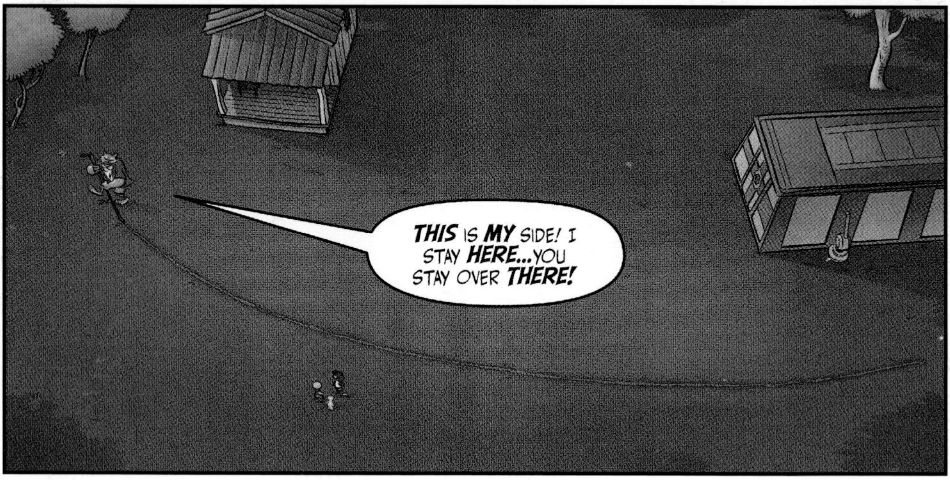
THIS IS MY SIDE! I STAY HERE...YOU STAY OVER THERE!

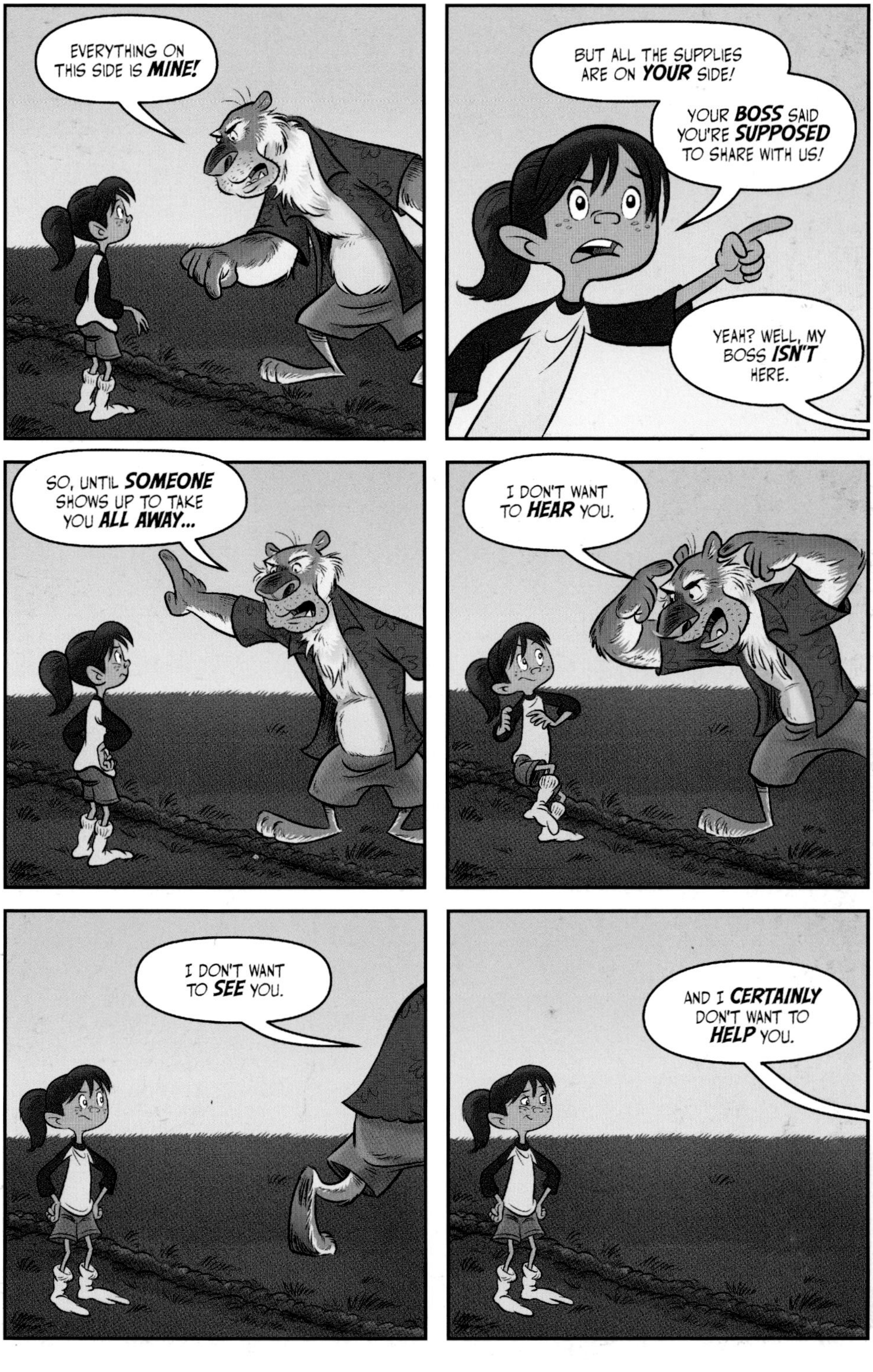
EVERYTHING ON THIS SIDE IS **MINE!**
BUT ALL THE SUPPLIES ARE ON **YOUR** SIDE!
YOUR **BOSS** SAID YOU'RE **SUPPOSED** TO SHARE WITH US!
YEAH? WELL, MY BOSS **ISN'T** HERE.
SO, UNTIL **SOMEONE** SHOWS UP TO TAKE YOU **ALL AWAY...**
I DON'T WANT TO **HEAR** YOU.
I DON'T WANT TO **SEE** YOU.
AND I **CERTAINLY** DON'T WANT TO **HELP** YOU.

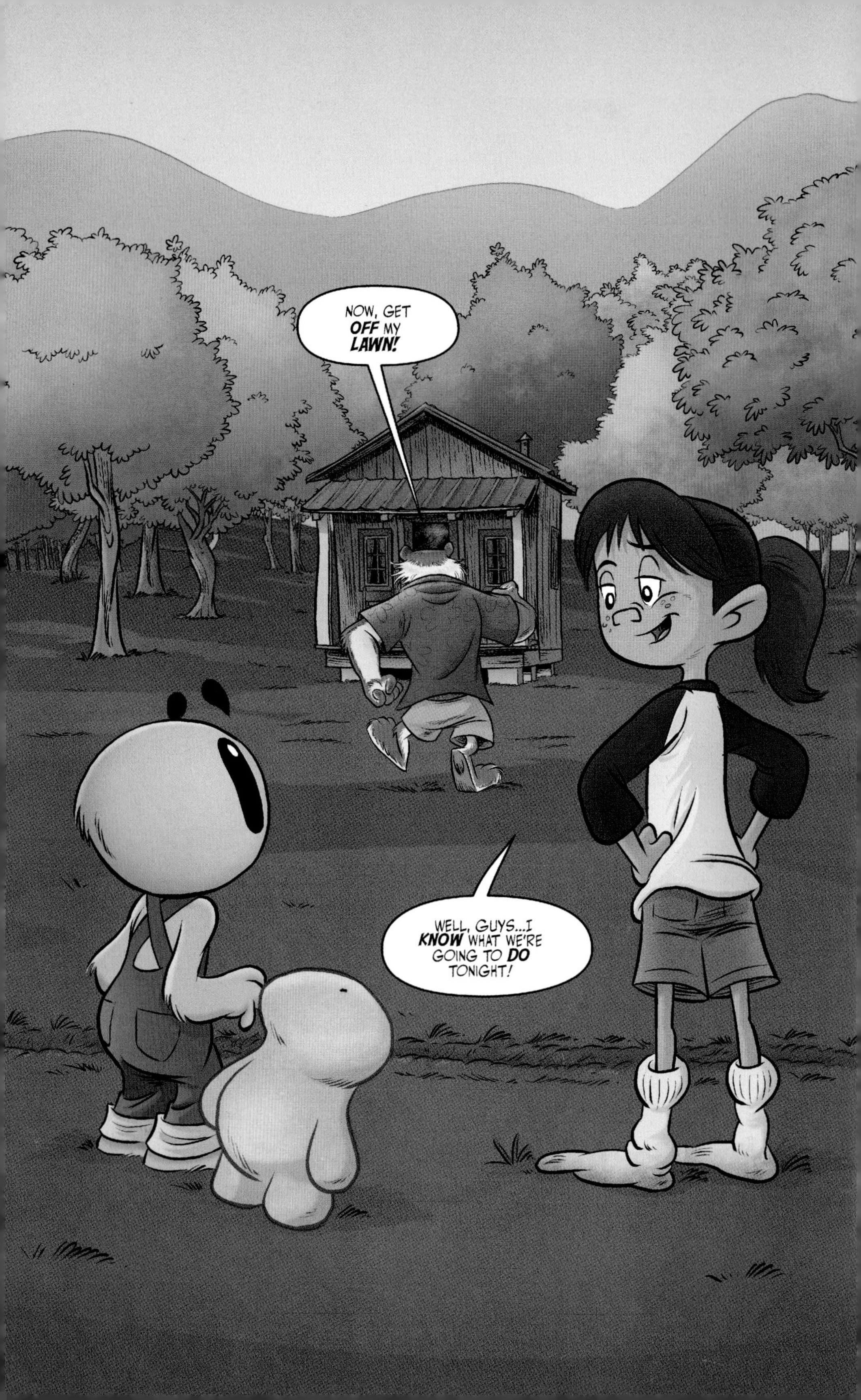
NOW, GET OFF MY LAWN!
WELL, GUYS...I KNOW WHAT WE'RE GOING TO DO TONIGHT!

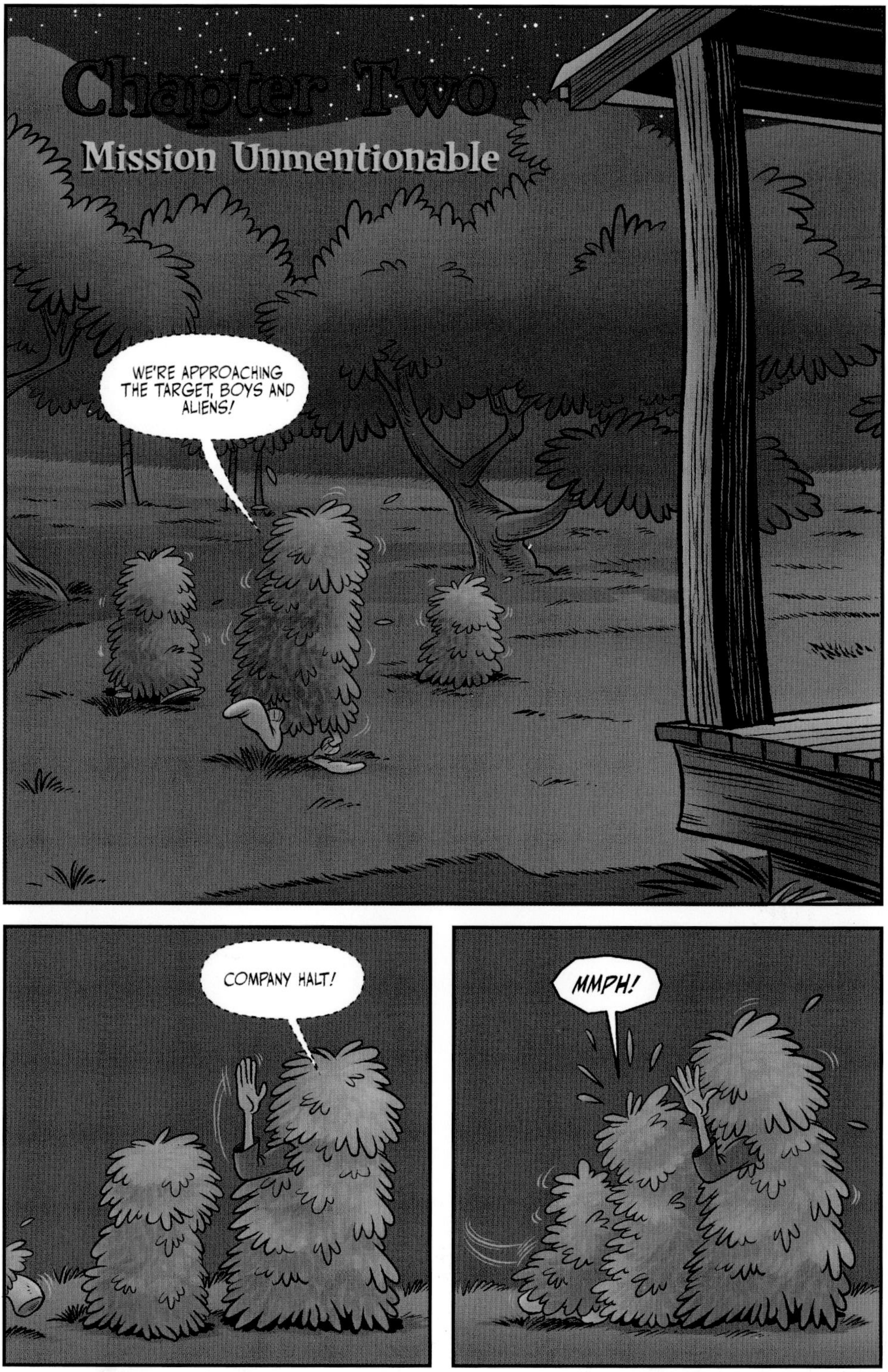
Chapter Two
Mission Unmentionable
WE'RE APPROACHING THE TARGET, BOYS AND ALIENS!
COMPANY HALT!
MMPH!

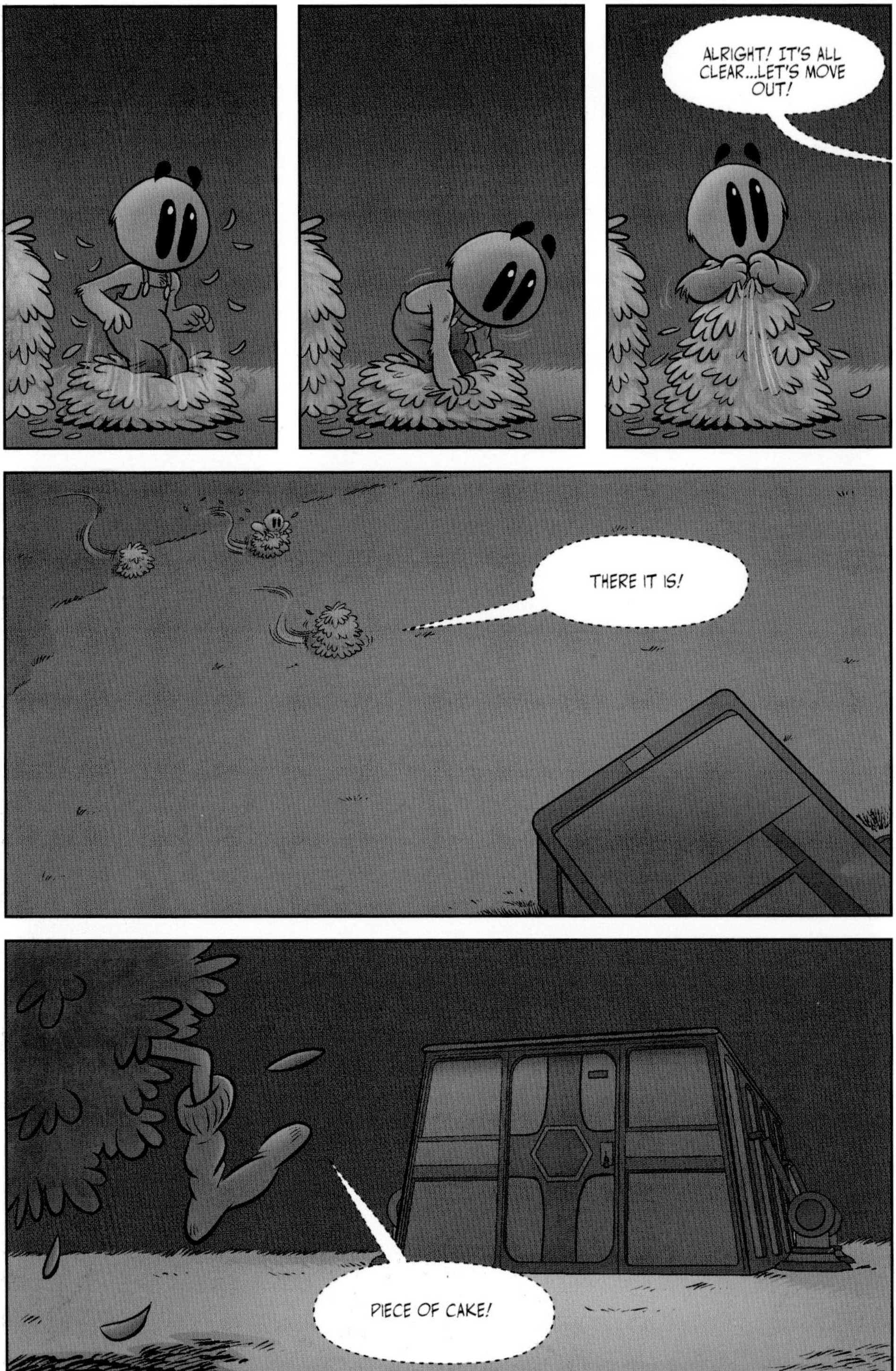

ALRIGHT! IT'S ALL CLEAR...LET'S MOVE OUT!
THERE IT IS!
PIECE OF CAKE!

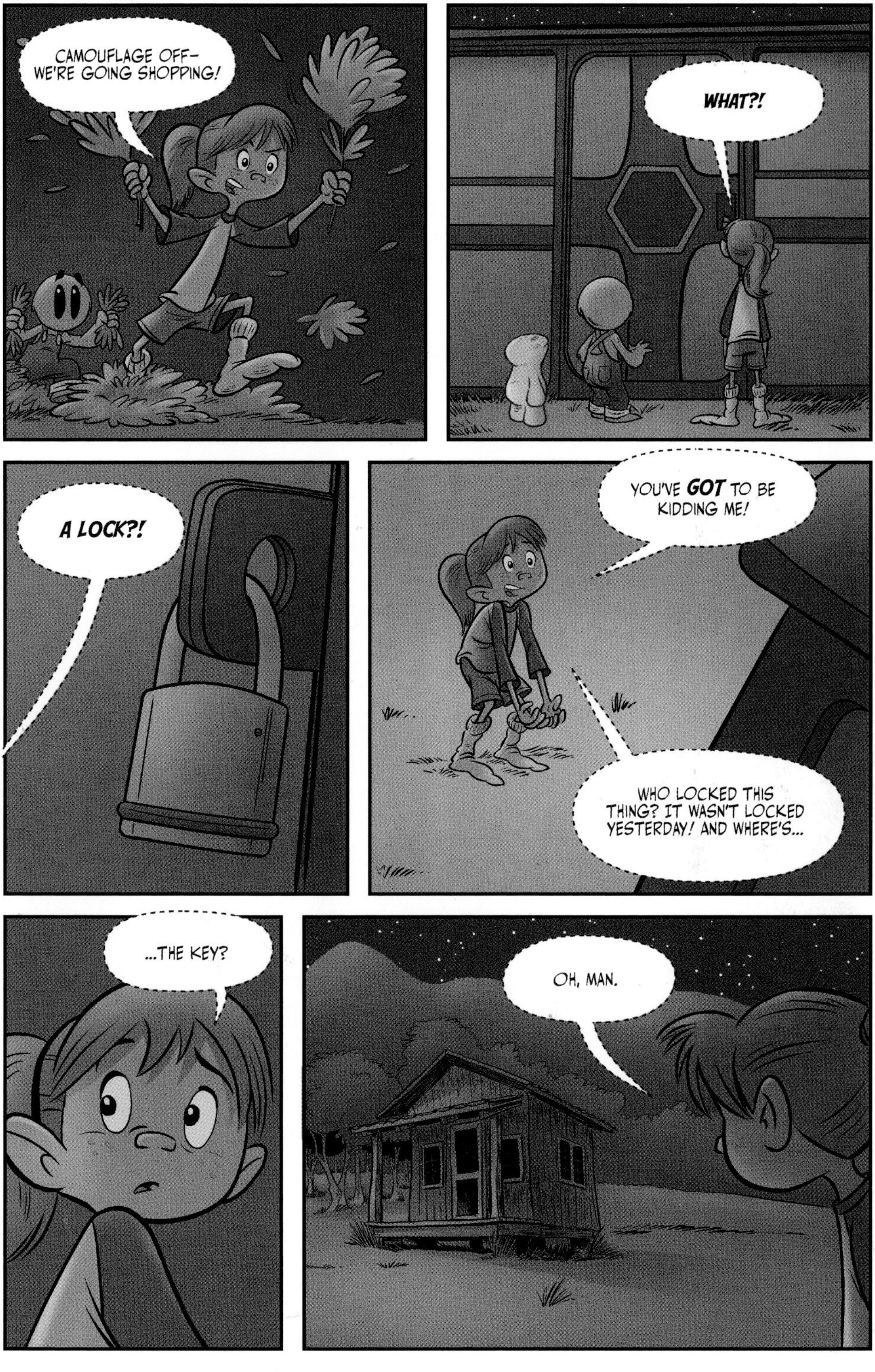
CAMOUFLAGE OFF-
WE'RE GOING SHOPPING!
WHAT?!
A LOCK?!
YOU'VE GOT TO BE KIDDING ME!
WHO LOCKED THIS THING? IT WASN'T LOCKED YESTERDAY! AND WHERE'S...
...THE KEY?
OH, MAN.

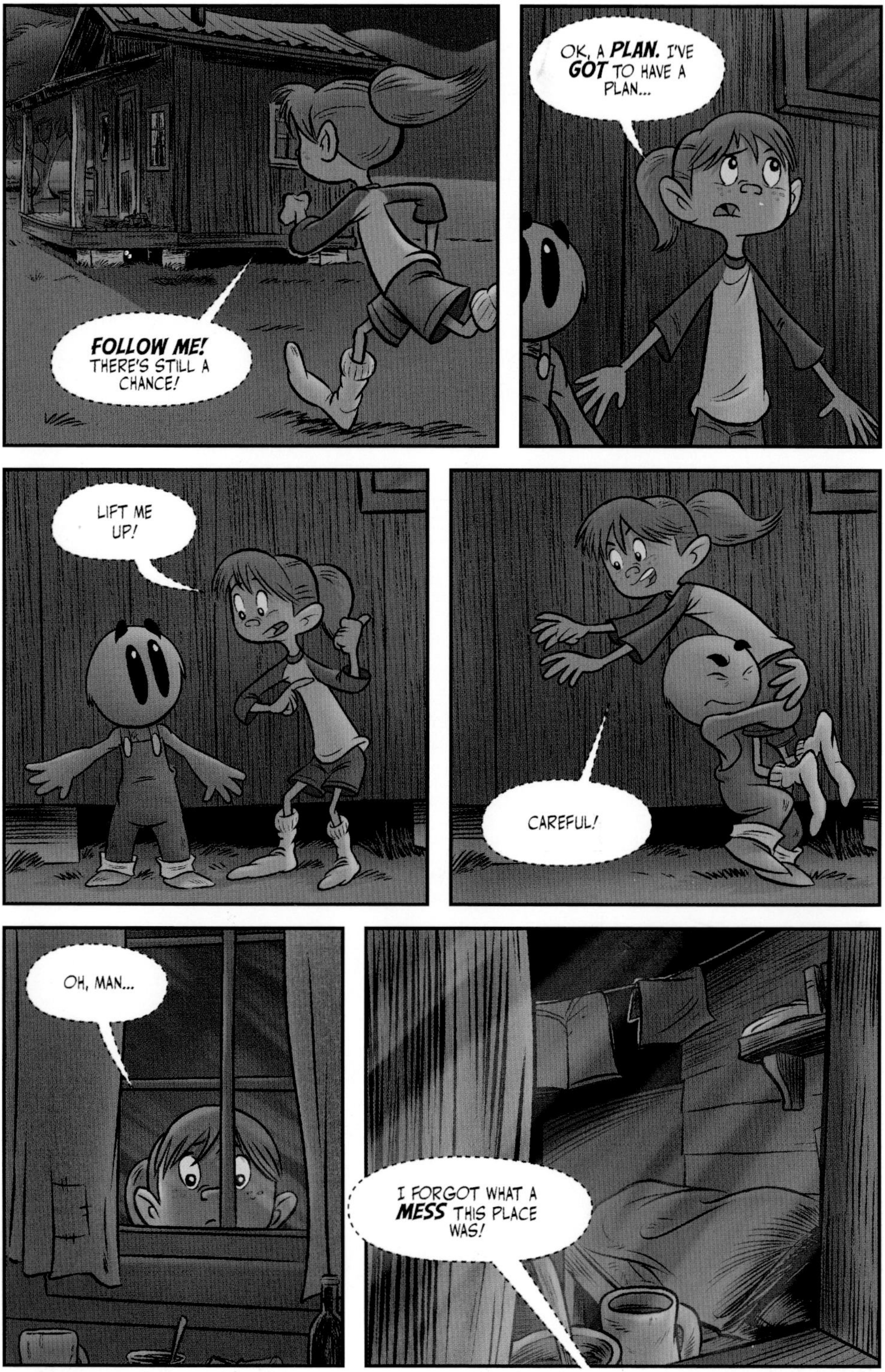
FOLLOW ME! THERE'S STILL A CHANCE!
OK, A PLAN. I'VE GOT TO HAVE A PLAN...
LIFT ME UP!
CAREFUL!
OH, MAN...
I FORGOT WHAT A MESS THIS PLACE WAS!

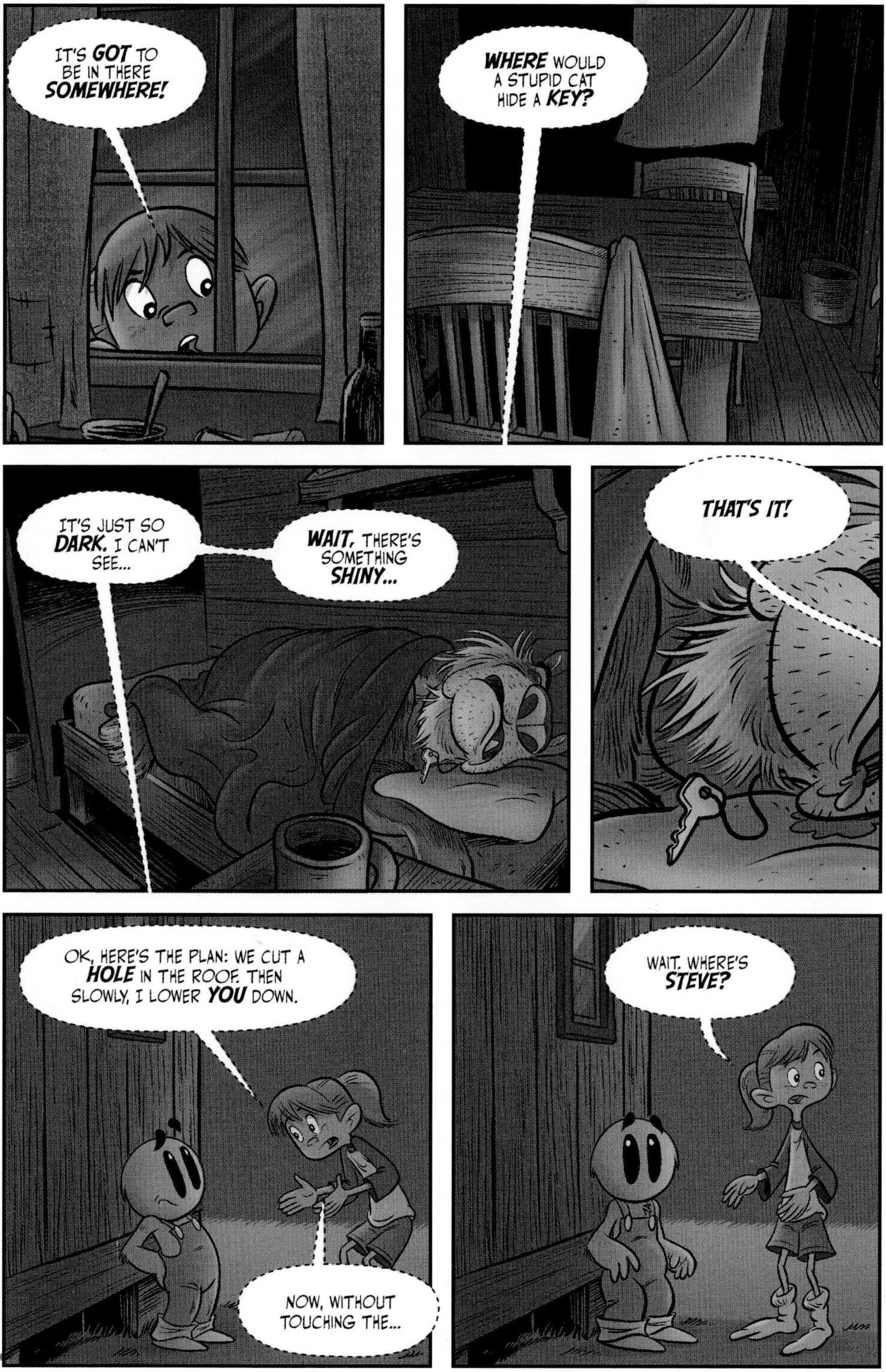
IT'S GOT TO BE IN THERE SOMEWHERE!
WHERE WOULD A STUPID CAT HIDE A KEY?
IT'S JUST SO DARK. I CAN'T SEE...
WAIT, THERE'S SOMETHING SHINY...
THAT'S IT!
OK, HERE'S THE PLAN: WE CUT A HOLE IN THE ROOF. THEN SLOWLY, I LOWER YOU DOWN.
NOW, WITHOUT TOUCHING THE...
WAIT. WHERE'S STEVE?

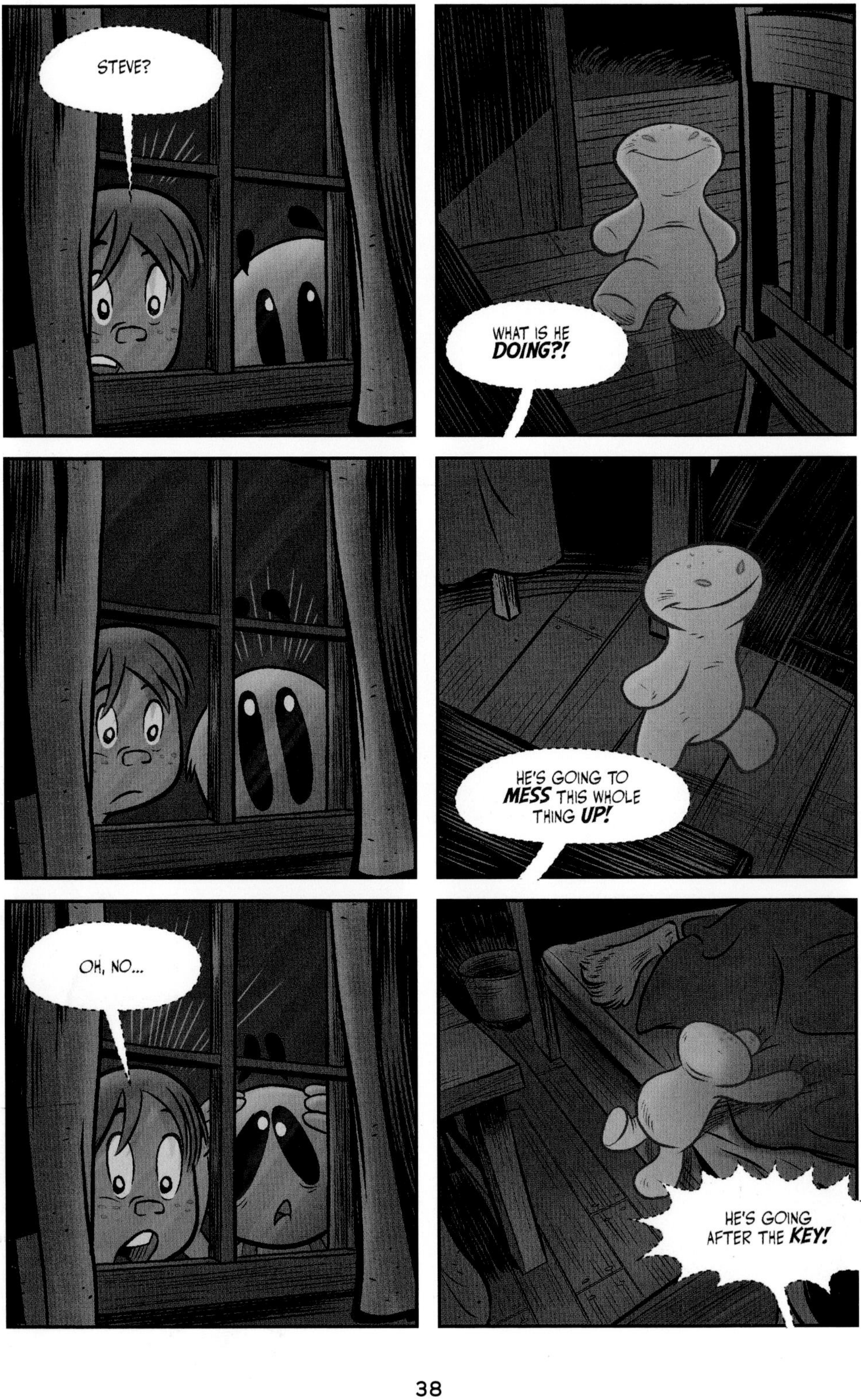
STEVE?
WHAT IS HE DOING?!
HE'S GOING TO MESS THIS WHOLE THING UP!
OH, NO...
HE'S GOING AFTER THE KEY!

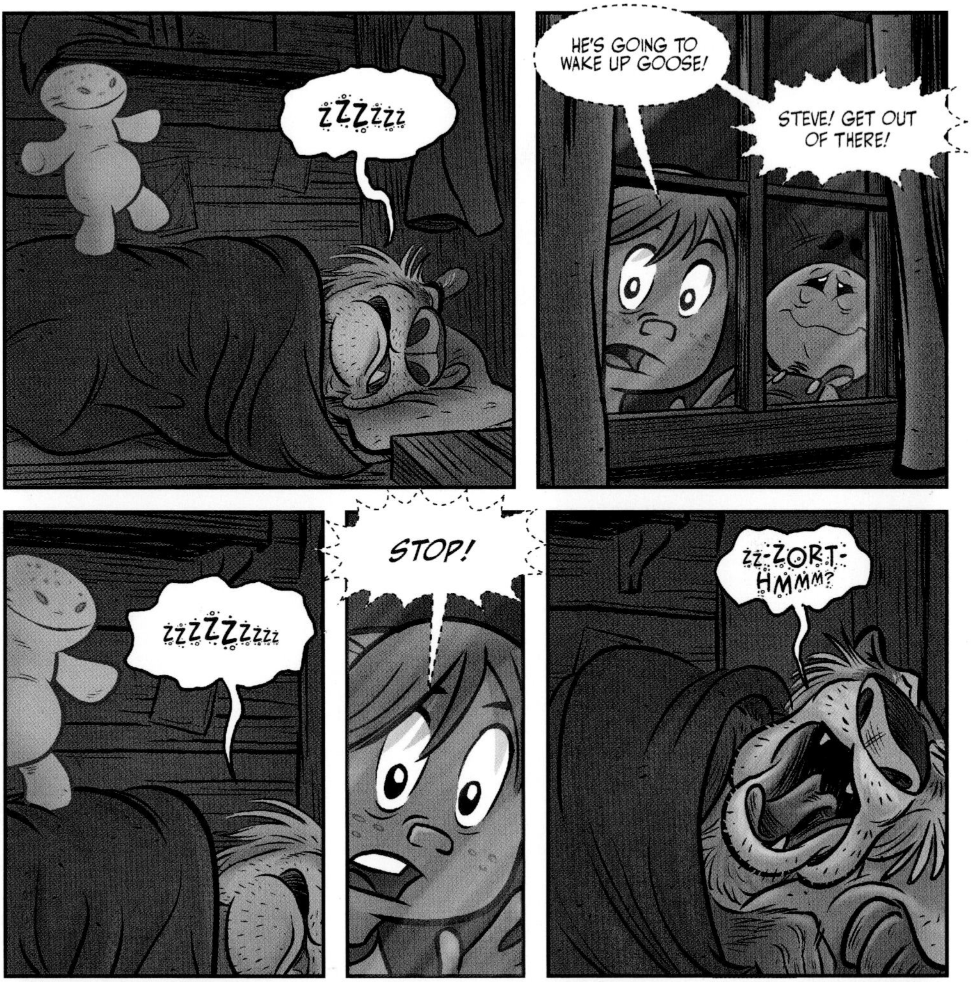
ZZZzzz
HE'S GOING TO WAKE UP GOOSE!
STEVE! GET OUT OF THERE!
ZzzZZzzz
STOP!
ZZ-ZORT-HMMM?
WHA..?!
AIEEE-AHHHH!!

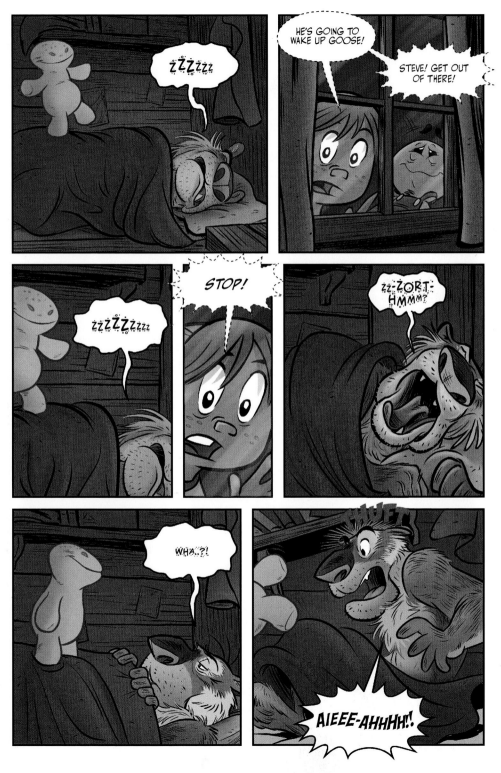

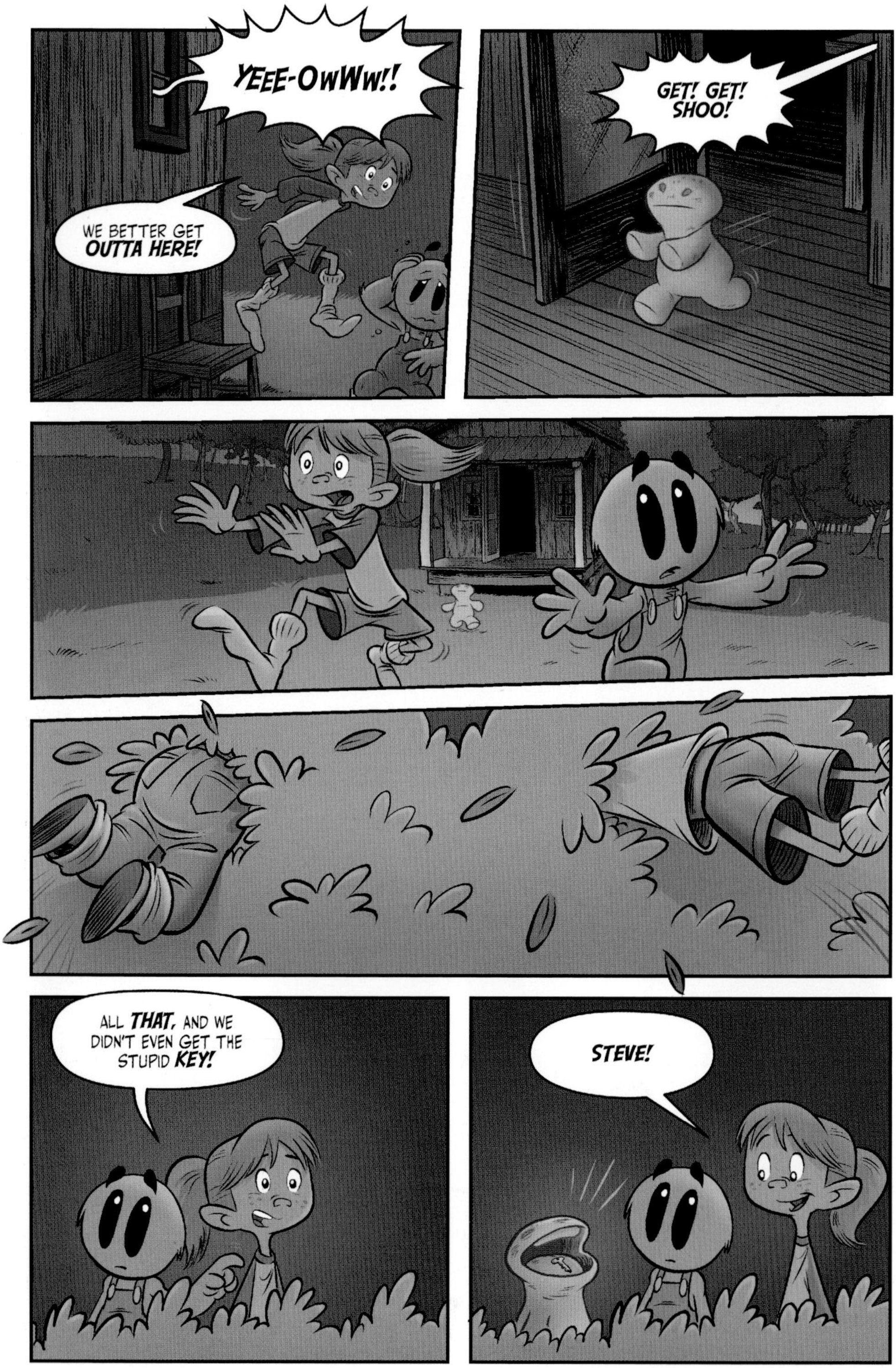
YEEE-OWWW!!
WE BETTER GET OUTTA HERE!
GET! GET! SHOO!
ALL THAT, AND WE DIDN'T EVEN GET THE STUPID KEY!
STEVE!

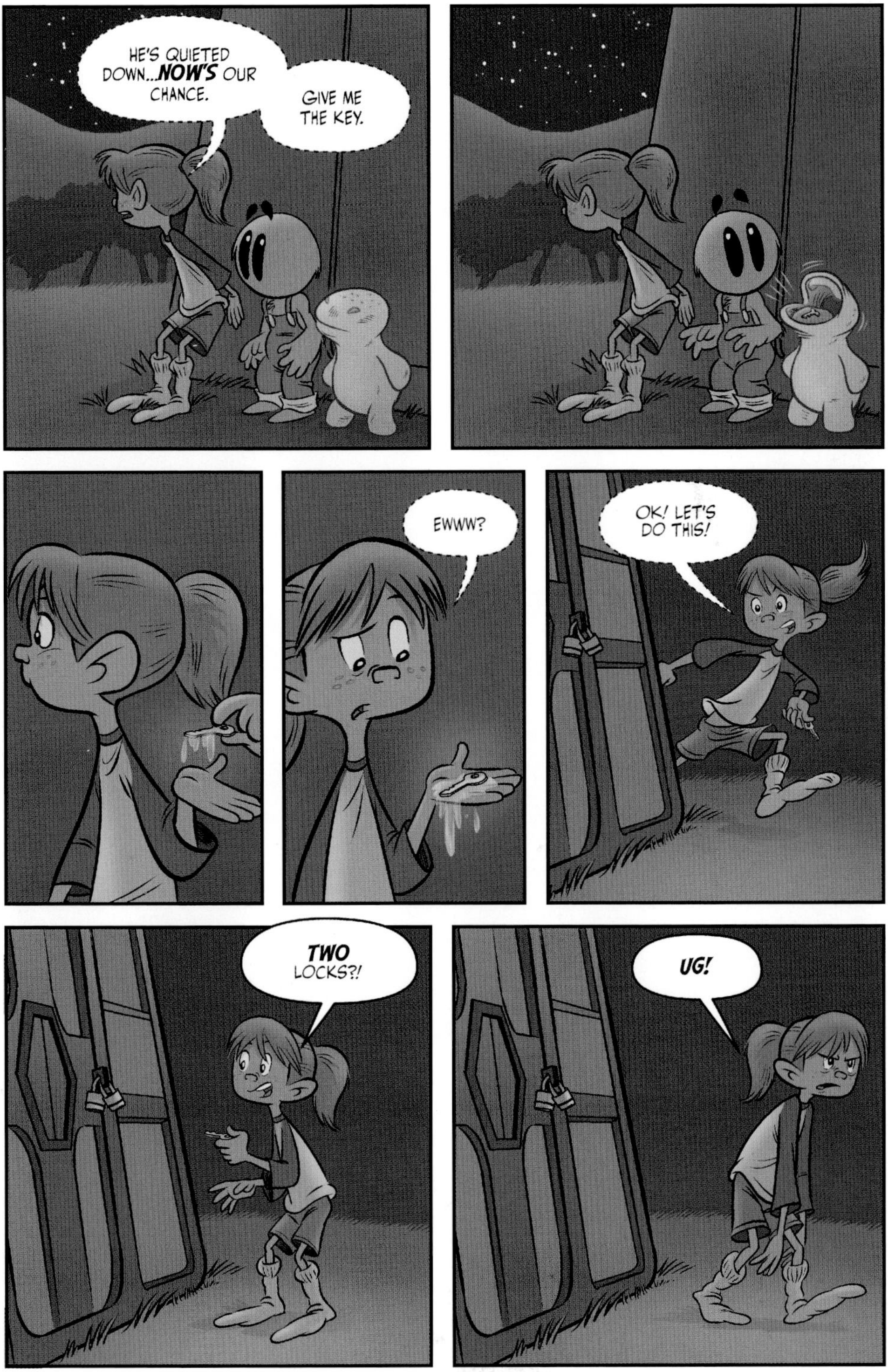
HE'S QUIETED DOWN...NOW'S OUR CHANCE.
GIVE ME THE KEY.
EWWW?
OK! LET'S DO THIS!
TWO LOCKS?!
UG!

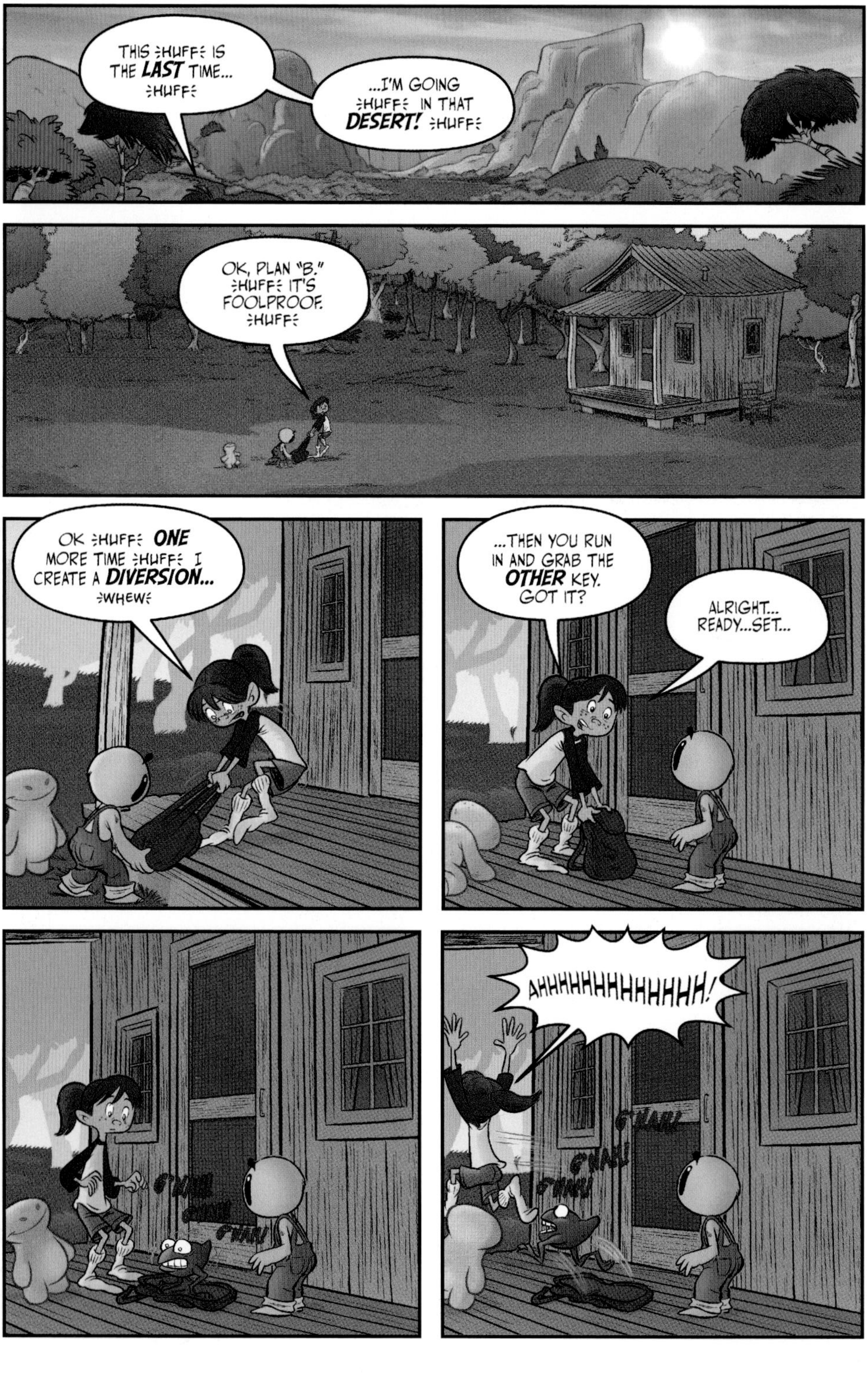
THIS ⸗HUFF⸗ IS THE **LAST** TIME... ⸗HUFF⸗
...I'M GOING ⸗HUFF⸗ IN THAT **DESERT!** ⸗HUFF⸗
OK, PLAN "B." ⸗HUFF⸗ IT'S FOOLPROOF. ⸗HUFF⸗
OK ⸗HUFF⸗ **ONE** MORE TIME ⸗HUFF⸗ I CREATE A **DIVERSION...** ⸗WHEW⸗
...THEN YOU RUN IN AND GRAB THE **OTHER** KEY. GOT IT?
ALRIGHT... READY...SET...
G'NAH!
AHHHHHHHHHHHHH!
G'NAH!
G'NAH!
G'NAH!

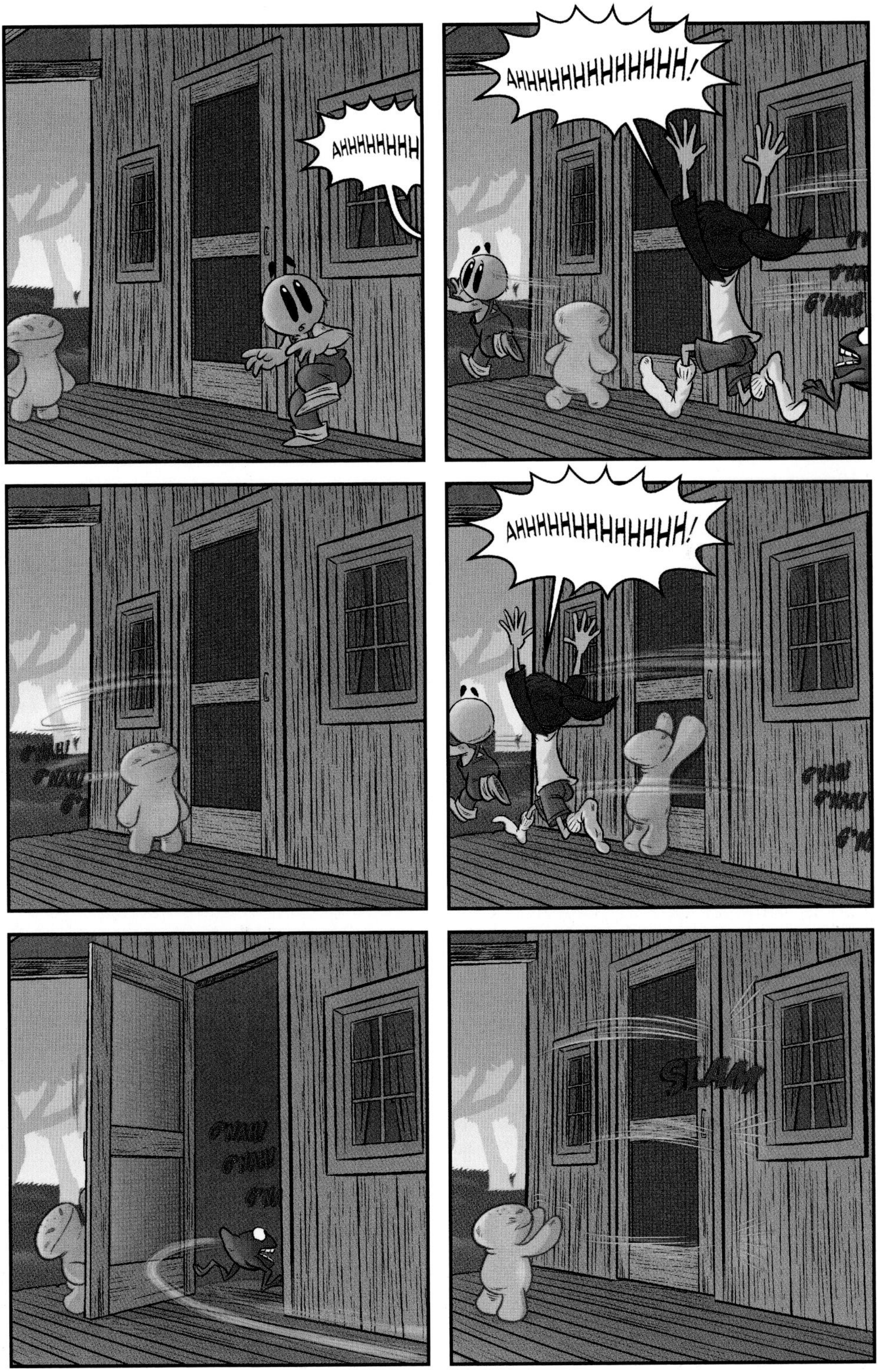
AHHHHHHHH
AHHHHHHHHHHHHHH!
AHHHHHHHHHHHHHH!

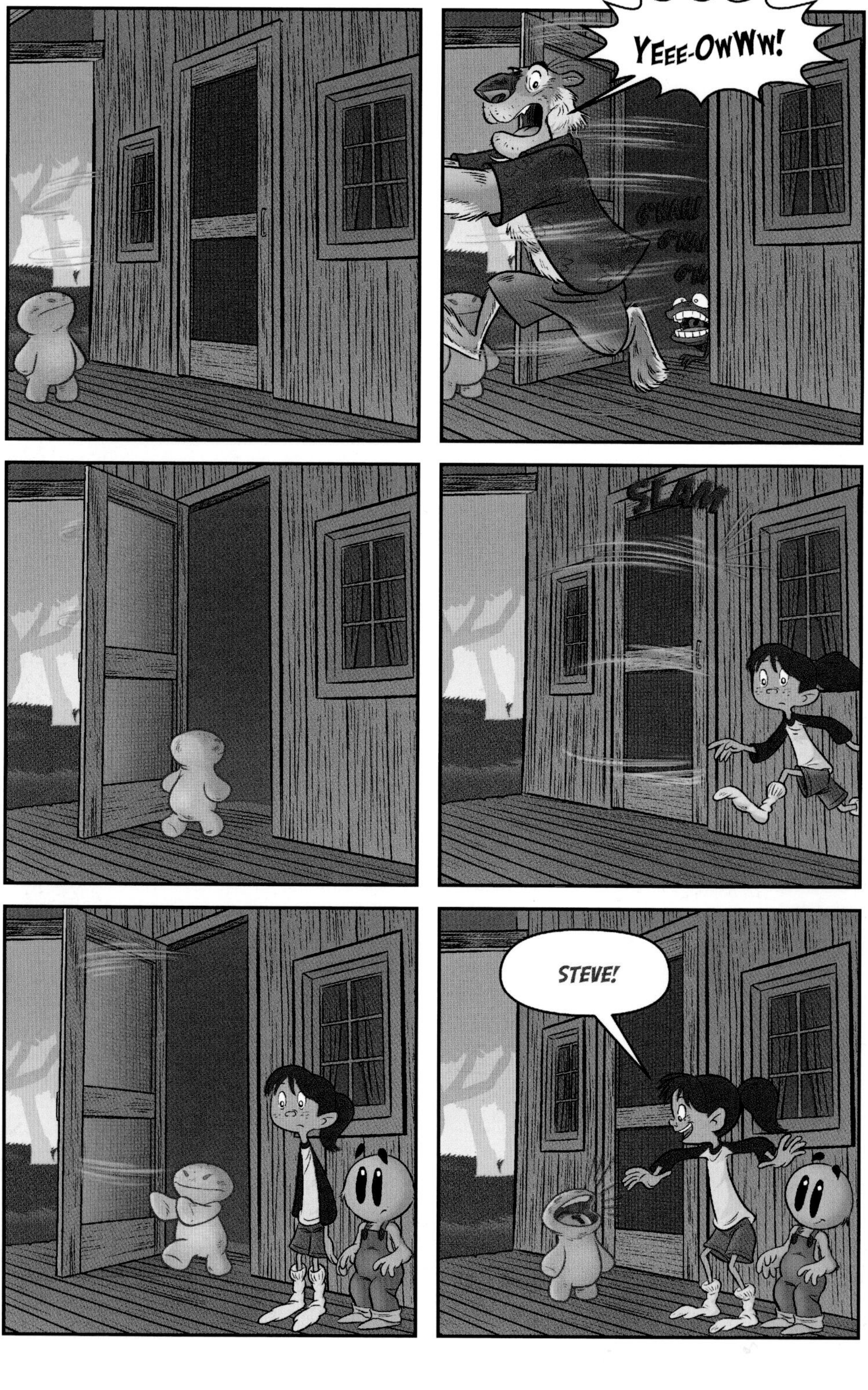
YEEE-OWWW!
SLAM
STEVE!

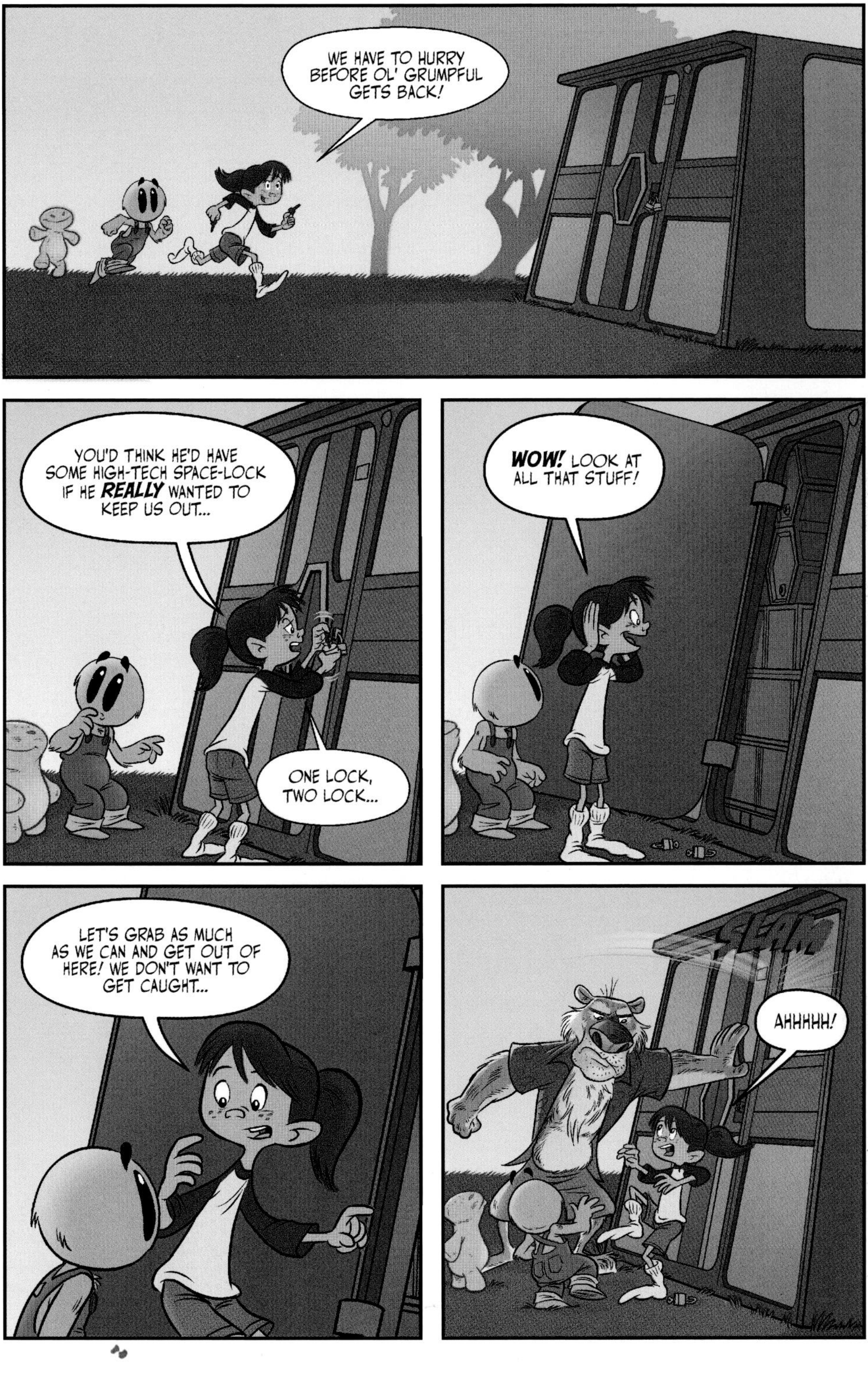
WE HAVE TO HURRY BEFORE OL' GRUMPFUL GETS BACK!
YOU'D THINK HE'D HAVE SOME HIGH-TECH SPACE-LOCK IF HE REALLY WANTED TO KEEP US OUT...
ONE LOCK, TWO LOCK...
WOW! LOOK AT ALL THAT STUFF!
LET'S GRAB AS MUCH AS WE CAN AND GET OUT OF HERE! WE DON'T WANT TO GET CAUGHT...
SLAM
AHHHHH!

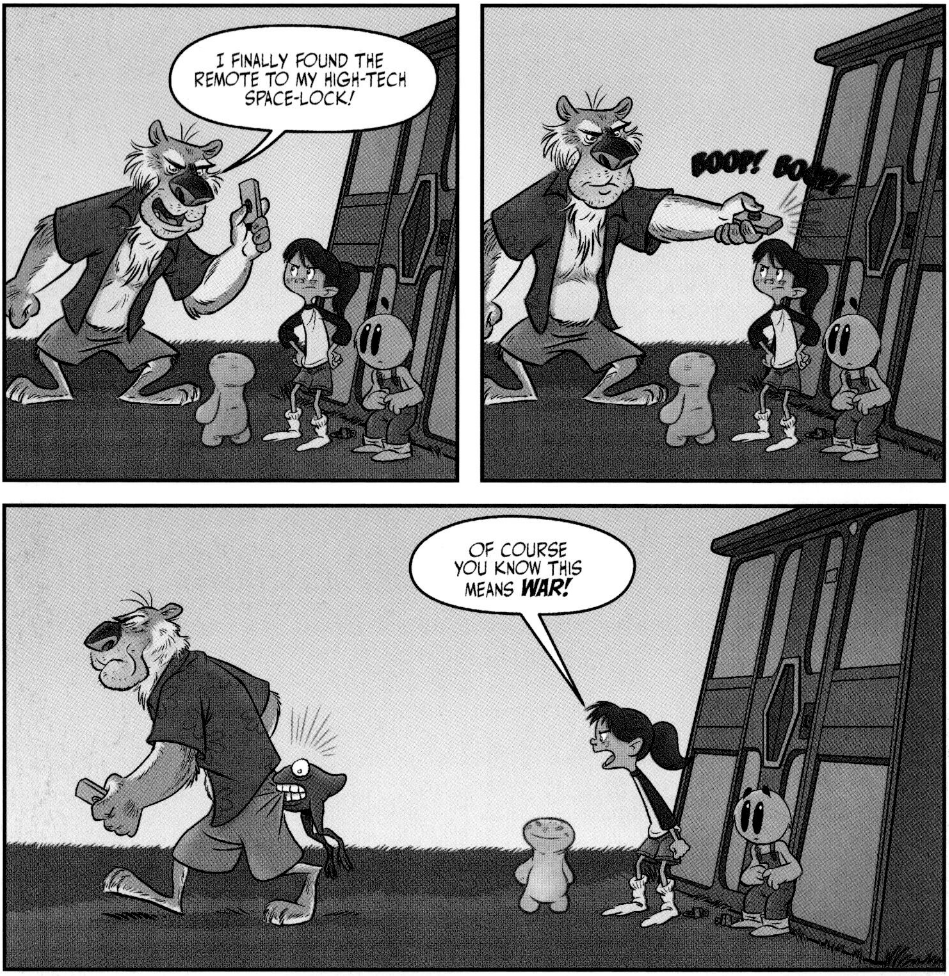
I FINALLY FOUND THE REMOTE TO MY HIGH-TECH SPACE-LOCK!
BOOP! BOOP!
OF COURSE YOU KNOW THIS MEANS **WAR!**
I, UH, HEARD SOME RABBIT SAY THAT ON TV!
WELL, C'MON...
IF WE'RE GOING TO DO PLAN "C," WE'RE GOING TO NEED A LITTLE MORE HELP!

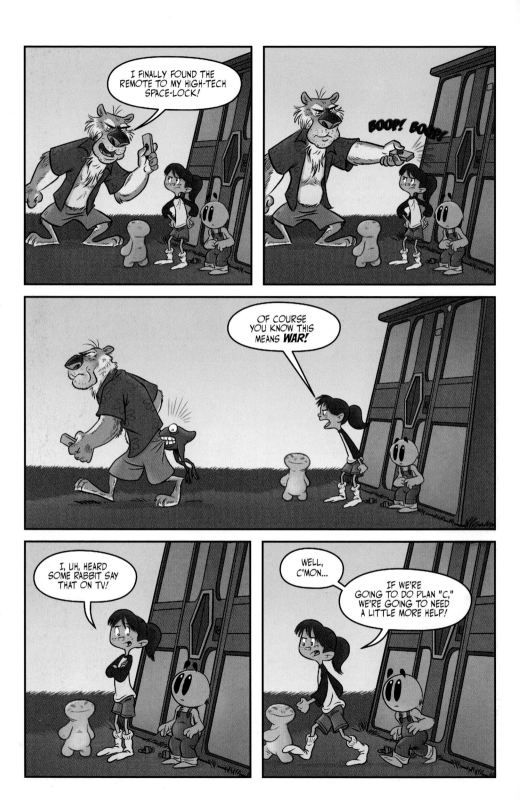

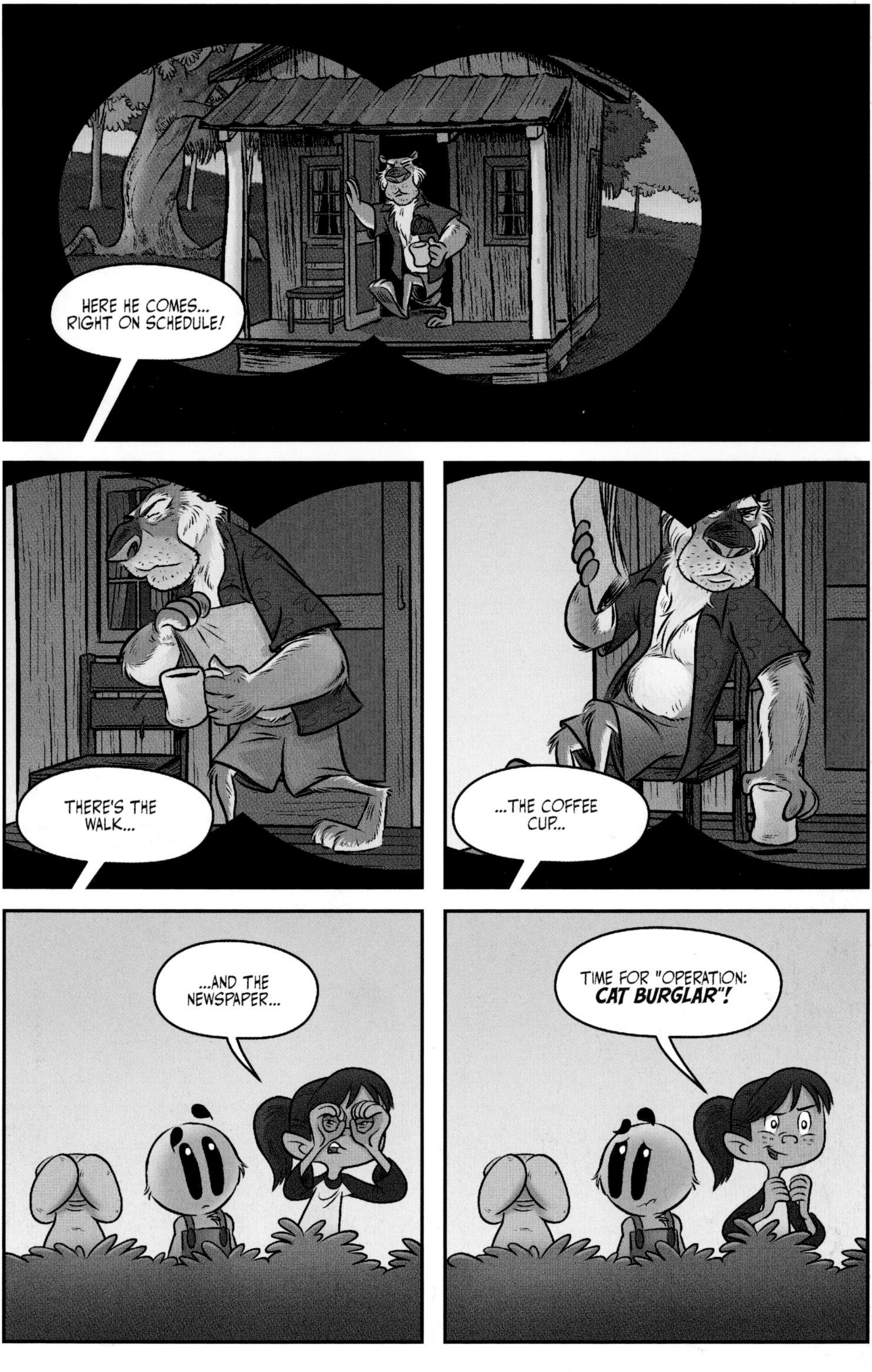
HERE HE COMES...
RIGHT ON SCHEDULE!
THERE'S THE WALK...
...THE COFFEE CUP...
...AND THE NEWSPAPER...
TIME FOR "OPERATION: CAT BURGLAR"!

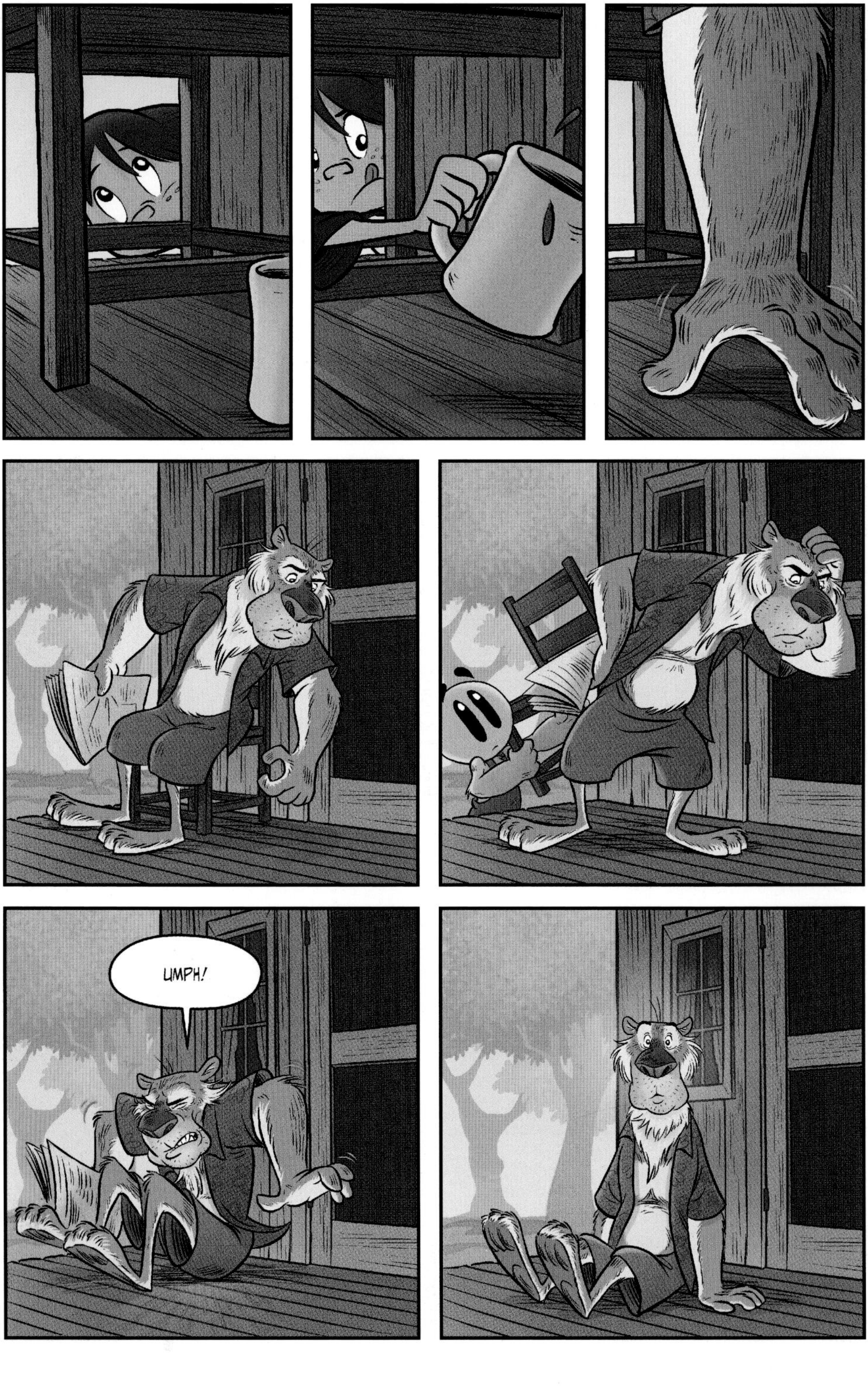
UMPH!

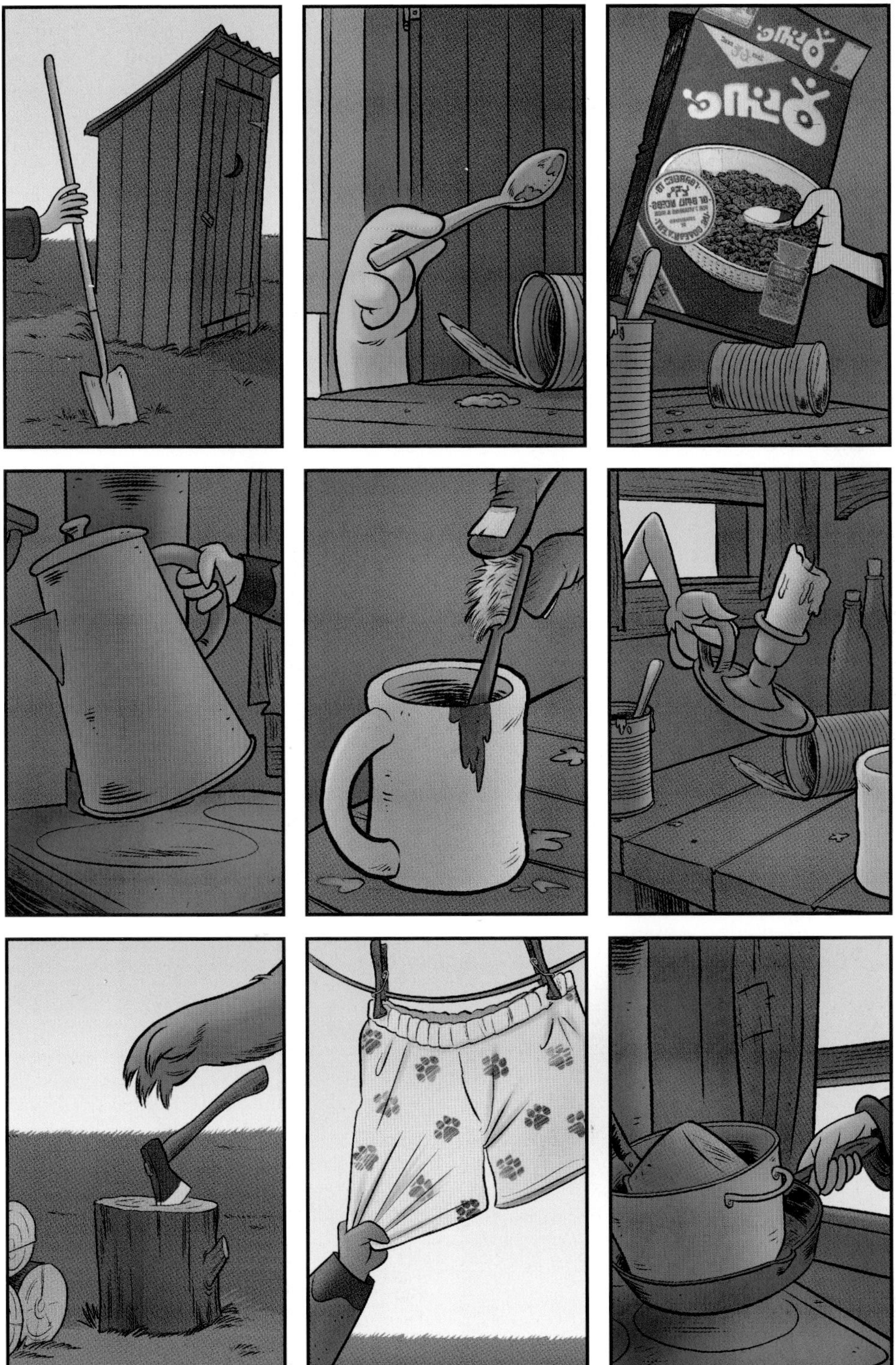

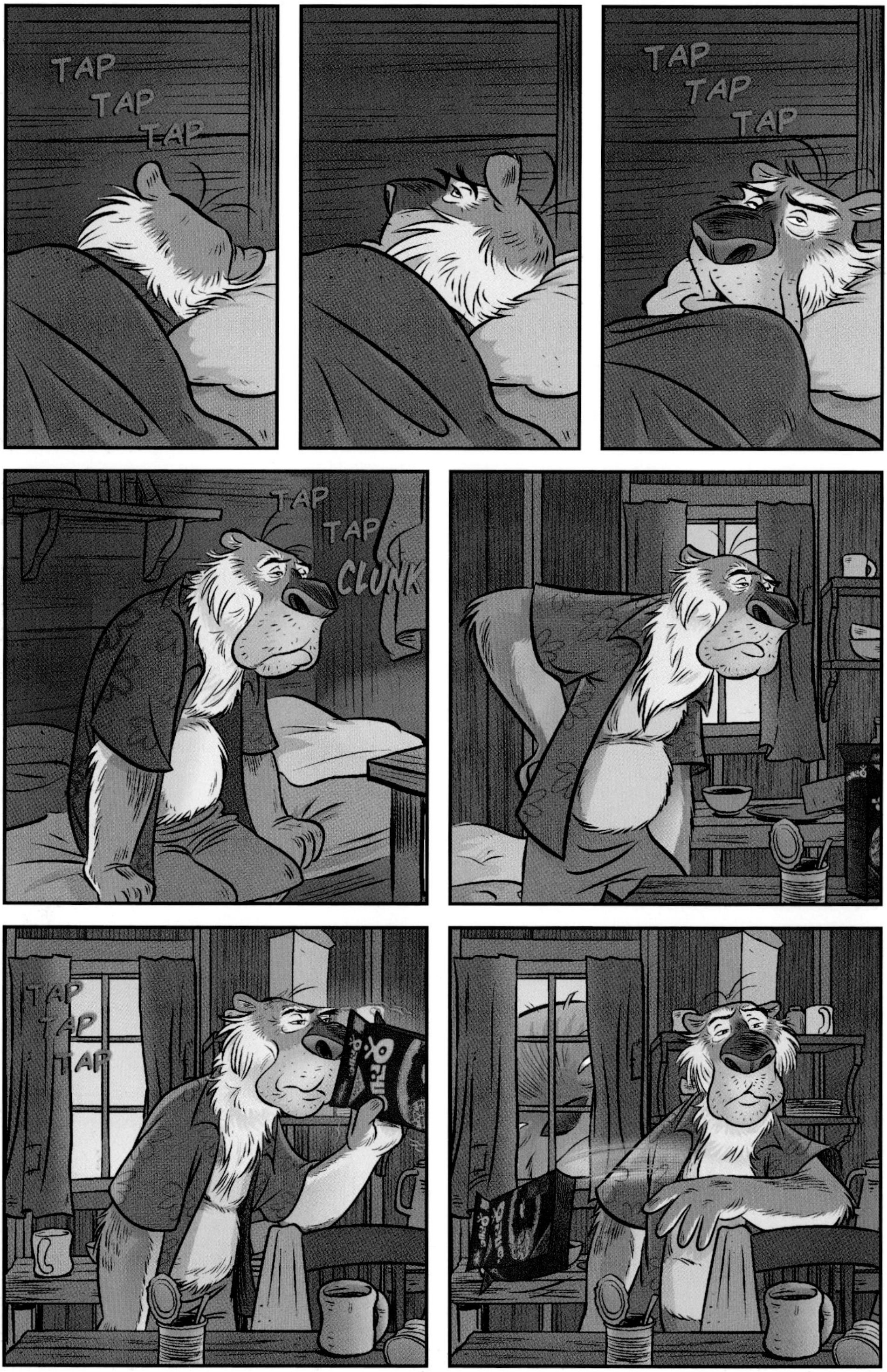
TAP
TAP
TAP
TAP
TAP
TAP
TAP
TAP
CLUNK
TAP
TAP
TAP

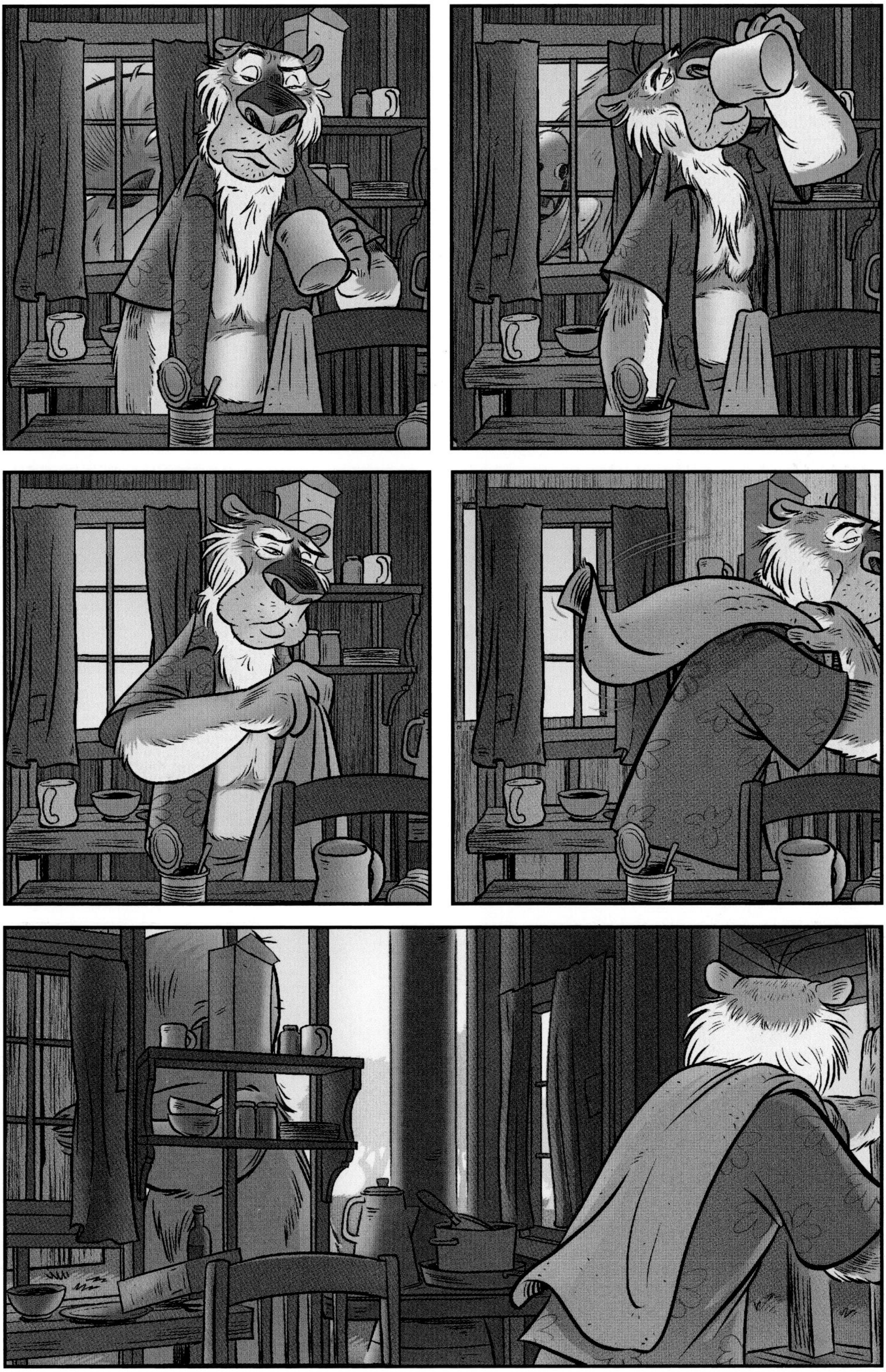

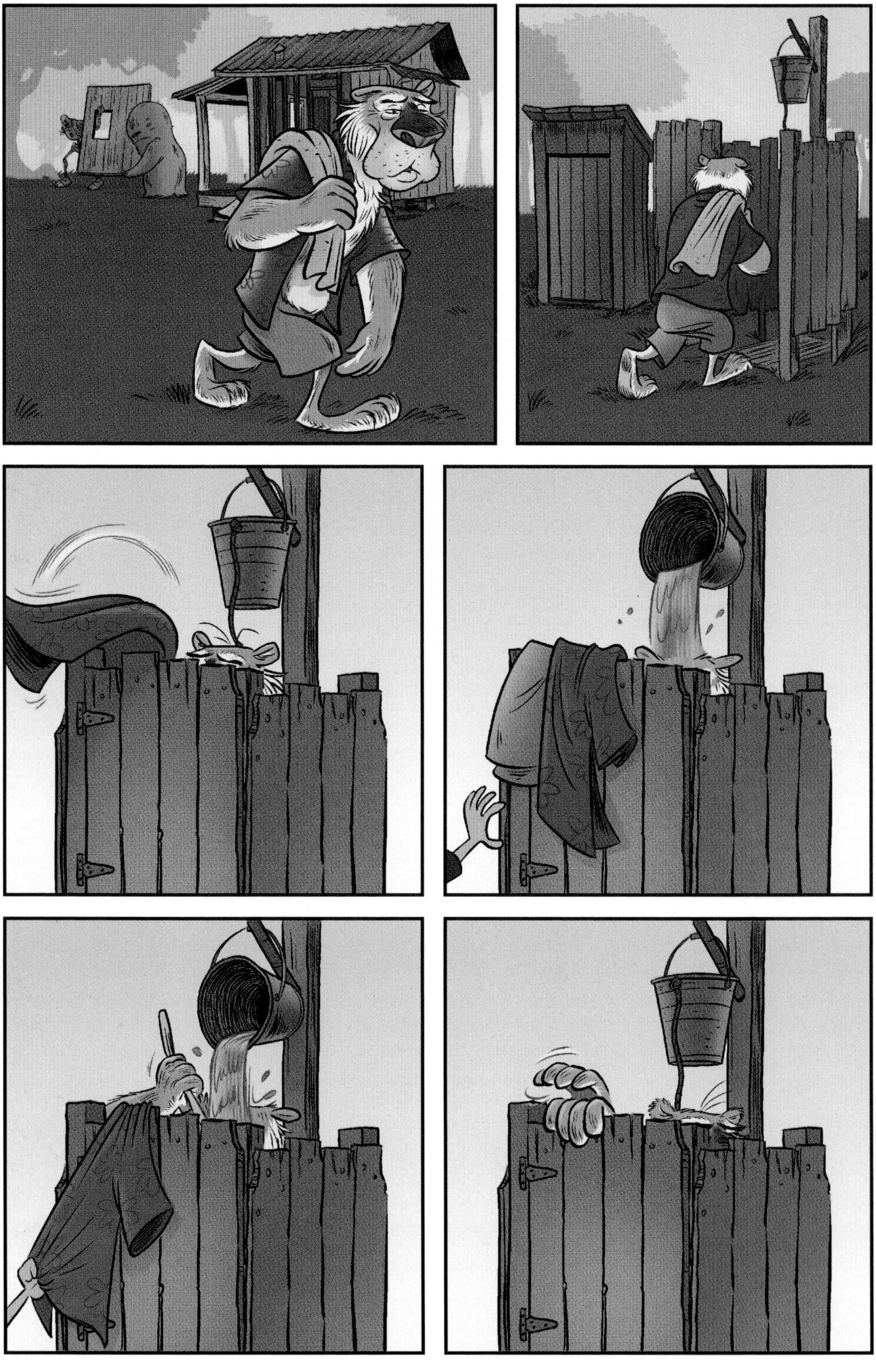

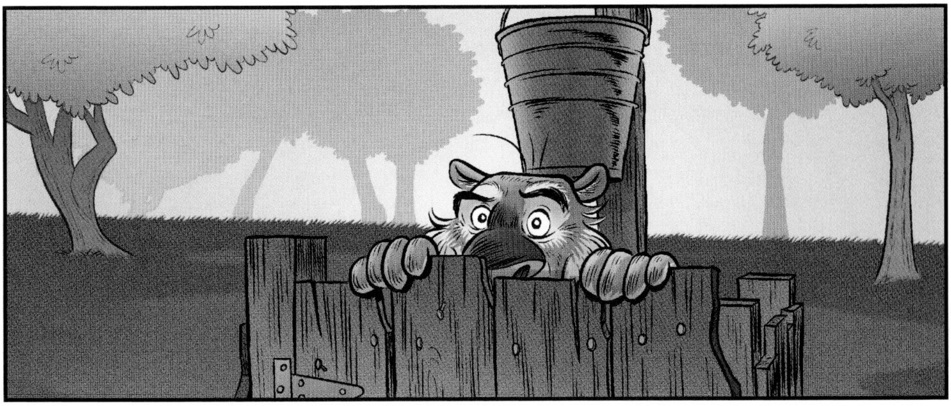

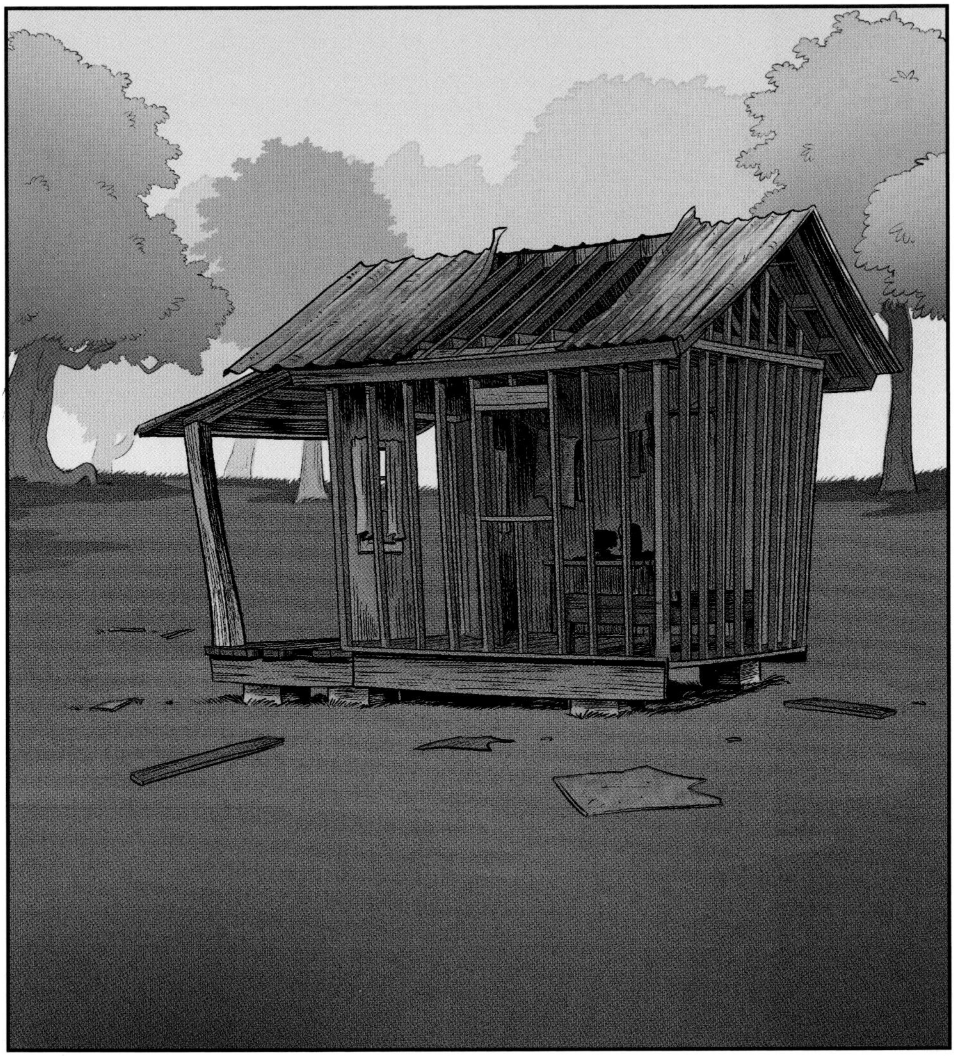

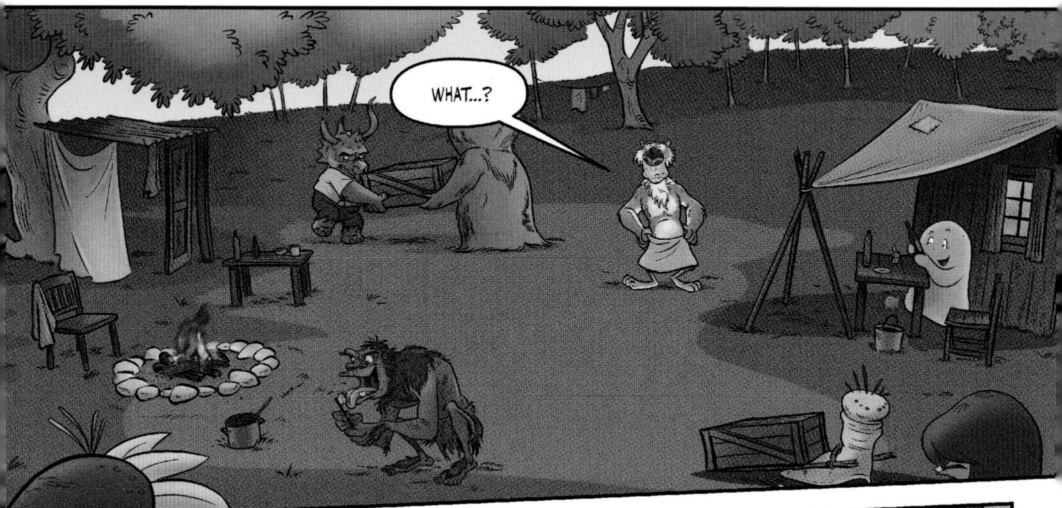
WHAT...?

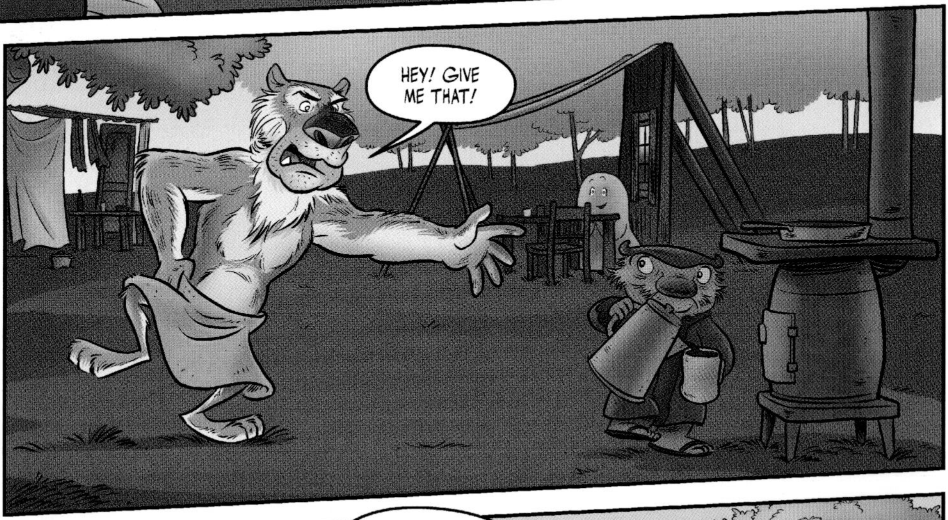
HEY! GIVE ME THAT!

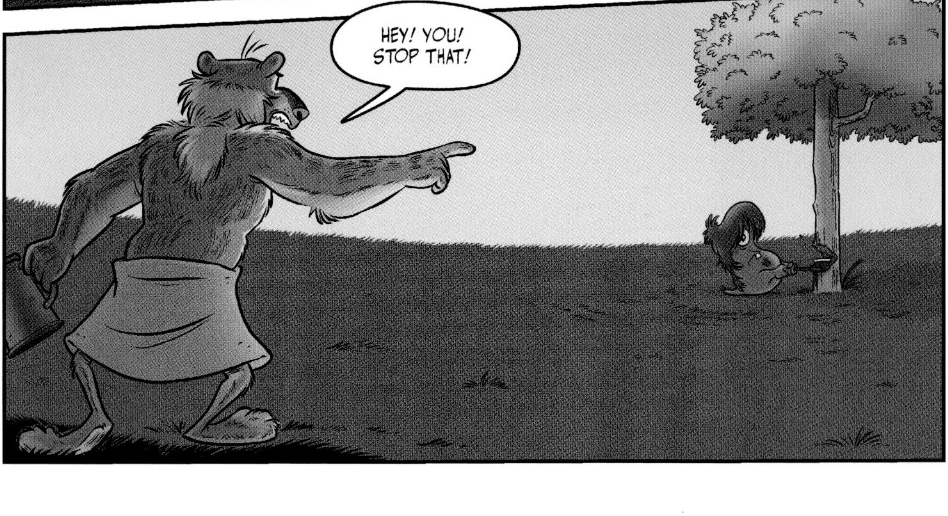
HEY! YOU! STOP THAT!

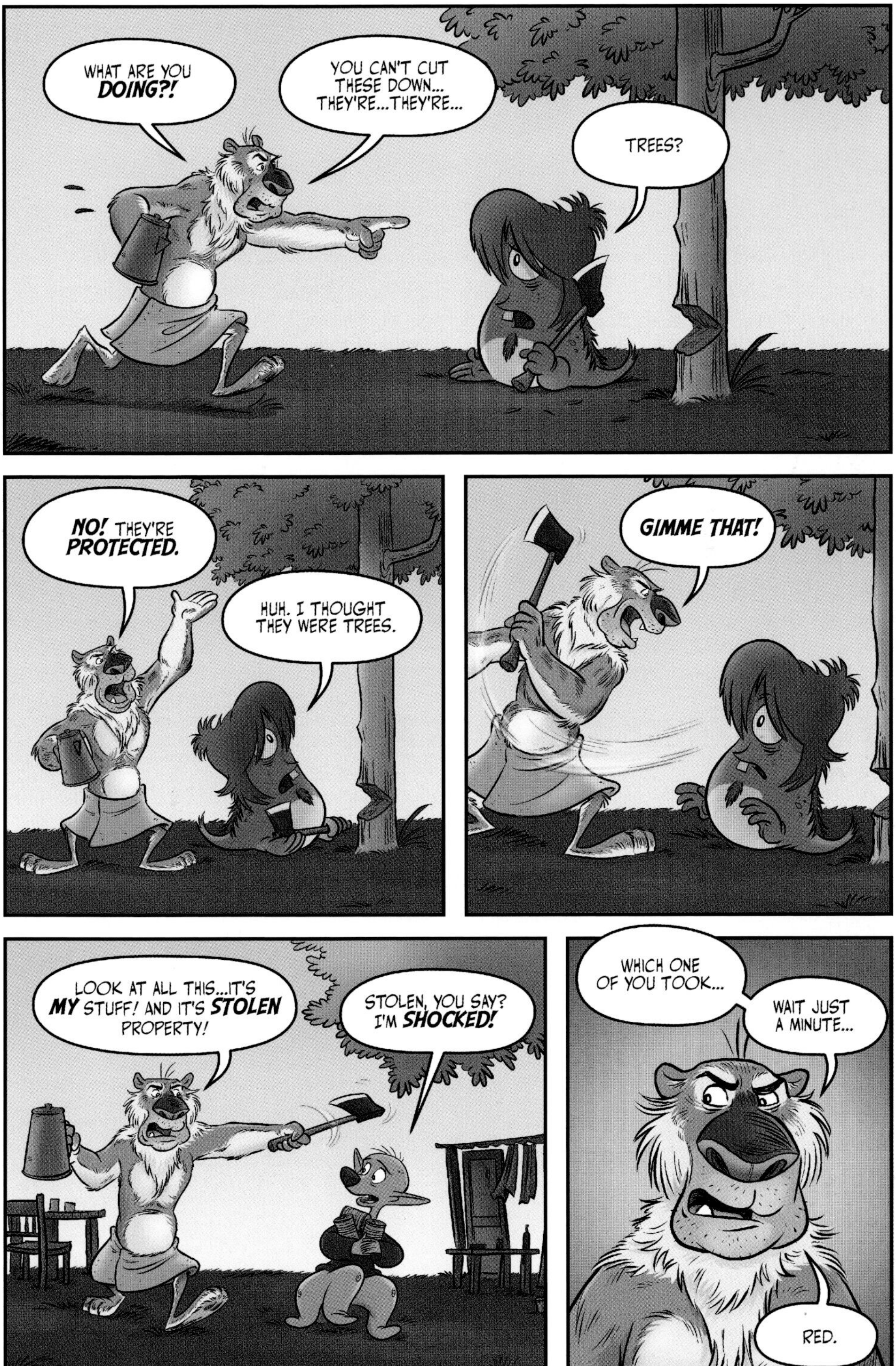
WHAT ARE YOU DOING?!
YOU CAN'T CUT THESE DOWN... THEY'RE...THEY'RE...
TREES?
NO! THEY'RE PROTECTED.
HUH. I THOUGHT THEY WERE TREES.
GIMME THAT!
LOOK AT ALL THIS...IT'S MY STUFF! AND IT'S STOLEN PROPERTY!
STOLEN, YOU SAY? I'M SHOCKED!
WHICH ONE OF YOU TOOK...
WAIT JUST A MINUTE...
RED.

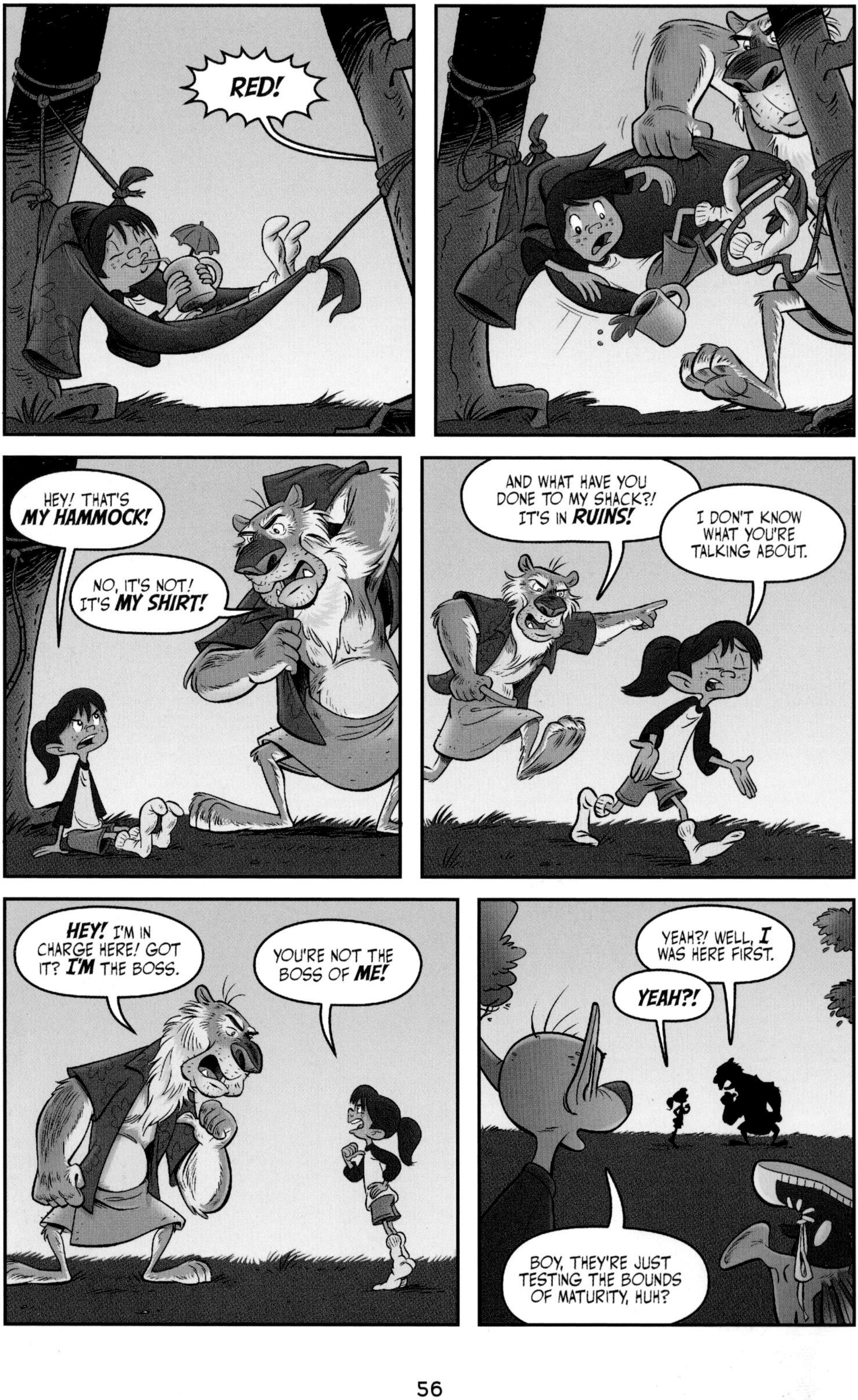
RED!
HEY! THAT'S MY HAMMOCK!
NO, IT'S NOT! IT'S MY SHIRT!
AND WHAT HAVE YOU DONE TO MY SHACK?! IT'S IN RUINS!
I DON'T KNOW WHAT YOU'RE TALKING ABOUT.
HEY! I'M IN CHARGE HERE! GOT IT? I'M THE BOSS.
YOU'RE NOT THE BOSS OF ME!
YEAH?! WELL, I WAS HERE FIRST.
YEAH?!
BOY, THEY'RE JUST TESTING THE BOUNDS OF MATURITY, HUH?

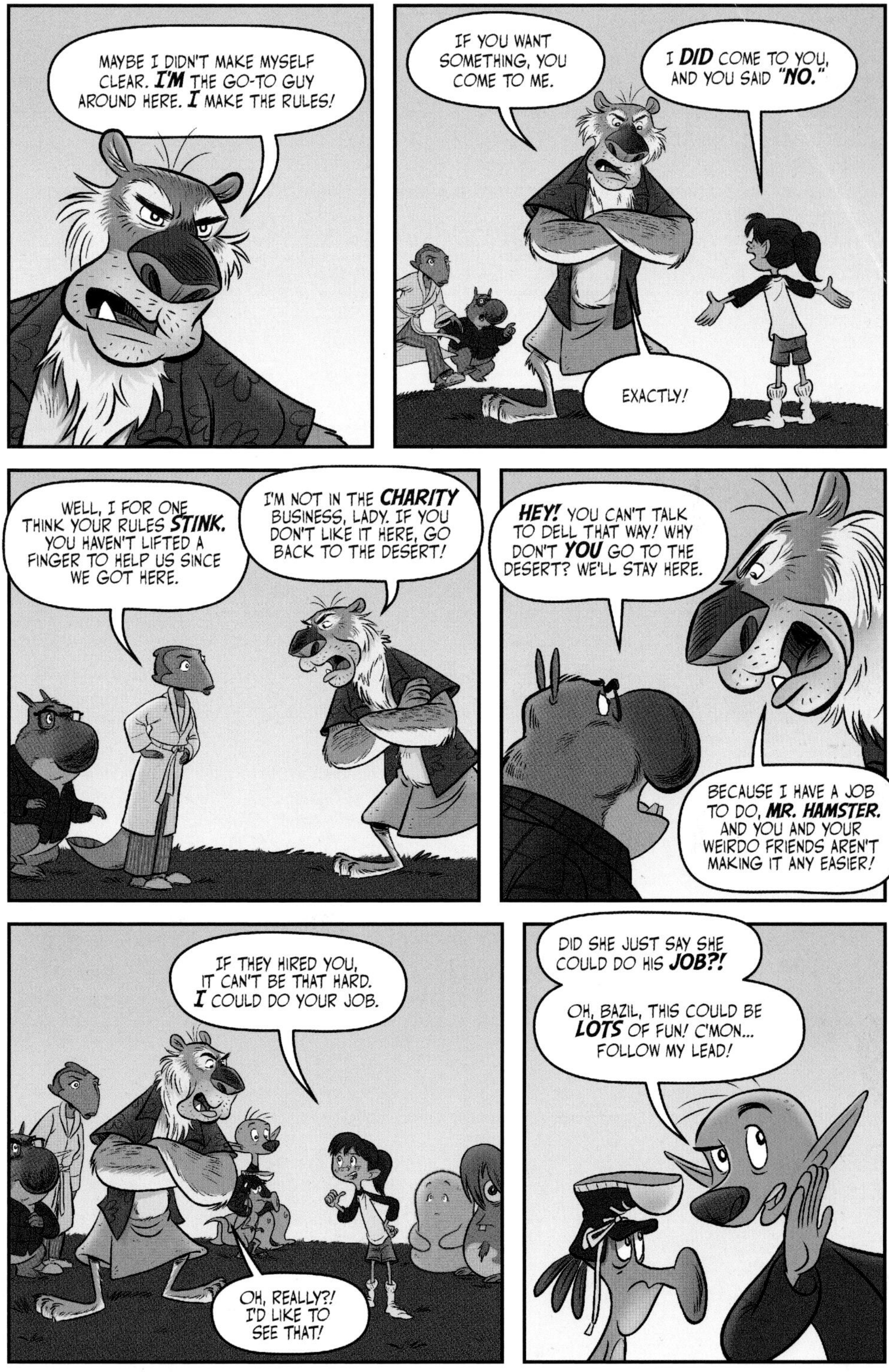
MAYBE I DIDN'T MAKE MYSELF CLEAR. I'M THE GO-TO GUY AROUND HERE. I MAKE THE RULES!
IF YOU WANT SOMETHING, YOU COME TO ME.
I DID COME TO YOU, AND YOU SAID "NO."
EXACTLY!
WELL, I FOR ONE THINK YOUR RULES STINK. YOU HAVEN'T LIFTED A FINGER TO HELP US SINCE WE GOT HERE.
I'M NOT IN THE CHARITY BUSINESS, LADY. IF YOU DON'T LIKE IT HERE, GO BACK TO THE DESERT!
HEY! YOU CAN'T TALK TO DELL THAT WAY! WHY DON'T YOU GO TO THE DESERT? WE'LL STAY HERE.
BECAUSE I HAVE A JOB TO DO, MR. HAMSTER. AND YOU AND YOUR WEIRDO FRIENDS AREN'T MAKING IT ANY EASIER!
IF THEY HIRED YOU, IT CAN'T BE THAT HARD. I COULD DO YOUR JOB.
OH, REALLY?! I'D LIKE TO SEE THAT!
DID SHE JUST SAY SHE COULD DO HIS JOB?!
OH, BAZIL, THIS COULD BE LOTS OF FUN! C'MON... FOLLOW MY LEAD!

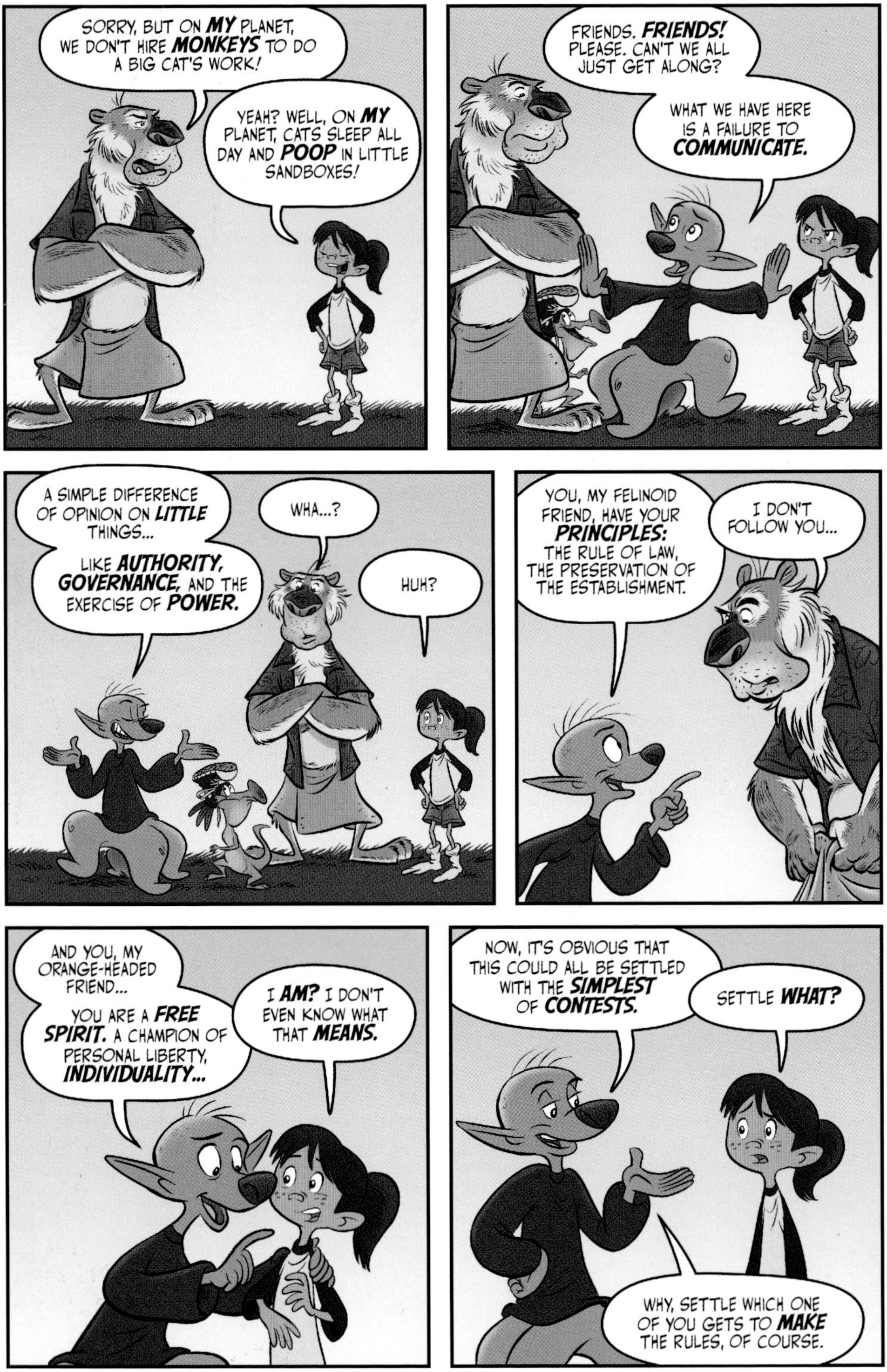
SORRY, BUT ON MY PLANET, WE DON'T HIRE MONKEYS TO DO A BIG CAT'S WORK!
YEAH? WELL, ON MY PLANET, CATS SLEEP ALL DAY AND POOP IN LITTLE SANDBOXES!
FRIENDS. FRIENDS! PLEASE. CAN'T WE ALL JUST GET ALONG?
WHAT WE HAVE HERE IS A FAILURE TO COMMUNICATE.
A SIMPLE DIFFERENCE OF OPINION ON LITTLE THINGS...
LIKE AUTHORITY, GOVERNANCE, AND THE EXERCISE OF POWER.
WHA...?
HUH?
YOU, MY FELINOID FRIEND, HAVE YOUR PRINCIPLES: THE RULE OF LAW, THE PRESERVATION OF THE ESTABLISHMENT.
I DON'T FOLLOW YOU...
AND YOU, MY ORANGE-HEADED FRIEND...
YOU ARE A FREE SPIRIT. A CHAMPION OF PERSONAL LIBERTY, INDIVIDUALITY...
I AM? I DON'T EVEN KNOW WHAT THAT MEANS.
NOW, IT'S OBVIOUS THAT THIS COULD ALL BE SETTLED WITH THE SIMPLEST OF CONTESTS.
SETTLE WHAT?
WHY, SETTLE WHICH ONE OF YOU GETS TO MAKE THE RULES, OF COURSE.

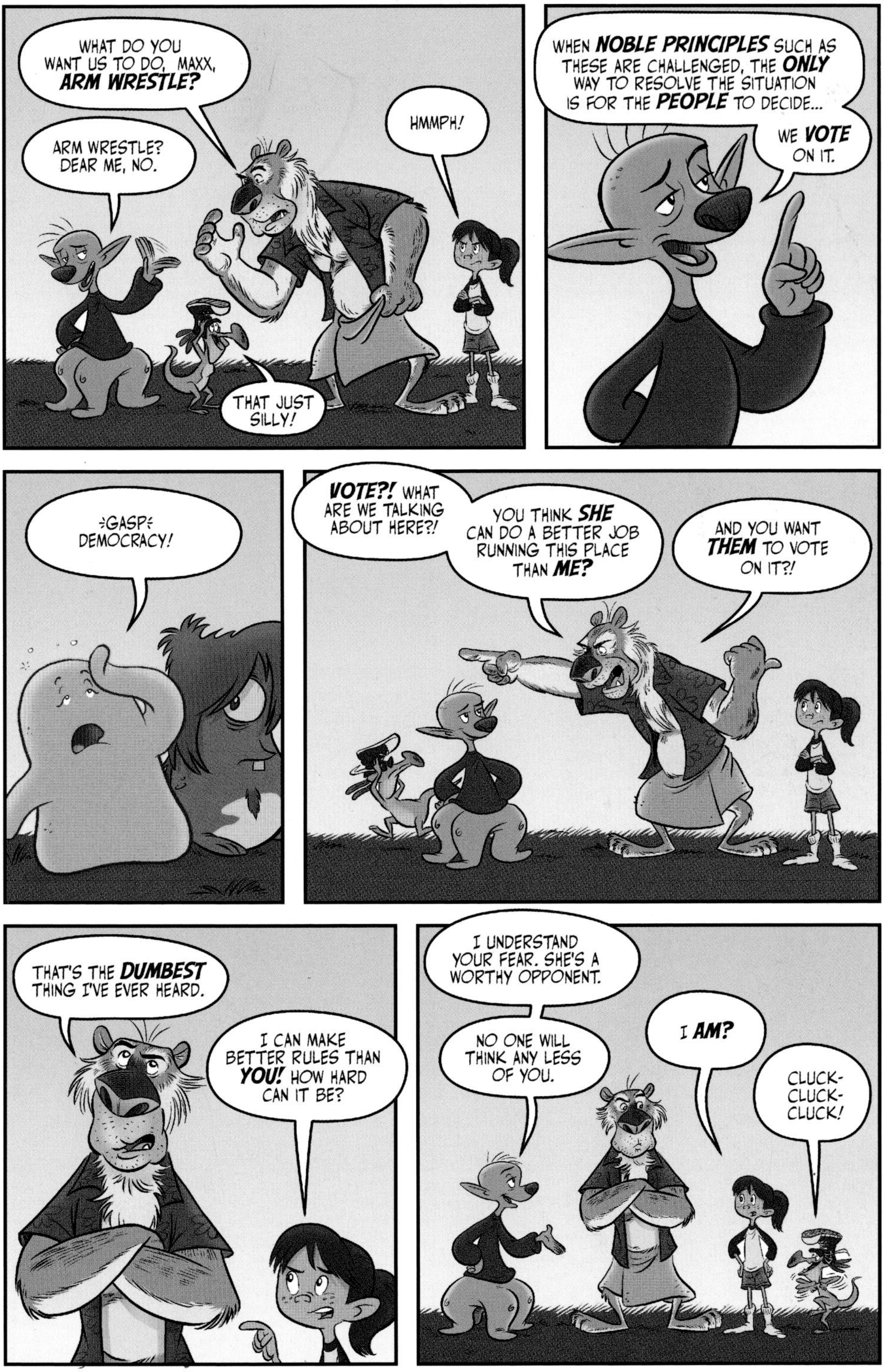
WHAT DO YOU WANT US TO DO, MAXX, ARM WRESTLE?
ARM WRESTLE? DEAR ME, NO.
HMMPH!
THAT JUST SILLY!
WHEN NOBLE PRINCIPLES SUCH AS THESE ARE CHALLENGED, THE ONLY WAY TO RESOLVE THE SITUATION IS FOR THE PEOPLE TO DECIDE...
WE VOTE ON IT.
GASP DEMOCRACY!
VOTE?! WHAT ARE WE TALKING ABOUT HERE?!
YOU THINK SHE CAN DO A BETTER JOB RUNNING THIS PLACE THAN ME?
AND YOU WANT THEM TO VOTE ON IT?!
THAT'S THE DUMBEST THING I'VE EVER HEARD.
I CAN MAKE BETTER RULES THAN YOU! HOW HARD CAN IT BE?
I UNDERSTAND YOUR FEAR. SHE'S A WORTHY OPPONENT.
NO ONE WILL THINK ANY LESS OF YOU.
I AM?
CLUCK-CLUCK-CLUCK!

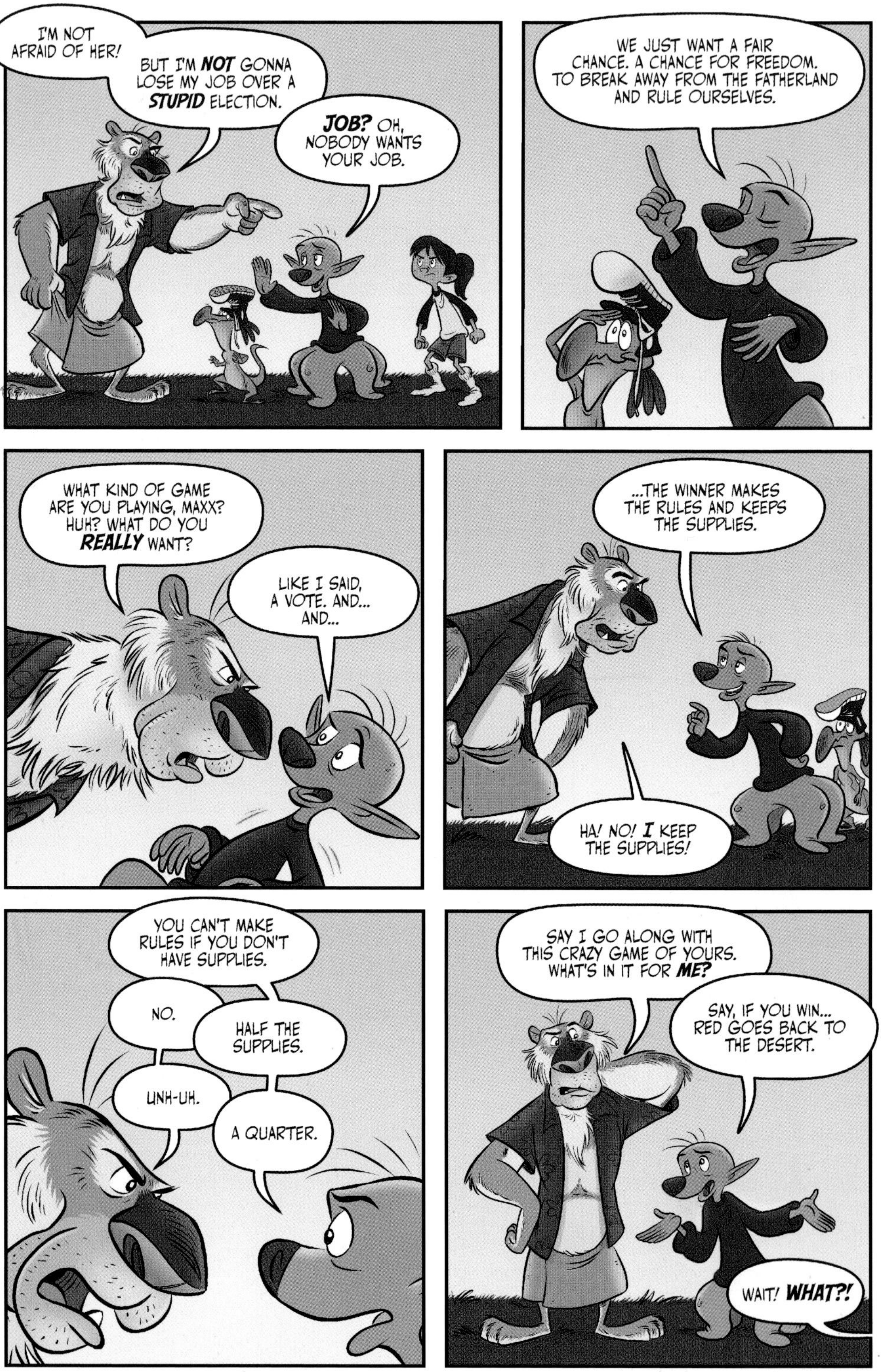
I'M NOT AFRAID OF HER!
BUT I'M **NOT** GONNA LOSE MY JOB OVER A **STUPID** ELECTION.
JOB? OH, NOBODY WANTS YOUR JOB.
WE JUST WANT A FAIR CHANCE. A CHANCE FOR FREEDOM. TO BREAK AWAY FROM THE FATHERLAND AND RULE OURSELVES.
WHAT KIND OF GAME ARE YOU PLAYING, MAXX? HUH? WHAT DO YOU **REALLY** WANT?
LIKE I SAID, A VOTE. AND... AND...
...THE WINNER MAKES THE RULES AND KEEPS THE SUPPLIES.
HA! NO! **I** KEEP THE SUPPLIES!
YOU CAN'T MAKE RULES IF YOU DON'T HAVE SUPPLIES.
NO.
HALF THE SUPPLIES.
UNH-UH.
A QUARTER.
SAY I GO ALONG WITH THIS CRAZY GAME OF YOURS. WHAT'S IN IT FOR **ME?**
SAY, IF YOU WIN... RED GOES BACK TO THE DESERT.
WAIT! **WHAT?!**

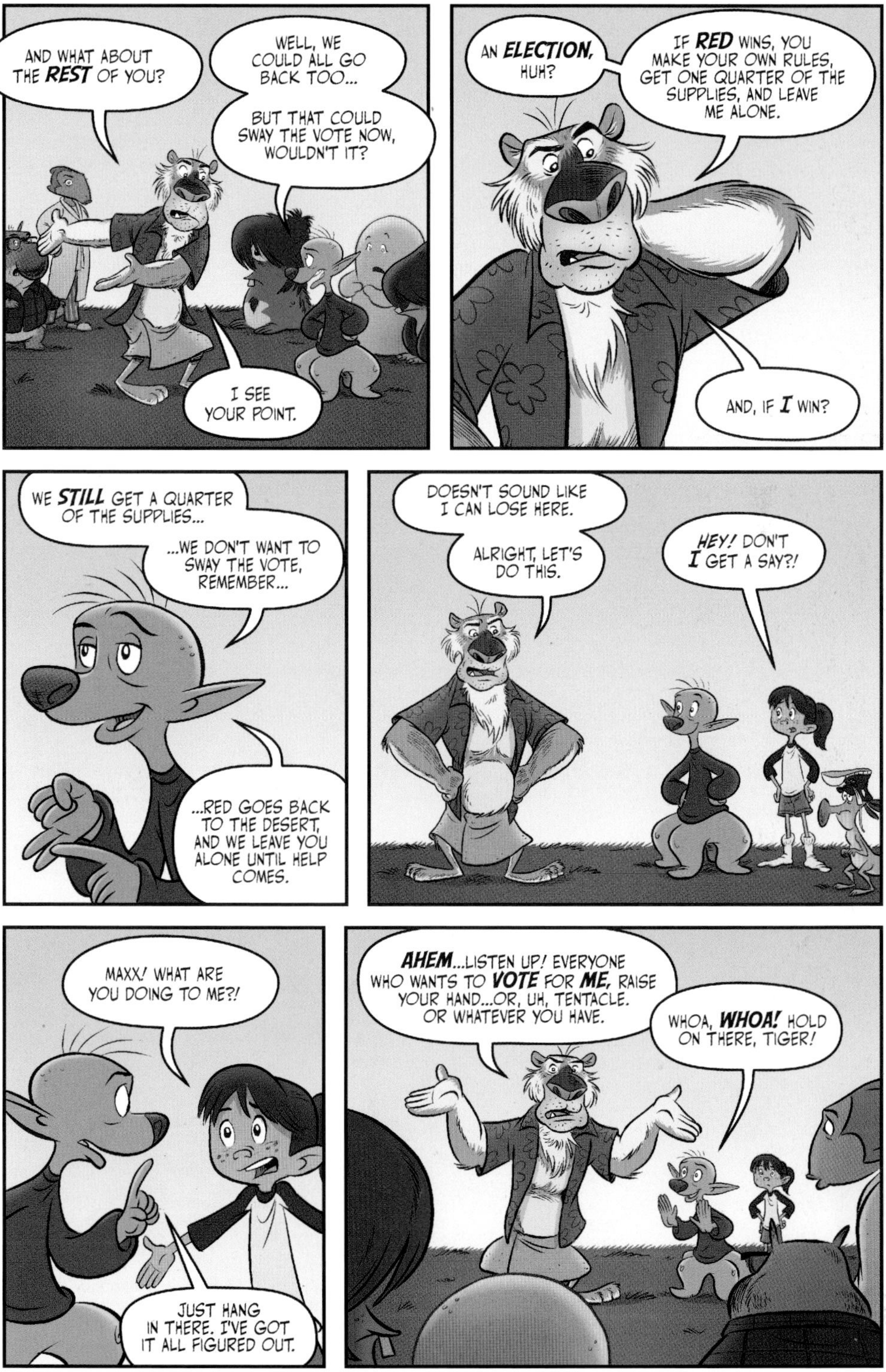
AND WHAT ABOUT THE REST OF YOU?
WELL, WE COULD ALL GO BACK TOO...
BUT THAT COULD SWAY THE VOTE NOW, WOULDN'T IT?
I SEE YOUR POINT.
AN ELECTION, HUH?
IF RED WINS, YOU MAKE YOUR OWN RULES, GET ONE QUARTER OF THE SUPPLIES, AND LEAVE ME ALONE.
AND, IF I WIN?
WE STILL GET A QUARTER OF THE SUPPLIES...
...WE DON'T WANT TO SWAY THE VOTE, REMEMBER...
...RED GOES BACK TO THE DESERT, AND WE LEAVE YOU ALONE UNTIL HELP COMES.
DOESN'T SOUND LIKE I CAN LOSE HERE.
ALRIGHT, LET'S DO THIS.
HEY! DON'T I GET A SAY?!
MAXX! WHAT ARE YOU DOING TO ME?!
JUST HANG IN THERE. I'VE GOT IT ALL FIGURED OUT.
AHEM...LISTEN UP! EVERYONE WHO WANTS TO VOTE FOR ME, RAISE YOUR HAND...OR, UH, TENTACLE. OR WHATEVER YOU HAVE.
WHOA, WHOA! HOLD ON THERE, TIGER!

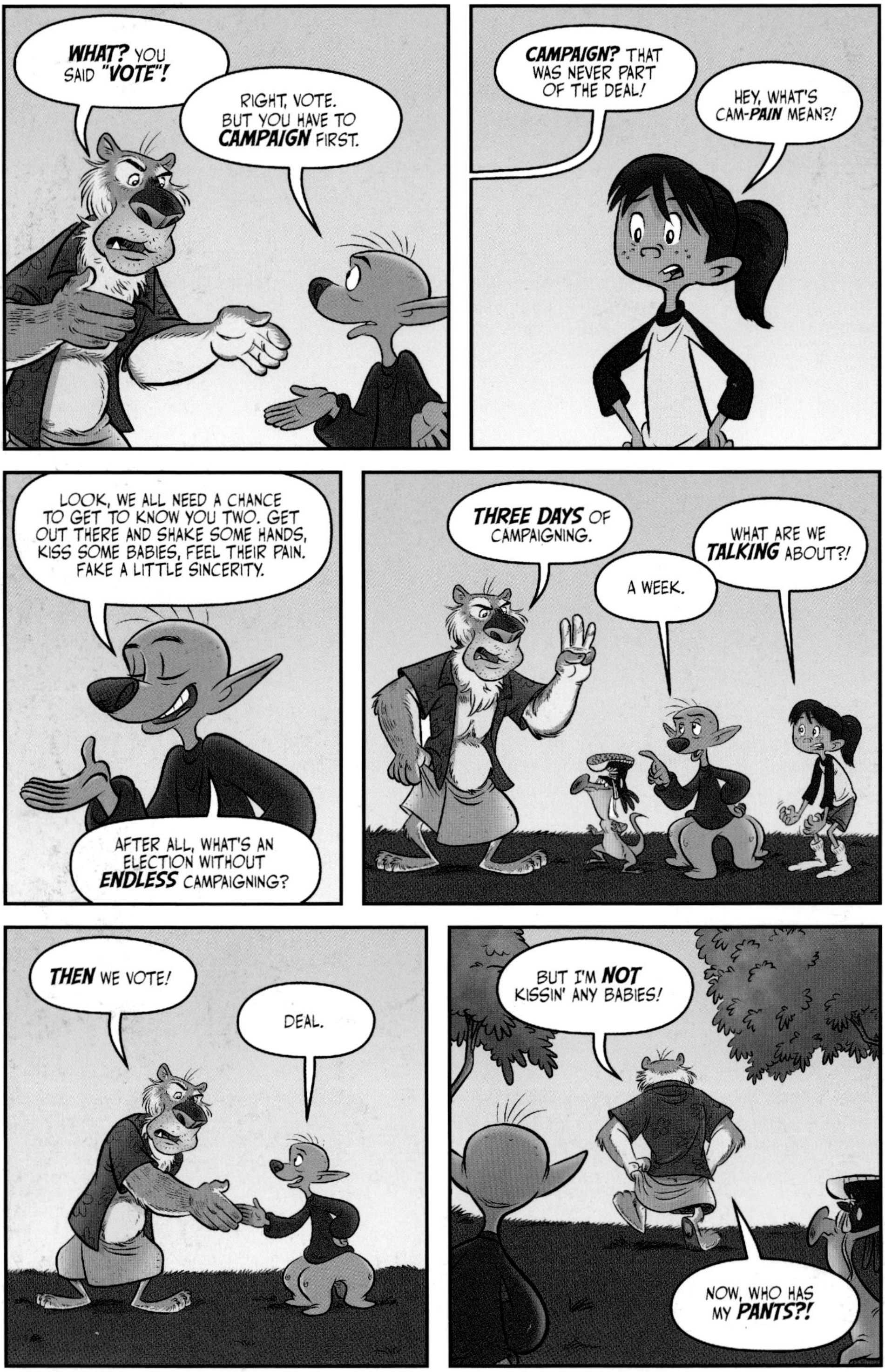
WHAT? YOU SAID "VOTE"!
RIGHT, VOTE. BUT YOU HAVE TO CAMPAIGN FIRST.
CAMPAIGN? THAT WAS NEVER PART OF THE DEAL!
HEY, WHAT'S CAM-PAIN MEAN?!
LOOK, WE ALL NEED A CHANCE TO GET TO KNOW YOU TWO. GET OUT THERE AND SHAKE SOME HANDS, KISS SOME BABIES, FEEL THEIR PAIN. FAKE A LITTLE SINCERITY.
AFTER ALL, WHAT'S AN ELECTION WITHOUT ENDLESS CAMPAIGNING?
THREE DAYS OF CAMPAIGNING.
A WEEK.
WHAT ARE WE TALKING ABOUT?!
THEN WE VOTE!
DEAL.
BUT I'M NOT KISSIN' ANY BABIES!
NOW, WHO HAS MY PANTS?!

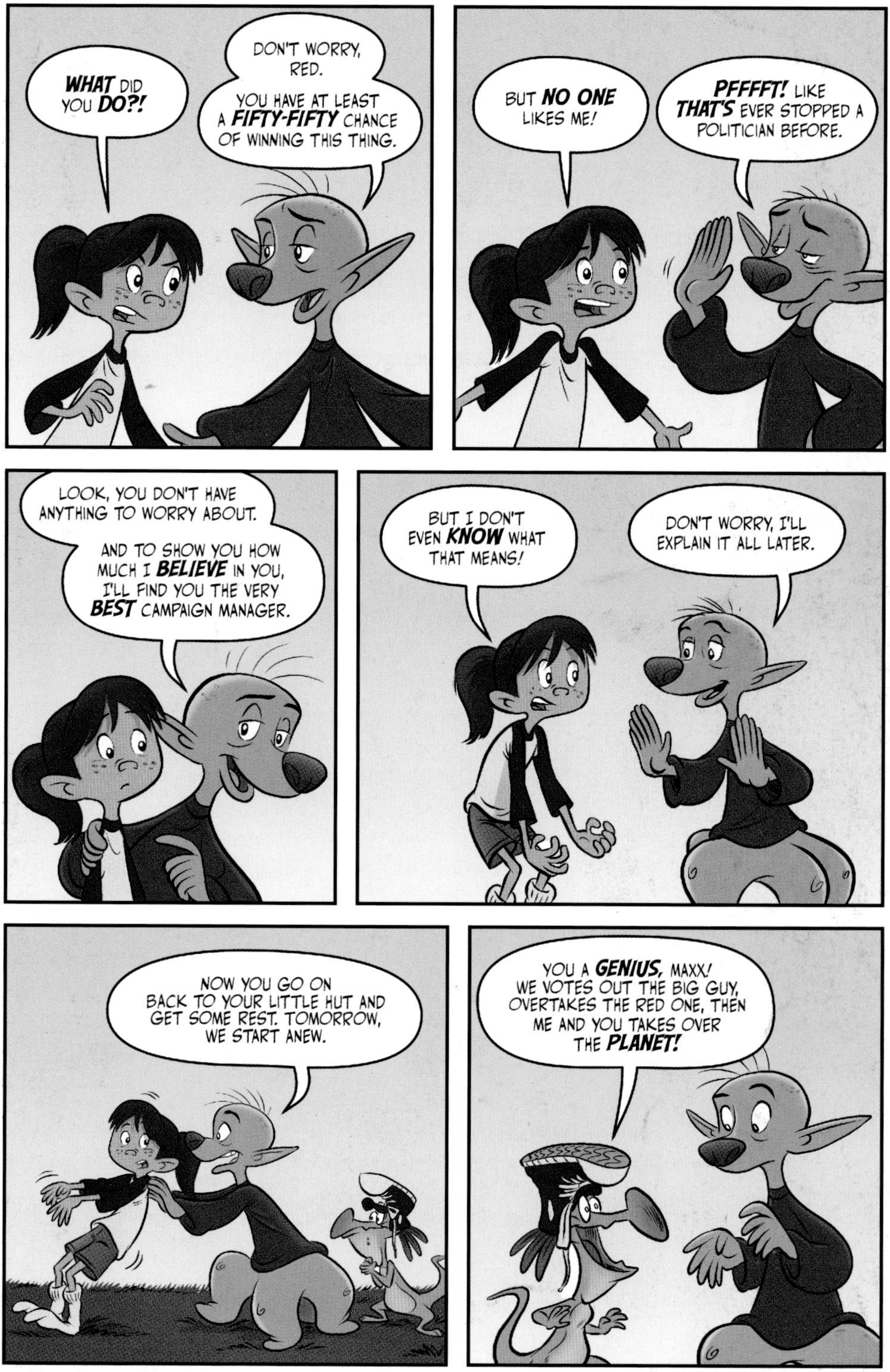
WHAT DID YOU DO?!
DON'T WORRY, RED.
YOU HAVE AT LEAST A FIFTY-FIFTY CHANCE OF WINNING THIS THING.
BUT NO ONE LIKES ME!
PFFFFT! LIKE THAT'S EVER STOPPED A POLITICIAN BEFORE.
LOOK, YOU DON'T HAVE ANYTHING TO WORRY ABOUT.
AND TO SHOW YOU HOW MUCH I BELIEVE IN YOU, I'LL FIND YOU THE VERY BEST CAMPAIGN MANAGER.
BUT I DON'T EVEN KNOW WHAT THAT MEANS!
DON'T WORRY, I'LL EXPLAIN IT ALL LATER.
NOW YOU GO ON BACK TO YOUR LITTLE HUT AND GET SOME REST. TOMORROW, WE START ANEW.
YOU A GENIUS, MAXX! WE VOTES OUT THE BIG GUY, OVERTAKES THE RED ONE, THEN ME AND YOU TAKES OVER THE PLANET!

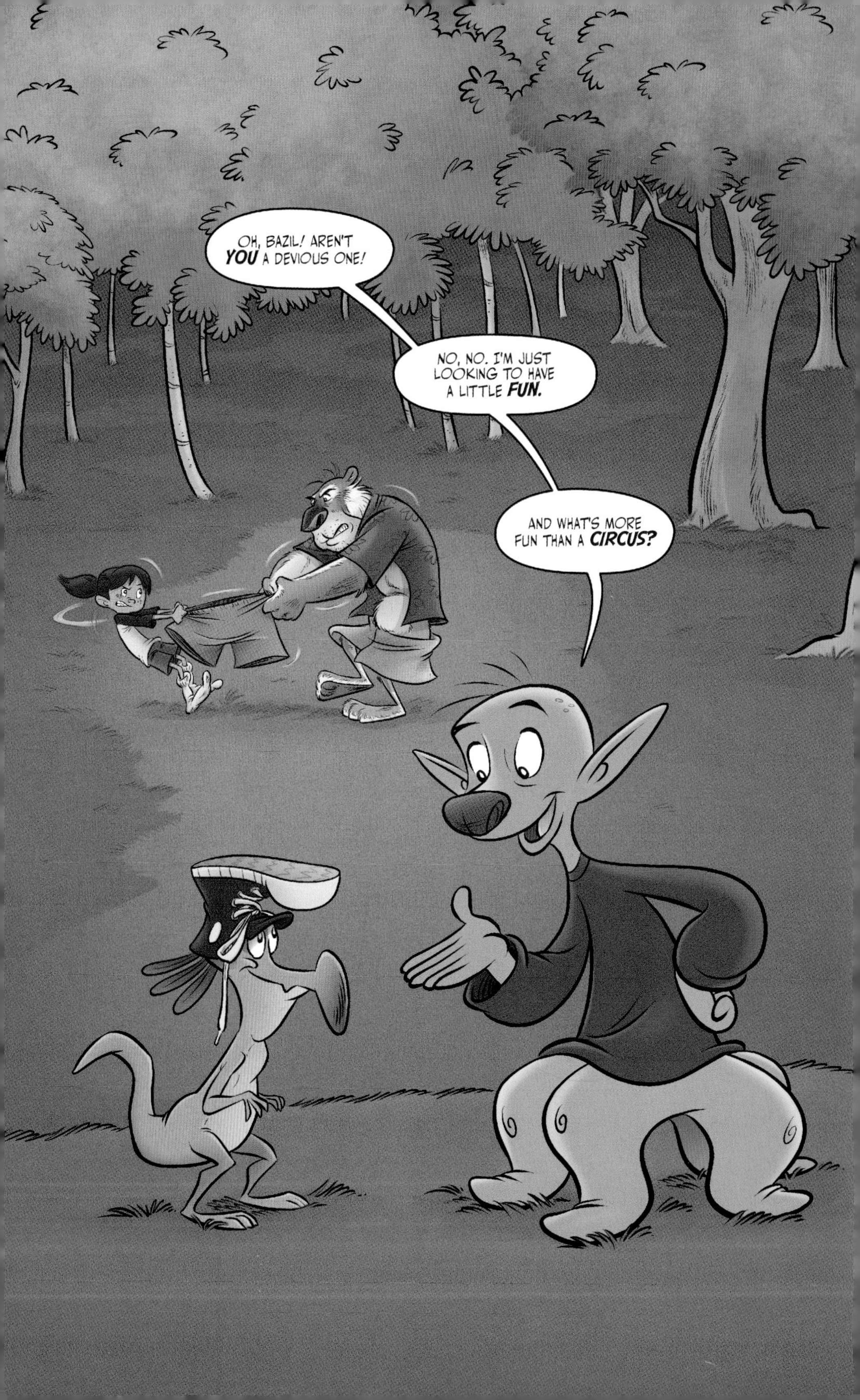
OH, BAZIL! AREN'T YOU A DEVIOUS ONE!
NO, NO. I'M JUST LOOKING TO HAVE A LITTLE FUN.
AND WHAT'S MORE FUN THAN A CIRCUS?

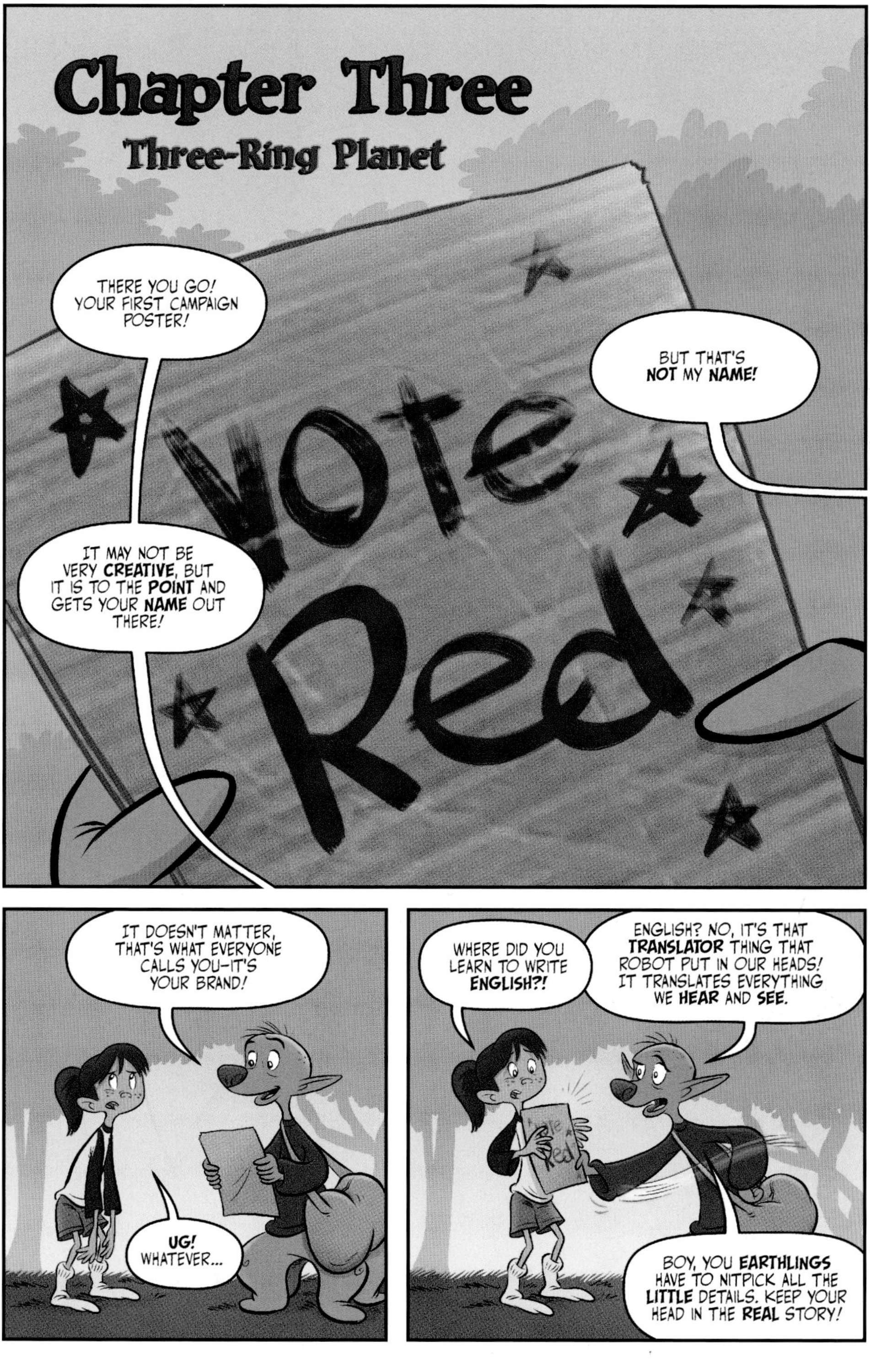
Chapter Three
Three-Ring Planet
THERE YOU GO! YOUR FIRST CAMPAIGN POSTER!
BUT THAT'S NOT MY NAME!
Vote Red
IT MAY NOT BE VERY CREATIVE, BUT IT IS TO THE POINT AND GETS YOUR NAME OUT THERE!
IT DOESN'T MATTER, THAT'S WHAT EVERYONE CALLS YOU—IT'S YOUR BRAND!
UG! WHATEVER...
WHERE DID YOU LEARN TO WRITE ENGLISH?!
ENGLISH? NO, IT'S THAT TRANSLATOR THING THAT ROBOT PUT IN OUR HEADS! IT TRANSLATES EVERYTHING WE HEAR AND SEE.
BOY, YOU EARTHLINGS HAVE TO NITPICK ALL THE LITTLE DETAILS. KEEP YOUR HEAD IN THE REAL STORY!

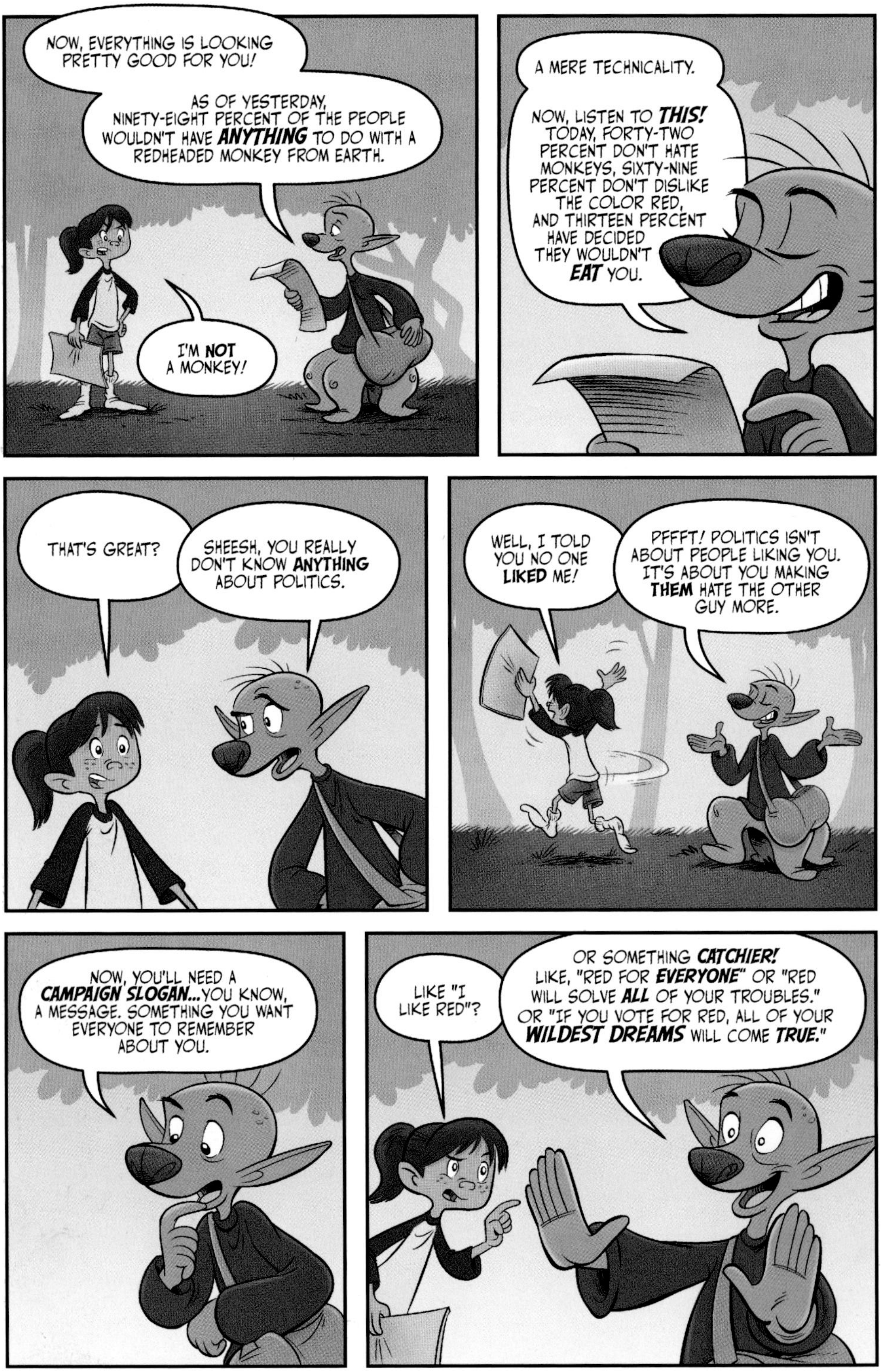
NOW, EVERYTHING IS LOOKING PRETTY GOOD FOR YOU!
AS OF YESTERDAY, NINETY-EIGHT PERCENT OF THE PEOPLE WOULDN'T HAVE **ANYTHING** TO DO WITH A REDHEADED MONKEY FROM EARTH.
I'M **NOT** A MONKEY!
A MERE TECHNICALITY.
NOW, LISTEN TO **THIS!** TODAY, FORTY-TWO PERCENT DON'T HATE MONKEYS, SIXTY-NINE PERCENT DON'T DISLIKE THE COLOR RED, AND THIRTEEN PERCENT HAVE DECIDED THEY WOULDN'T **EAT** YOU.
THAT'S GREAT?
SHEESH, YOU REALLY DON'T KNOW **ANYTHING** ABOUT POLITICS.
WELL, I TOLD YOU NO ONE **LIKED** ME!
PFFFT! POLITICS ISN'T ABOUT PEOPLE LIKING YOU. IT'S ABOUT YOU MAKING **THEM** HATE THE OTHER GUY MORE.
NOW, YOU'LL NEED A **CAMPAIGN SLOGAN...** YOU KNOW, A MESSAGE. SOMETHING YOU WANT EVERYONE TO REMEMBER ABOUT YOU.
LIKE "I LIKE RED"?
OR SOMETHING **CATCHIER!** LIKE, "RED FOR **EVERYONE**" OR "RED WILL SOLVE **ALL** OF YOUR TROUBLES." OR "IF YOU VOTE FOR RED, ALL OF YOUR **WILDEST DREAMS** WILL COME **TRUE.**"

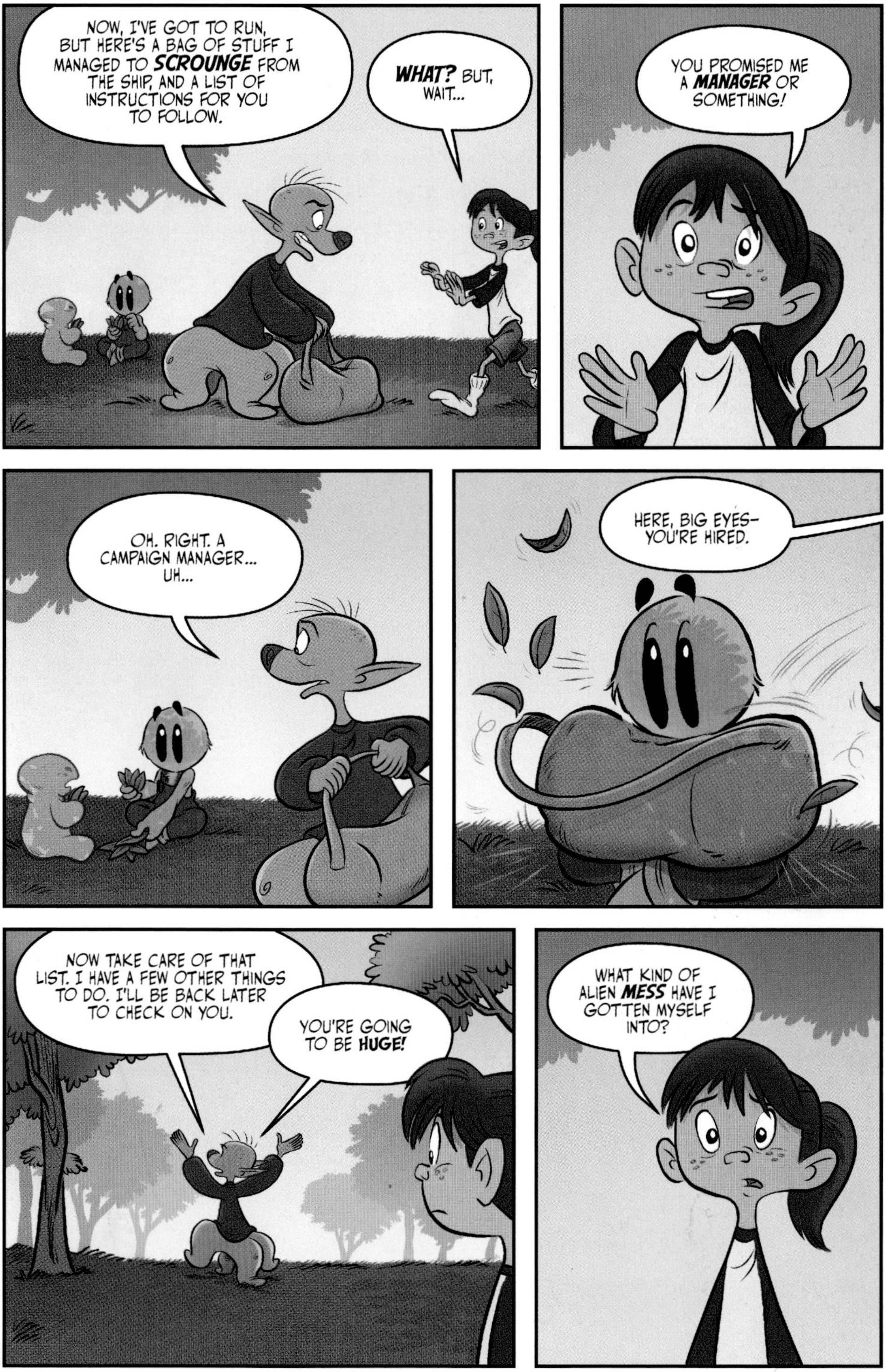
NOW, I'VE GOT TO RUN, BUT HERE'S A BAG OF STUFF I MANAGED TO **SCROUNGE** FROM THE SHIP, AND A LIST OF INSTRUCTIONS FOR YOU TO FOLLOW.
WHAT? BUT, WAIT...
YOU PROMISED ME A **MANAGER** OR SOMETHING!
OH. RIGHT. A CAMPAIGN MANAGER... UH...
HERE, BIG EYES-YOU'RE HIRED.
NOW TAKE CARE OF THAT LIST. I HAVE A FEW OTHER THINGS TO DO. I'LL BE BACK LATER TO CHECK ON YOU.
YOU'RE GOING TO BE **HUGE!**
WHAT KIND OF ALIEN **MESS** HAVE I GOTTEN MYSELF INTO?

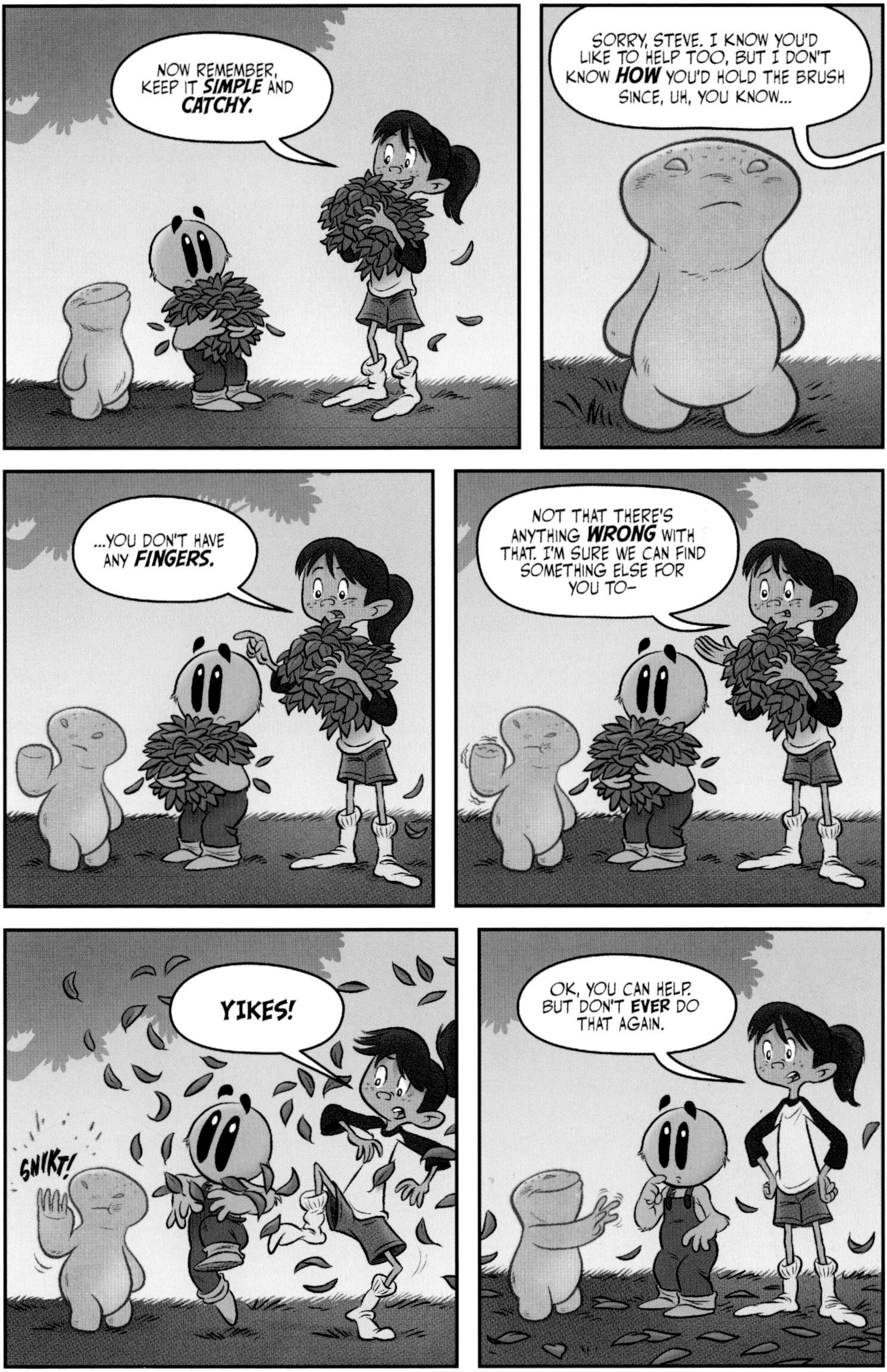
NOW REMEMBER, KEEP IT SIMPLE AND CATCHY.
SORRY, STEVE. I KNOW YOU'D LIKE TO HELP TOO, BUT I DON'T KNOW HOW YOU'D HOLD THE BRUSH SINCE, UH, YOU KNOW...
...YOU DON'T HAVE ANY FINGERS.
NOT THAT THERE'S ANYTHING WRONG WITH THAT. I'M SURE WE CAN FIND SOMETHING ELSE FOR YOU TO–
SNIKT!
YIKES!
OK, YOU CAN HELP. BUT DON'T EVER DO THAT AGAIN.

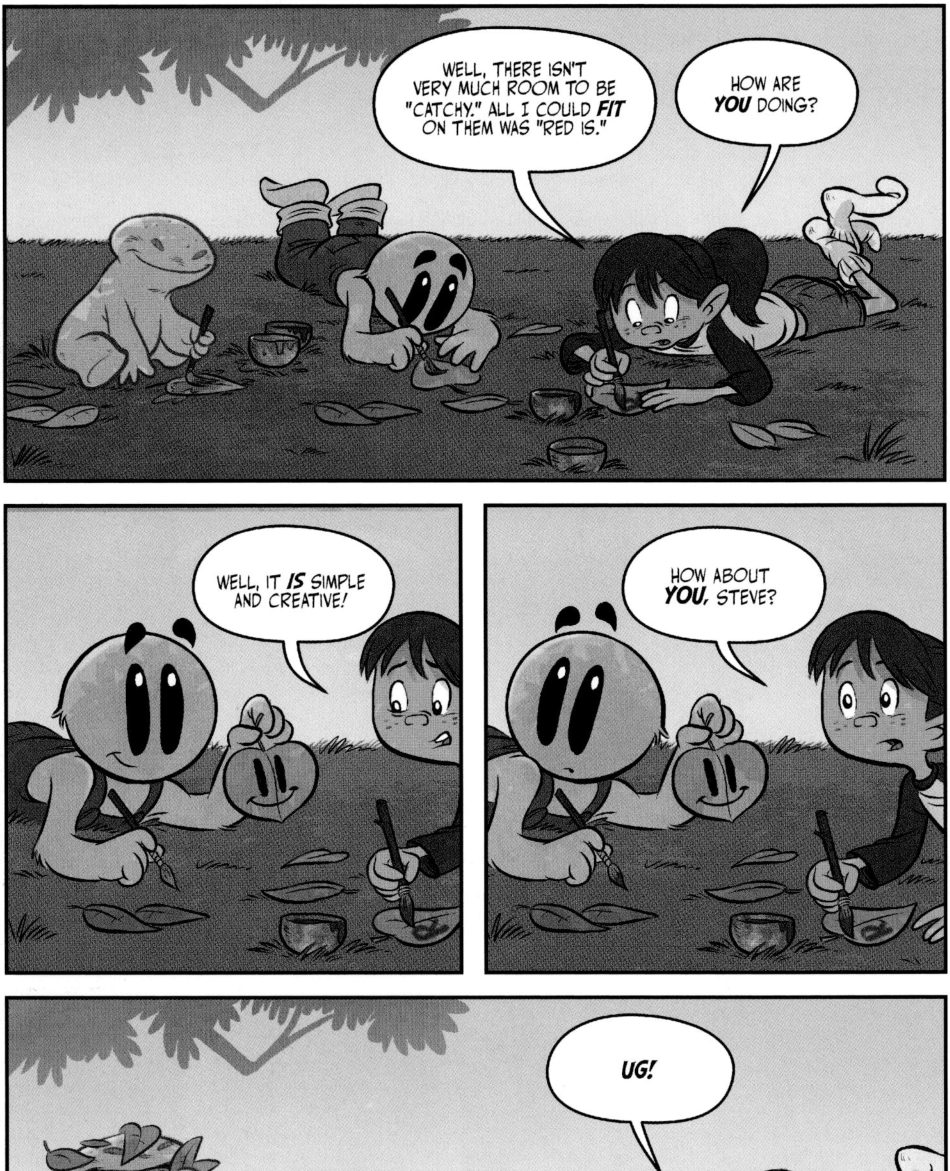

WELL, THERE ISN'T VERY MUCH ROOM TO BE "CATCHY." ALL I COULD *FIT* ON THEM WAS "RED IS."
HOW ARE *YOU* DOING?
WELL, IT *IS* SIMPLE AND CREATIVE!
HOW ABOUT *YOU*, STEVE?
UG!

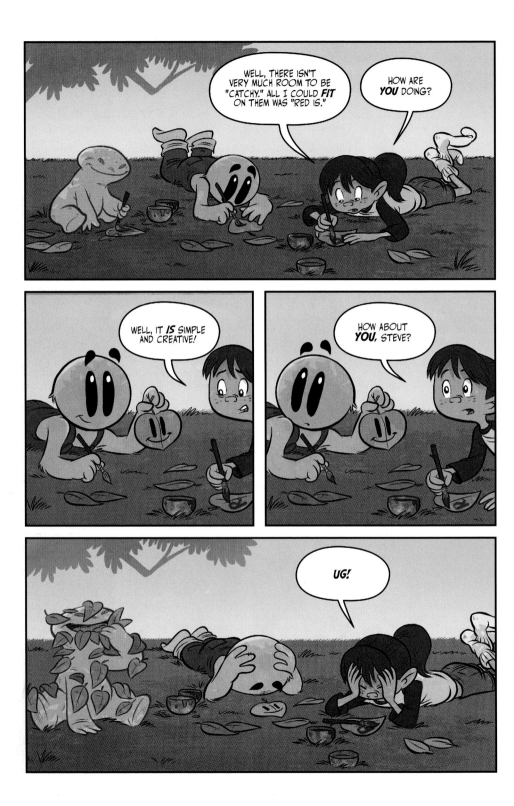

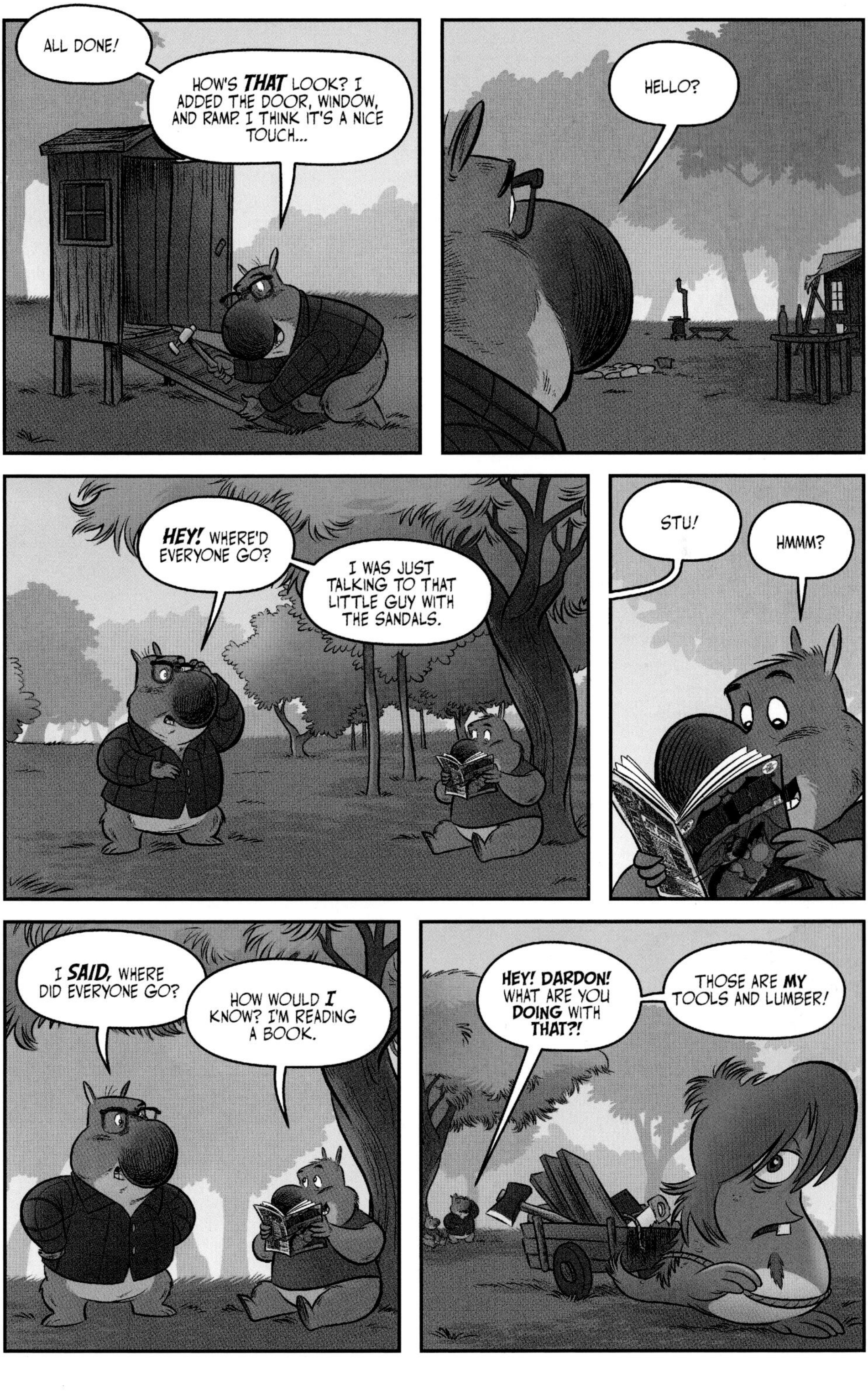
ALL DONE!
HOW'S **THAT** LOOK? I ADDED THE DOOR, WINDOW, AND RAMP. I THINK IT'S A NICE TOUCH...
HELLO?
HEY! WHERE'D EVERYONE GO?
I WAS JUST TALKING TO THAT LITTLE GUY WITH THE SANDALS.
STU!
HMMM?
I **SAID,** WHERE DID EVERYONE GO?
HOW WOULD **I** KNOW? I'M READING A BOOK.
HEY! DARDON! WHAT ARE YOU **DOING** WITH **THAT?!**
THOSE ARE **MY** TOOLS AND LUMBER!

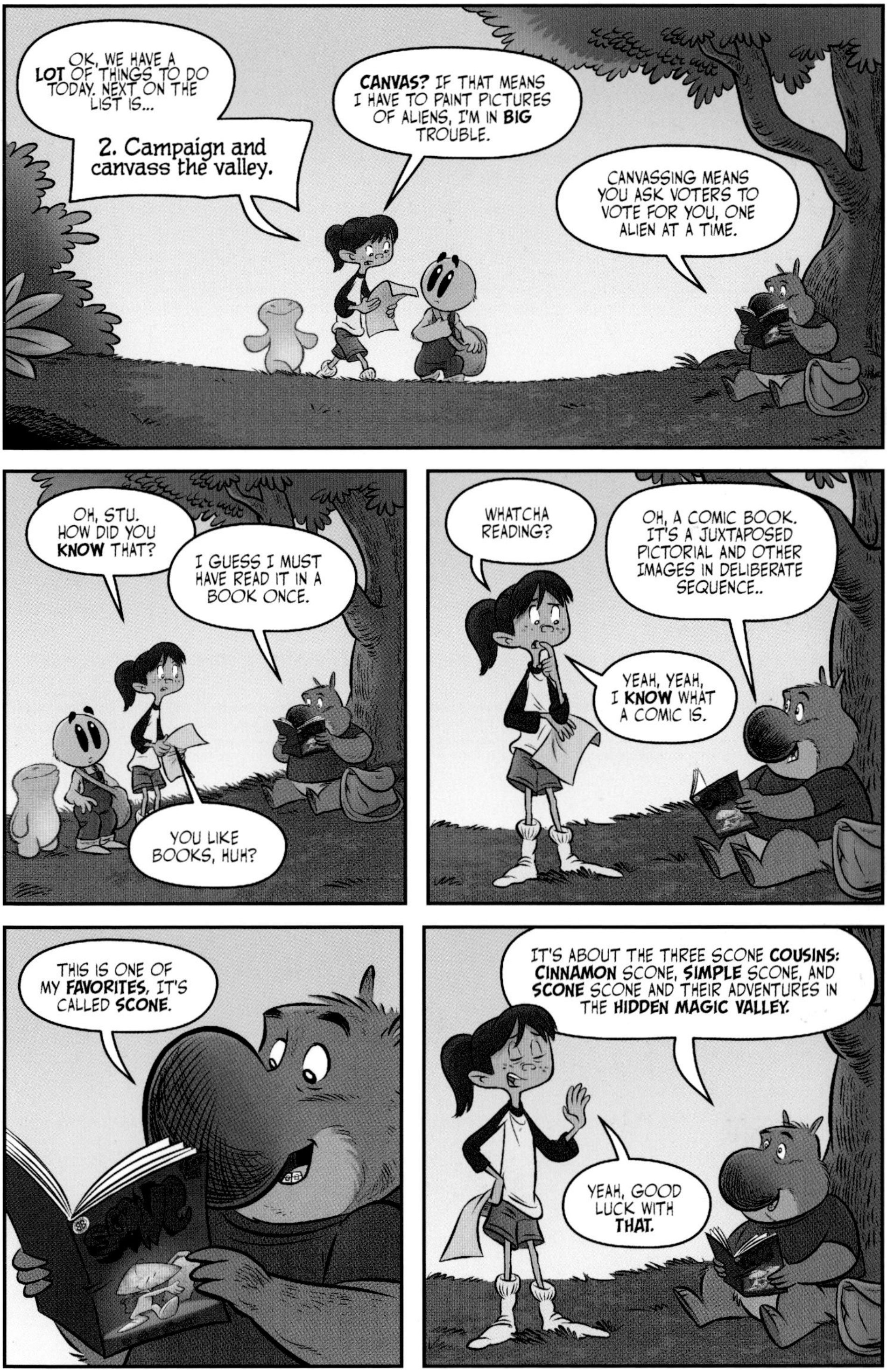
OK, WE HAVE A LOT OF THINGS TO DO TODAY. NEXT ON THE LIST IS...
2. Campaign and canvass the valley.
CANVAS? IF THAT MEANS I HAVE TO PAINT PICTURES OF ALIENS, I'M IN BIG TROUBLE.
CANVASSING MEANS YOU ASK VOTERS TO VOTE FOR YOU, ONE ALIEN AT A TIME.
OH, STU. HOW DID YOU KNOW THAT?
I GUESS I MUST HAVE READ IT IN A BOOK ONCE.
YOU LIKE BOOKS, HUH?
WHATCHA READING?
OH, A COMIC BOOK. IT'S A JUXTAPOSED PICTORIAL AND OTHER IMAGES IN DELIBERATE SEQUENCE..
YEAH, YEAH, I KNOW WHAT A COMIC IS.
THIS IS ONE OF MY FAVORITES, IT'S CALLED SCONE.
IT'S ABOUT THE THREE SCONE COUSINS: CINNAMON SCONE, SIMPLE SCONE, AND SCONE SCONE AND THEIR ADVENTURES IN THE HIDDEN MAGIC VALLEY.
YEAH, GOOD LUCK WITH THAT.

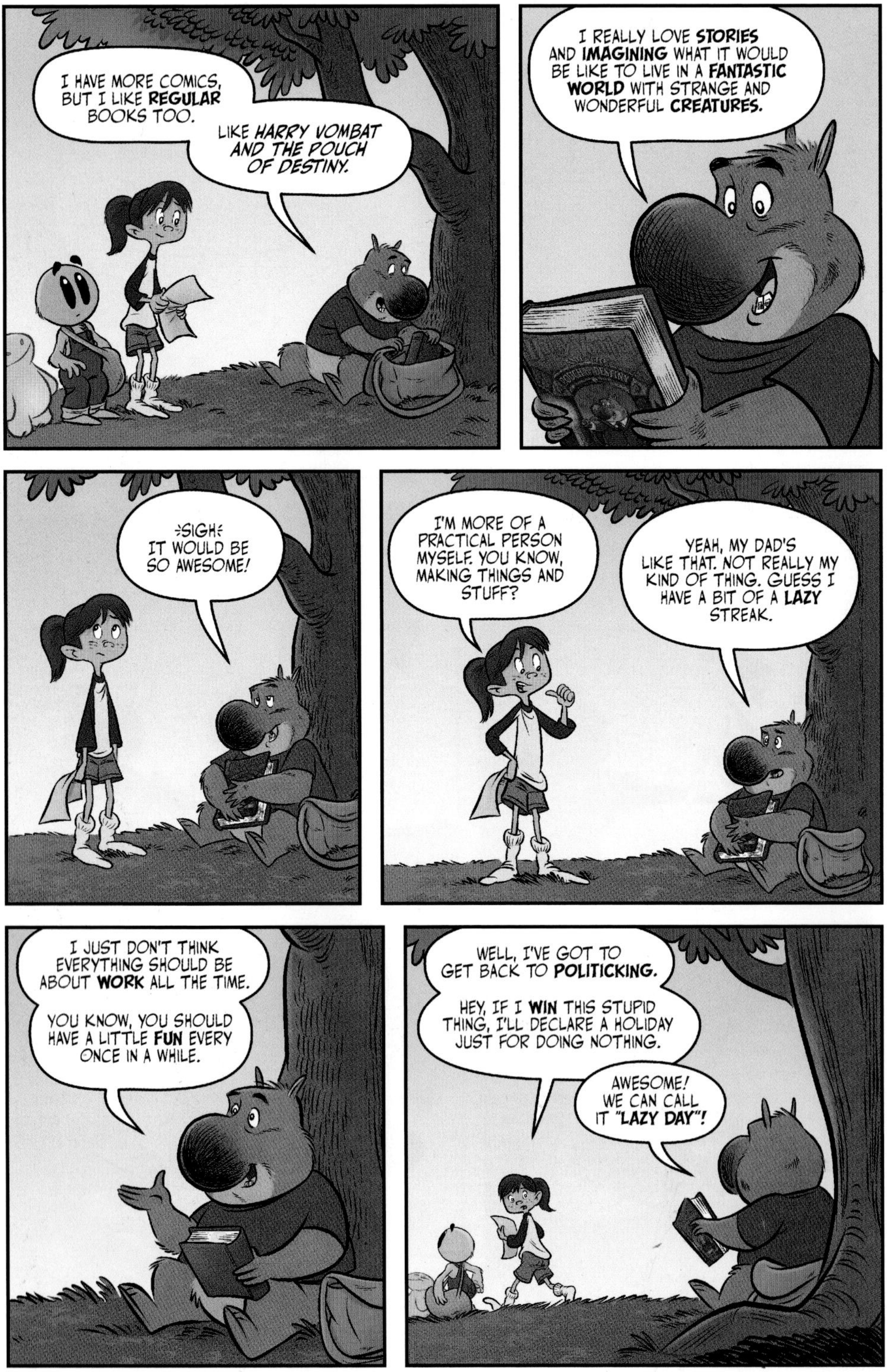

I HAVE MORE COMICS, BUT I LIKE REGULAR BOOKS TOO.
LIKE HARRY VOMBAT AND THE POUCH OF DESTINY.
I REALLY LOVE STORIES AND IMAGINING WHAT IT WOULD BE LIKE TO LIVE IN A FANTASTIC WORLD WITH STRANGE AND WONDERFUL CREATURES.
SIGH
IT WOULD BE SO AWESOME!
I'M MORE OF A PRACTICAL PERSON MYSELF. YOU KNOW, MAKING THINGS AND STUFF?
YEAH, MY DAD'S LIKE THAT. NOT REALLY MY KIND OF THING. GUESS I HAVE A BIT OF A LAZY STREAK.
I JUST DON'T THINK EVERYTHING SHOULD BE ABOUT WORK ALL THE TIME.
YOU KNOW, YOU SHOULD HAVE A LITTLE FUN EVERY ONCE IN A WHILE.
WELL, I'VE GOT TO GET BACK TO POLITICKING.
HEY, IF I WIN THIS STUPID THING, I'LL DECLARE A HOLIDAY JUST FOR DOING NOTHING.
AWESOME! WE CAN CALL IT "LAZY DAY"!

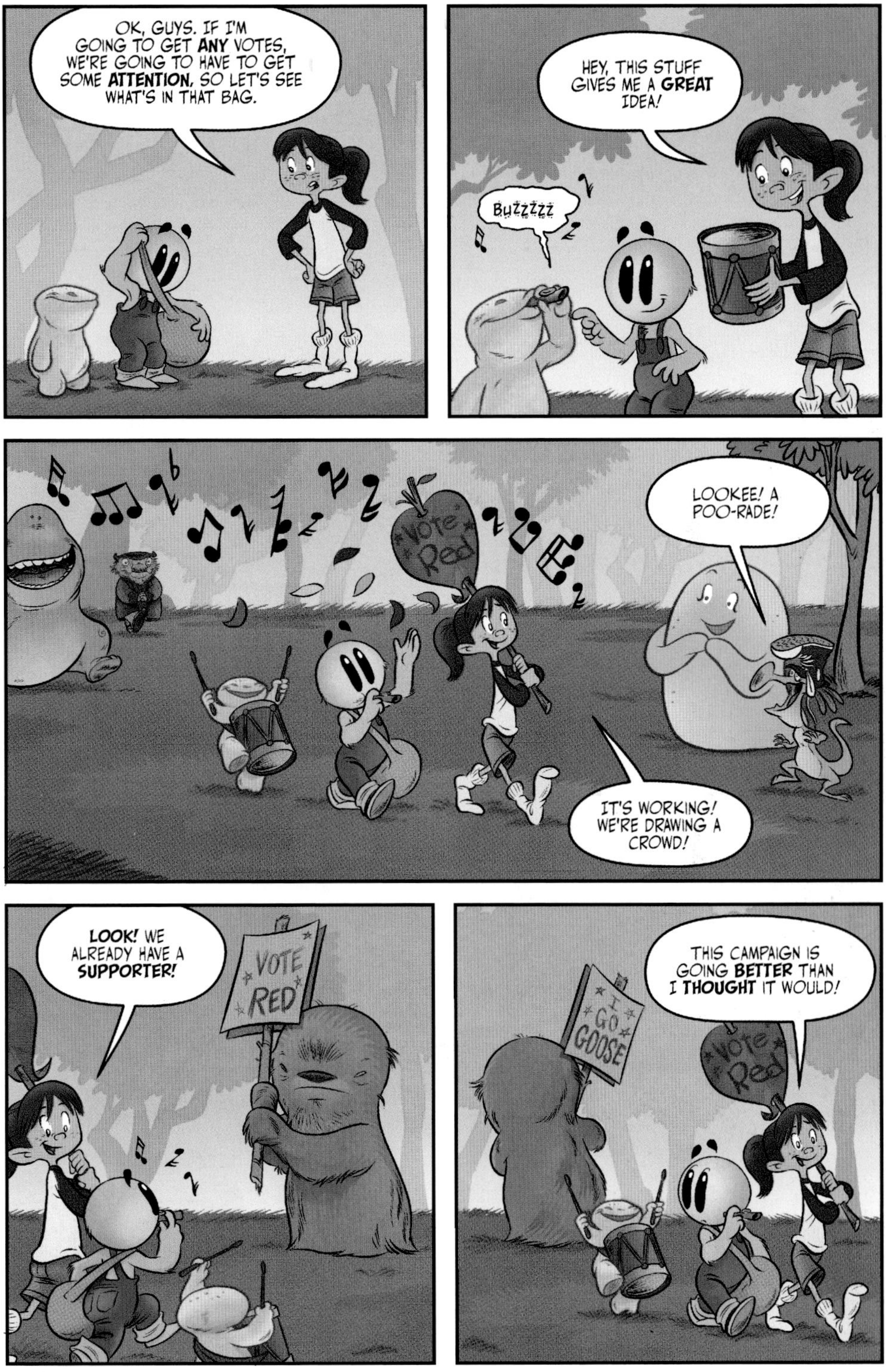
OK, GUYS. IF I'M GOING TO GET **ANY** VOTES, WE'RE GOING TO HAVE TO GET SOME **ATTENTION**, SO LET'S SEE WHAT'S IN THAT BAG.
HEY, THIS STUFF GIVES ME A **GREAT** IDEA!
BUZZZZZ
VOTE RED
LOOKEE! A POO-RADE!
IT'S WORKING! WE'RE DRAWING A CROWD!
LOOK! WE ALREADY HAVE A **SUPPORTER!**
VOTE RED
THIS CAMPAIGN IS GOING **BETTER** THAN I **THOUGHT** IT WOULD!
I GO GOOSE
VOTE RED

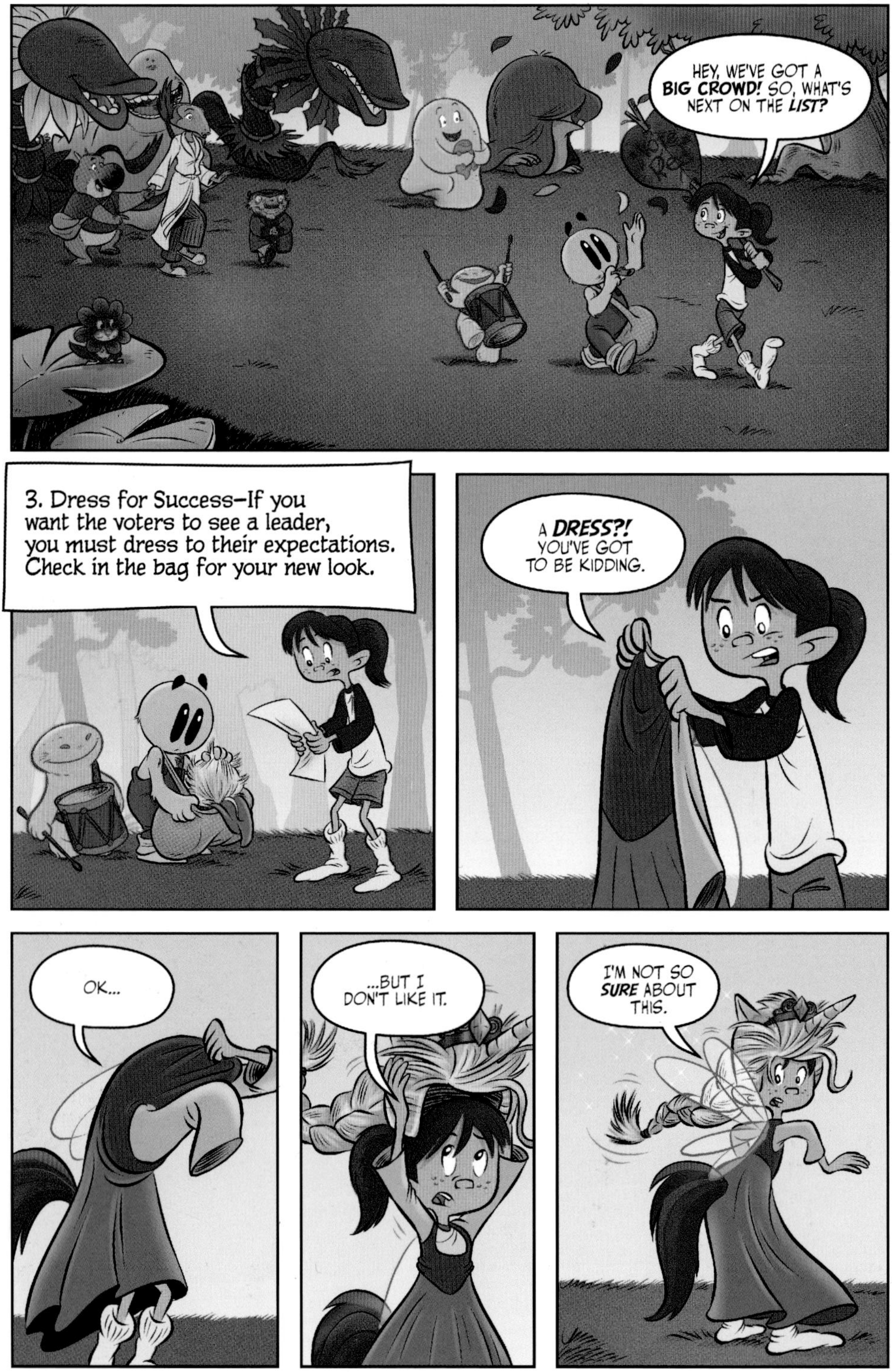
HEY, WE'VE GOT A BIG CROWD! SO, WHAT'S NEXT ON THE LIST?
3. Dress for Success—If you want the voters to see a leader, you must dress to their expectations. Check in the bag for your new look.
A DRESS?! YOU'VE GOT TO BE KIDDING.
OK...
...BUT I DON'T LIKE IT.
I'M NOT SO SURE ABOUT THIS.

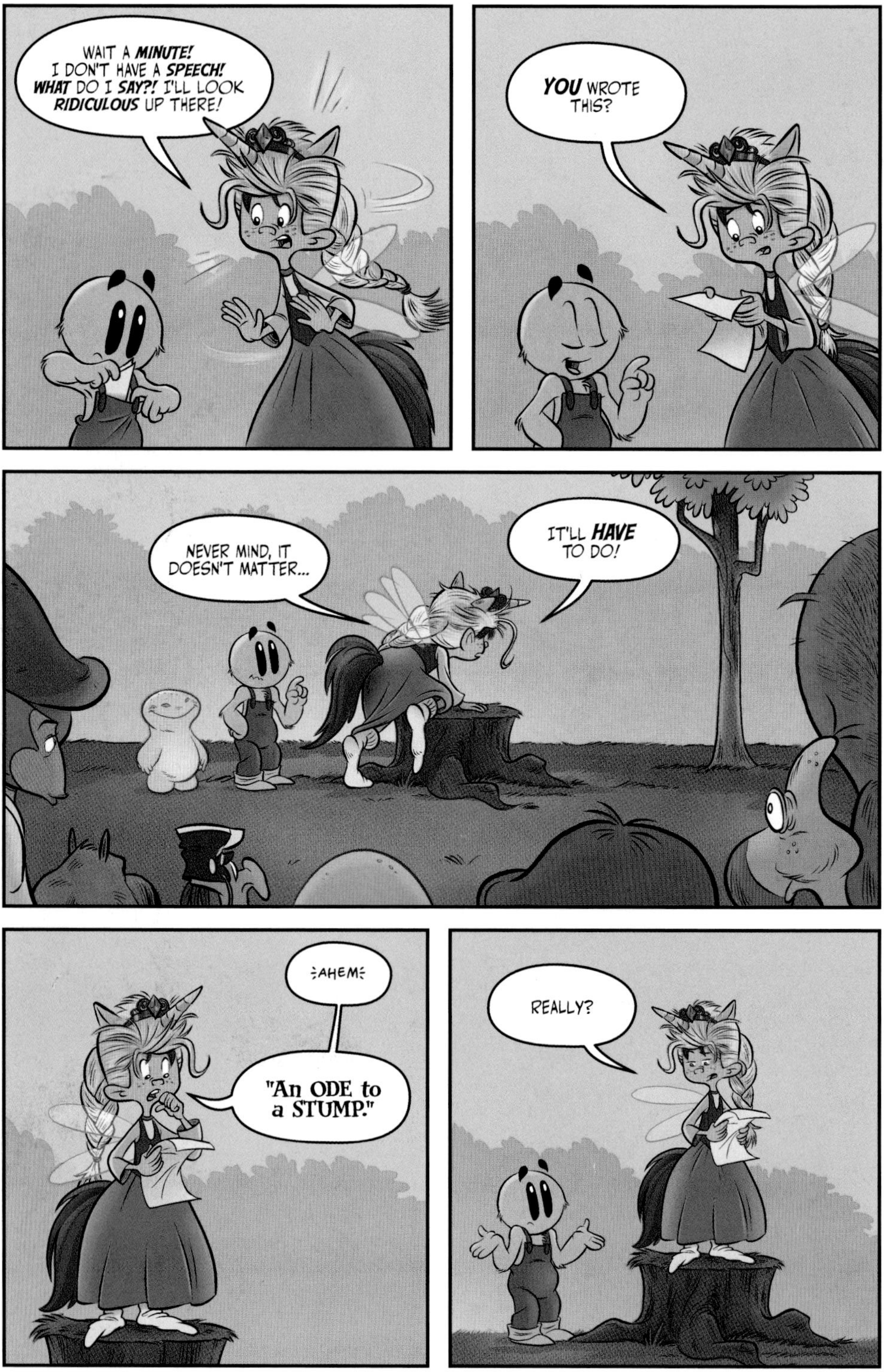
WAIT A MINUTE! I DON'T HAVE A SPEECH! WHAT DO I SAY?! I'LL LOOK RIDICULOUS UP THERE!
YOU WROTE THIS?
NEVER MIND, IT DOESN'T MATTER...
IT'LL HAVE TO DO!
AHEM
"An ODE to a STUMP."
REALLY?

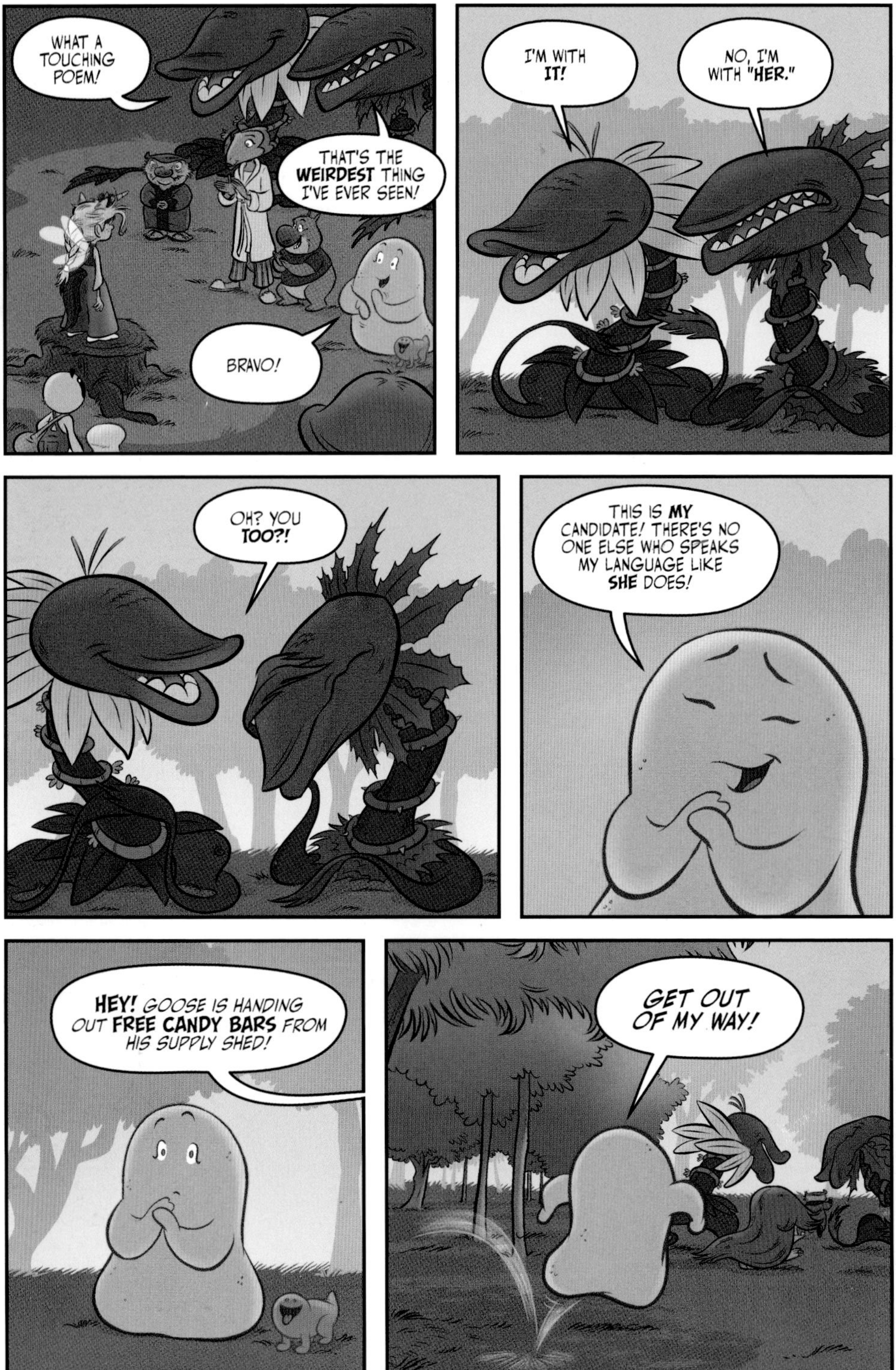
WHAT A TOUCHING POEM!
THAT'S THE **WEIRDEST** THING I'VE EVER SEEN!
BRAVO!
I'M WITH **IT!**
NO, I'M WITH **"HER."**
OH? YOU **TOO?!**
THIS IS **MY** CANDIDATE! THERE'S NO ONE ELSE WHO SPEAKS MY LANGUAGE LIKE **SHE** DOES!
HEY! *GOOSE IS HANDING OUT* **FREE CANDY BARS** *FROM HIS SUPPLY SHED!*
GET OUT OF MY WAY!

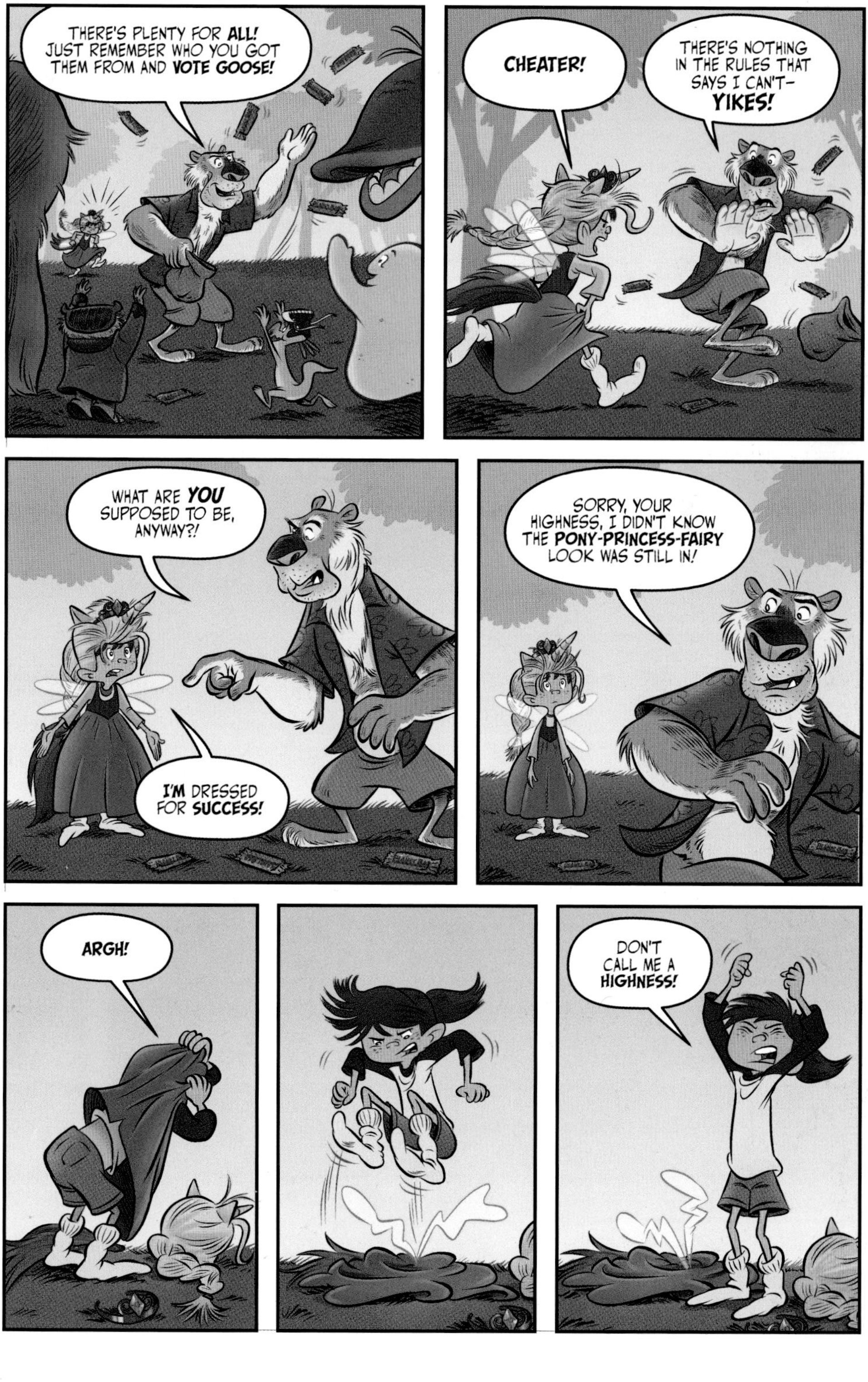
THERE'S PLENTY FOR ALL! JUST REMEMBER WHO YOU GOT THEM FROM AND VOTE GOOSE!
CHEATER!
THERE'S NOTHING IN THE RULES THAT SAYS I CAN'T— YIKES!
WHAT ARE YOU SUPPOSED TO BE, ANYWAY?!
I'M DRESSED FOR SUCCESS!
SORRY, YOUR HIGHNESS, I DIDN'T KNOW THE PONY-PRINCESS-FAIRY LOOK WAS STILL IN!
ARGH!
DON'T CALL ME A HIGHNESS!

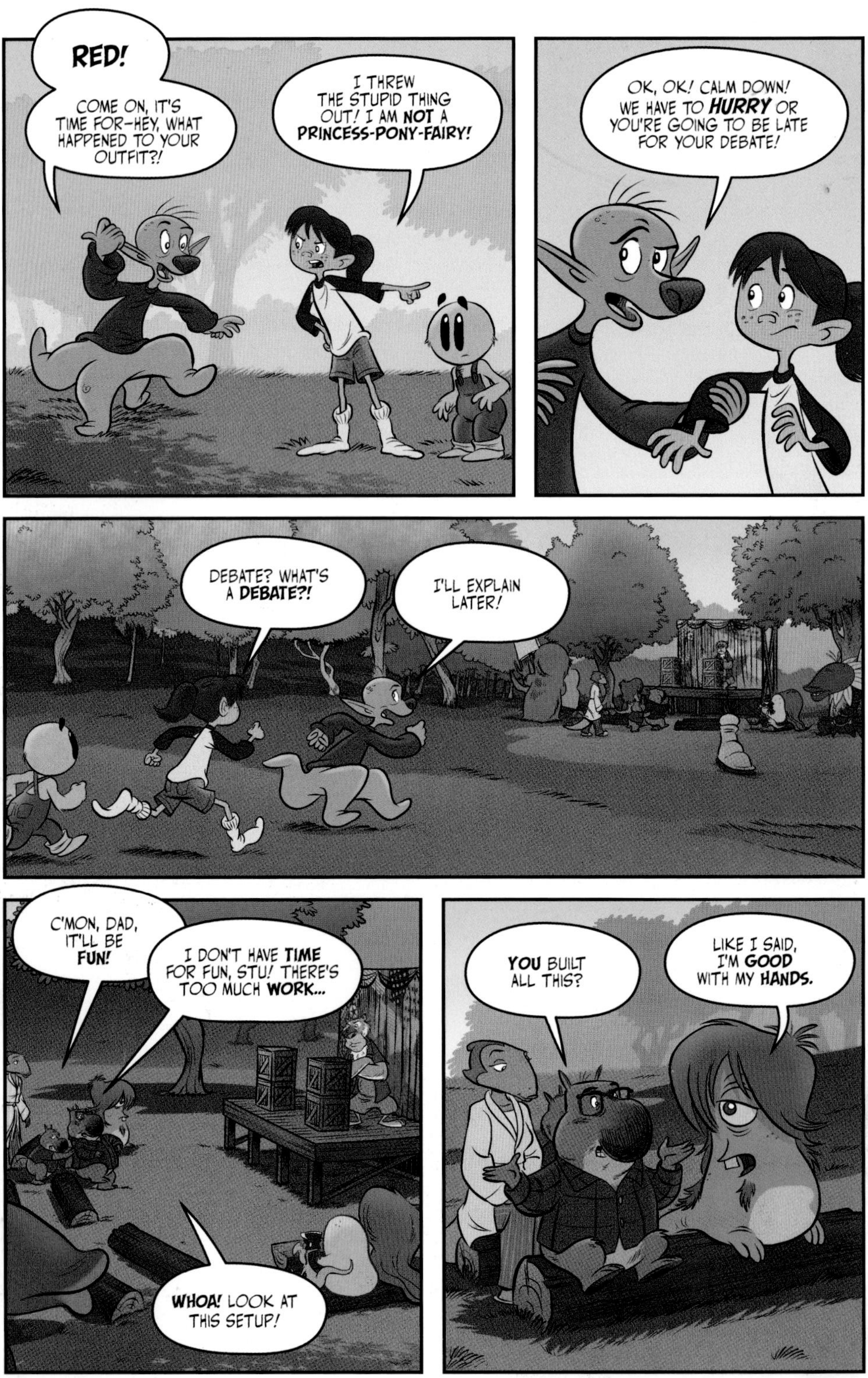
RED!
COME ON, IT'S TIME FOR–HEY, WHAT HAPPENED TO YOUR OUTFIT?!
I THREW THE STUPID THING OUT! I AM NOT A PRINCESS-PONY-FAIRY!
OK, OK! CALM DOWN! WE HAVE TO HURRY OR YOU'RE GOING TO BE LATE FOR YOUR DEBATE!
DEBATE? WHAT'S A DEBATE?!
I'LL EXPLAIN LATER!
C'MON, DAD, IT'LL BE FUN!
I DON'T HAVE TIME FOR FUN, STU! THERE'S TOO MUCH WORK...
WHOA! LOOK AT THIS SETUP!
YOU BUILT ALL THIS?
LIKE I SAID, I'M GOOD WITH MY HANDS.

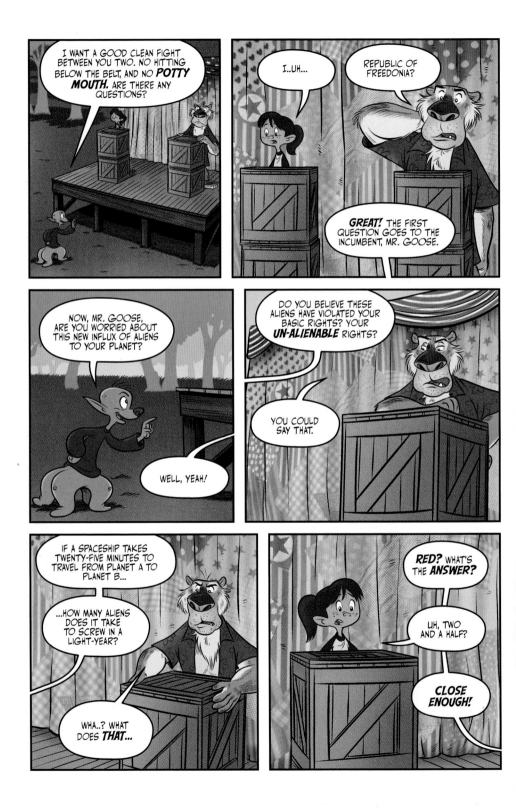

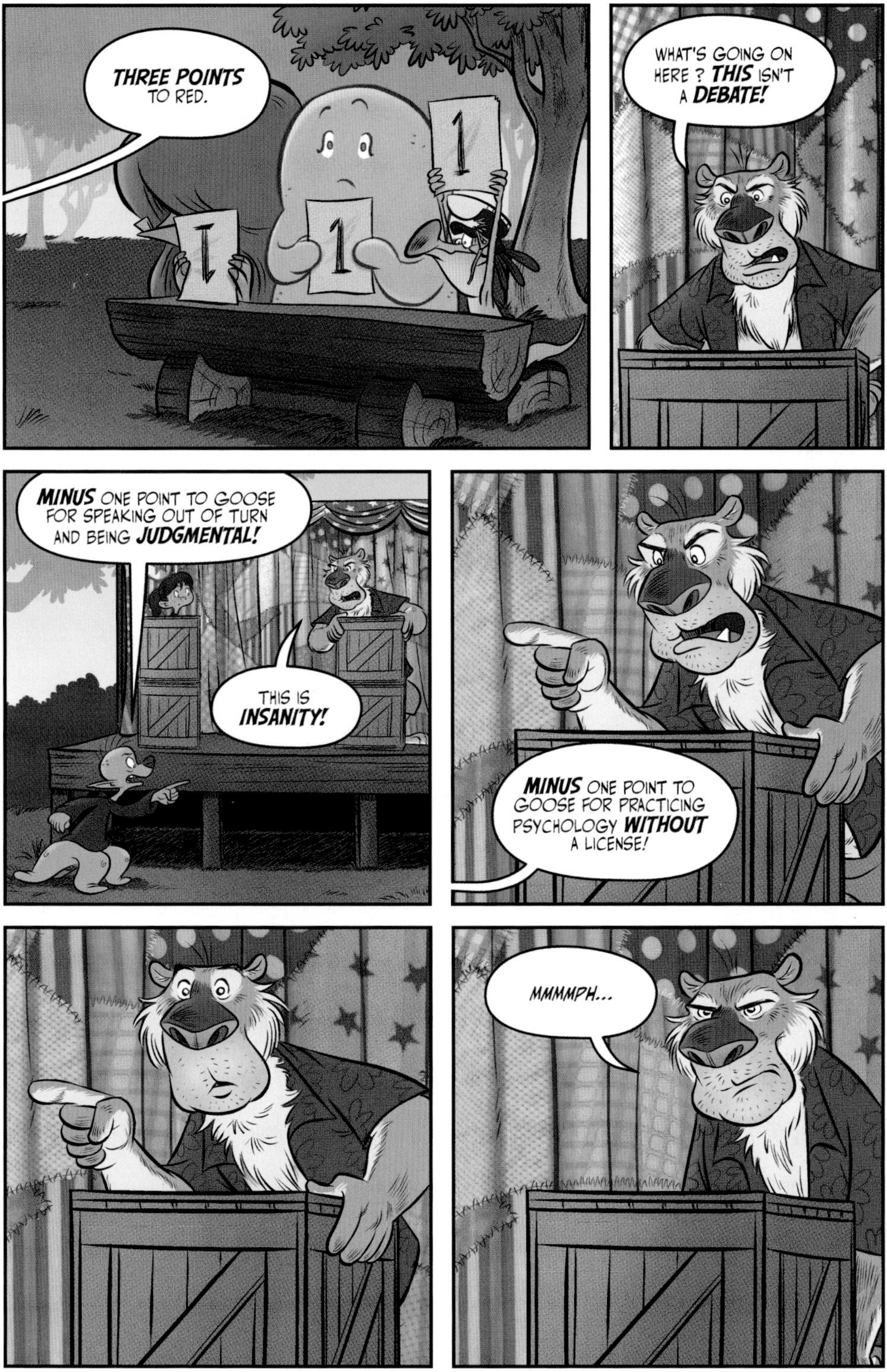
THREE POINTS TO RED.
WHAT'S GOING ON HERE ? THIS ISN'T A DEBATE!
MINUS ONE POINT TO GOOSE FOR SPEAKING OUT OF TURN AND BEING JUDGMENTAL!
THIS IS INSANITY!
MINUS ONE POINT TO GOOSE FOR PRACTICING PSYCHOLOGY WITHOUT A LICENSE!
MMMMPH...

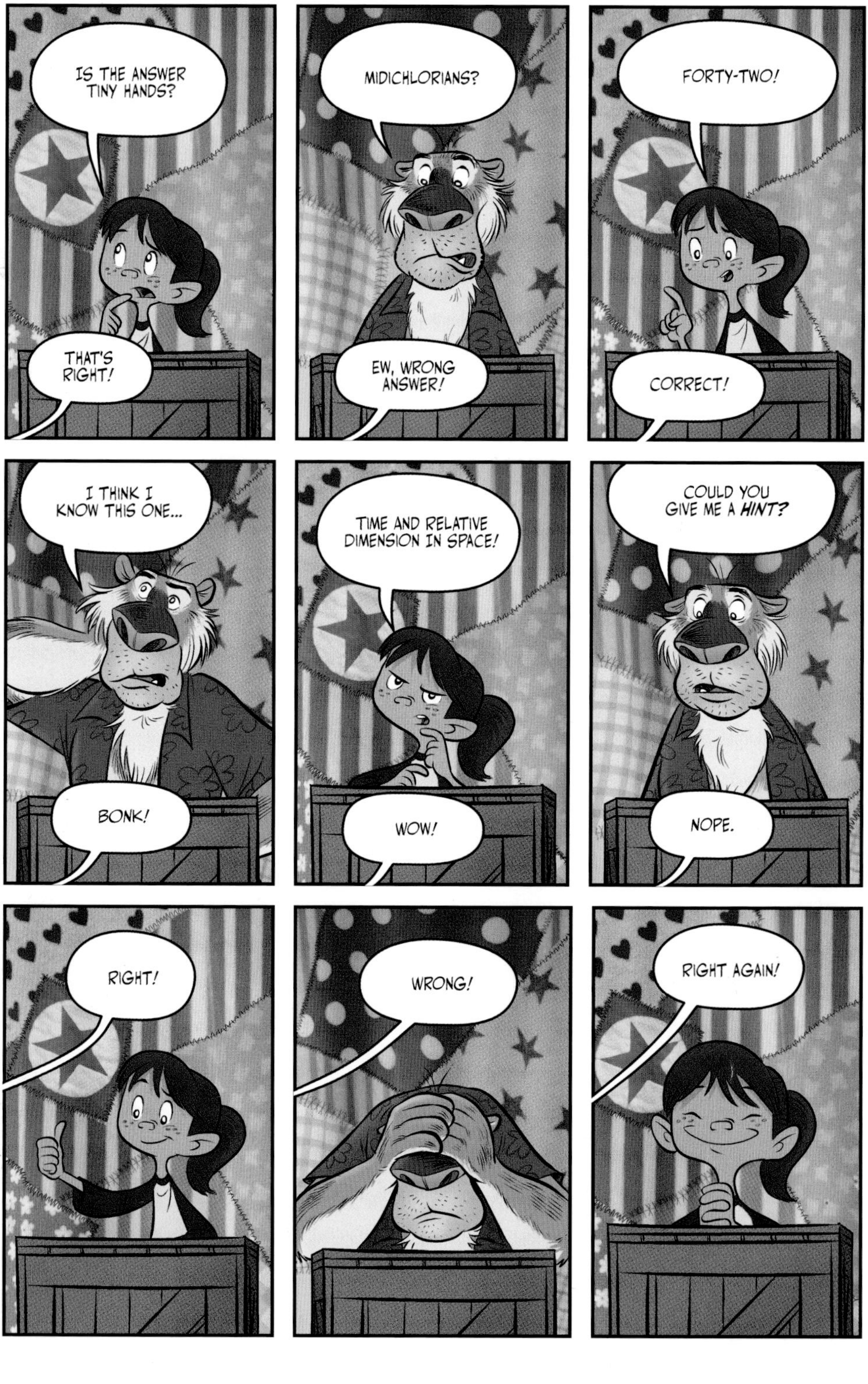
IS THE ANSWER TINY HANDS?
THAT'S RIGHT!
MIDICHLORIANS?
EW, WRONG ANSWER!
FORTY-TWO!
CORRECT!
I THINK I KNOW THIS ONE...
BONK!
TIME AND RELATIVE DIMENSION IN SPACE!
WOW!
COULD YOU GIVE ME A *HINT?*
NOPE.
RIGHT!
WRONG!
RIGHT AGAIN!

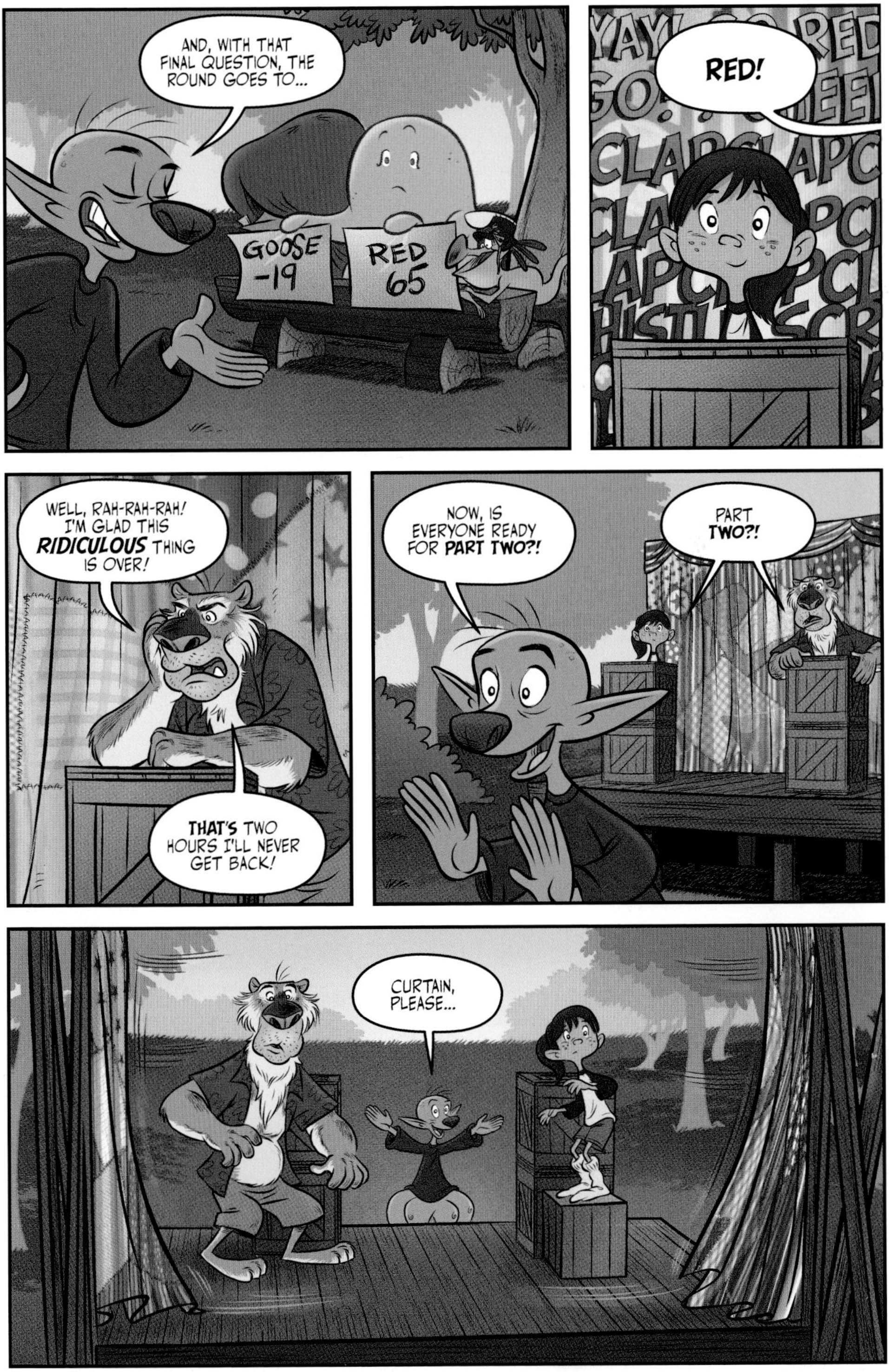
AND, WITH THAT FINAL QUESTION, THE ROUND GOES TO...
GOOSE -19
RED 65
RED!
WELL, RAH-RAH-RAH! I'M GLAD THIS RIDICULOUS THING IS OVER!
THAT'S TWO HOURS I'LL NEVER GET BACK!
NOW, IS EVERYONE READY FOR PART TWO?!
PART TWO?!
CURTAIN, PLEASE...

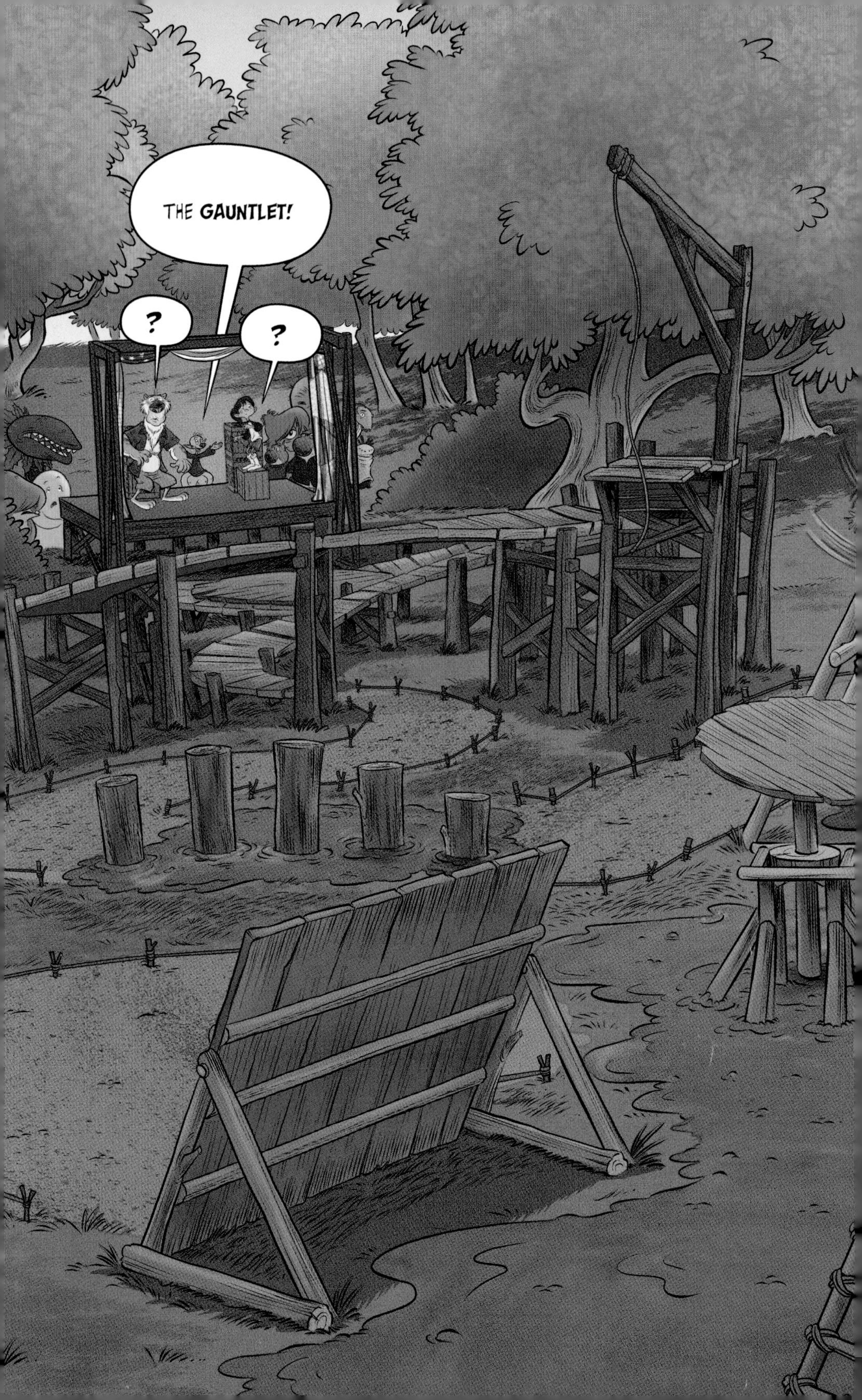
?
THE GAUNTLET!
?

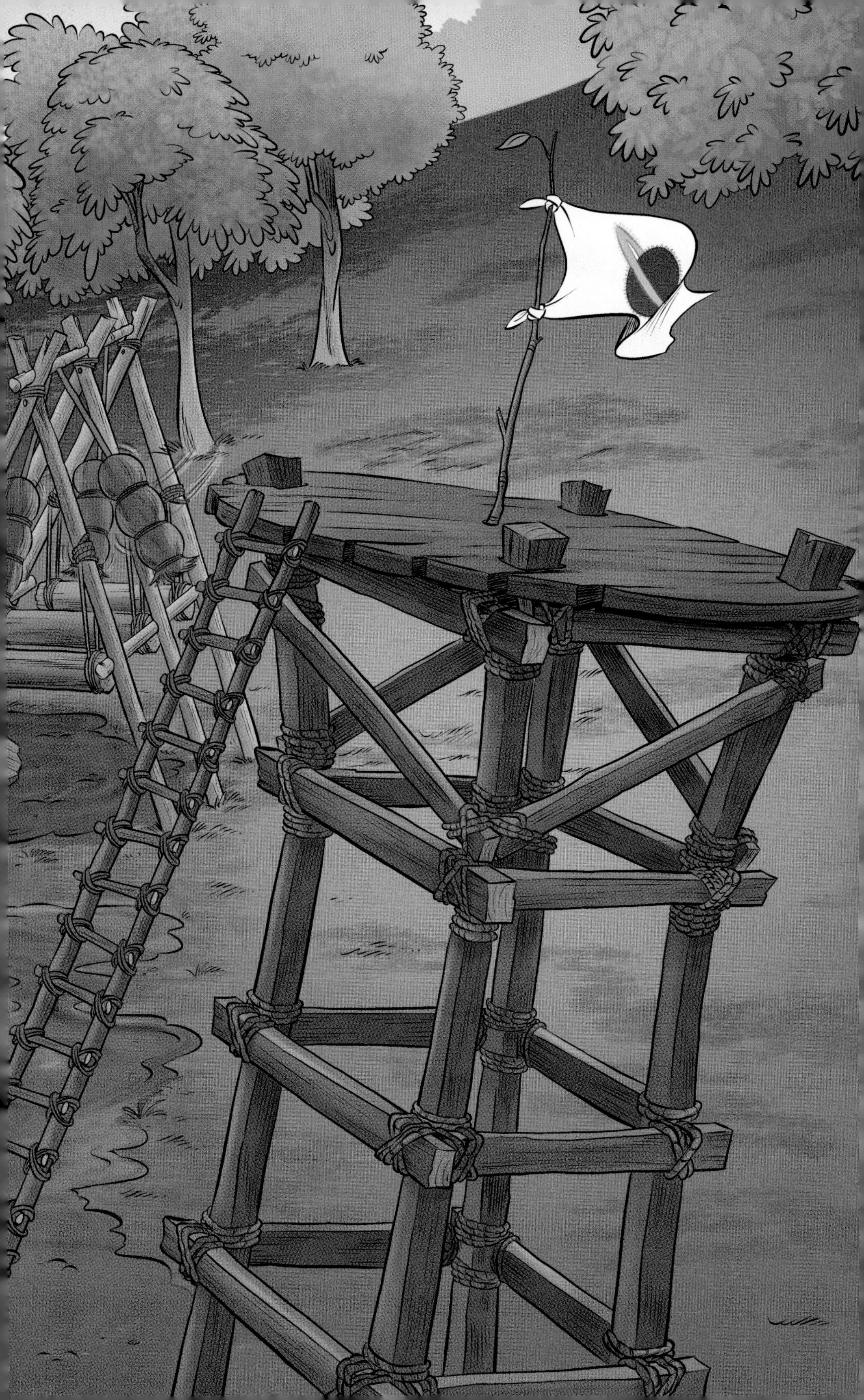

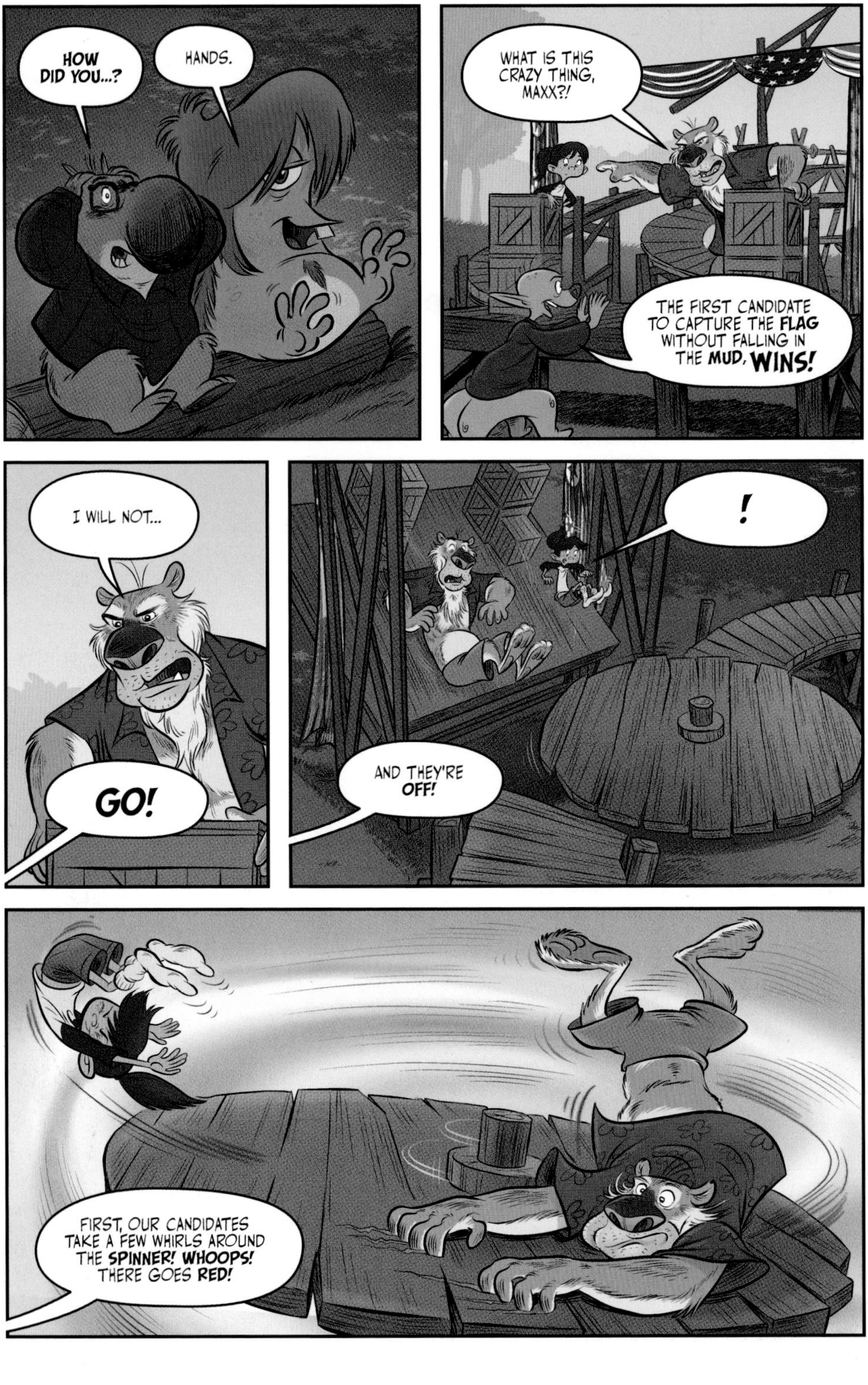
HOW DID YOU...?
HANDS.
WHAT IS THIS CRAZY THING, MAXX?!
THE FIRST CANDIDATE TO CAPTURE THE **FLAG** WITHOUT FALLING IN THE **MUD, WINS!**
I WILL NOT...
GO!
!
AND THEY'RE **OFF!**
FIRST, OUR CANDIDATES TAKE A FEW WHIRLS AROUND THE **SPINNER! WHOOPS!** THERE GOES **RED!**

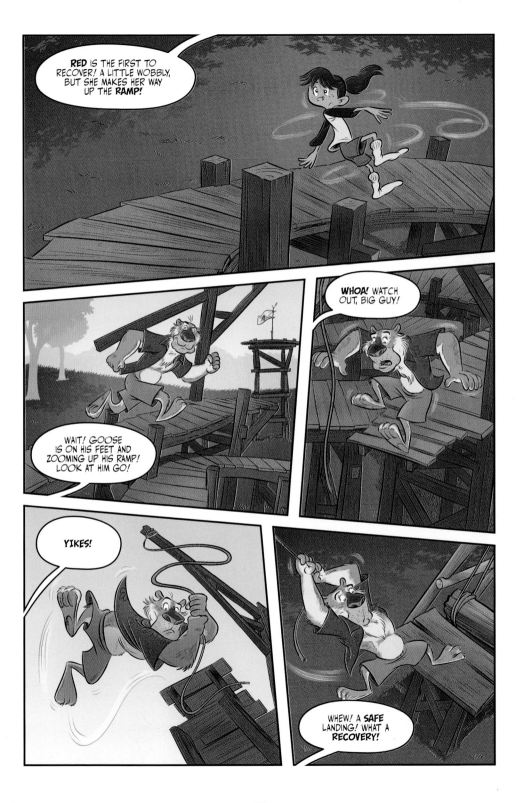

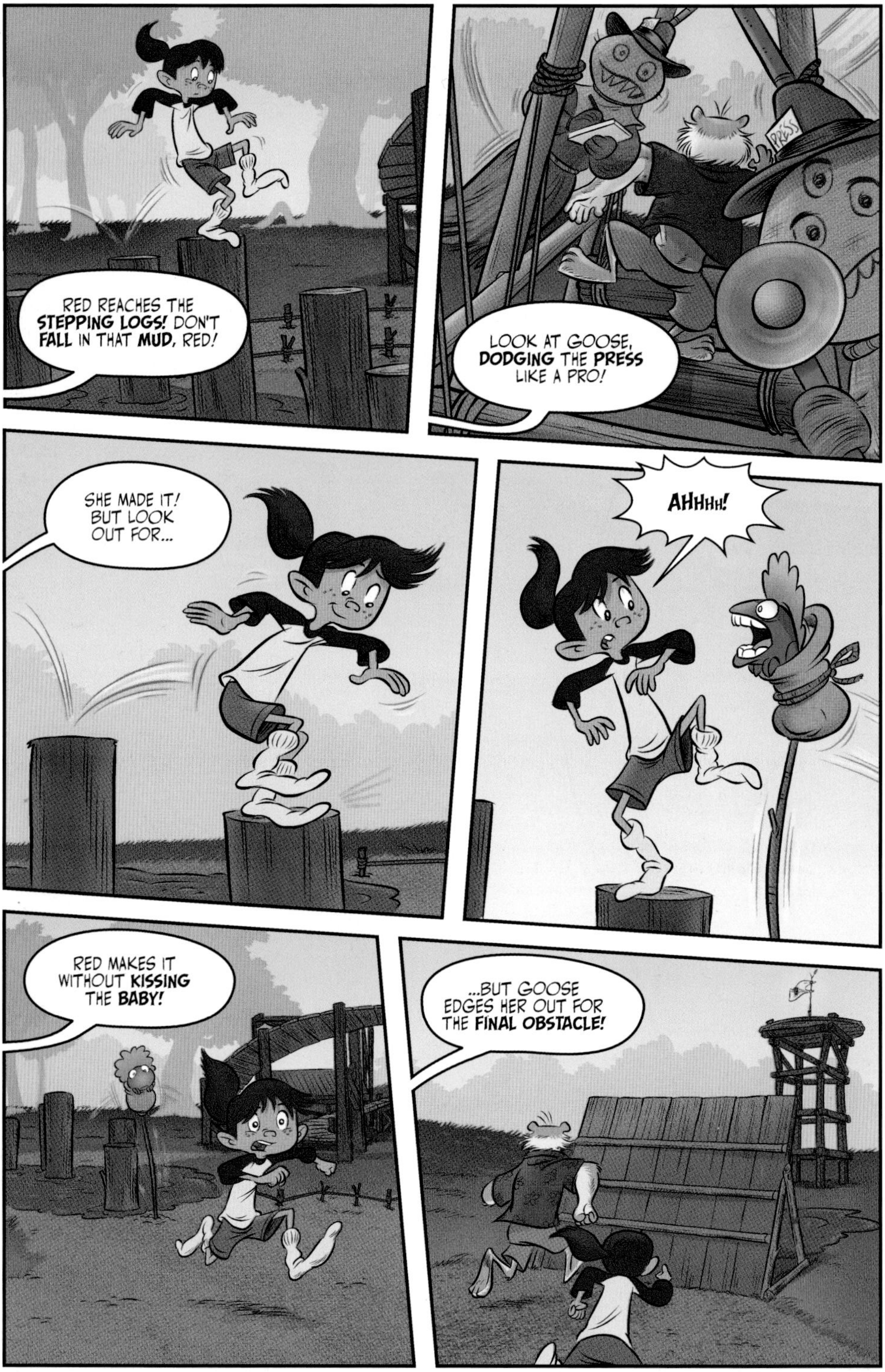
RED REACHES THE STEPPING LOGS! DON'T FALL IN THAT MUD, RED!
LOOK AT GOOSE, DODGING THE PRESS LIKE A PRO!
PRESS
SHE MADE IT! BUT LOOK OUT FOR...
AHHHH!
RED MAKES IT WITHOUT KISSING THE BABY!
...BUT GOOSE EDGES HER OUT FOR THE FINAL OBSTACLE!

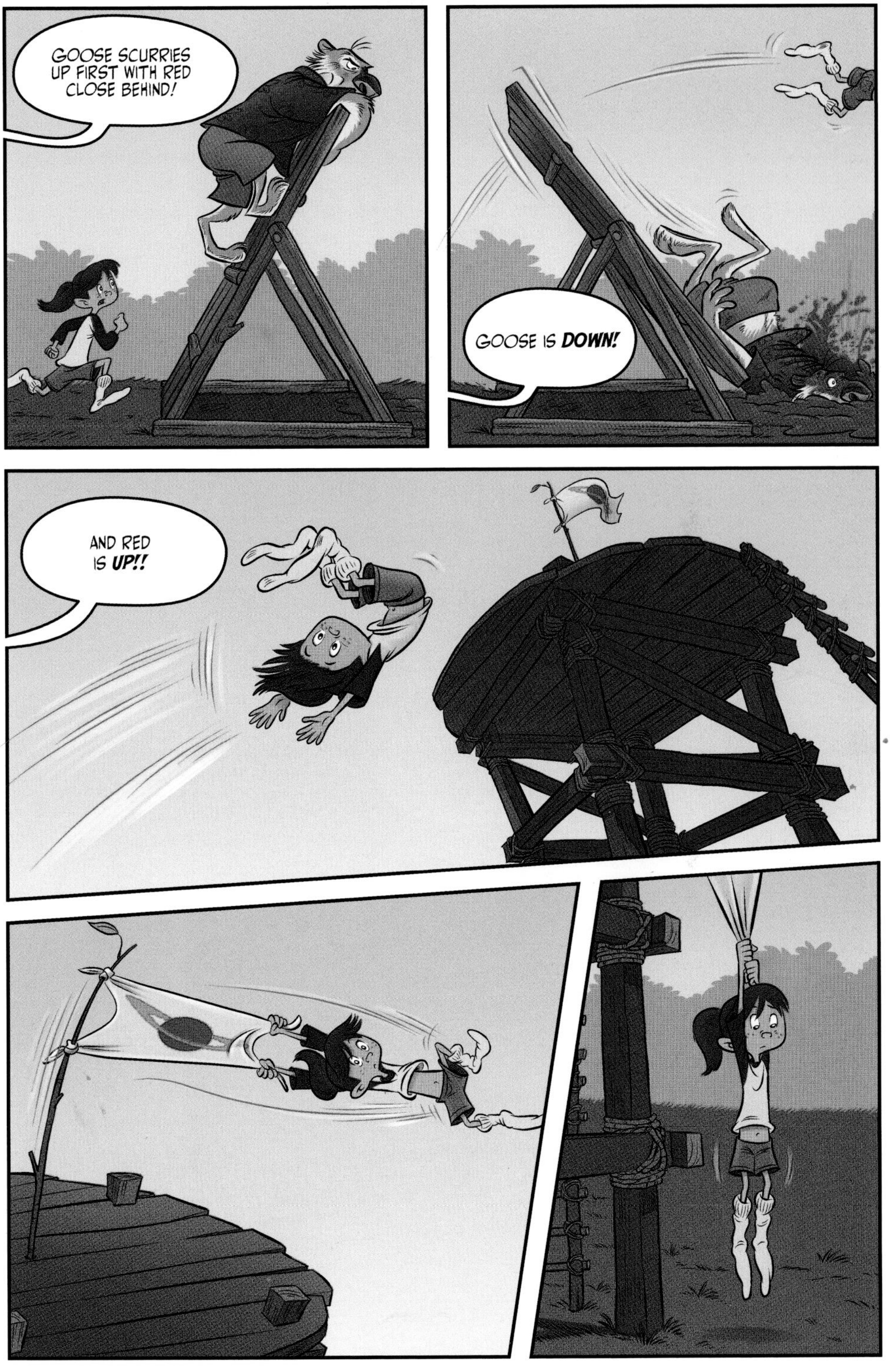
GOOSE SCURRIES UP FIRST WITH RED CLOSE BEHIND!
GOOSE IS **DOWN!**
AND RED IS **UP!!**

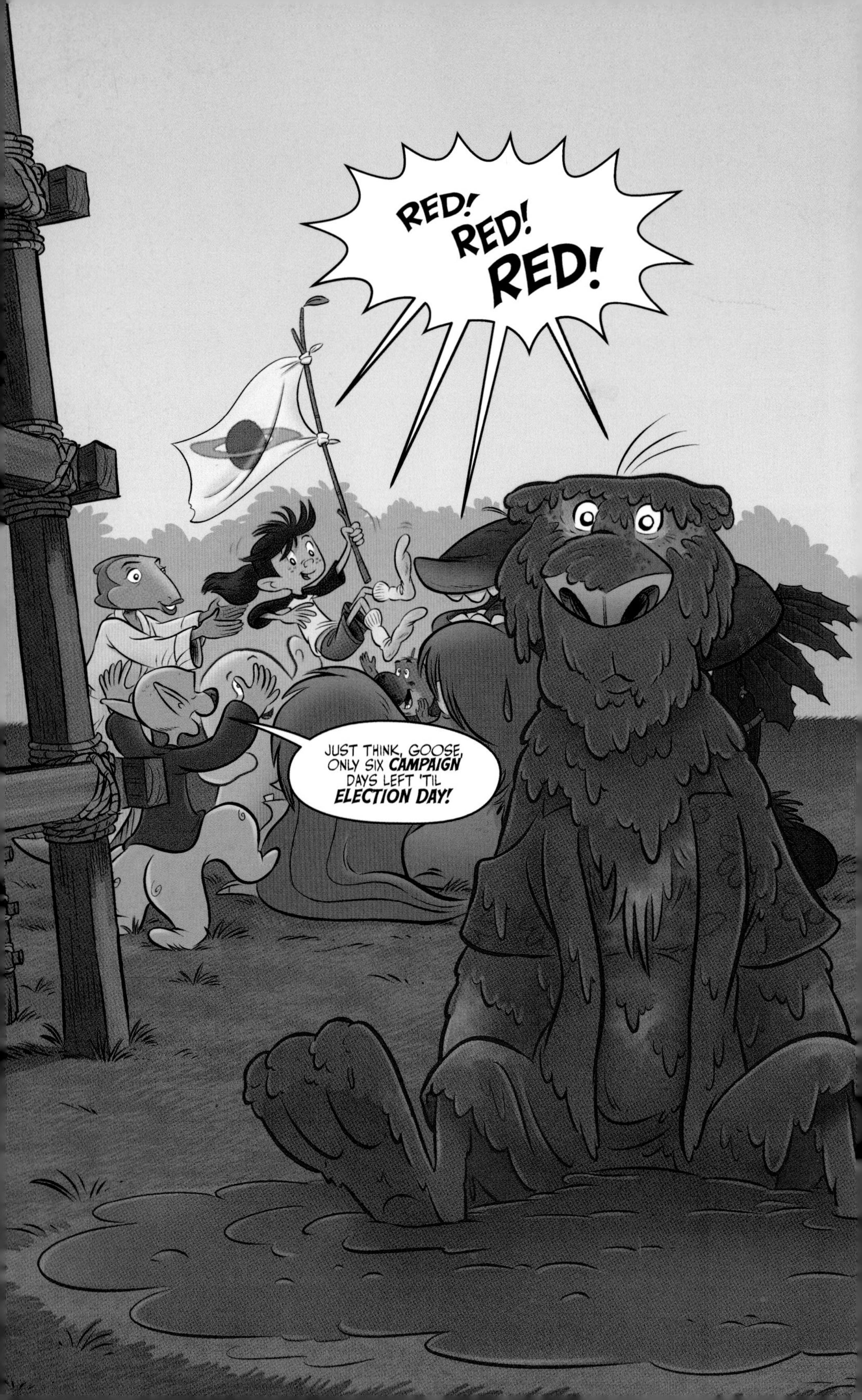
RED! RED! RED!
JUST THINK, GOOSE, ONLY SIX CAMPAIGN DAYS LEFT 'TIL ELECTION DAY!

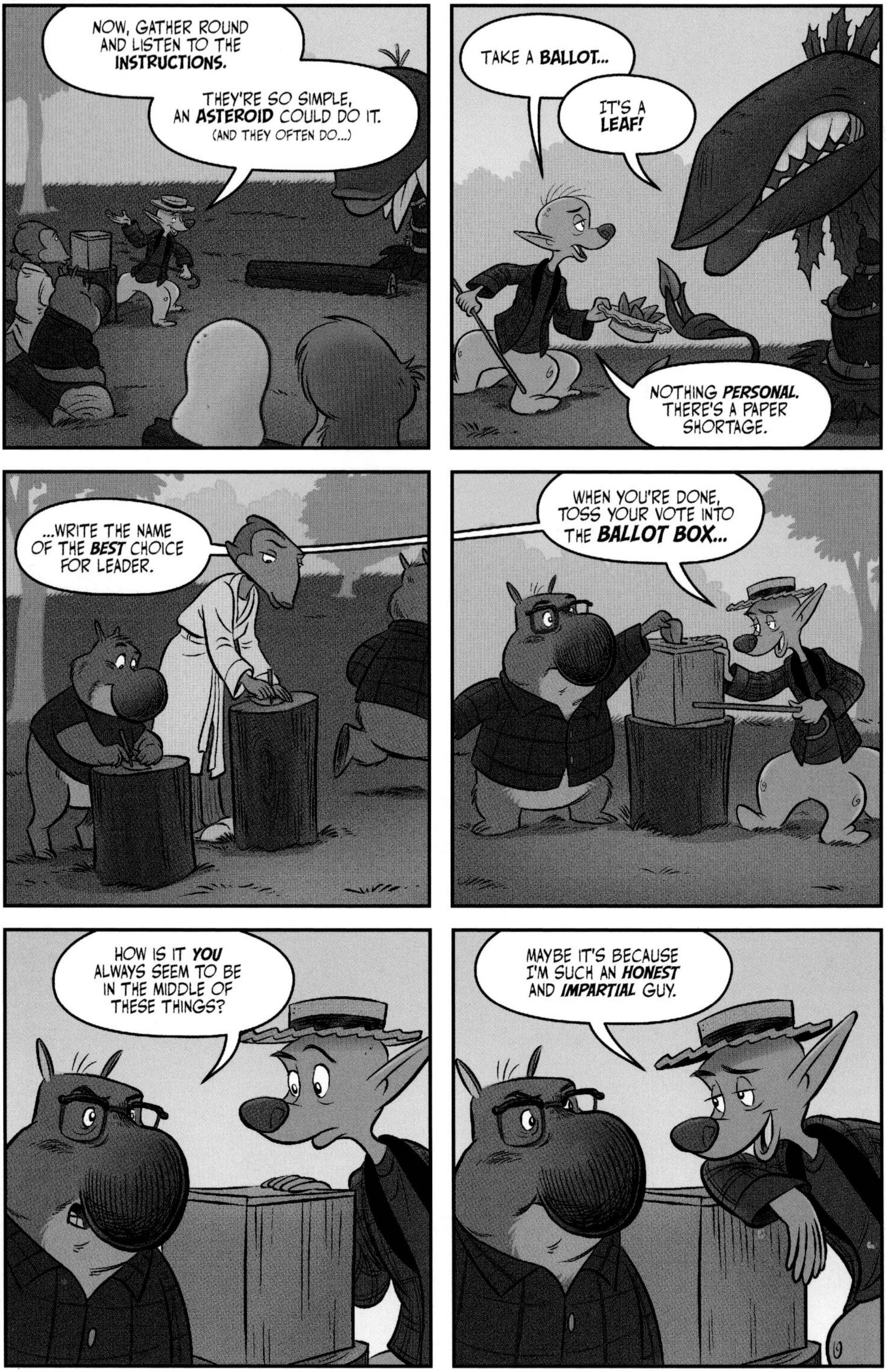
NOW, GATHER ROUND AND LISTEN TO THE **INSTRUCTIONS.**
THEY'RE SO SIMPLE, AN **ASTEROID** COULD DO IT. (AND THEY OFTEN DO...)
TAKE A **BALLOT...**
IT'S A **LEAF!**
NOTHING ***PERSONAL.*** THERE'S A PAPER SHORTAGE.
...WRITE THE NAME OF THE ***BEST*** CHOICE FOR LEADER.
WHEN YOU'RE DONE, TOSS YOUR VOTE INTO THE **BALLOT BOX...**
HOW IS IT ***YOU*** ALWAYS SEEM TO BE IN THE MIDDLE OF THESE THINGS?
MAYBE IT'S BECAUSE I'M SUCH AN ***HONEST*** AND ***IMPARTIAL*** GUY.

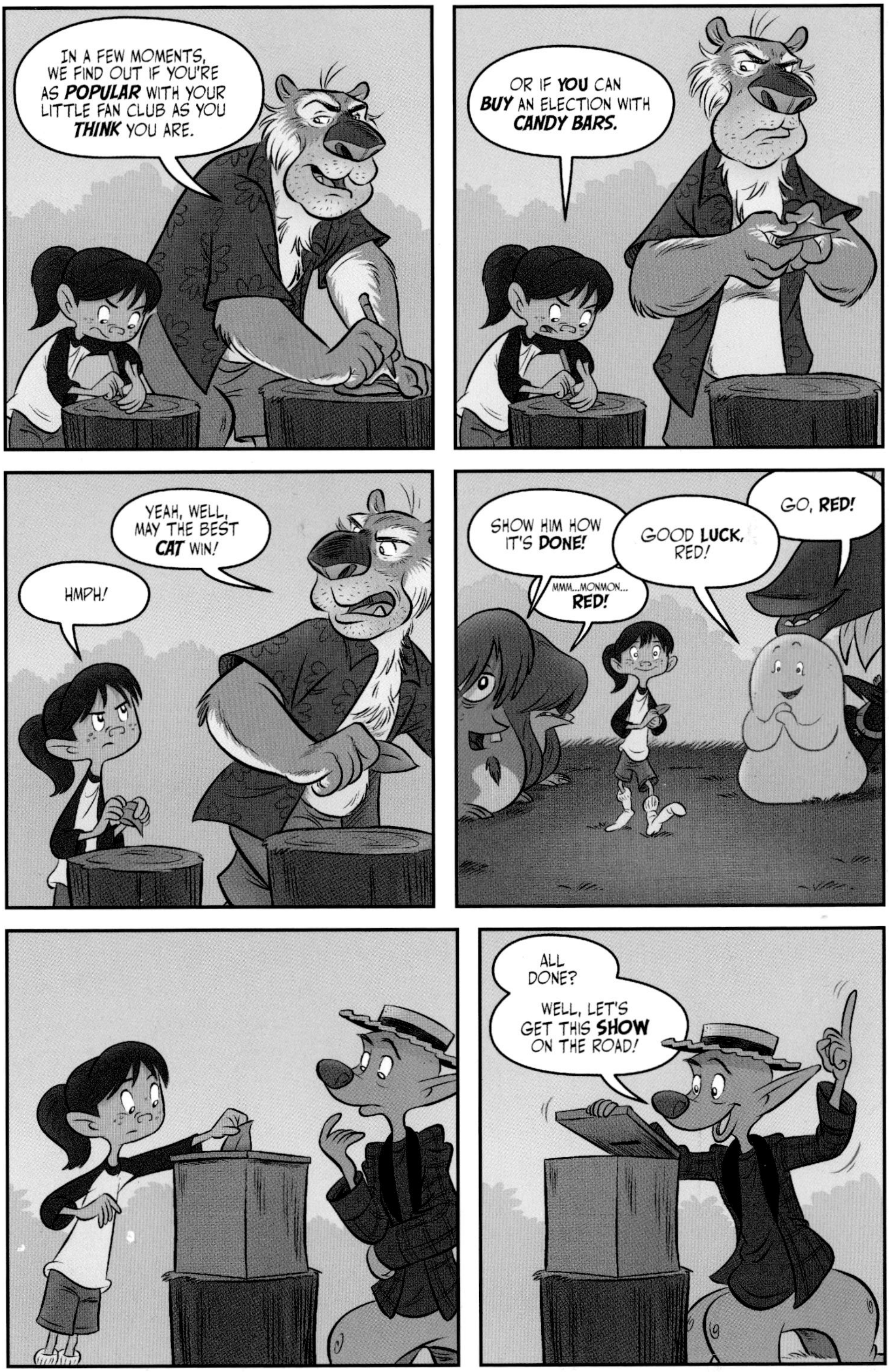
IN A FEW MOMENTS, WE FIND OUT IF YOU'RE AS **POPULAR** WITH YOUR LITTLE FAN CLUB AS YOU **THINK** YOU ARE.
OR IF **YOU** CAN **BUY** AN ELECTION WITH **CANDY BARS.**
YEAH, WELL, MAY THE BEST **CAT** WIN!
HMPH!
SHOW HIM HOW IT'S **DONE!**
GOOD **LUCK,** RED!
GO, **RED!**
MMM...MONMON... **RED!**
ALL DONE?
WELL, LET'S GET THIS **SHOW** ON THE ROAD!

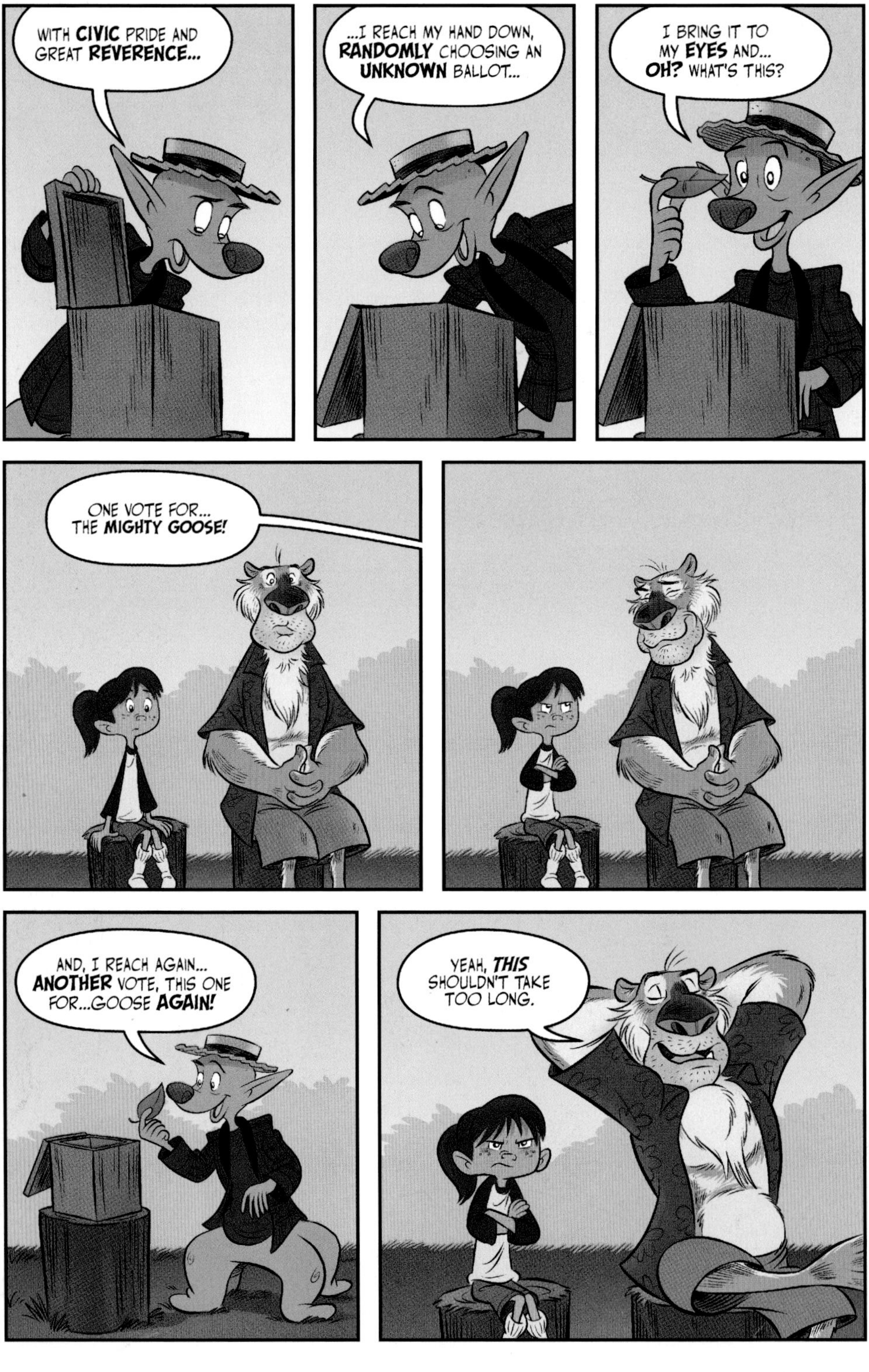
WITH CIVIC PRIDE AND GREAT REVERENCE...
...I REACH MY HAND DOWN, RANDOMLY CHOOSING AN UNKNOWN BALLOT...
I BRING IT TO MY EYES AND... OH? WHAT'S THIS?
ONE VOTE FOR... THE MIGHTY GOOSE!
AND, I REACH AGAIN... ANOTHER VOTE, THIS ONE FOR...GOOSE AGAIN!
YEAH, THIS SHOULDN'T TAKE TOO LONG.

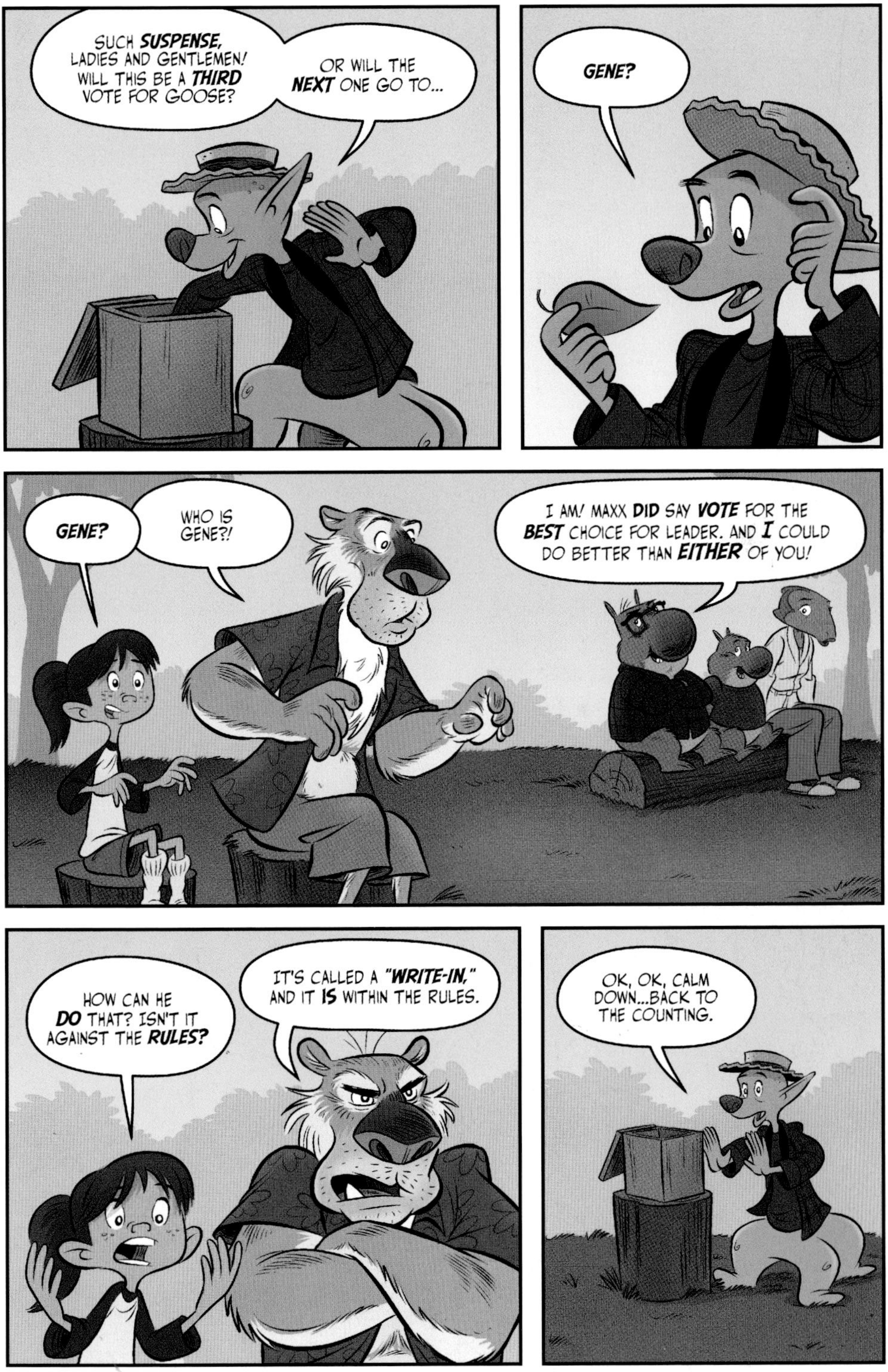
SUCH **SUSPENSE,** LADIES AND GENTLEMEN! WILL THIS BE A **THIRD** VOTE FOR GOOSE?
OR WILL THE **NEXT** ONE GO TO...
GENE?
GENE?
WHO IS GENE?!
I AM! MAXX **DID** SAY **VOTE** FOR THE **BEST** CHOICE FOR LEADER. AND **I** COULD DO BETTER THAN **EITHER** OF YOU!
HOW CAN HE **DO** THAT? ISN'T IT AGAINST THE **RULES?**
IT'S CALLED A **"WRITE-IN,"** AND IT **IS** WITHIN THE RULES.
OK, OK, CALM DOWN...BACK TO THE COUNTING.

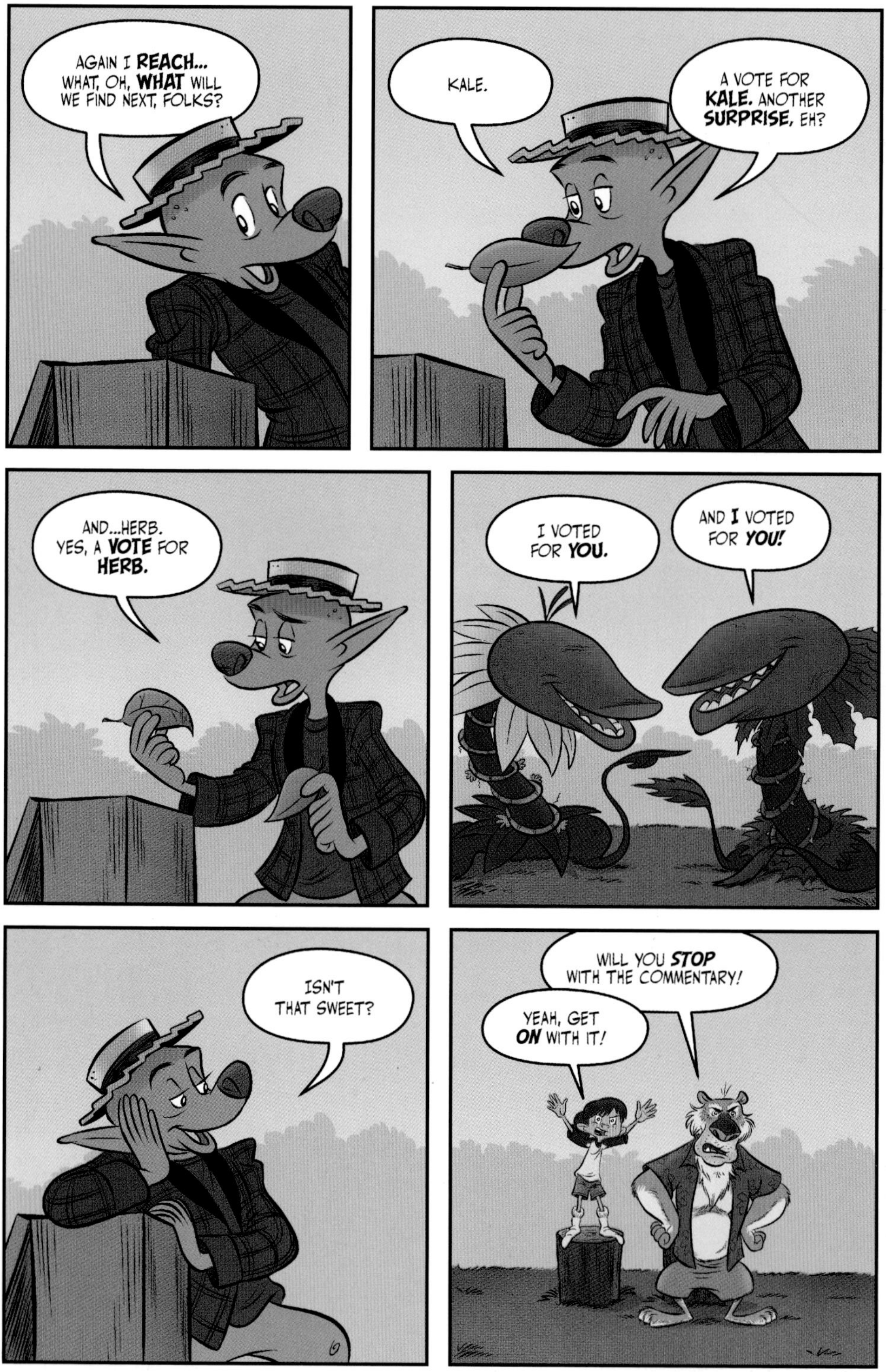
AGAIN I REACH... WHAT, OH, WHAT WILL WE FIND NEXT, FOLKS?
KALE.
A VOTE FOR KALE. ANOTHER SURPRISE, EH?
AND...HERB. YES, A VOTE FOR HERB.
I VOTED FOR YOU.
AND I VOTED FOR YOU!
ISN'T THAT SWEET?
WILL YOU STOP WITH THE COMMENTARY!
YEAH, GET ON WITH IT!

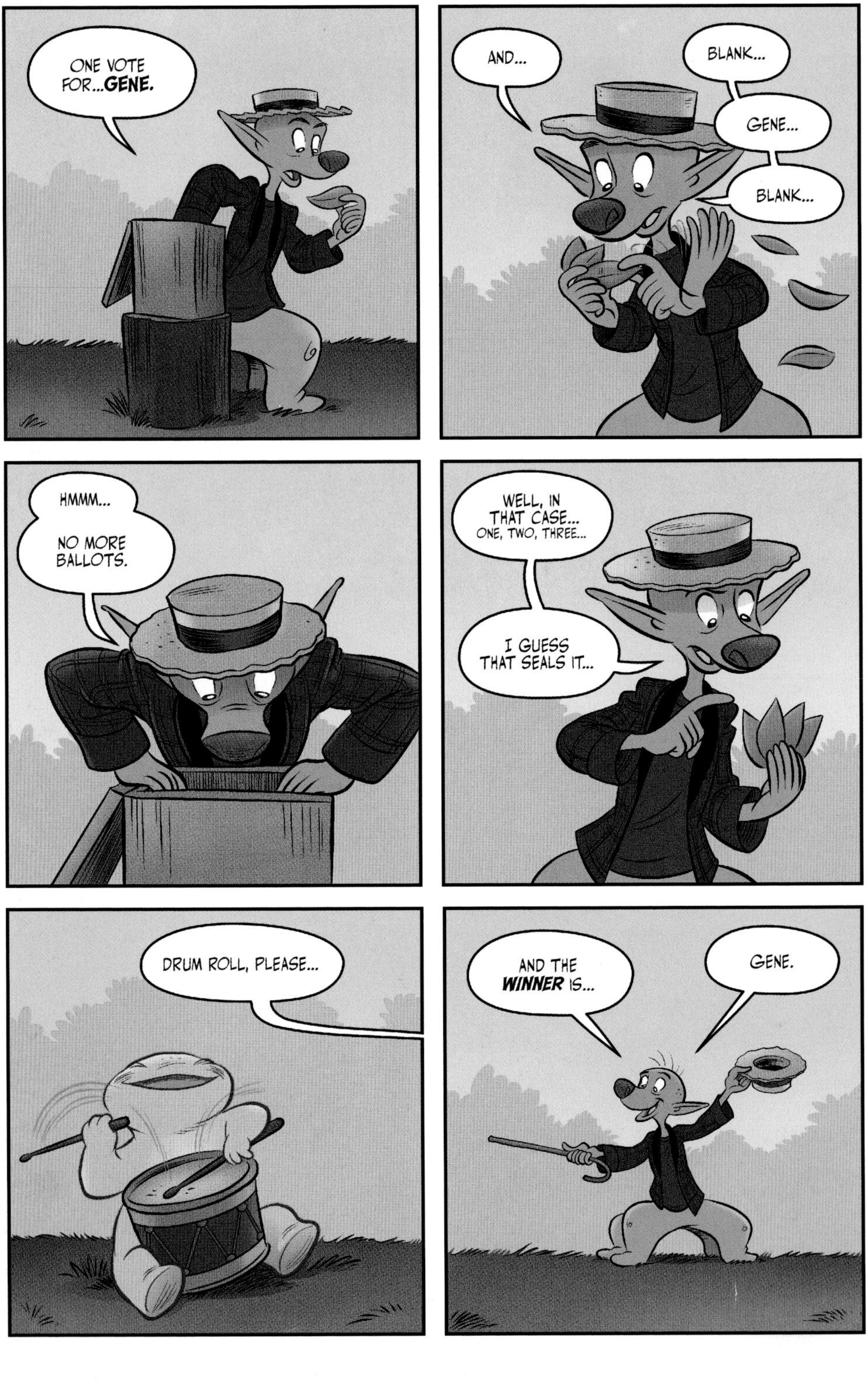
ONE VOTE FOR...**GENE.**
AND...
BLANK...
GENE...
BLANK...
HMMM...
NO MORE BALLOTS.
WELL, IN THAT CASE... ONE, TWO, THREE...
I GUESS THAT SEALS IT...
DRUM ROLL, PLEASE...
AND THE ***WINNER*** IS...
GENE.

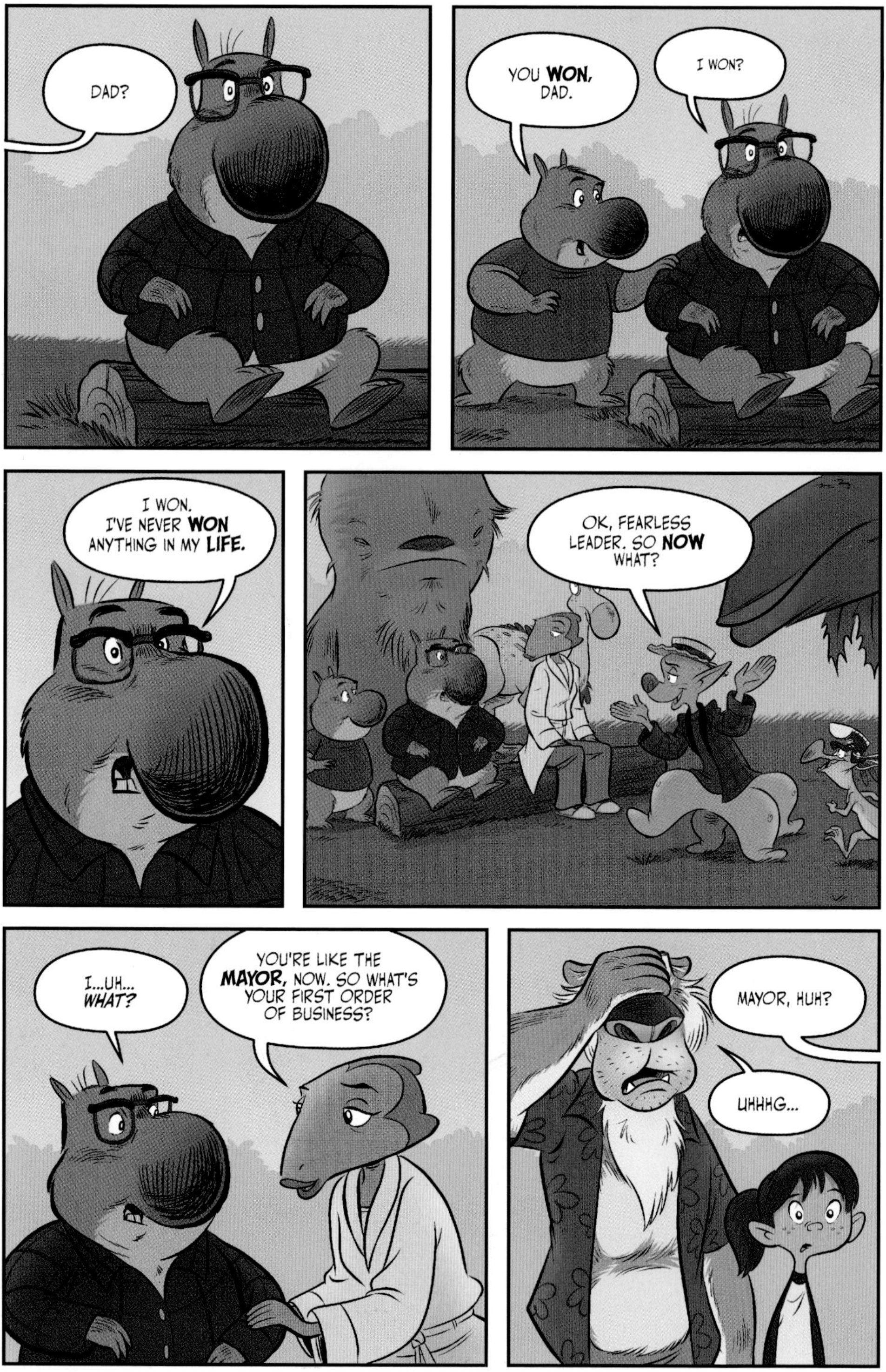
DAD?
YOU WON, DAD.
I WON?
I WON. I'VE NEVER WON ANYTHING IN MY LIFE.
OK, FEARLESS LEADER. SO NOW WHAT?
I...UH... WHAT?
YOU'RE LIKE THE MAYOR, NOW. SO WHAT'S YOUR FIRST ORDER OF BUSINESS?
MAYOR, HUH?
UHHHG...

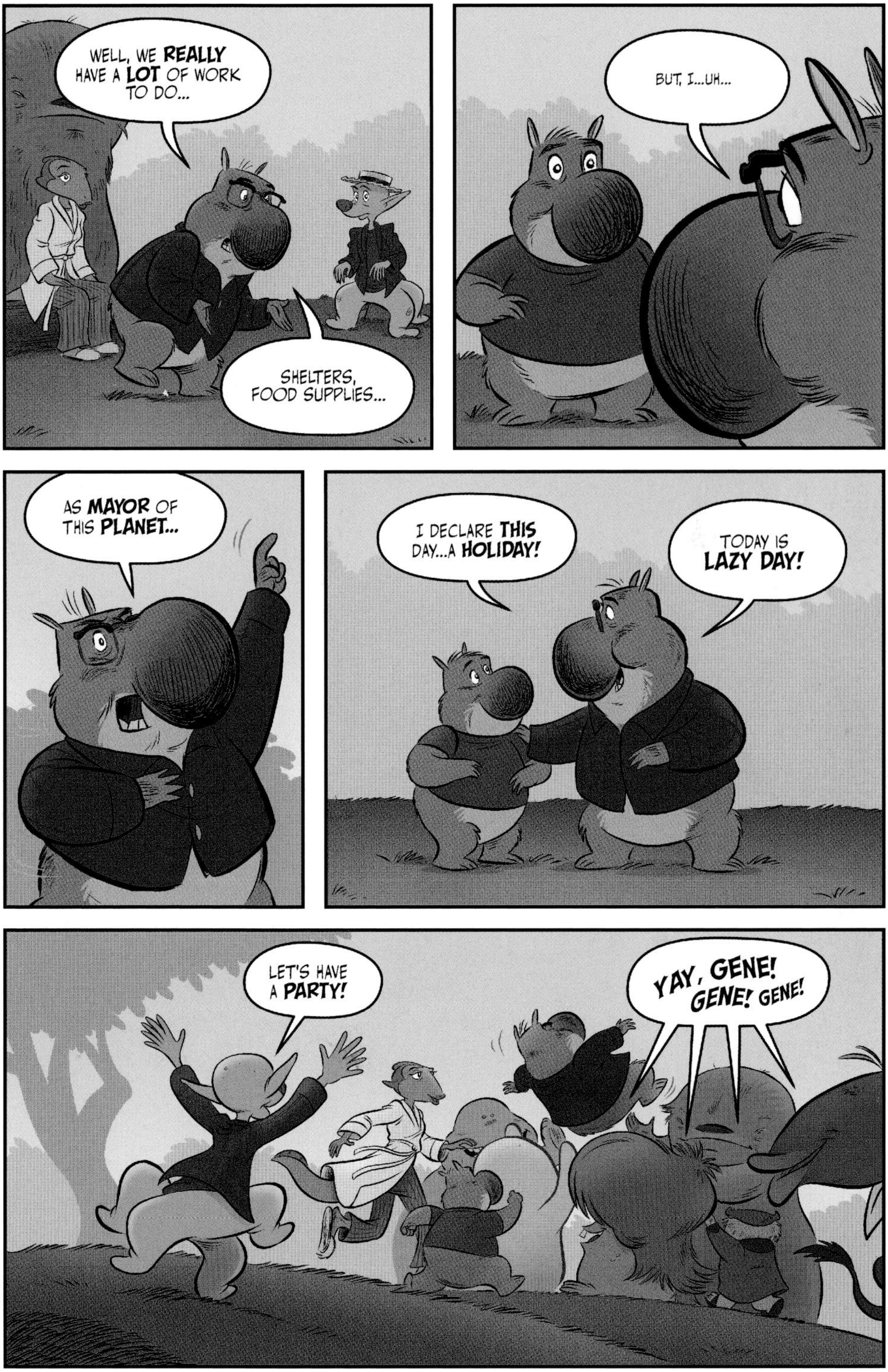
WELL, WE REALLY HAVE A LOT OF WORK TO DO...
SHELTERS, FOOD SUPPLIES...
BUT, I...UH...
AS MAYOR OF THIS PLANET...
I DECLARE THIS DAY...A HOLIDAY!
TODAY IS LAZY DAY!
LET'S HAVE A PARTY!
YAY, GENE! GENE! GENE!

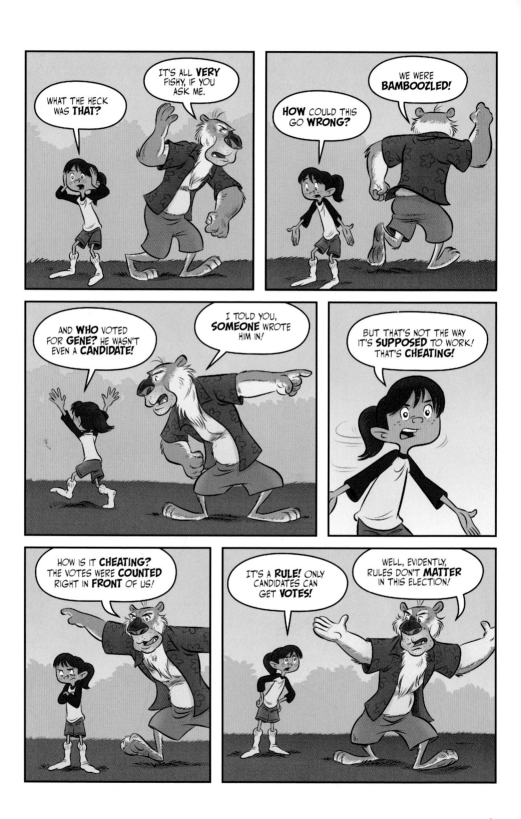

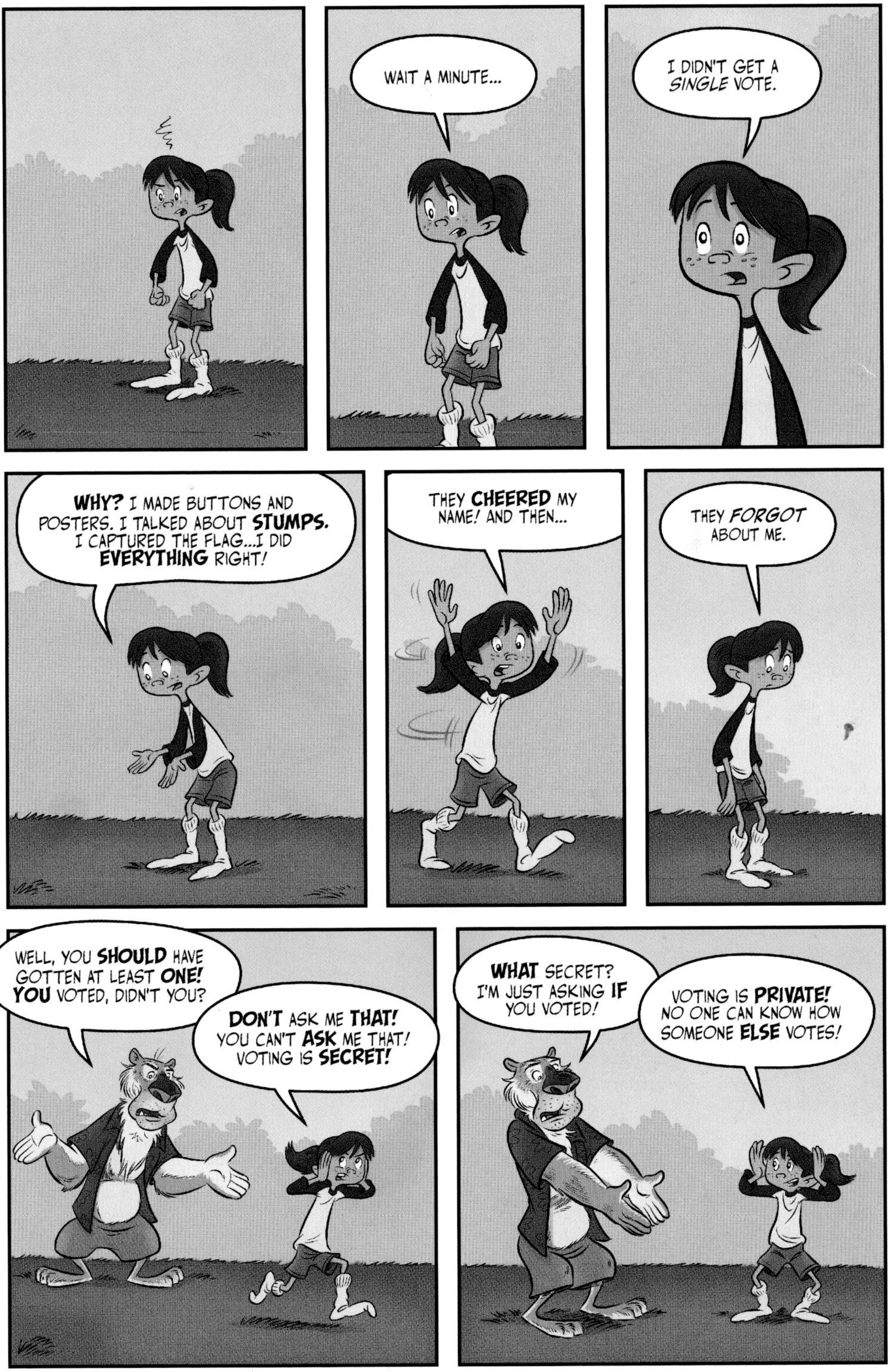
WAIT A MINUTE...
I DIDN'T GET A *SINGLE* VOTE.
WHY? I MADE BUTTONS AND POSTERS. I TALKED ABOUT **STUMPS.** I CAPTURED THE FLAG...I DID **EVERYTHING** RIGHT!
THEY **CHEERED** MY NAME! AND THEN...
THEY *FORGOT* ABOUT ME.
WELL, YOU **SHOULD** HAVE GOTTEN AT LEAST **ONE! YOU** VOTED, DIDN'T YOU?
DON'T ASK ME **THAT!** YOU CAN'T **ASK** ME THAT! VOTING IS **SECRET!**
WHAT SECRET? I'M JUST ASKING **IF** YOU VOTED!
VOTING IS **PRIVATE!** NO ONE CAN KNOW HOW SOMEONE **ELSE** VOTES!

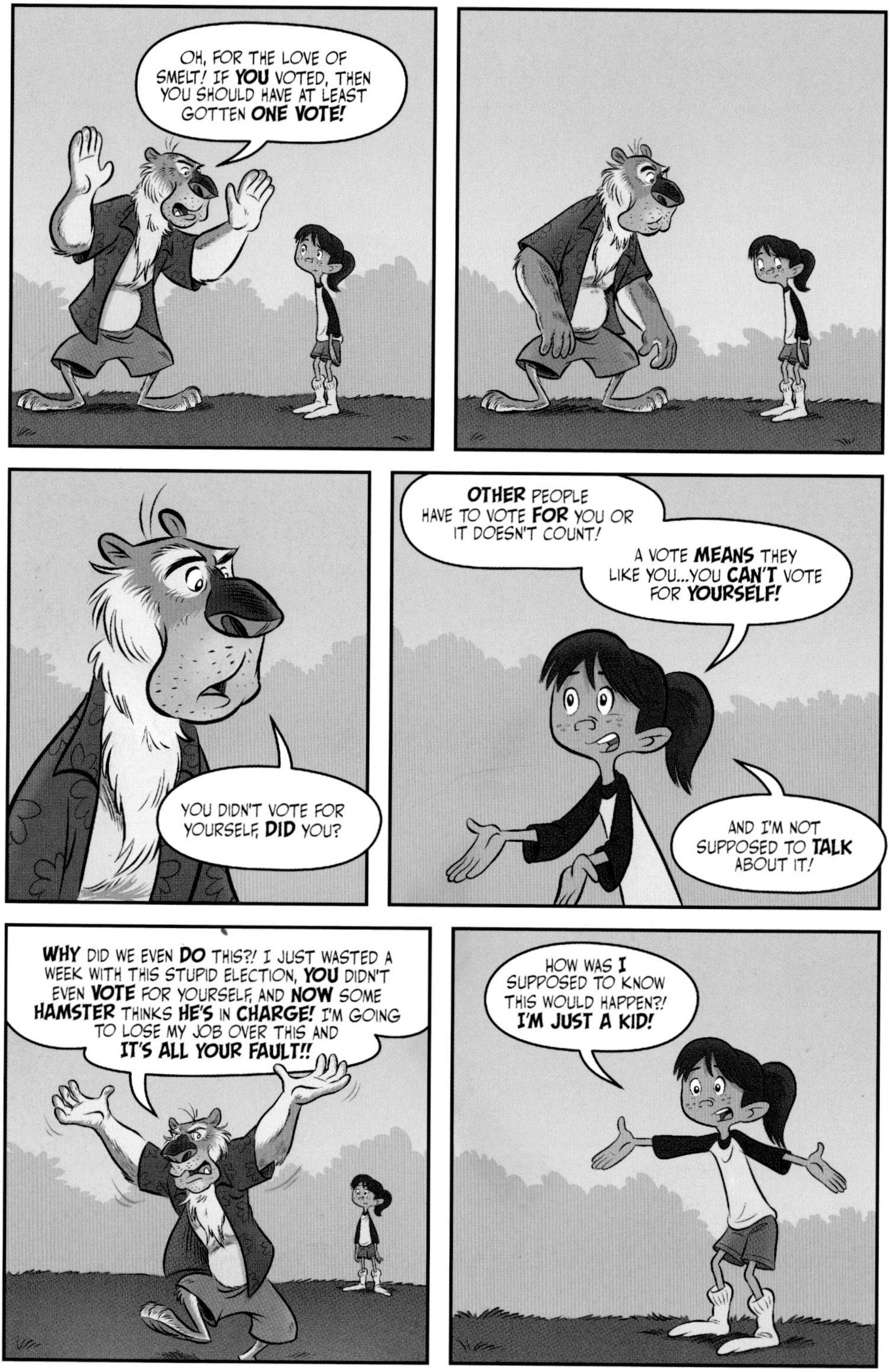
OH, FOR THE LOVE OF SMELT! IF **YOU** VOTED, THEN YOU SHOULD HAVE AT LEAST GOTTEN **ONE VOTE!**
YOU DIDN'T VOTE FOR YOURSELF, **DID** YOU?
OTHER PEOPLE HAVE TO VOTE **FOR** YOU OR IT DOESN'T COUNT!
A VOTE **MEANS** THEY LIKE YOU...YOU **CAN'T** VOTE FOR **YOURSELF!**
AND I'M NOT SUPPOSED TO **TALK** ABOUT IT!
WHY DID WE EVEN **DO** THIS?! I JUST WASTED A WEEK WITH THIS STUPID ELECTION, **YOU** DIDN'T EVEN **VOTE** FOR YOURSELF, AND **NOW** SOME **HAMSTER** THINKS **HE'S** IN **CHARGE!** I'M GOING TO LOSE MY JOB OVER THIS AND **IT'S ALL YOUR FAULT!!**
HOW WAS **I** SUPPOSED TO KNOW THIS WOULD HAPPEN?! **I'M JUST A KID!**

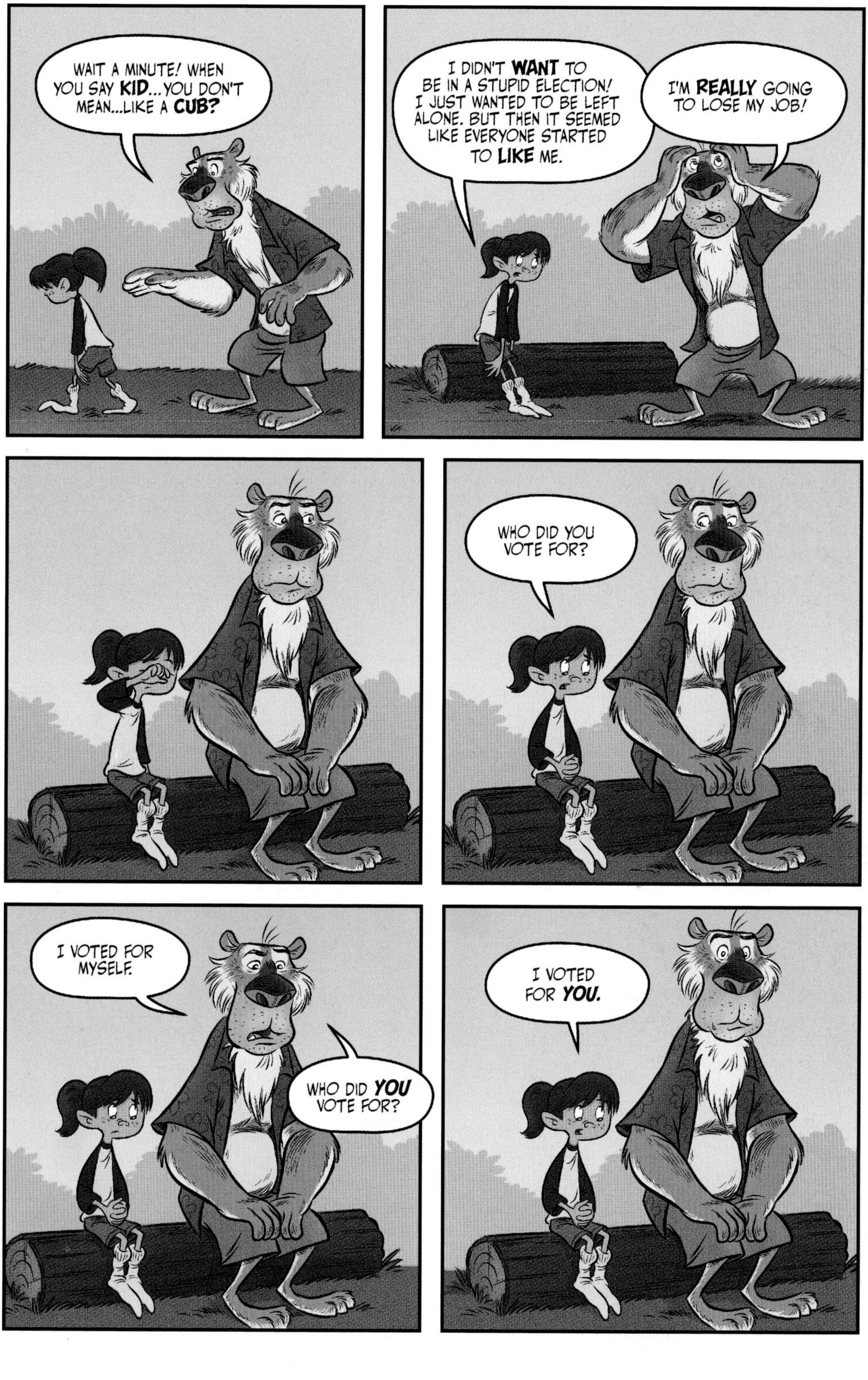
WAIT A MINUTE! WHEN YOU SAY KID...YOU DON'T MEAN...LIKE A CUB?
I DIDN'T WANT TO BE IN A STUPID ELECTION! I JUST WANTED TO BE LEFT ALONE. BUT THEN IT SEEMED LIKE EVERYONE STARTED TO LIKE ME.
I'M REALLY GOING TO LOSE MY JOB!
WHO DID YOU VOTE FOR?
I VOTED FOR MYSELF.
WHO DID YOU VOTE FOR?
I VOTED FOR YOU.

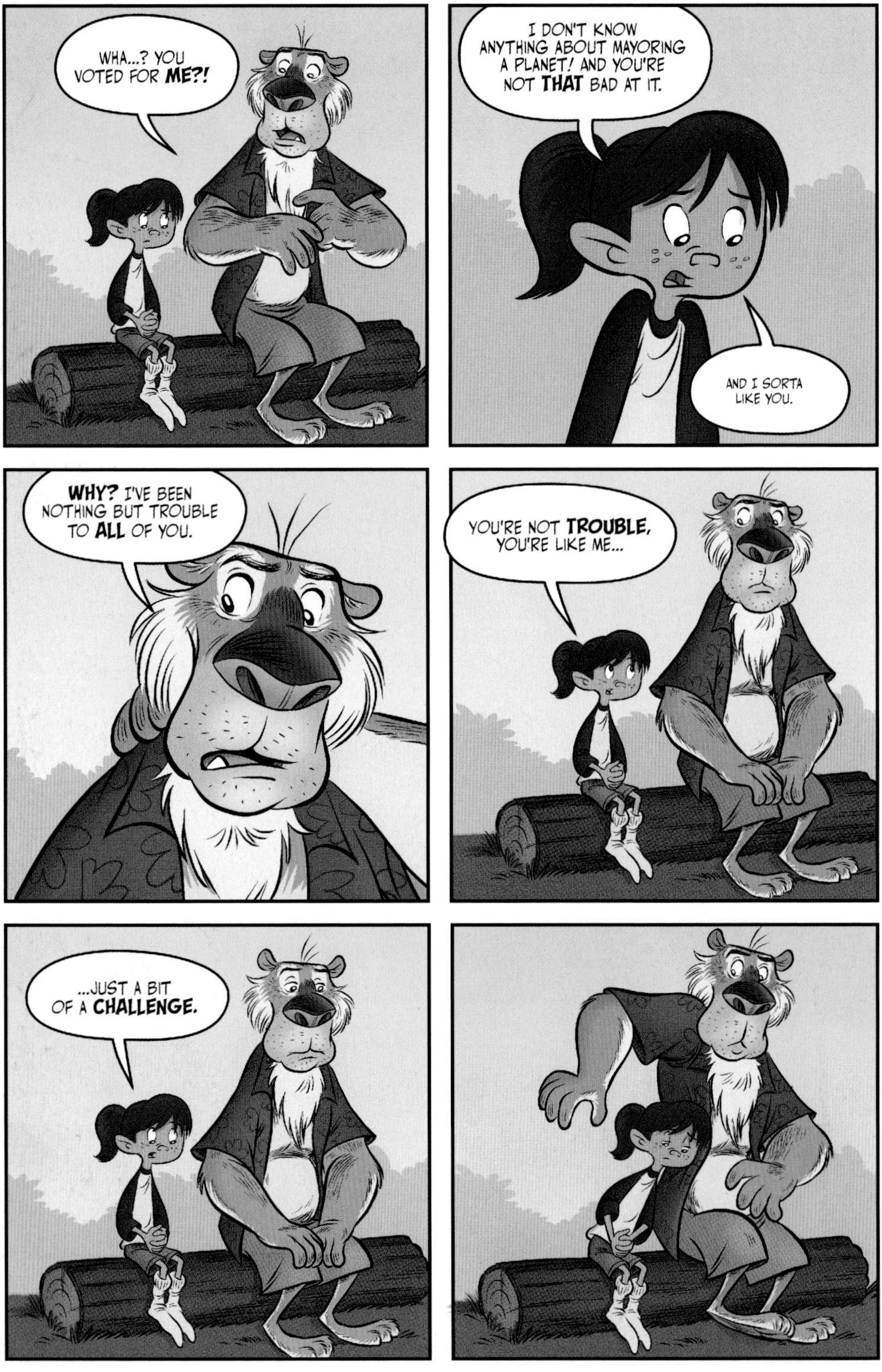
WHA...? YOU VOTED FOR ME?!
I DON'T KNOW ANYTHING ABOUT MAYORING A PLANET! AND YOU'RE NOT THAT BAD AT IT.
AND I SORTA LIKE YOU.
WHY? I'VE BEEN NOTHING BUT TROUBLE TO ALL OF YOU.
YOU'RE NOT TROUBLE, YOU'RE LIKE ME...
...JUST A BIT OF A CHALLENGE.

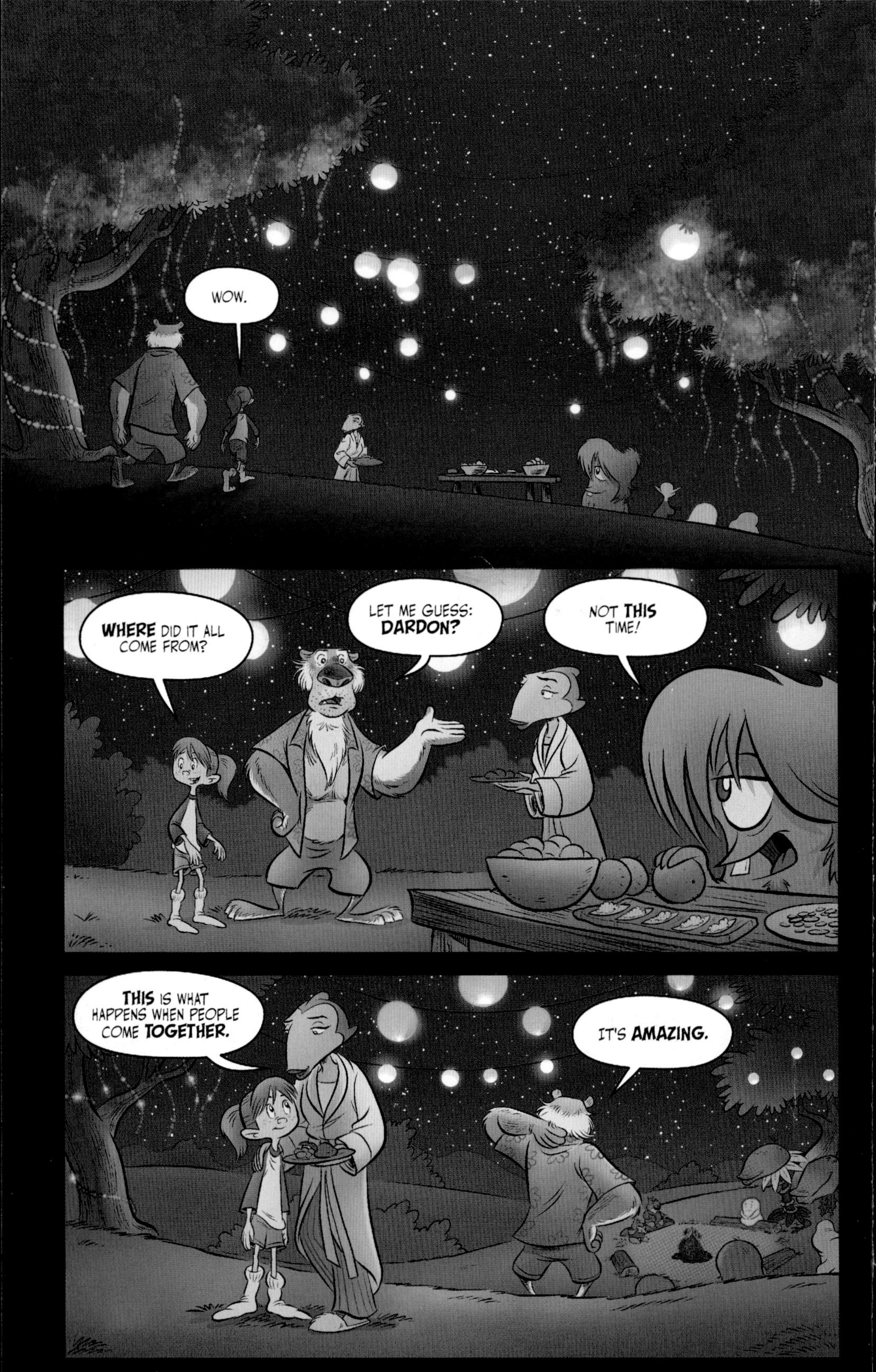
WOW.
WHERE DID IT ALL COME FROM?
LET ME GUESS: **DARDON?**
NOT **THIS** TIME!
THIS IS WHAT HAPPENS WHEN PEOPLE COME **TOGETHER.**
IT'S **AMAZING.**

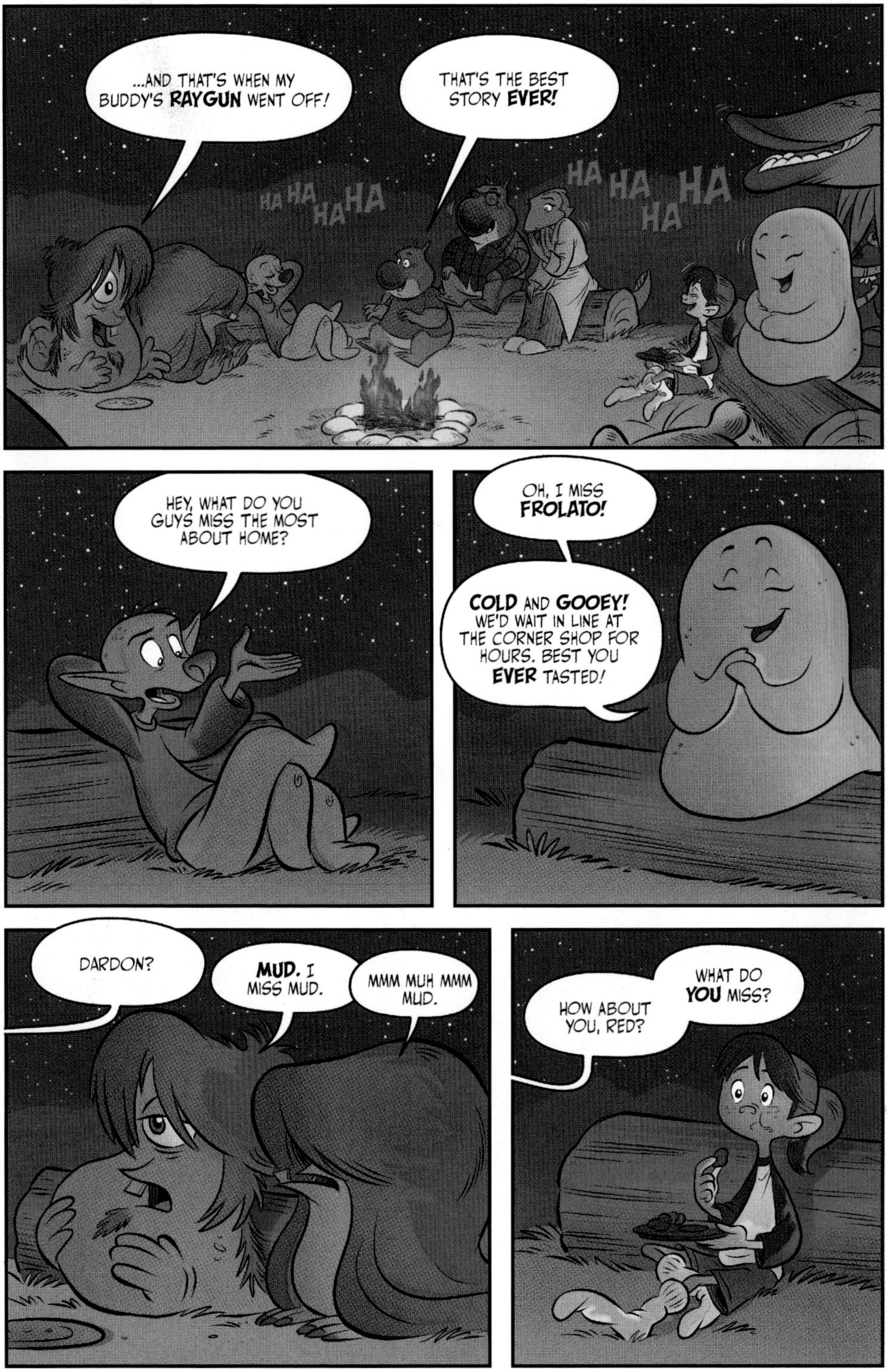
...AND THAT'S WHEN MY BUDDY'S **RAYGUN** WENT OFF!
THAT'S THE BEST STORY **EVER!**
HA HA HA HA
HA HA HA HA
HEY, WHAT DO YOU GUYS MISS THE MOST ABOUT HOME?
OH, I MISS **FROLATO!**
COLD AND **GOOEY!** WE'D WAIT IN LINE AT THE CORNER SHOP FOR HOURS. BEST YOU **EVER** TASTED!
DARDON?
MUD. I MISS MUD.
MMM MUH MMM MUD.
HOW ABOUT YOU, RED?
WHAT DO **YOU** MISS?

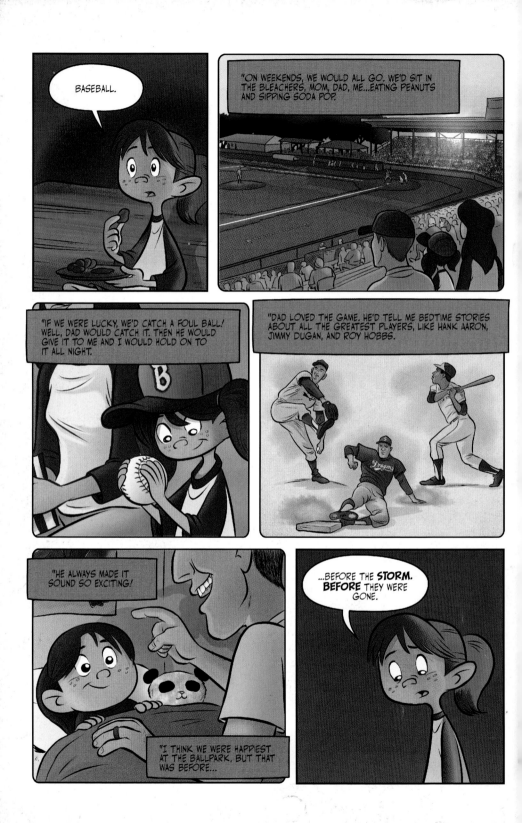

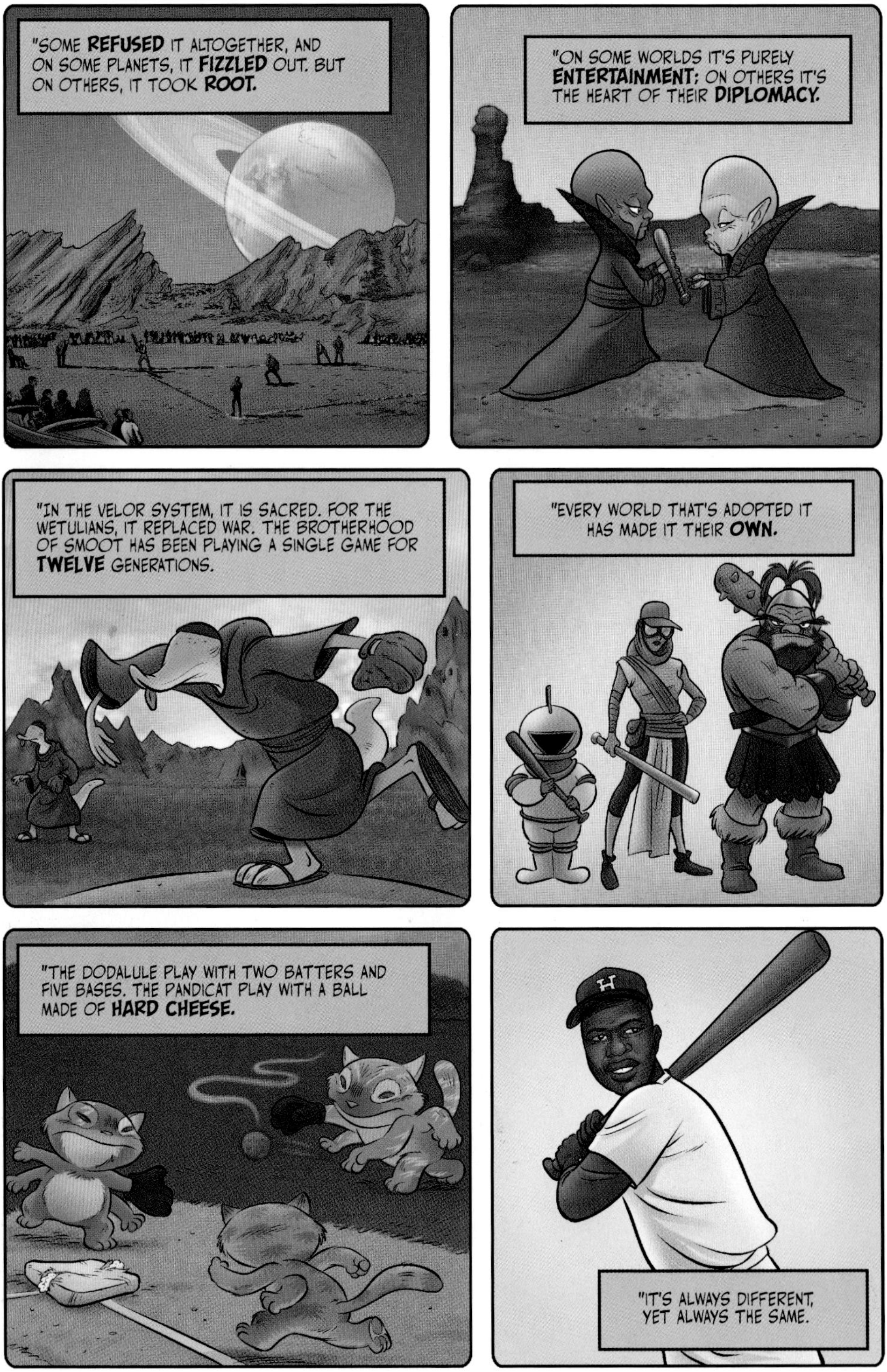
"SOME REFUSED IT ALTOGETHER, AND ON SOME PLANETS, IT FIZZLED OUT. BUT ON OTHERS, IT TOOK ROOT.
"ON SOME WORLDS IT'S PURELY ENTERTAINMENT; ON OTHERS IT'S THE HEART OF THEIR DIPLOMACY.
"IN THE VELOR SYSTEM, IT IS SACRED. FOR THE WETULIANS, IT REPLACED WAR. THE BROTHERHOOD OF SMOOT HAS BEEN PLAYING A SINGLE GAME FOR TWELVE GENERATIONS.
"EVERY WORLD THAT'S ADOPTED IT HAS MADE IT THEIR OWN.
"THE DODALULE PLAY WITH TWO BATTERS AND FIVE BASES. THE PANDICAT PLAY WITH A BALL MADE OF HARD CHEESE.
H
"IT'S ALWAYS DIFFERENT, YET ALWAYS THE SAME.

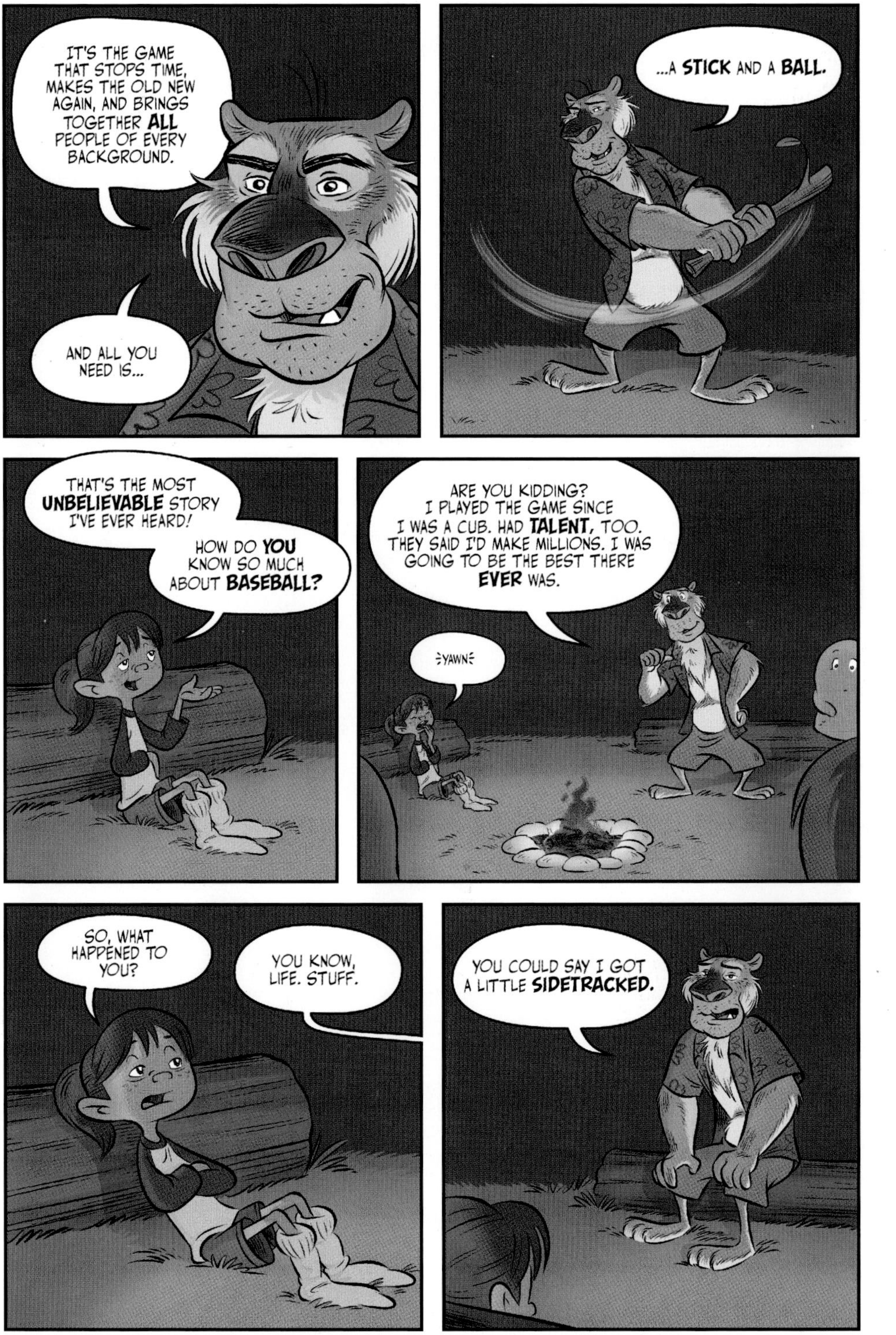
IT'S THE GAME THAT STOPS TIME, MAKES THE OLD NEW AGAIN, AND BRINGS TOGETHER ALL PEOPLE OF EVERY BACKGROUND.
AND ALL YOU NEED IS...
...A STICK AND A BALL.
THAT'S THE MOST UNBELIEVABLE STORY I'VE EVER HEARD!
HOW DO YOU KNOW SO MUCH ABOUT BASEBALL?
ARE YOU KIDDING? I PLAYED THE GAME SINCE I WAS A CUB. HAD TALENT, TOO. THEY SAID I'D MAKE MILLIONS. I WAS GOING TO BE THE BEST THERE EVER WAS.
YAWN
SO, WHAT HAPPENED TO YOU?
YOU KNOW, LIFE. STUFF.
YOU COULD SAY I GOT A LITTLE SIDETRACKED.

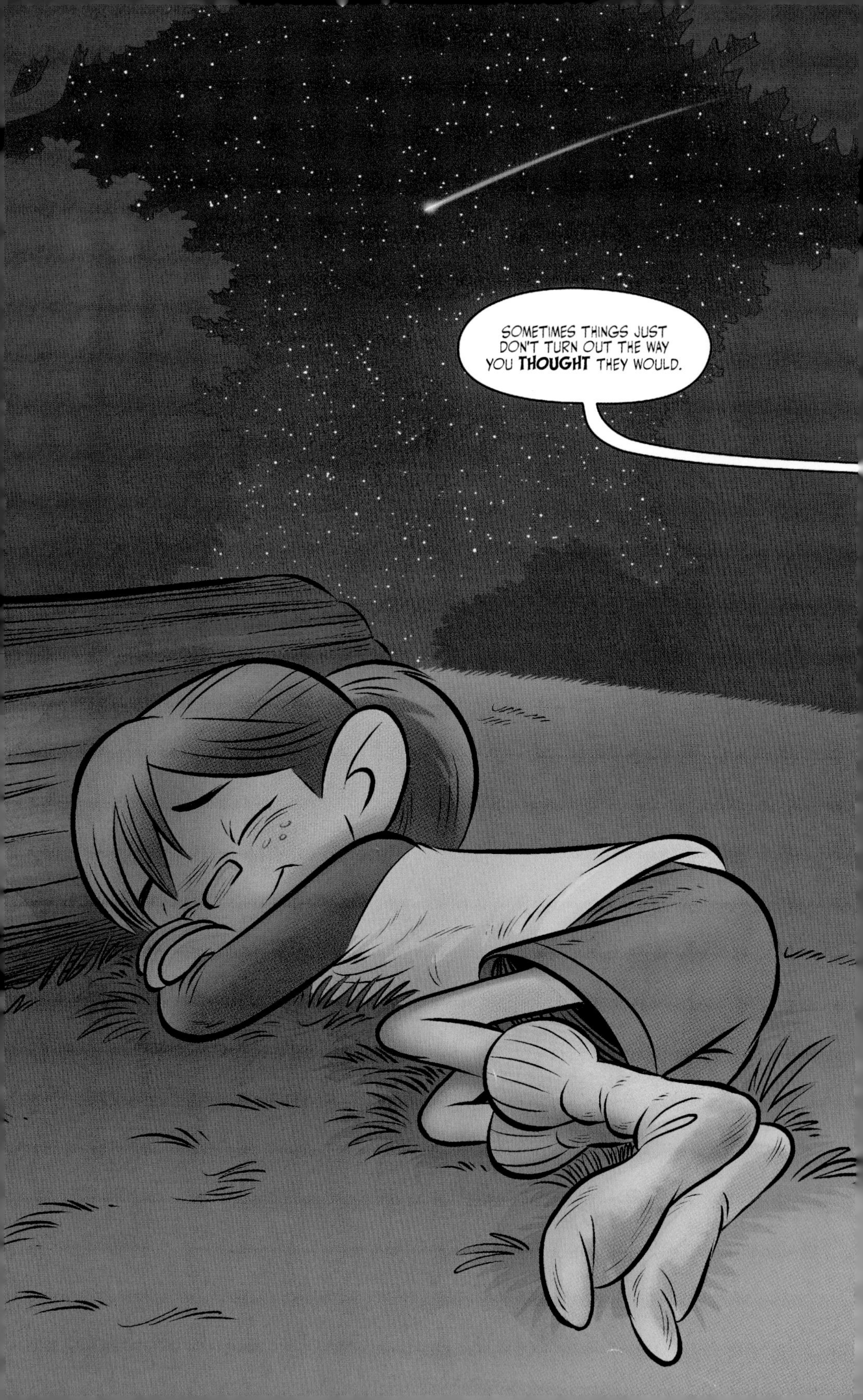
SOMETIMES THINGS JUST DON'T TURN OUT THE WAY YOU **THOUGHT** THEY WOULD.

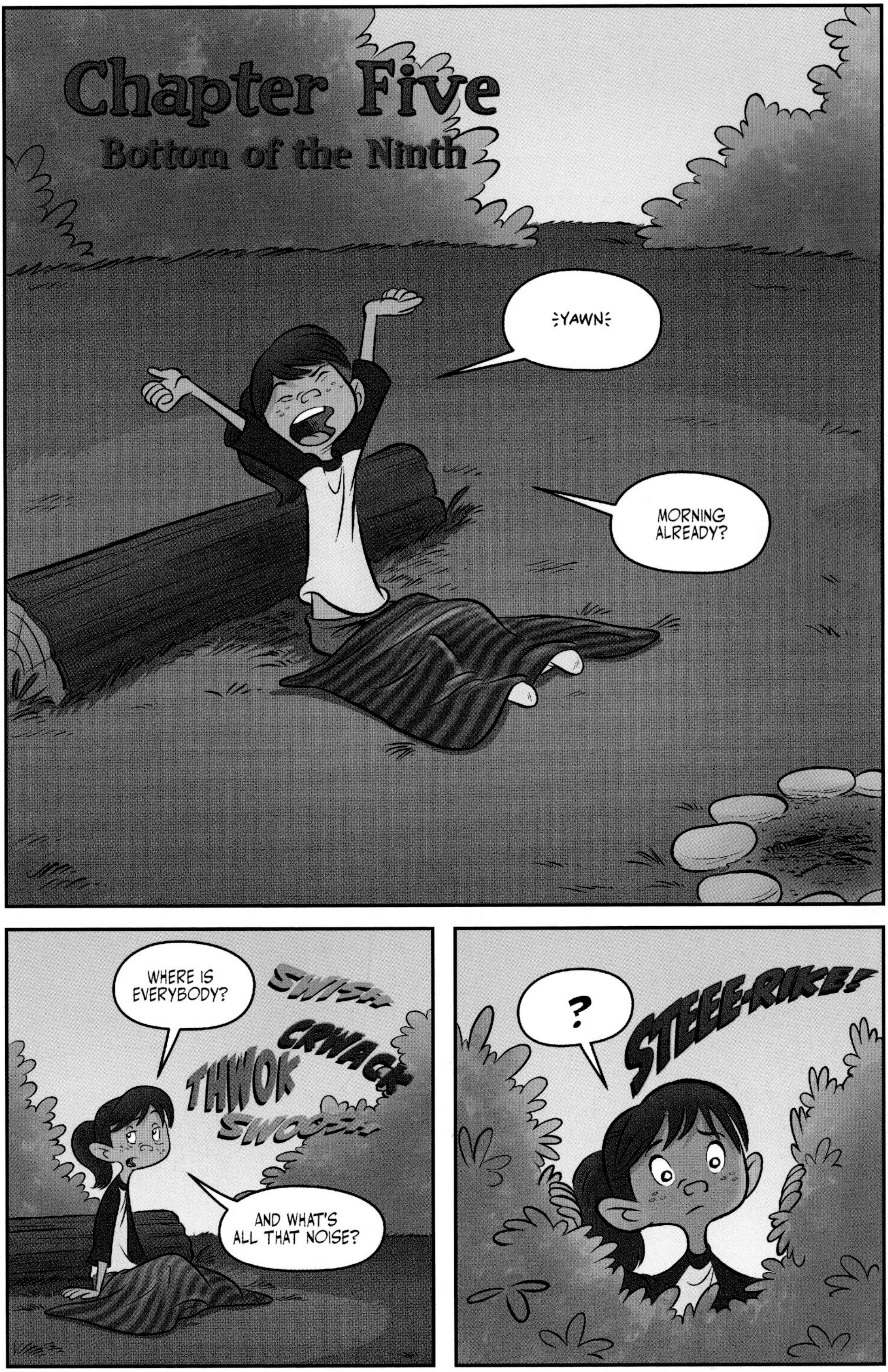
Chapter Five
Bottom of the Ninth
YAWN
MORNING ALREADY?
WHERE IS EVERYBODY?
SWISH
CRWACK
THWOK
SWOOSH
AND WHAT'S ALL THAT NOISE?
?
STEEE-RIKE!

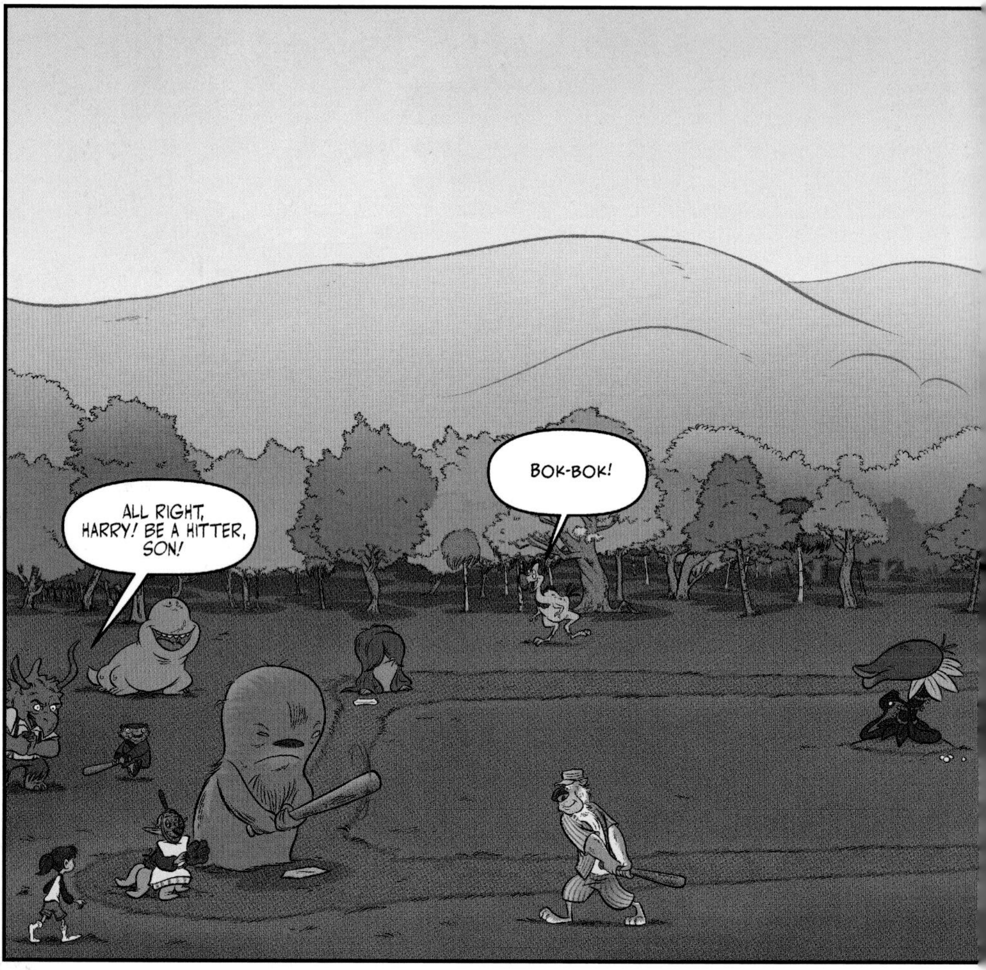
ALL RIGHT, HARRY! BE A HITTER, SON!
BOK-BOK!

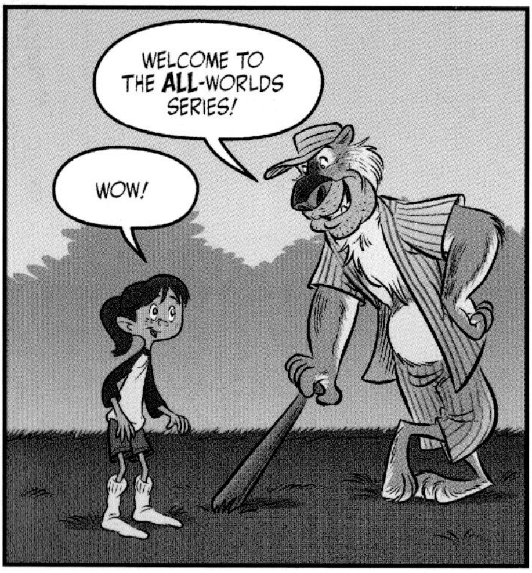
WELCOME TO THE **ALL**-WORLDS SERIES!
WOW!

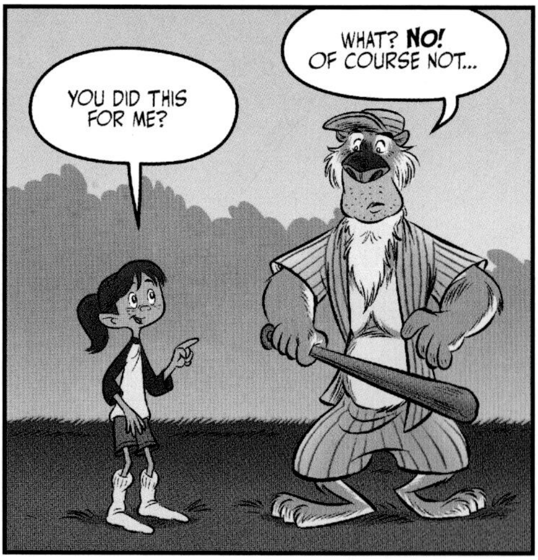
YOU DID THIS FOR ME?
WHAT? **NO!** OF COURSE NOT...

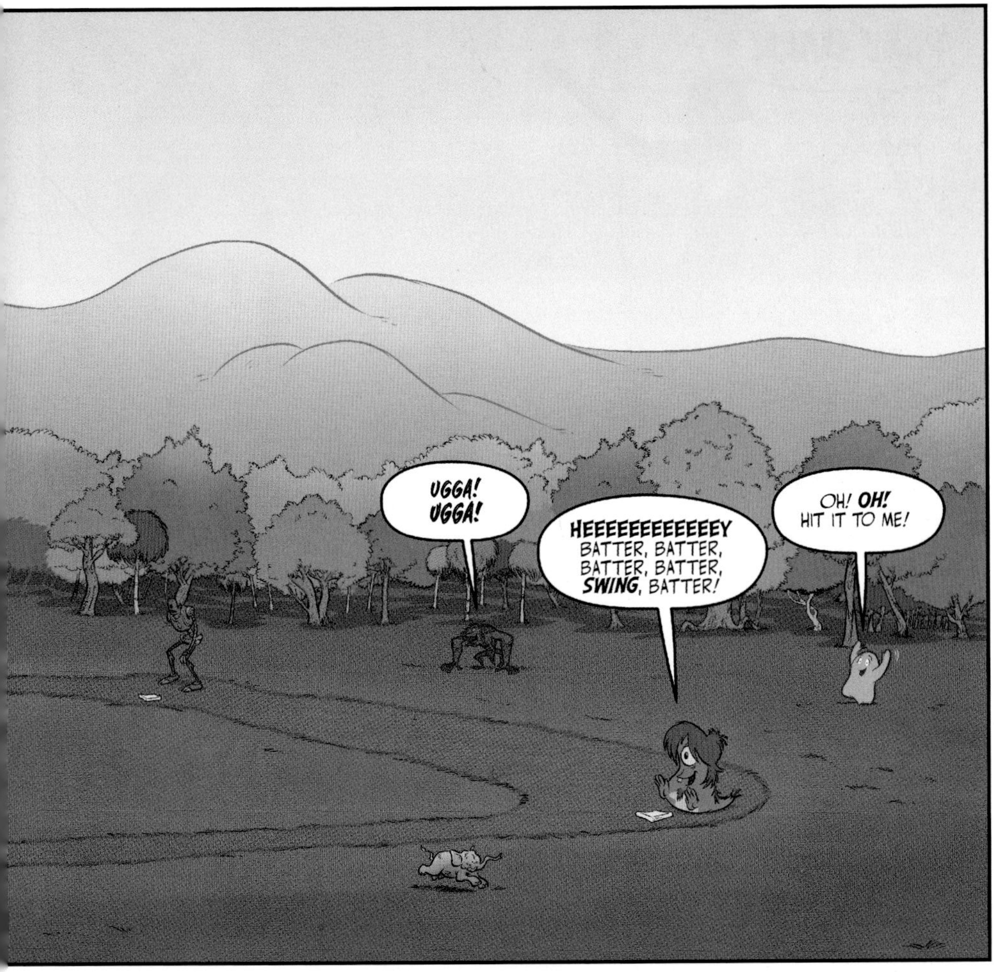
UGGA!
UGGA!
HEEEEEEEEEEEEY
BATTER, BATTER,
BATTER, BATTER,
SWING, BATTER!
OH! OH!
HIT IT TO ME!

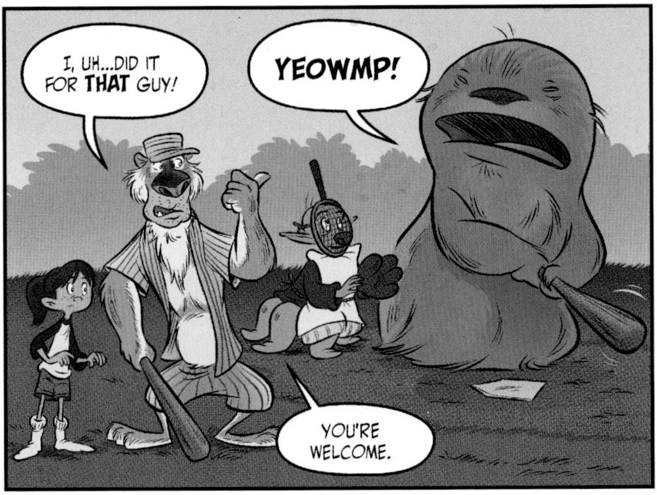
I, UH...DID IT
FOR THAT GUY!
YEOWMP!
YOU'RE
WELCOME.

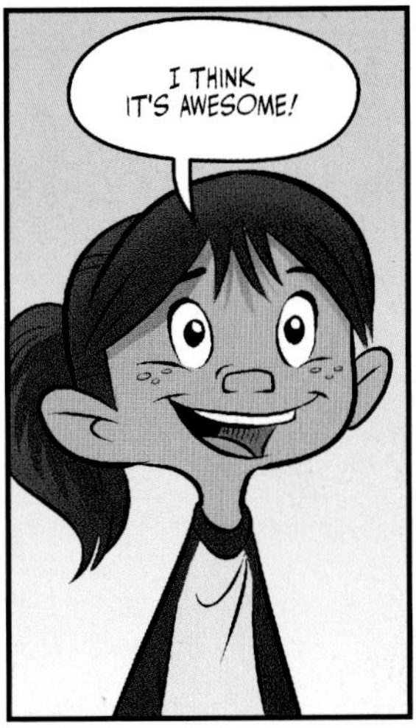
I THINK
IT'S AWESOME!

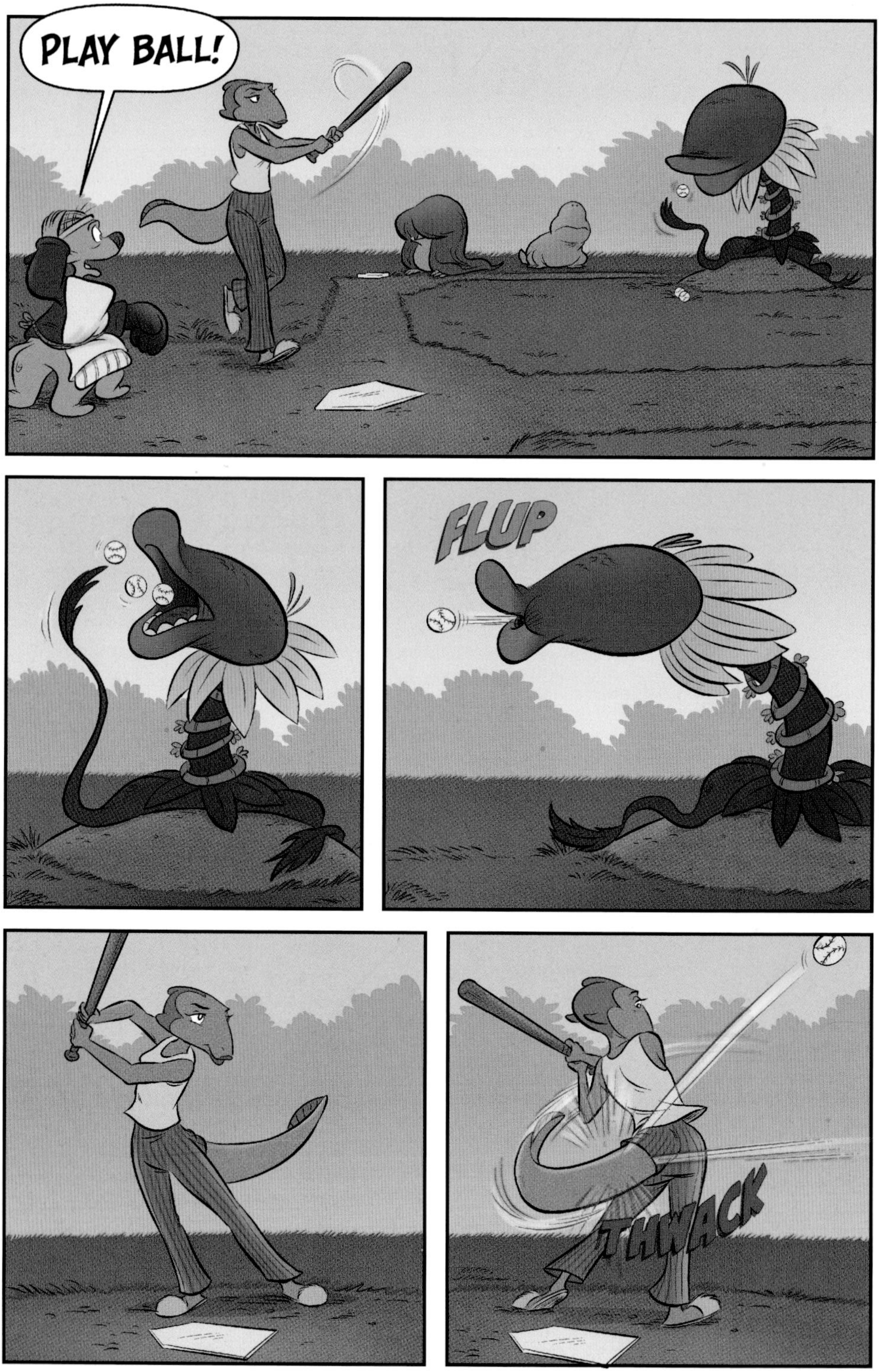
PLAY BALL!
FLUP
THWACK

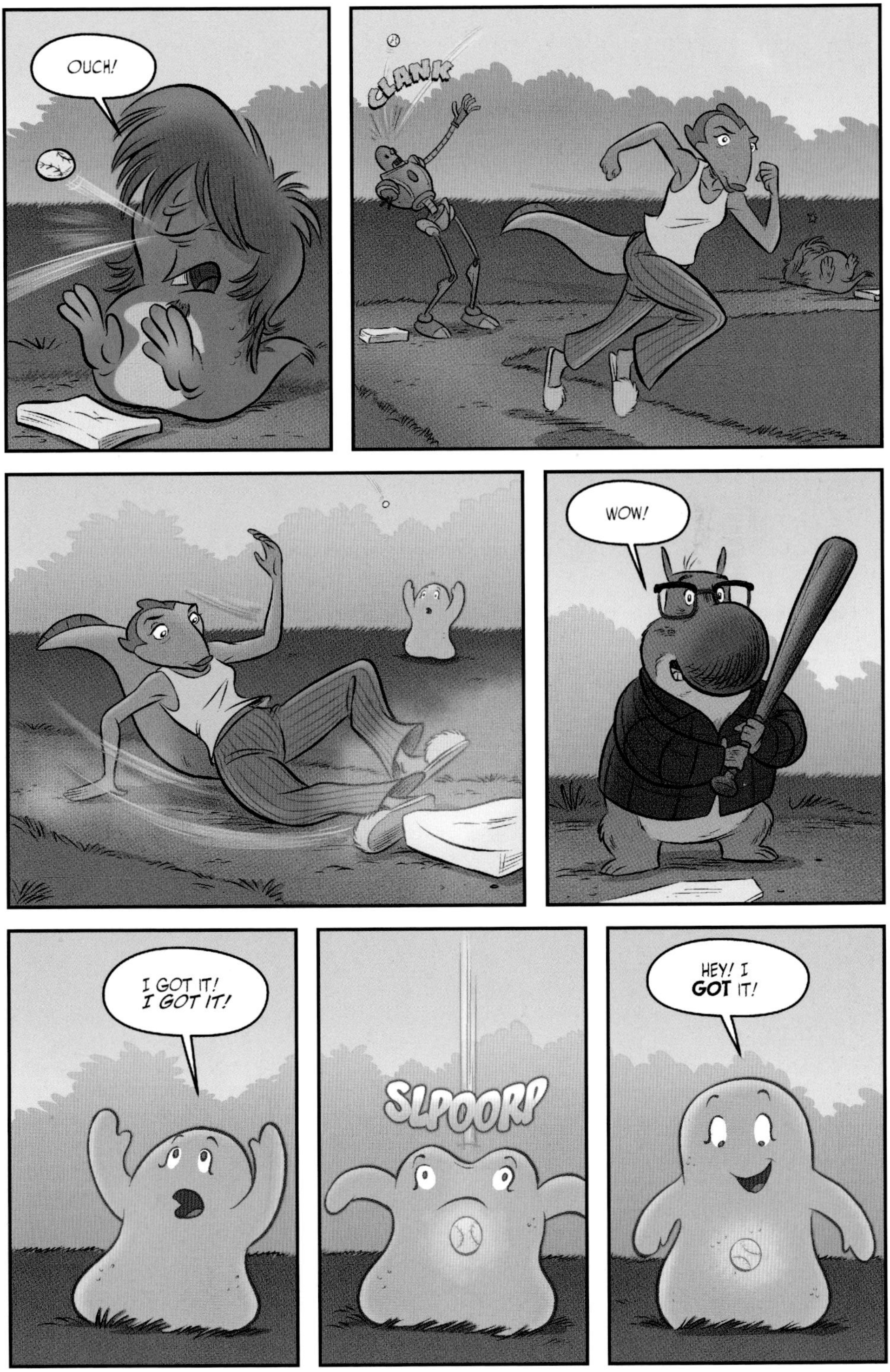
OUCH!
CLANK
WOW!
I GOT IT!
I GOT IT!
SLPOORP
HEY! I
GOT IT!

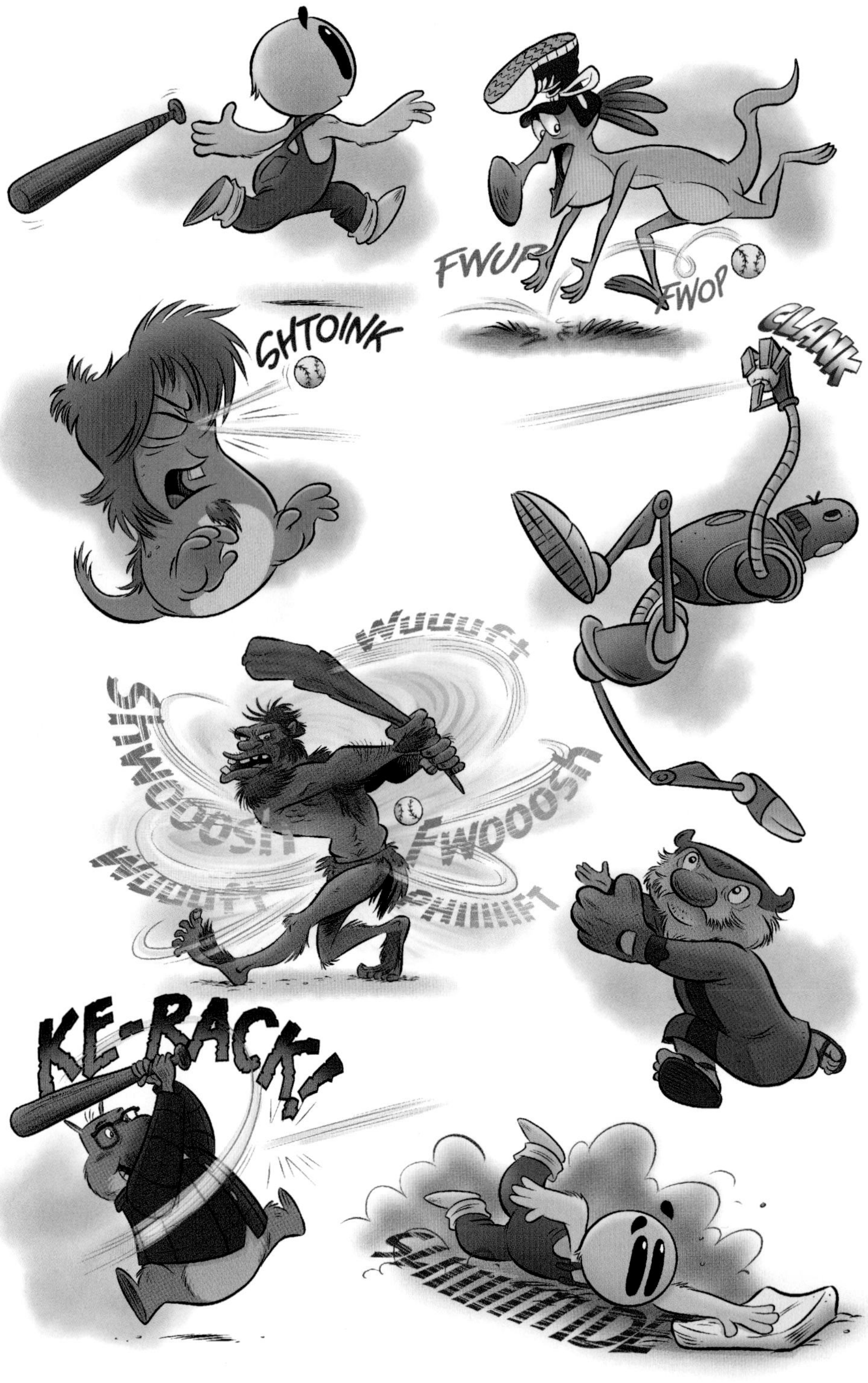
FWUF
FWOP
SHTOINK
CLANK
Wuuuft
Fwooosh
KE-RACK!

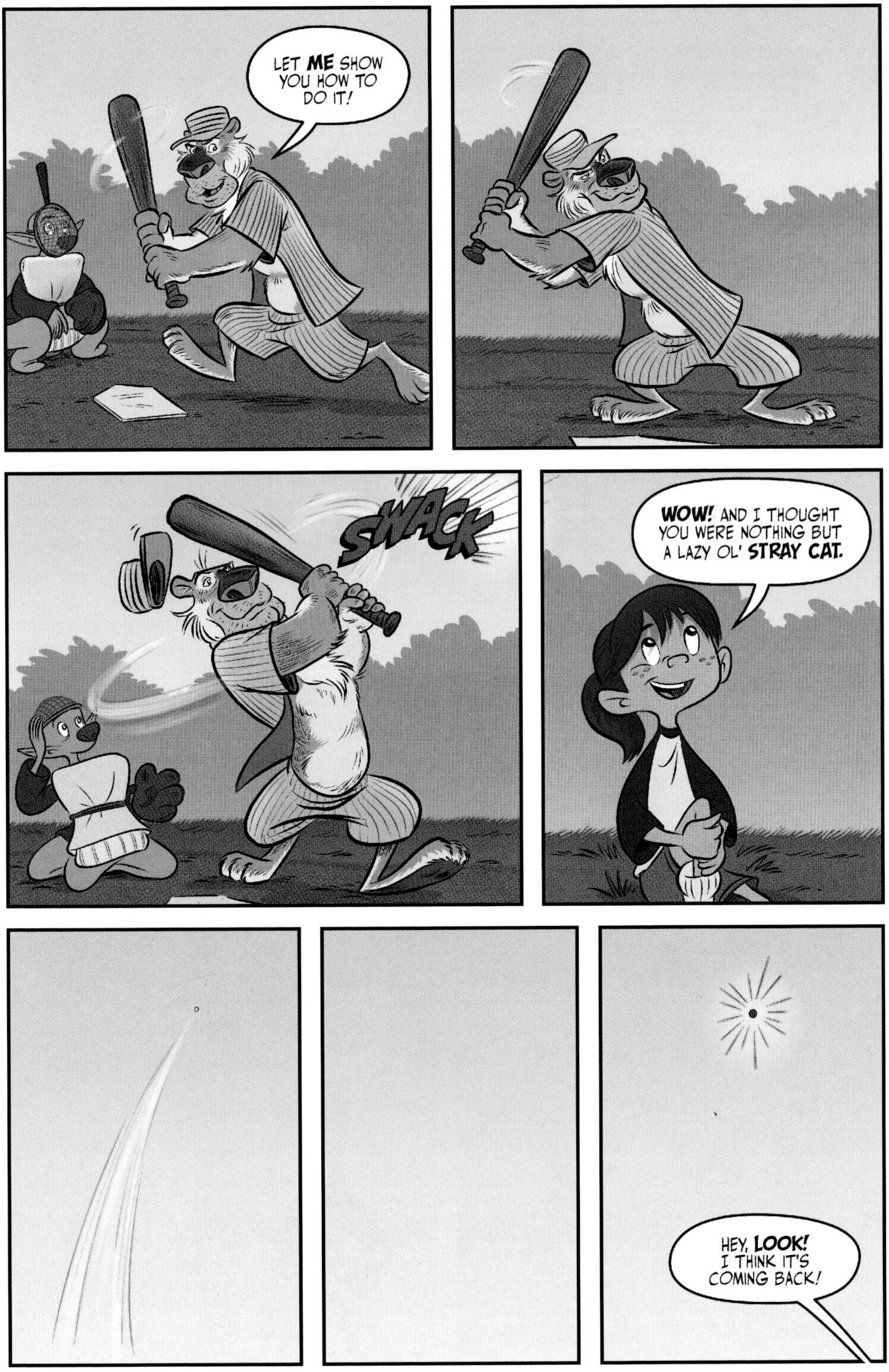
LET ME SHOW YOU HOW TO DO IT!
SWACK
WOW! AND I THOUGHT YOU WERE NOTHING BUT A LAZY OL' STRAY CAT.
HEY, LOOK! I THINK IT'S COMING BACK!

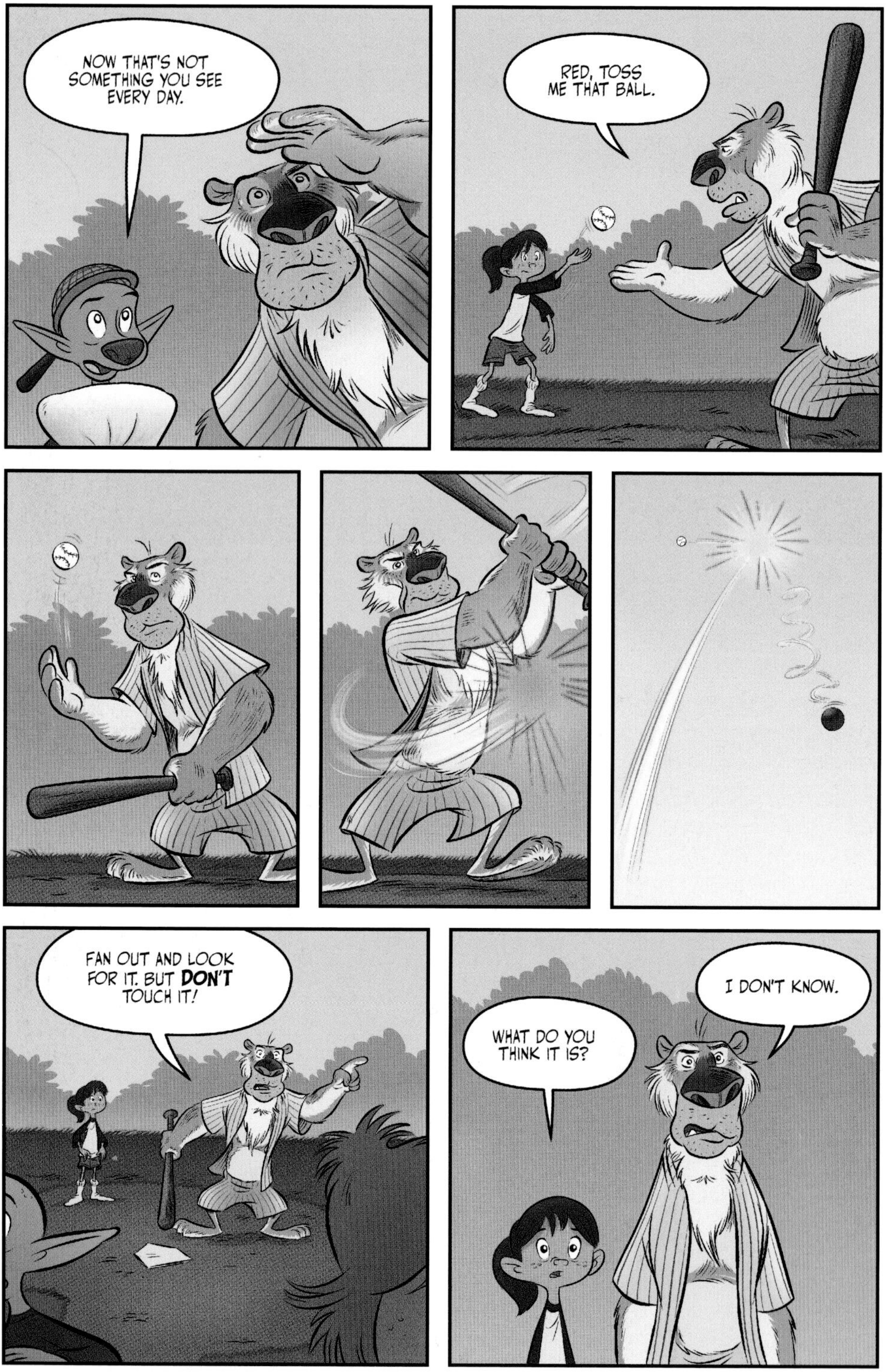
NOW THAT'S NOT SOMETHING YOU SEE EVERY DAY.
RED, TOSS ME THAT BALL.
FAN OUT AND LOOK FOR IT. BUT **DON'T** TOUCH IT!
WHAT DO YOU THINK IT IS?
I DON'T KNOW.

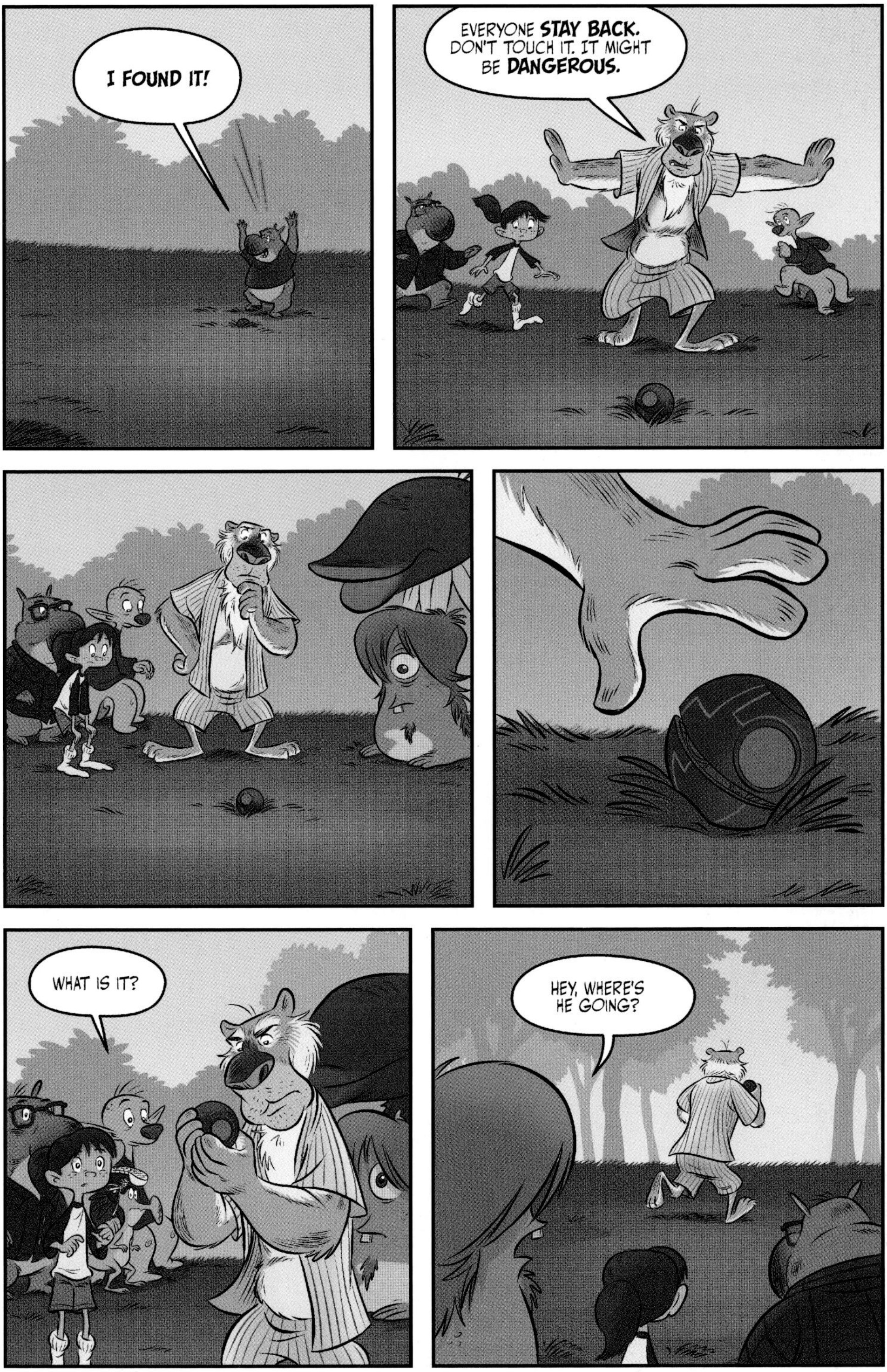
I FOUND IT!
EVERYONE STAY BACK. DON'T TOUCH IT. IT MIGHT BE DANGEROUS.
WHAT IS IT?
HEY, WHERE'S HE GOING?

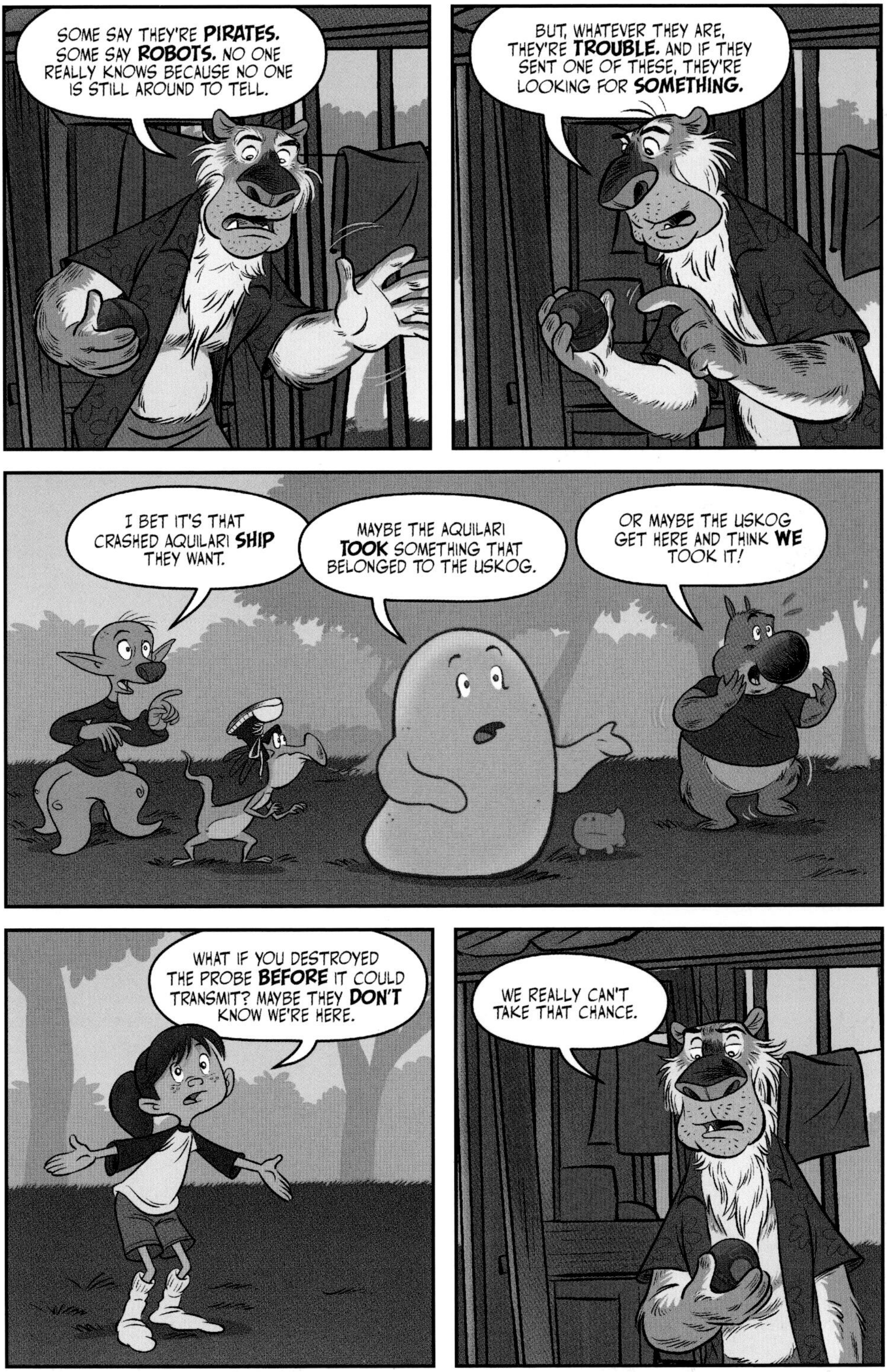
SOME SAY THEY'RE **PIRATES.** SOME SAY **ROBOTS.** NO ONE REALLY KNOWS BECAUSE NO ONE IS STILL AROUND TO TELL.
BUT, WHATEVER THEY ARE, THEY'RE **TROUBLE.** AND IF THEY SENT ONE OF THESE, THEY'RE LOOKING FOR **SOMETHING.**
I BET IT'S THAT CRASHED AQUILARI **SHIP** THEY WANT.
MAYBE THE AQUILARI **TOOK** SOMETHING THAT BELONGED TO THE USKOG.
OR MAYBE THE USKOG GET HERE AND THINK **WE** TOOK IT!
WHAT IF YOU DESTROYED THE PROBE **BEFORE** IT COULD TRANSMIT? MAYBE THEY **DON'T** KNOW WE'RE HERE.
WE REALLY CAN'T TAKE THAT CHANCE.

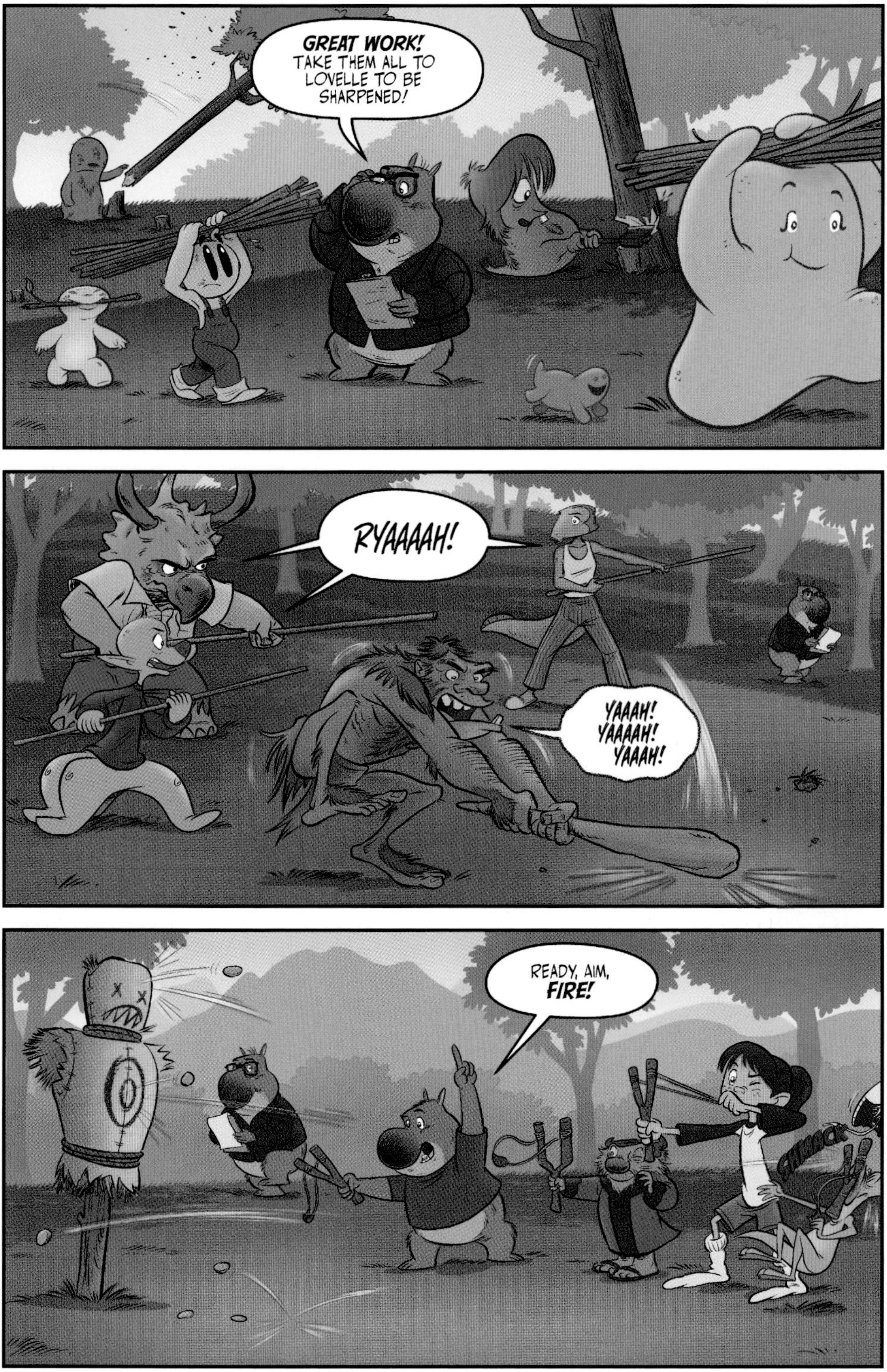
GREAT WORK! TAKE THEM ALL TO LOVELLE TO BE SHARPENED!
RYAAAAH!
YAAAH! YAAAAH! YAAAH!
READY, AIM, FIRE!

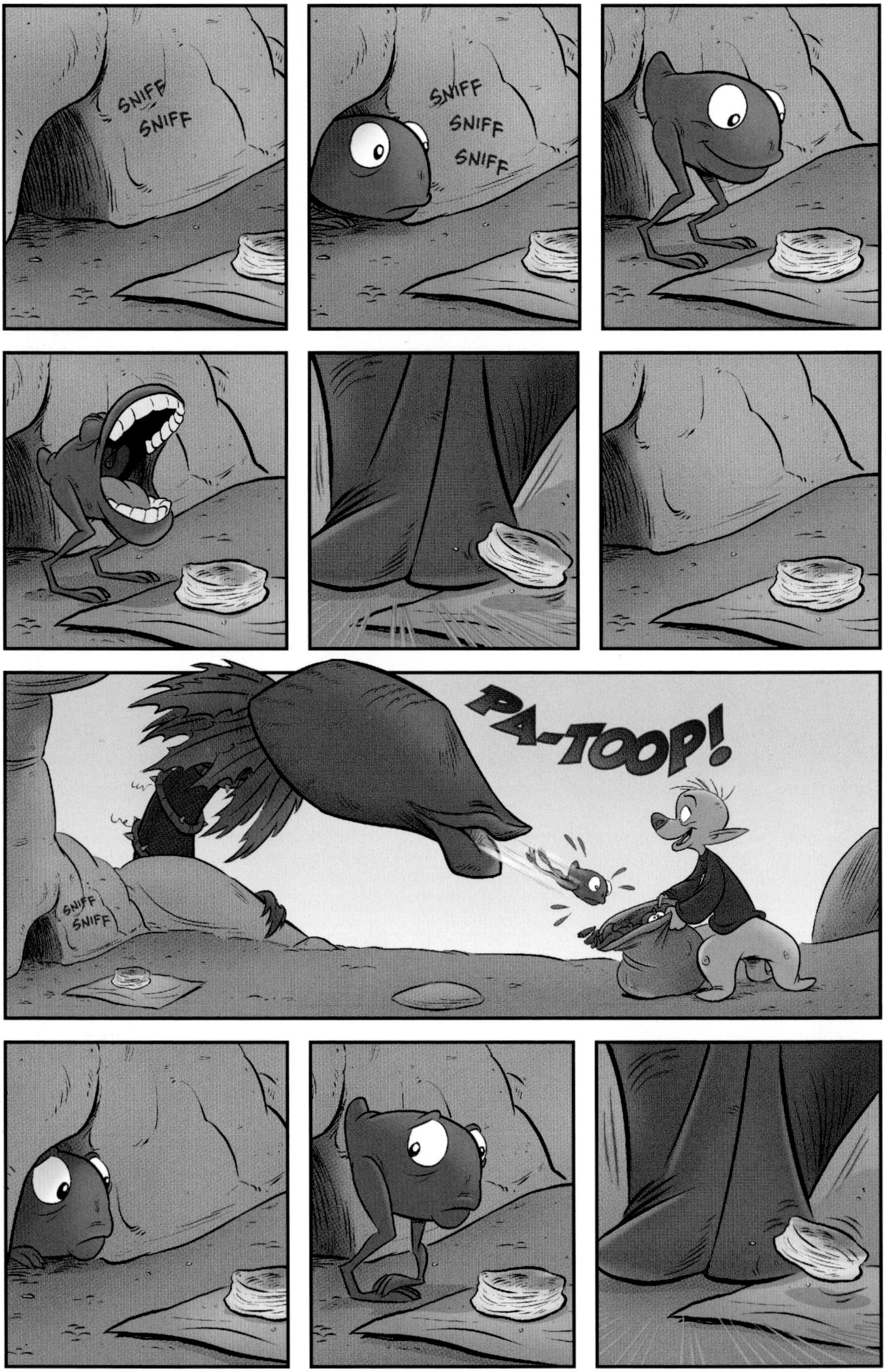
SNIFF
SNIFF
SNIFF
SNIFF
SNIFF
PA-TOOP!
SNIFF
SNIFF

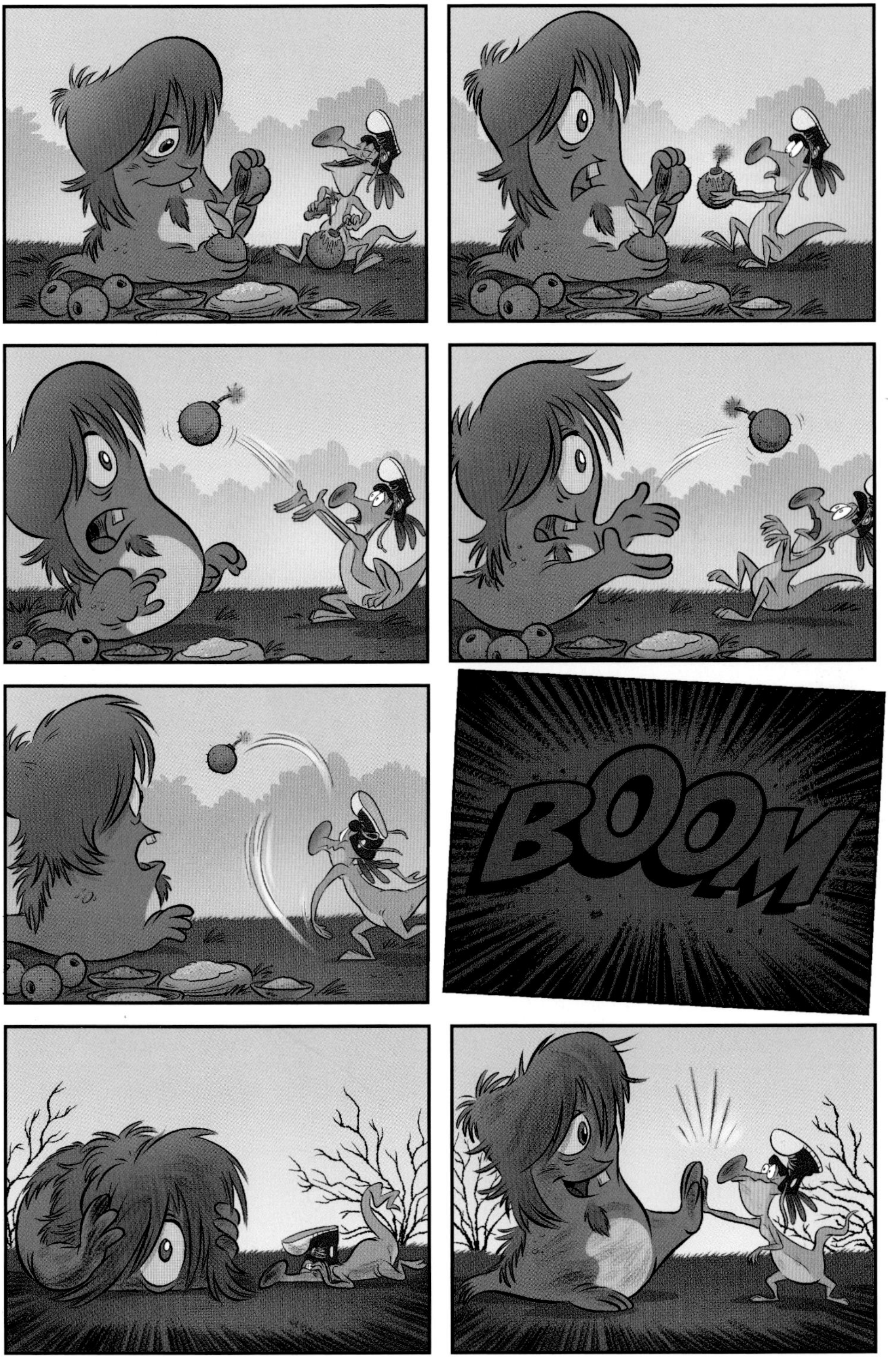
BOOM

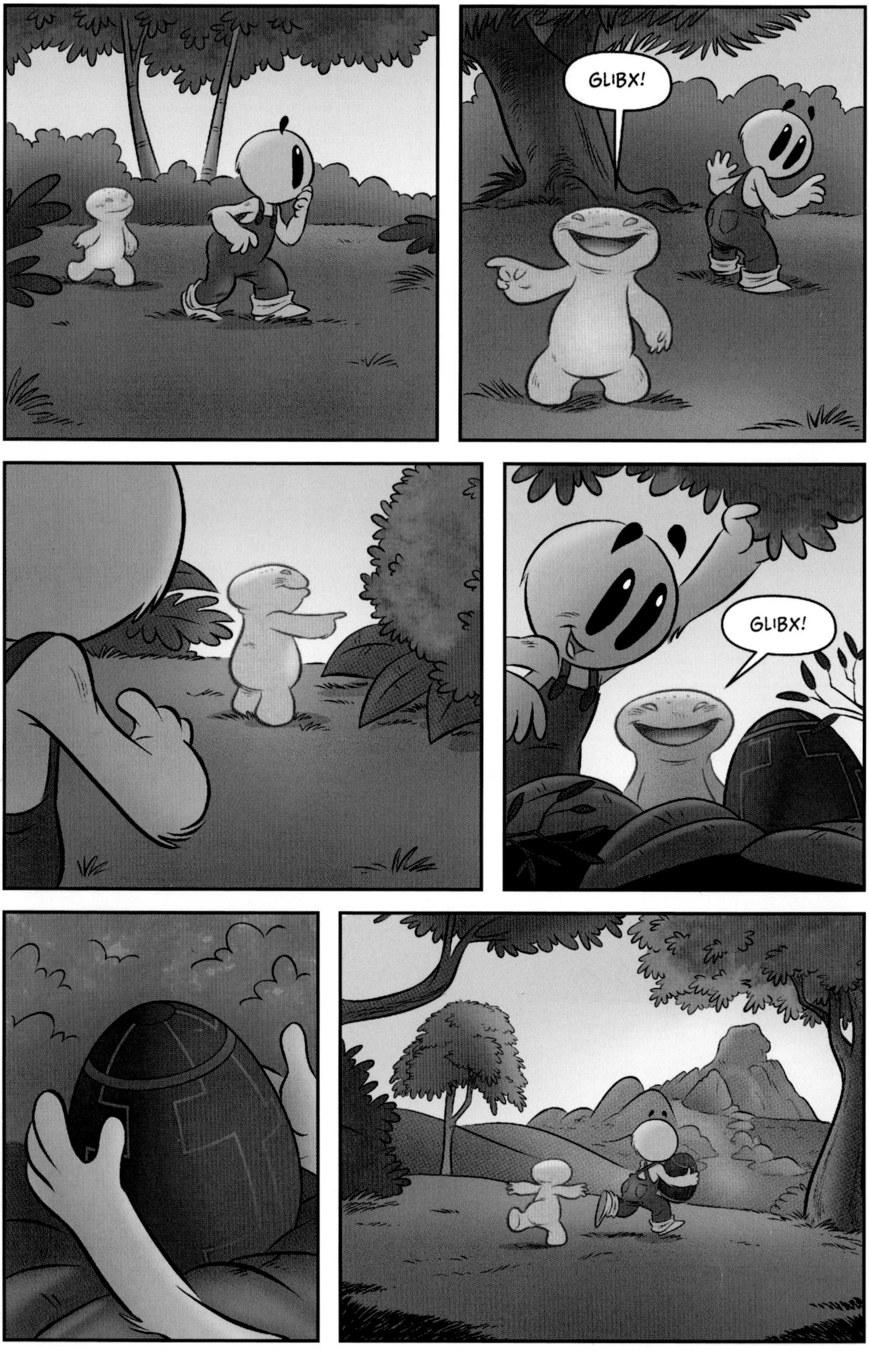
GLIBX!
GLIBX!

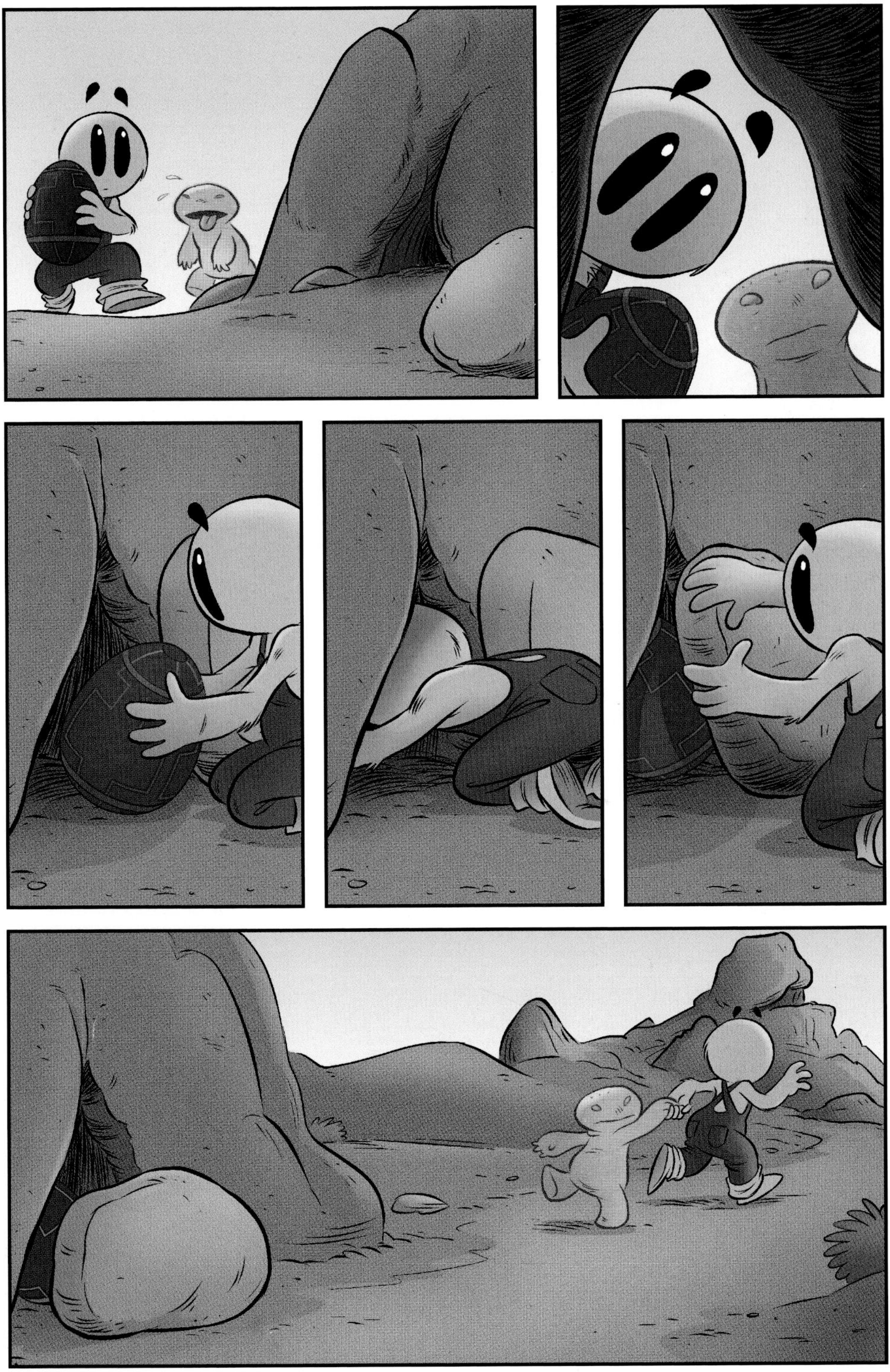

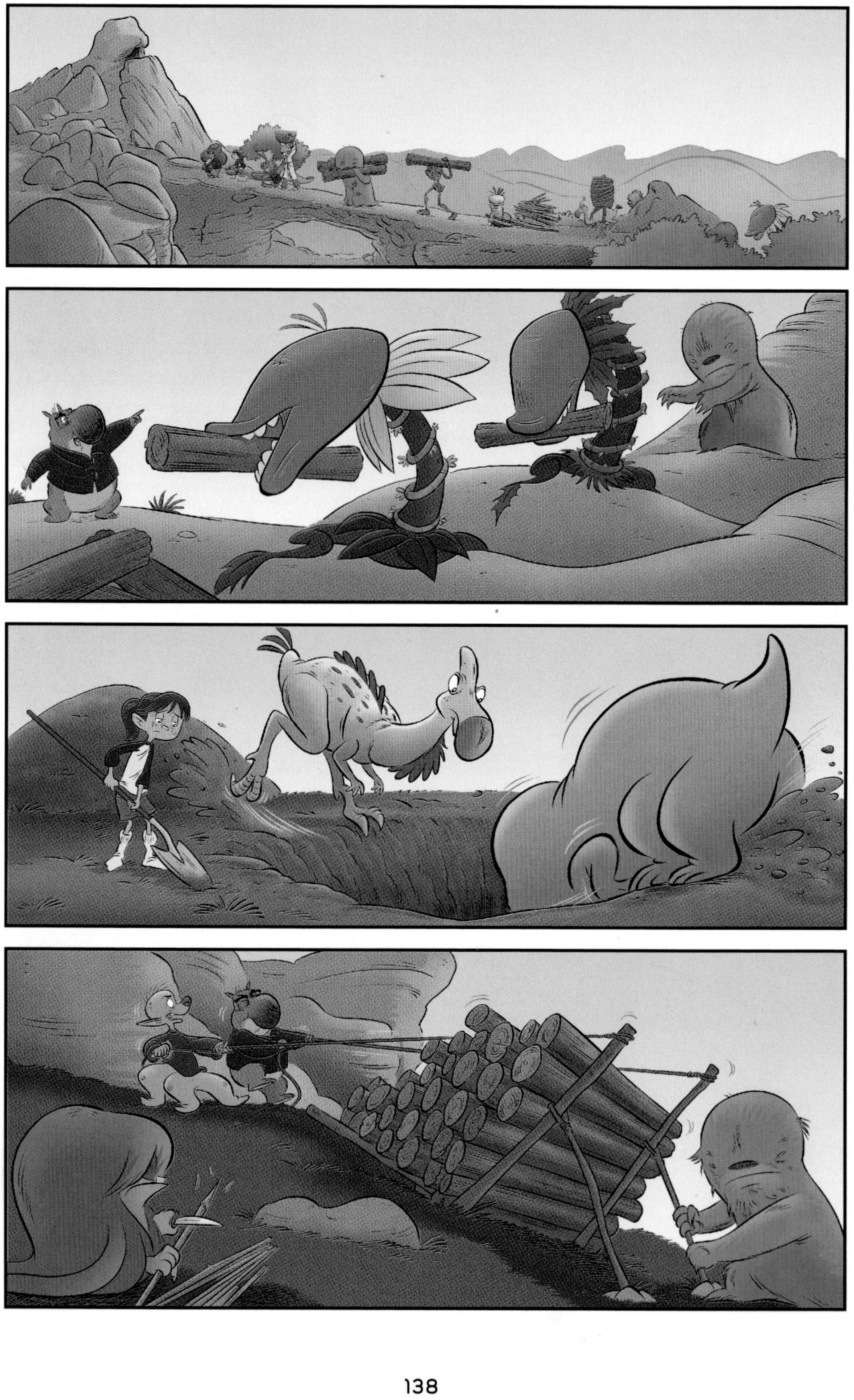

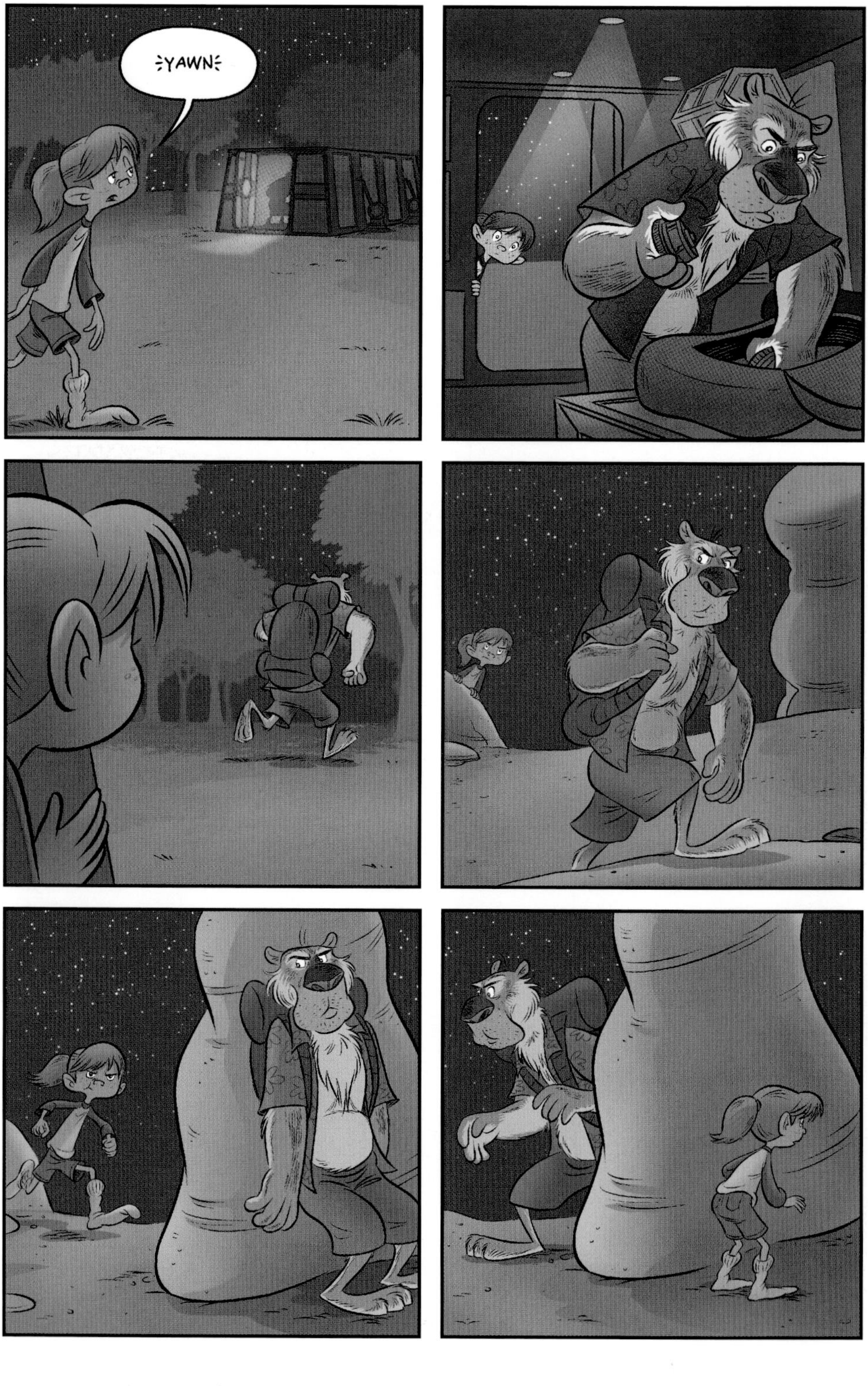
YAWN

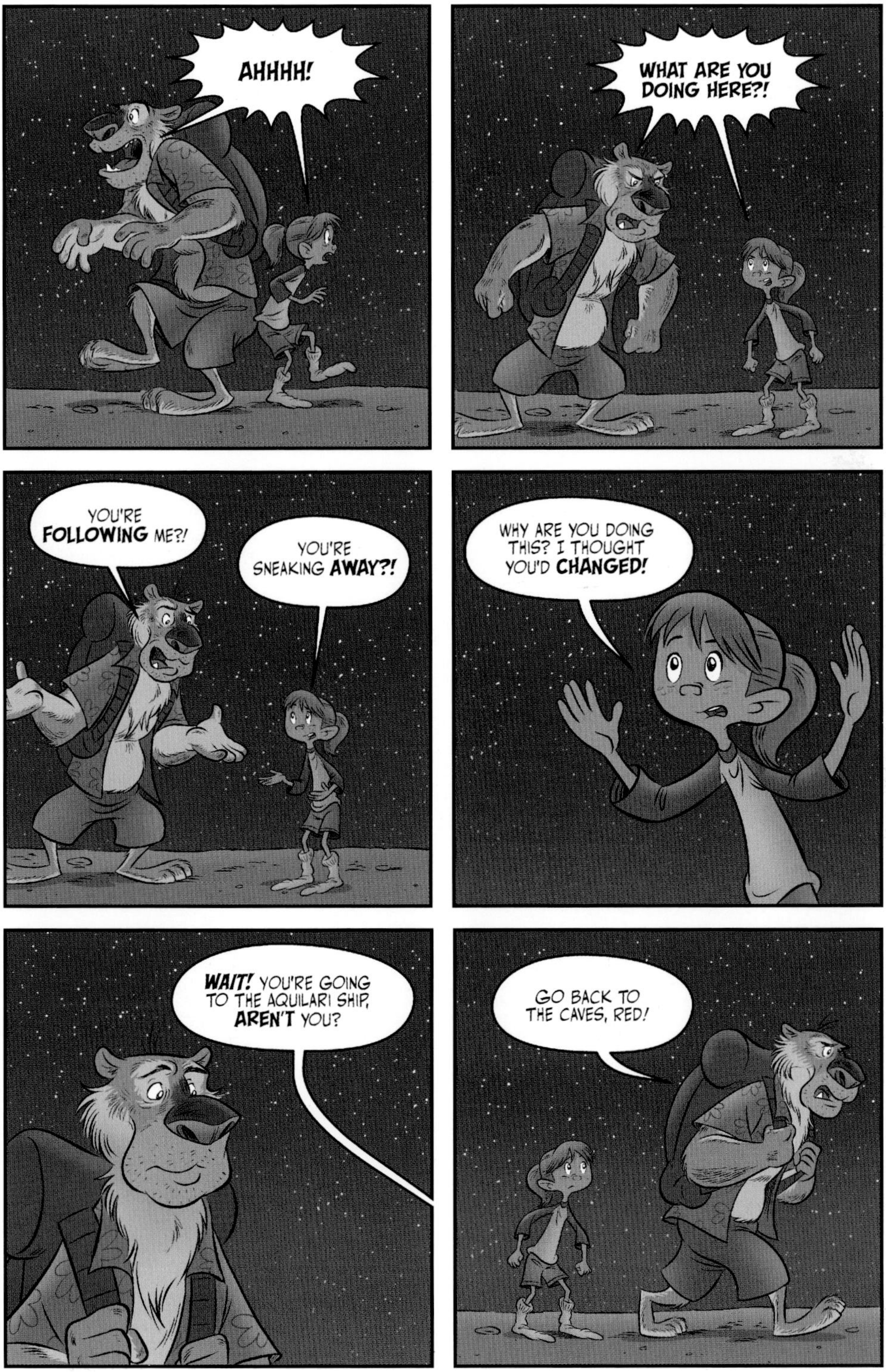
AHHHH!
WHAT ARE YOU DOING HERE?!
YOU'RE **FOLLOWING** ME?!
YOU'RE SNEAKING **AWAY?!**
WHY ARE YOU DOING THIS? I THOUGHT YOU'D **CHANGED!**
WAIT! YOU'RE GOING TO THE AQUILARI SHIP, **AREN'T** YOU?
GO BACK TO THE CAVES, RED!

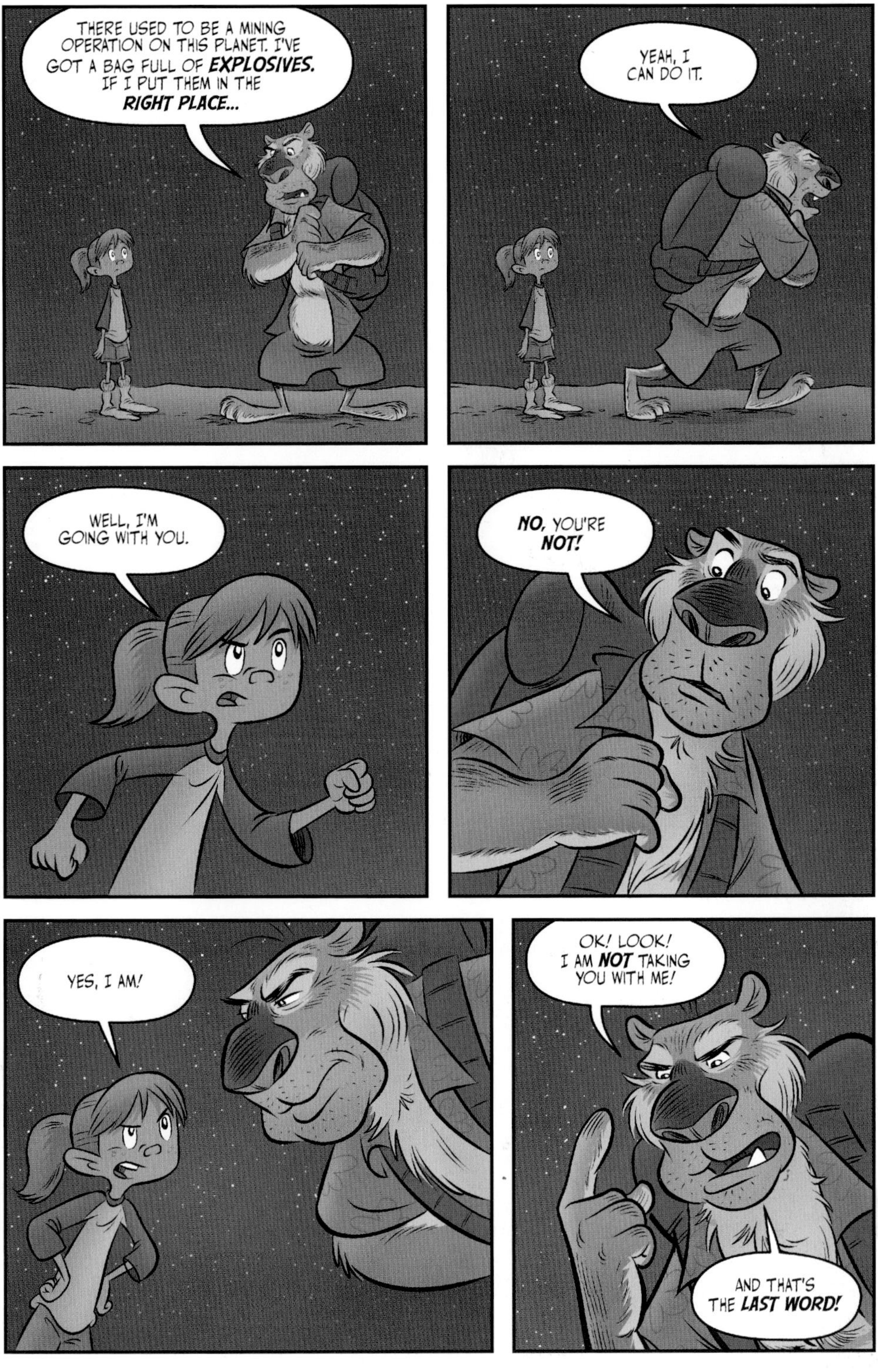

THERE USED TO BE A MINING OPERATION ON THIS PLANET. I'VE GOT A BAG FULL OF **EXPLOSIVES.** IF I PUT THEM IN THE **RIGHT PLACE...**
YEAH, I CAN DO IT.
WELL, I'M GOING WITH YOU.
NO, YOU'RE **NOT!**
YES, I AM!
OK! LOOK! I AM **NOT** TAKING YOU WITH ME!
AND THAT'S THE **LAST WORD!**

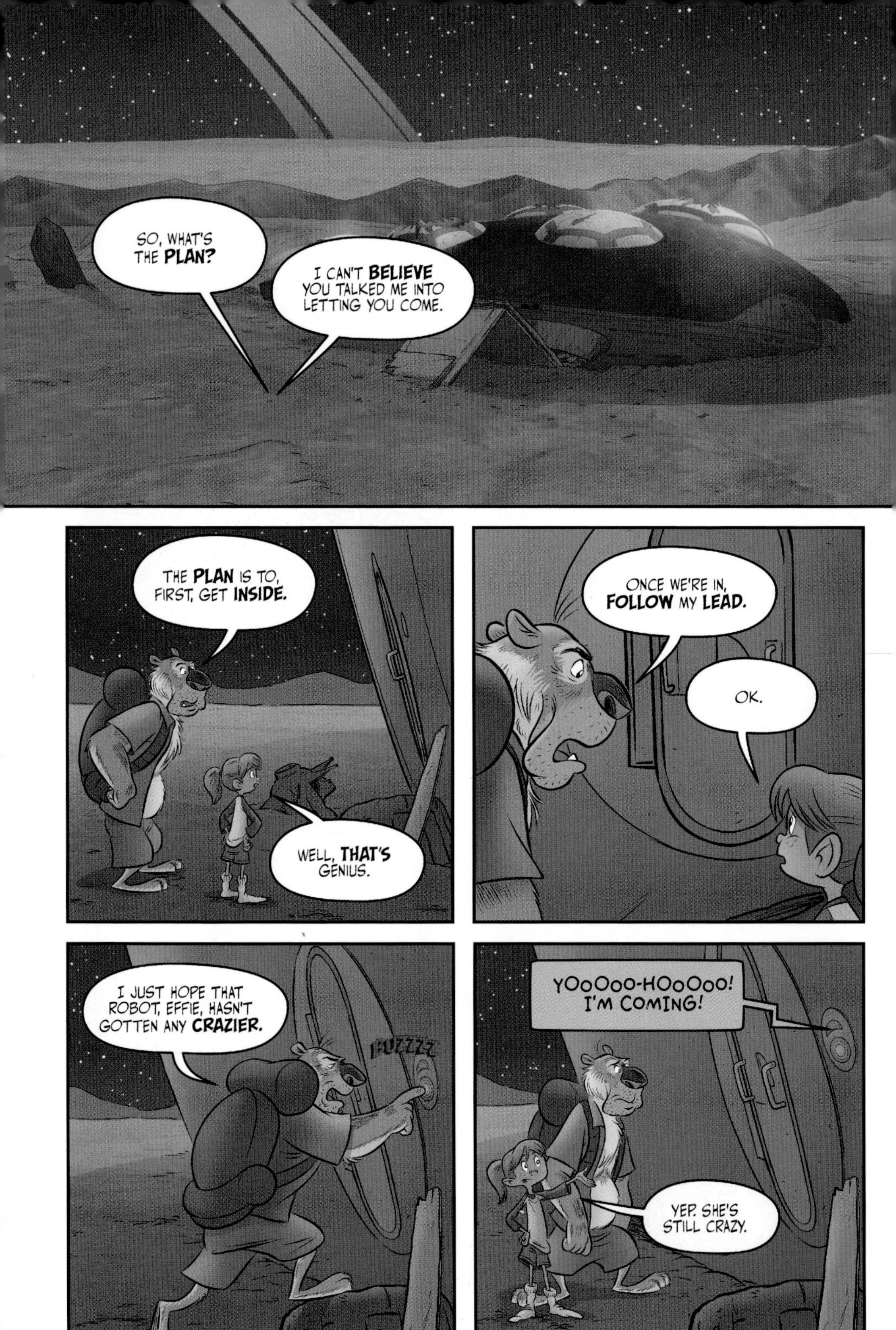
SO, WHAT'S THE PLAN?
I CAN'T BELIEVE YOU TALKED ME INTO LETTING YOU COME.
THE PLAN IS TO, FIRST, GET INSIDE.
WELL, THAT'S GENIUS.
ONCE WE'RE IN, FOLLOW MY LEAD.
OK.
I JUST HOPE THAT ROBOT, EFFIE, HASN'T GOTTEN ANY CRAZIER.
BUZZZZ
YOoOoO-HOoOoO! I'M COMING!
YEP. SHE'S STILL CRAZY.

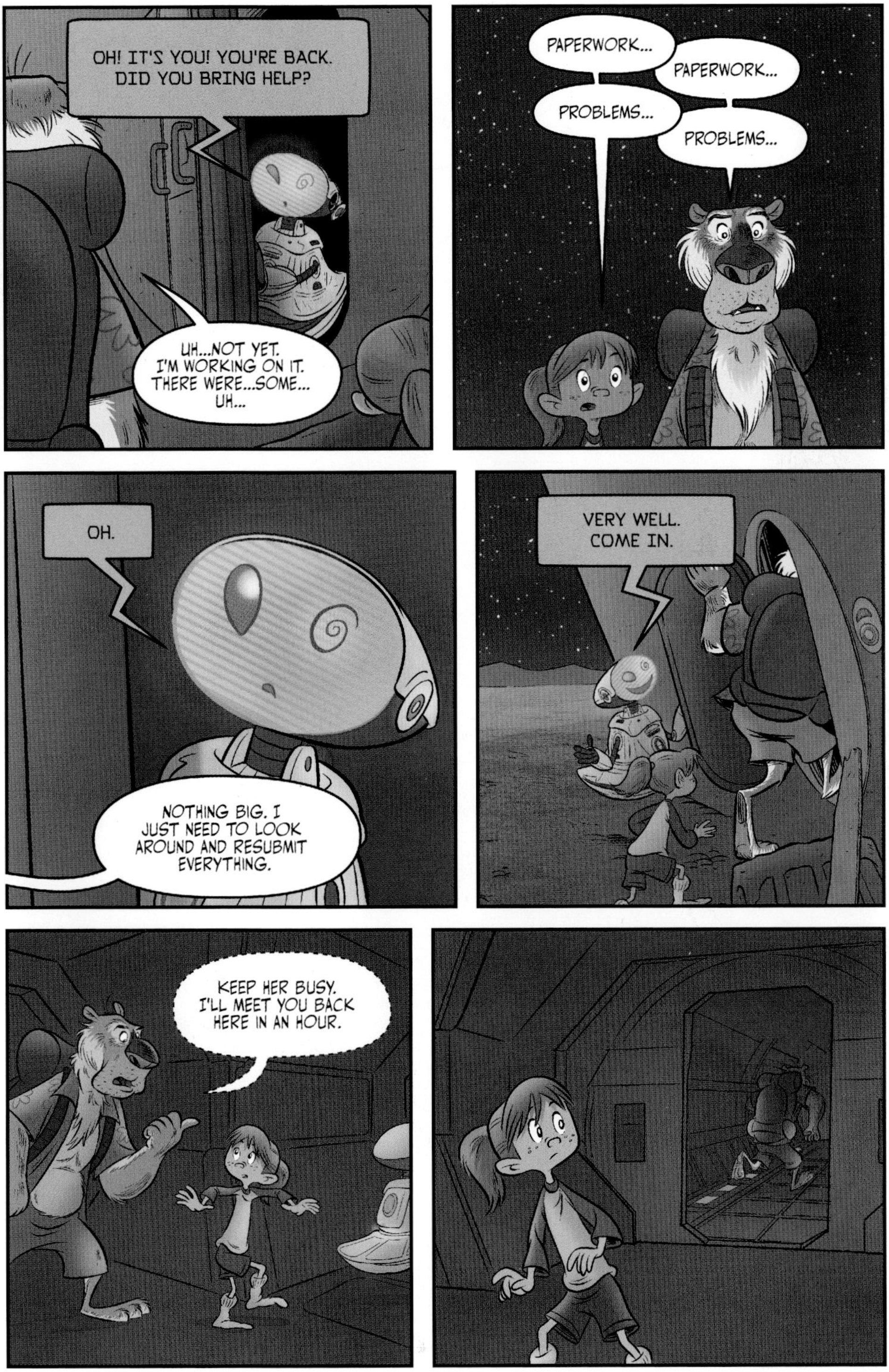
OH! IT'S YOU! YOU'RE BACK. DID YOU BRING HELP?
UH...NOT YET. I'M WORKING ON IT. THERE WERE...SOME... UH...
PAPERWORK...
PAPERWORK...
PROBLEMS...
PROBLEMS...
OH.
NOTHING BIG. I JUST NEED TO LOOK AROUND AND RESUBMIT EVERYTHING.
VERY WELL. COME IN.
KEEP HER BUSY. I'LL MEET YOU BACK HERE IN AN HOUR.

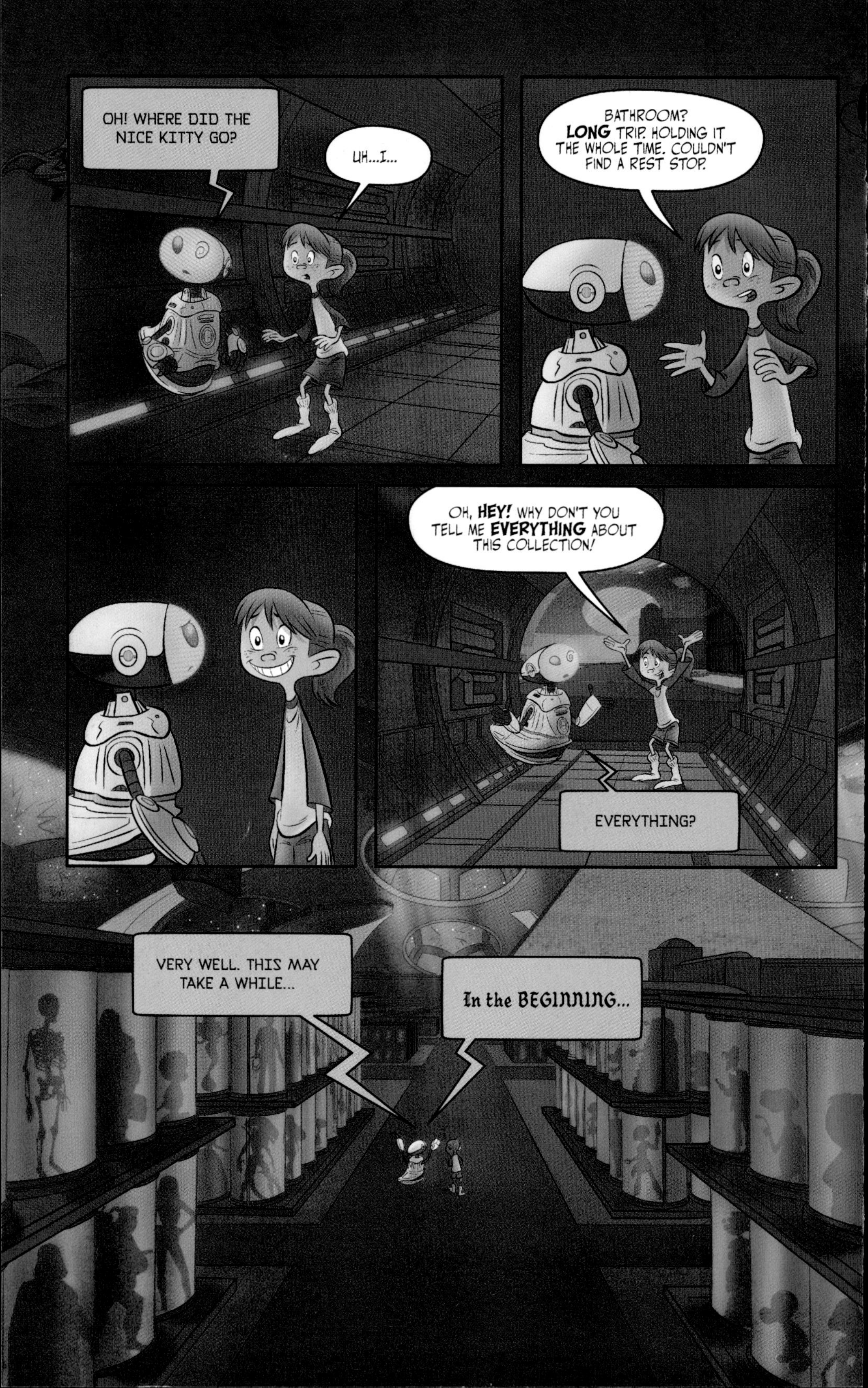
OH! WHERE DID THE NICE KITTY GO?
UH...I...
BATHROOM? **LONG** TRIP. HOLDING IT THE WHOLE TIME. COULDN'T FIND A REST STOP.
OH, **HEY!** WHY DON'T YOU TELL ME **EVERYTHING** ABOUT THIS COLLECTION!
EVERYTHING?
VERY WELL. THIS MAY TAKE A WHILE...
In the BEGINNING...

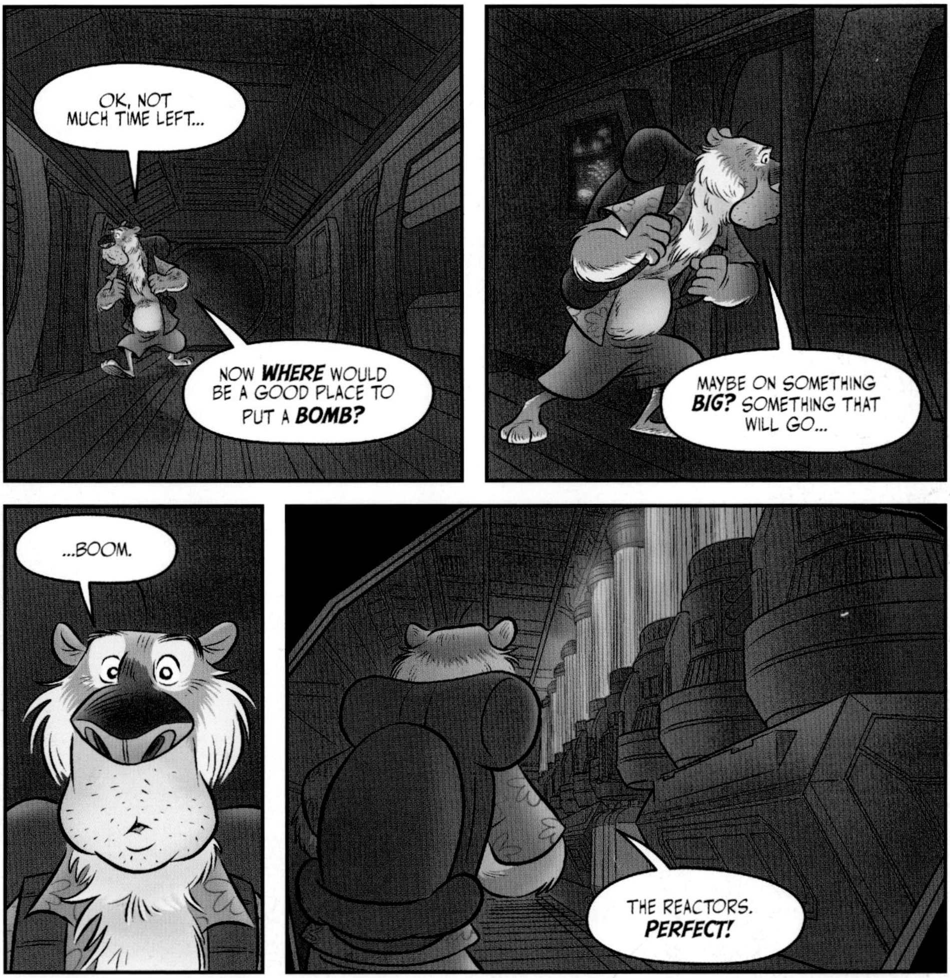
OK, NOT MUCH TIME LEFT...
NOW **WHERE** WOULD BE A GOOD PLACE TO PUT A **BOMB?**
MAYBE ON SOMETHING **BIG?** SOMETHING THAT WILL GO...
...BOOM.
THE REACTORS. **PERFECT!**
IF THIS ALL WORKS...
IT WILL CAUSE A CHAIN REACTION.
ONE DOWN... NINE TO GO.

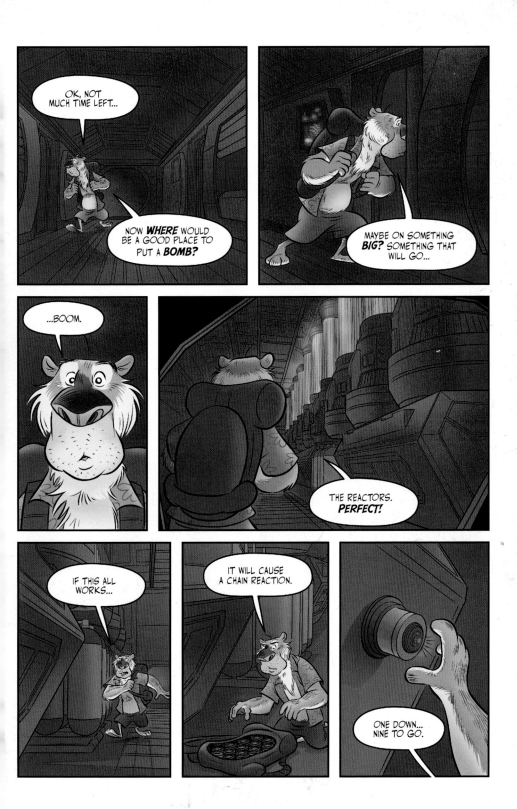

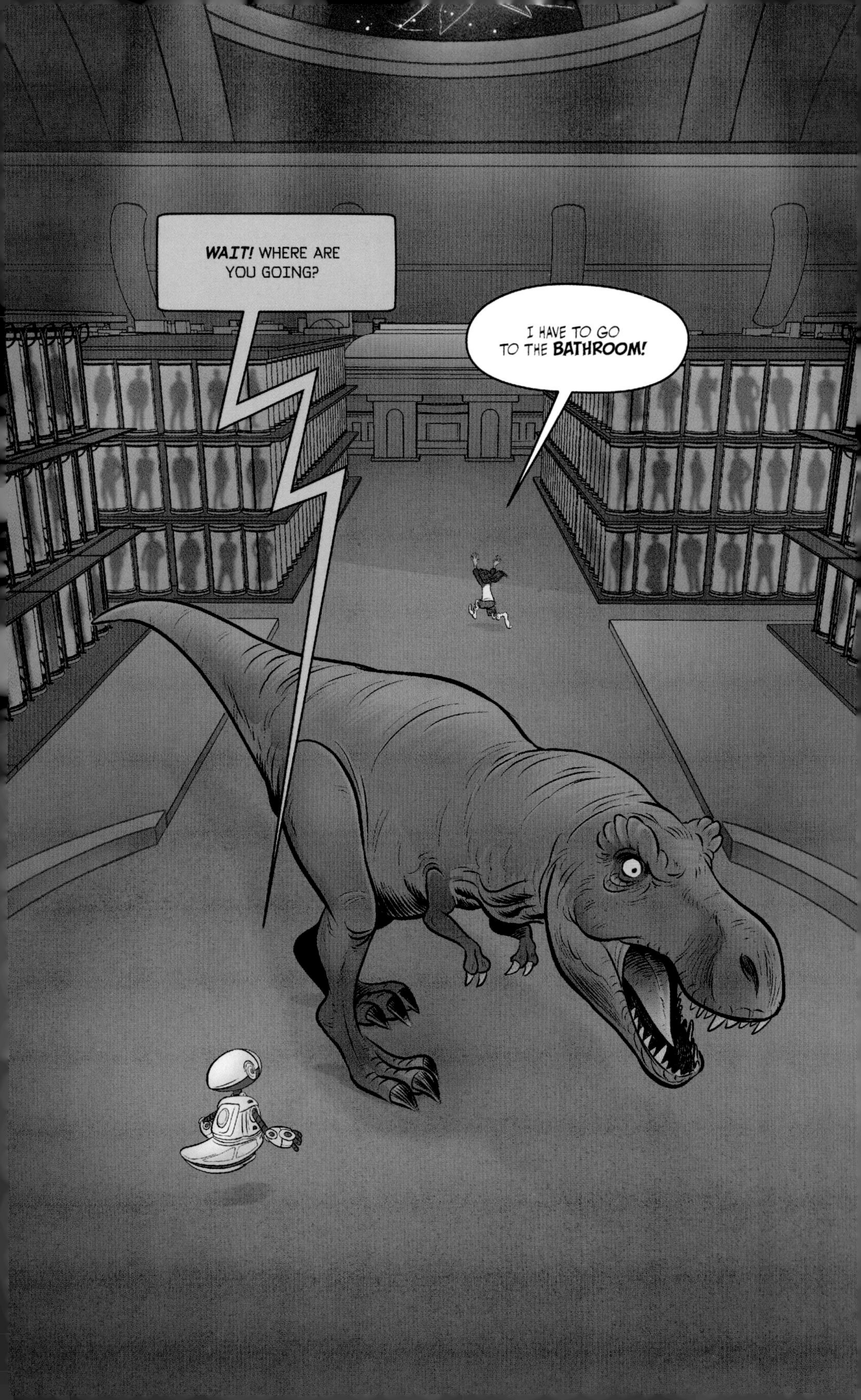
WAIT! WHERE ARE YOU GOING?
I HAVE TO GO TO THE BATHROOM!

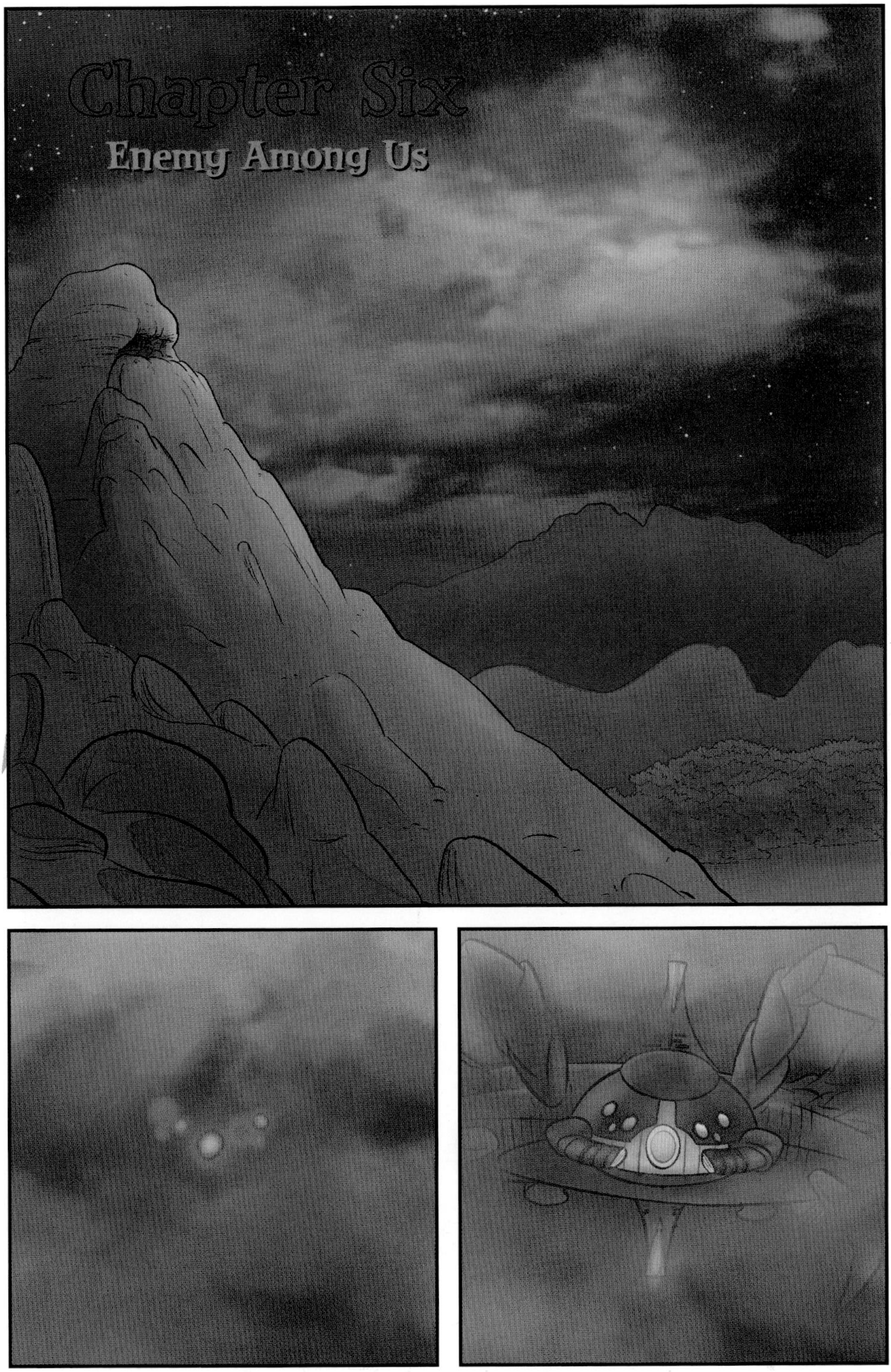
Chapter Six
Enemy Among Us

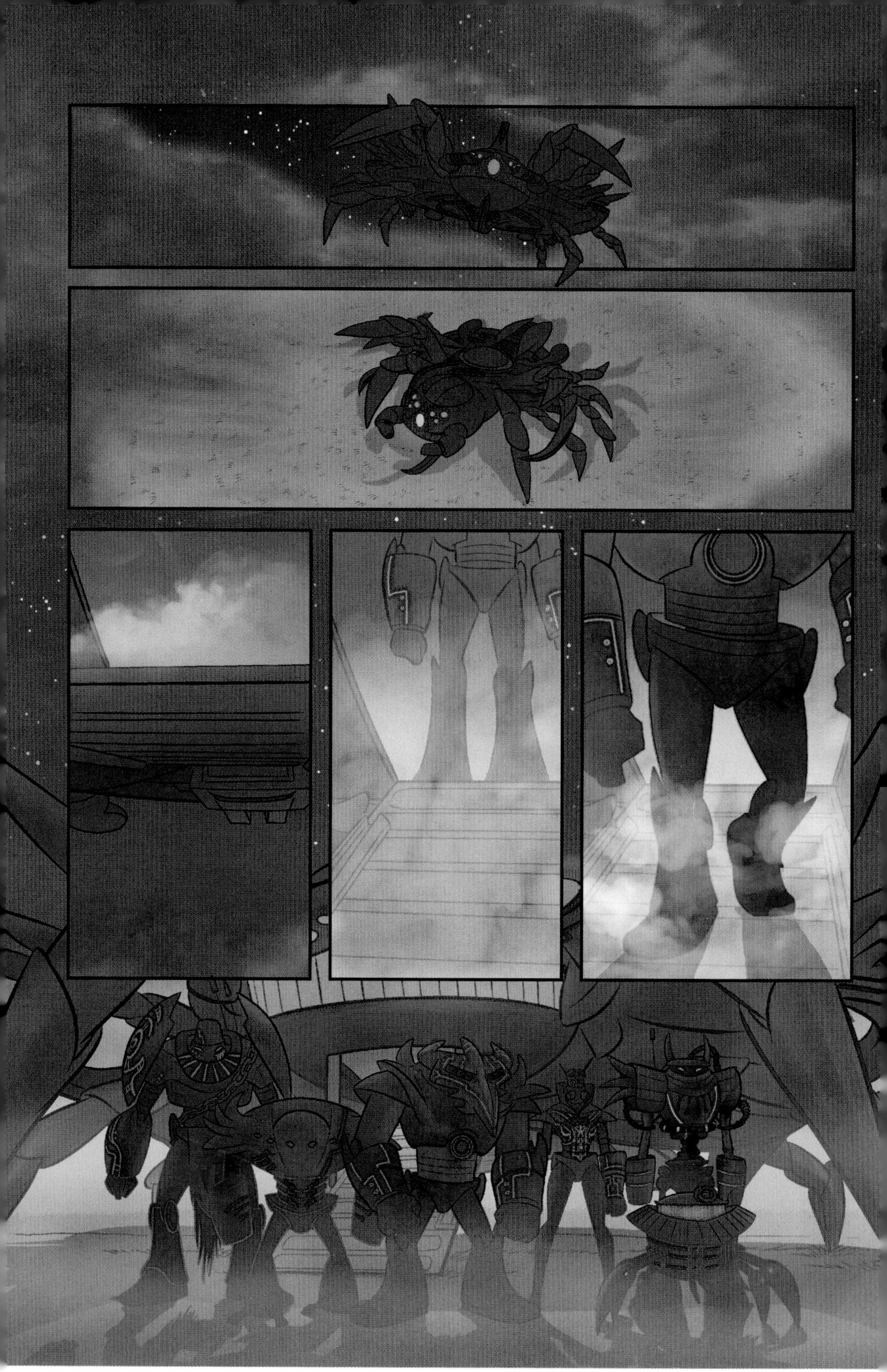

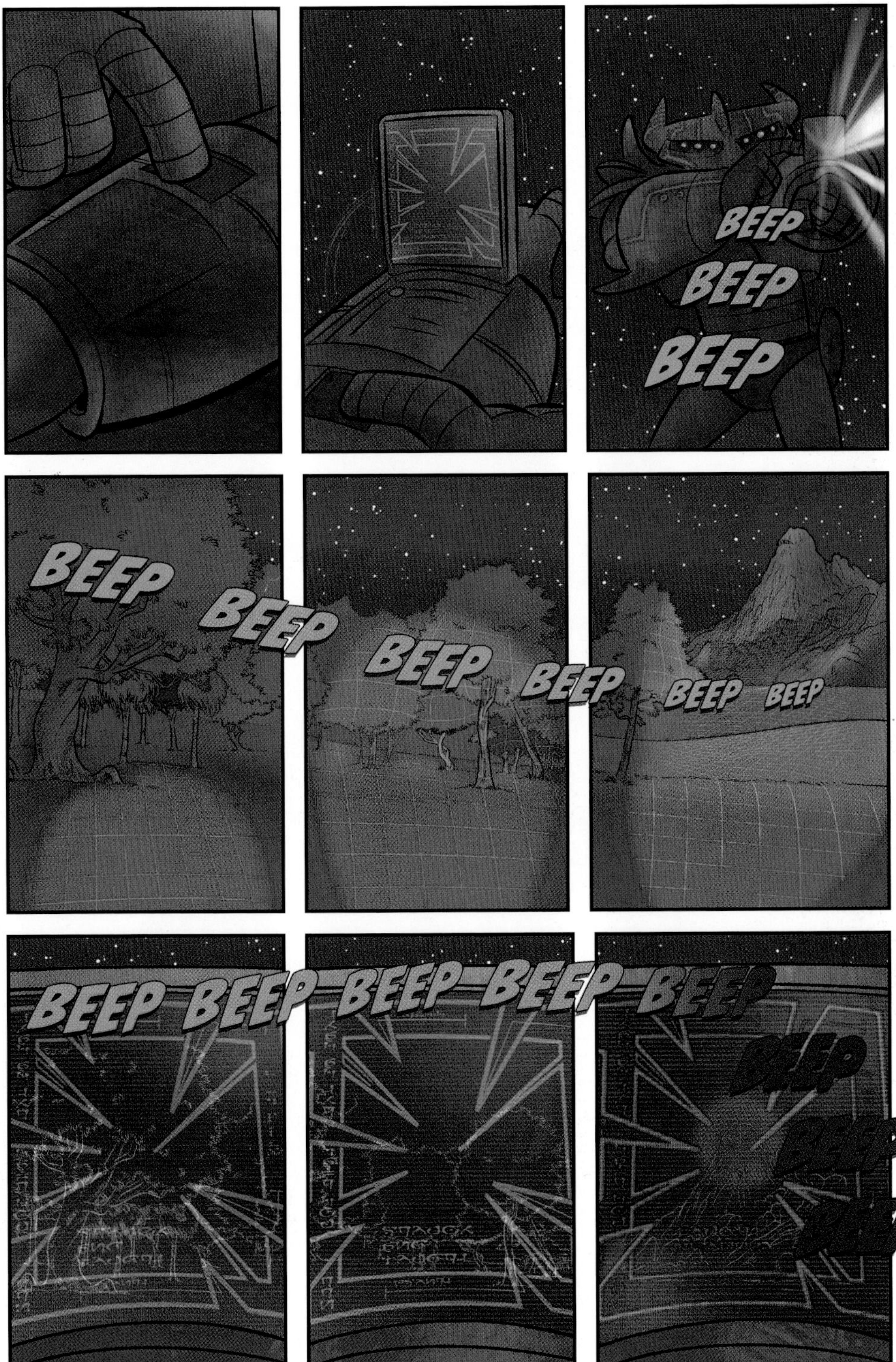
BEEP
BEEP
BEEP
BEEP
BEEP
BEEP
BEEP
BEEP
BEEP
BEEP
BEEP
BEEP
BEEP
BEEP

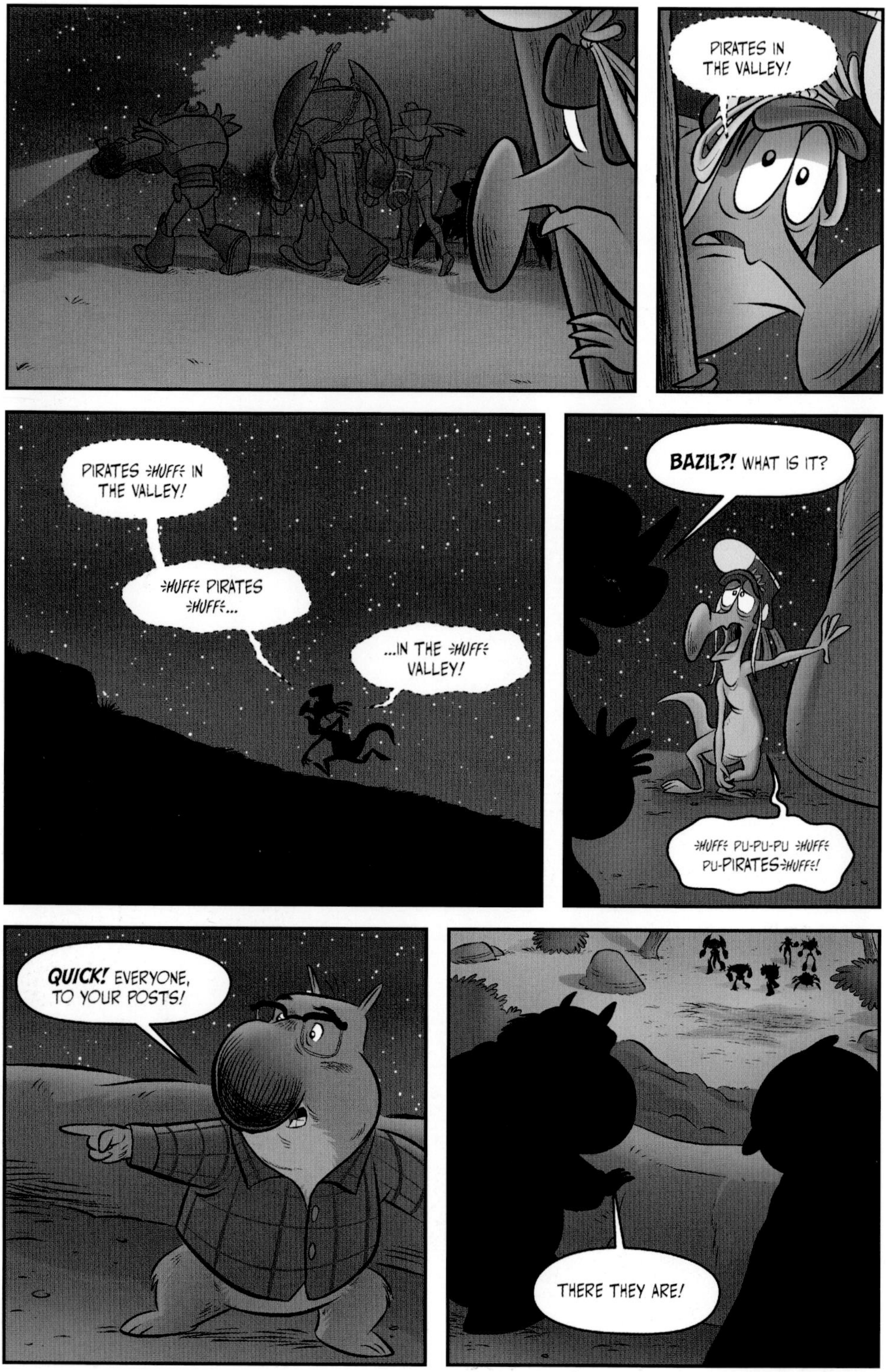
PIRATES IN THE VALLEY!
PIRATES ≠HUFF≠ IN THE VALLEY!
≠HUFF≠ PIRATES ≠HUFF≠...
...IN THE ≠HUFF≠ VALLEY!
BAZIL?! WHAT IS IT?
≠HUFF≠ PU-PU-PU ≠HUFF≠ PU-PIRATES≠HUFF≠!
QUICK! EVERYONE, TO YOUR POSTS!
THERE THEY ARE!

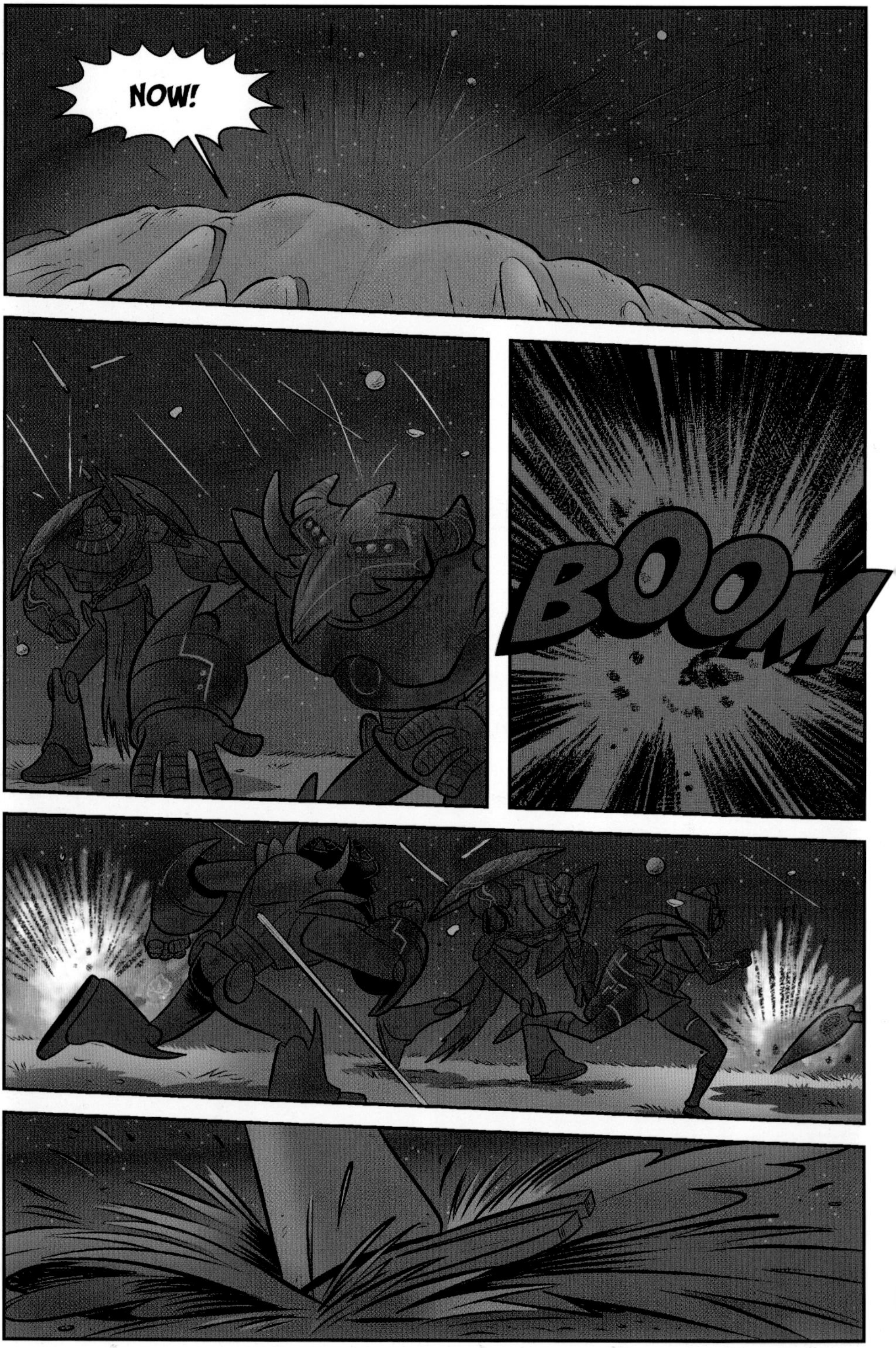
NOW!
BOOM

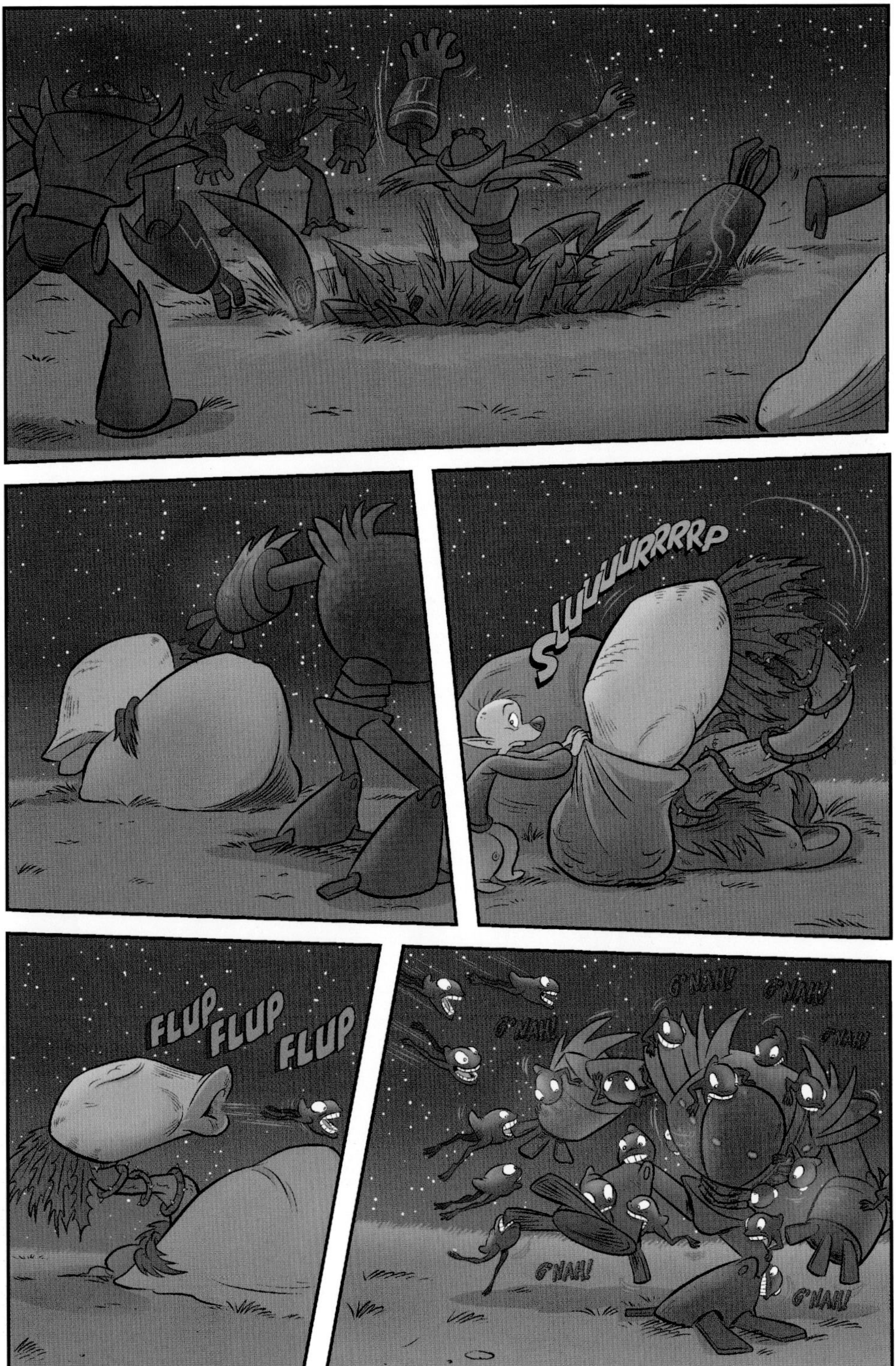
SLUUUURRRRP
FLUP
FLUP
FLUP
G'NAH!
G'NAH!
G'NAH!
G'NAH!
G'NAH!
G'NAH!

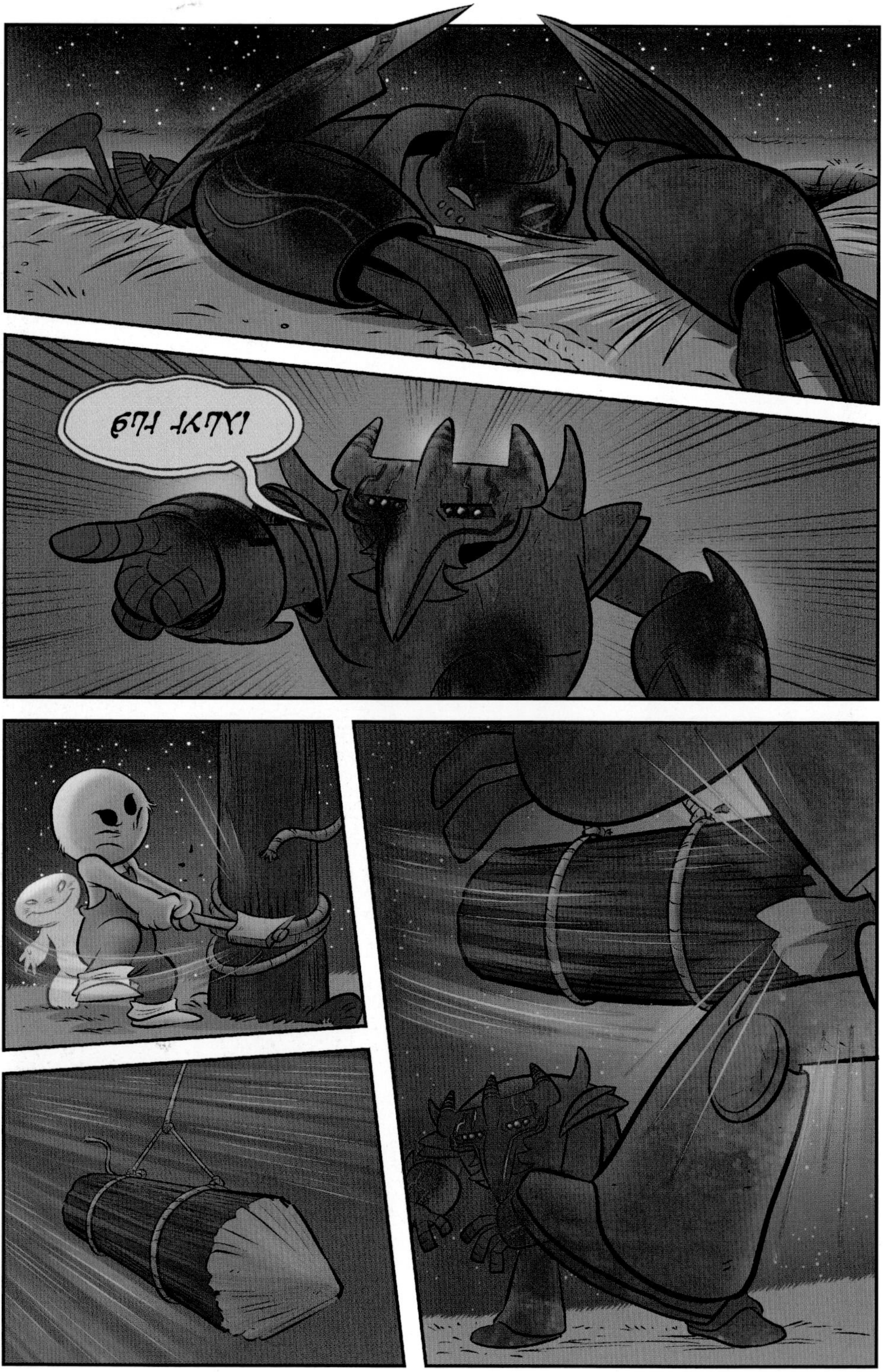

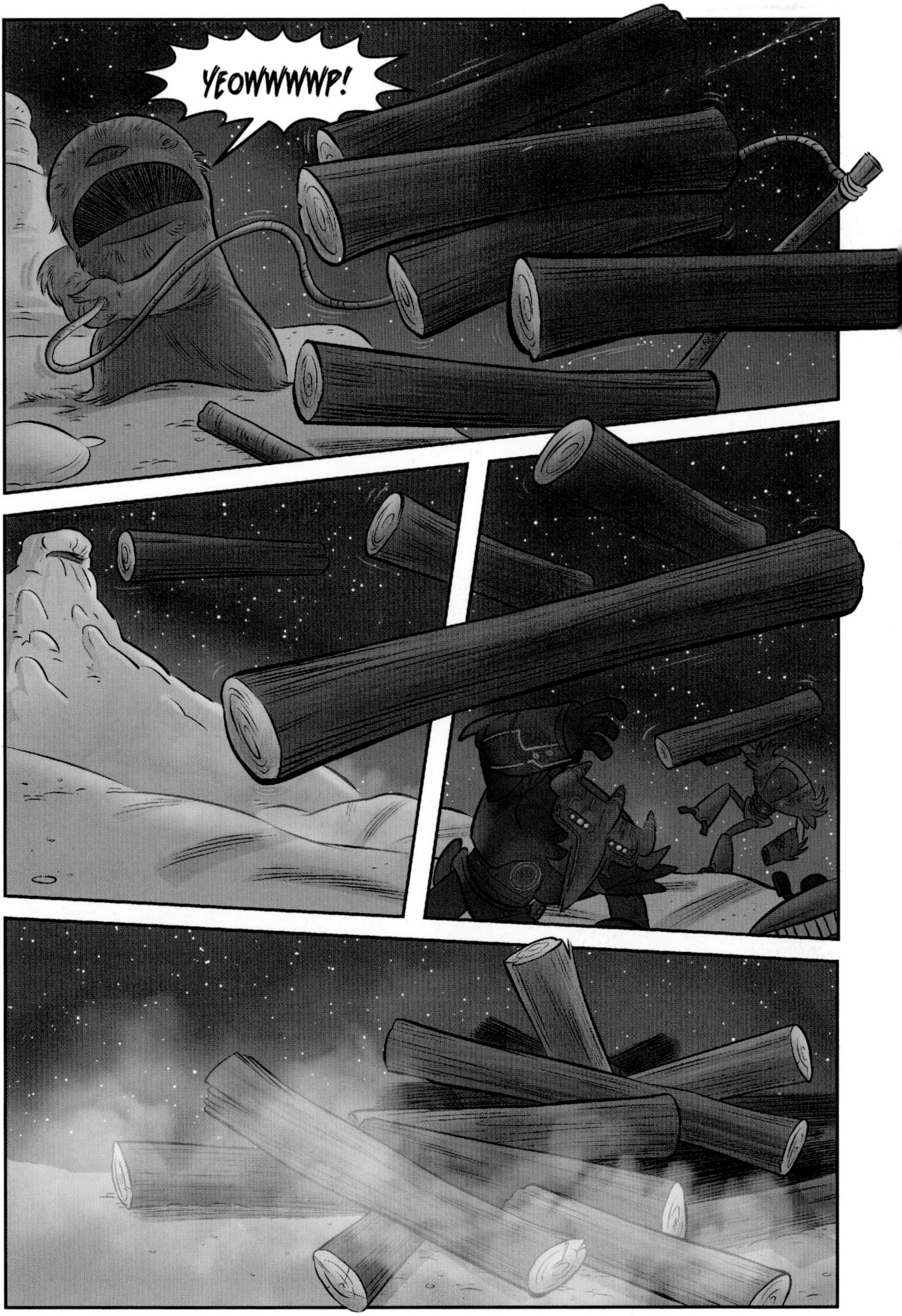
YEOWWWWP!

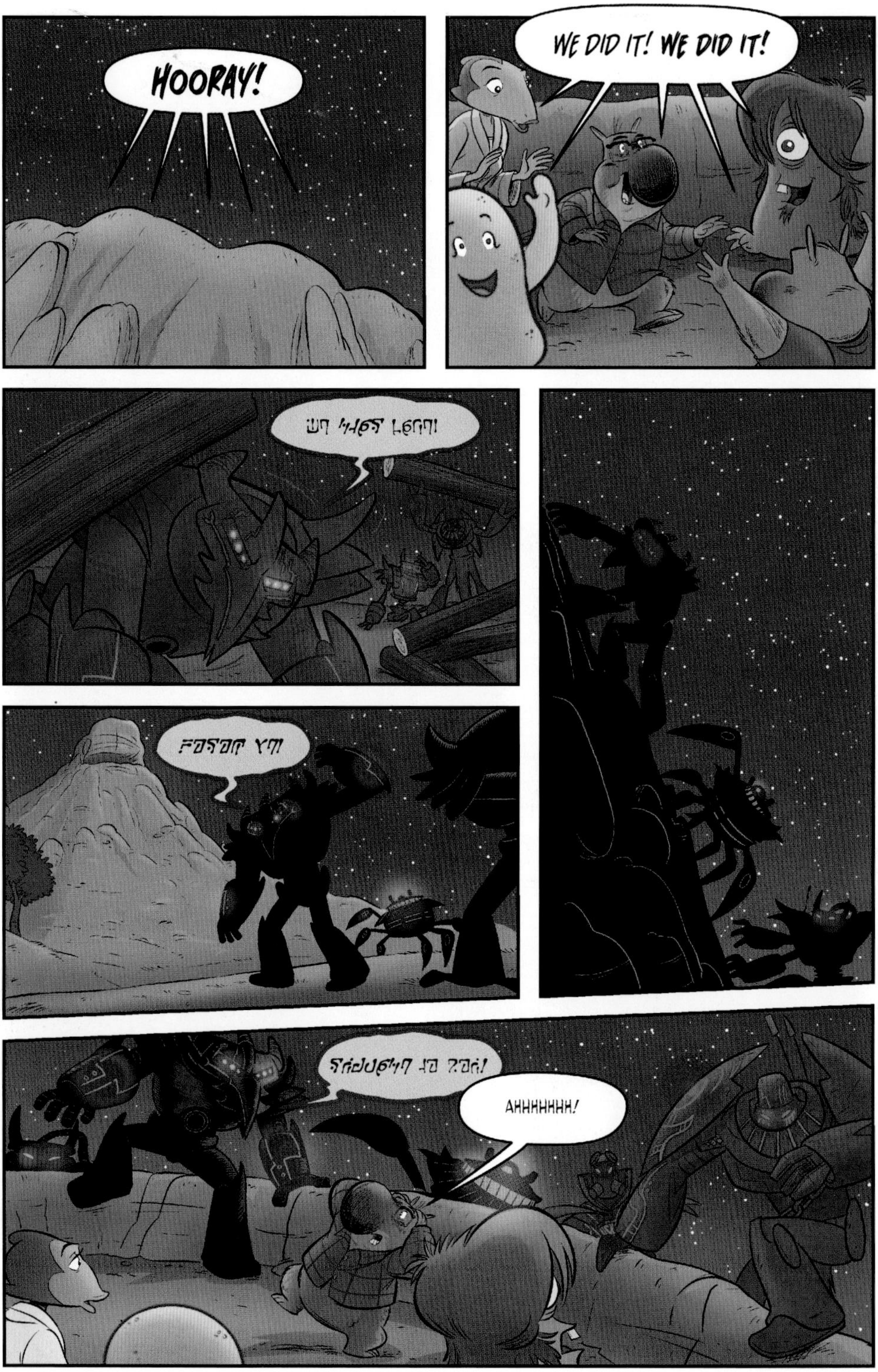
HOORAY!
WE DID IT! WE DID IT!
AHHHHHHH!

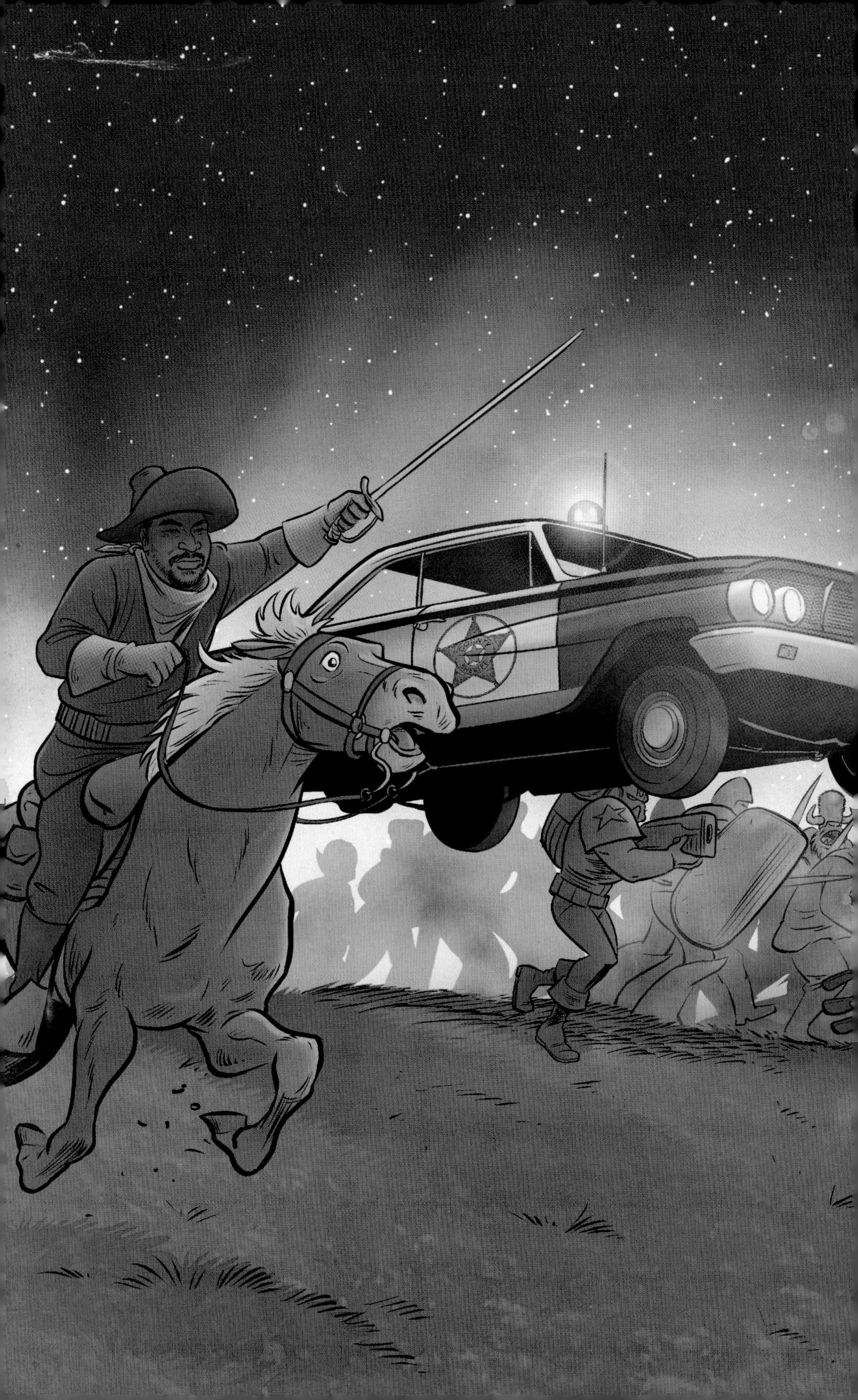
COUNTY
SHERIFF

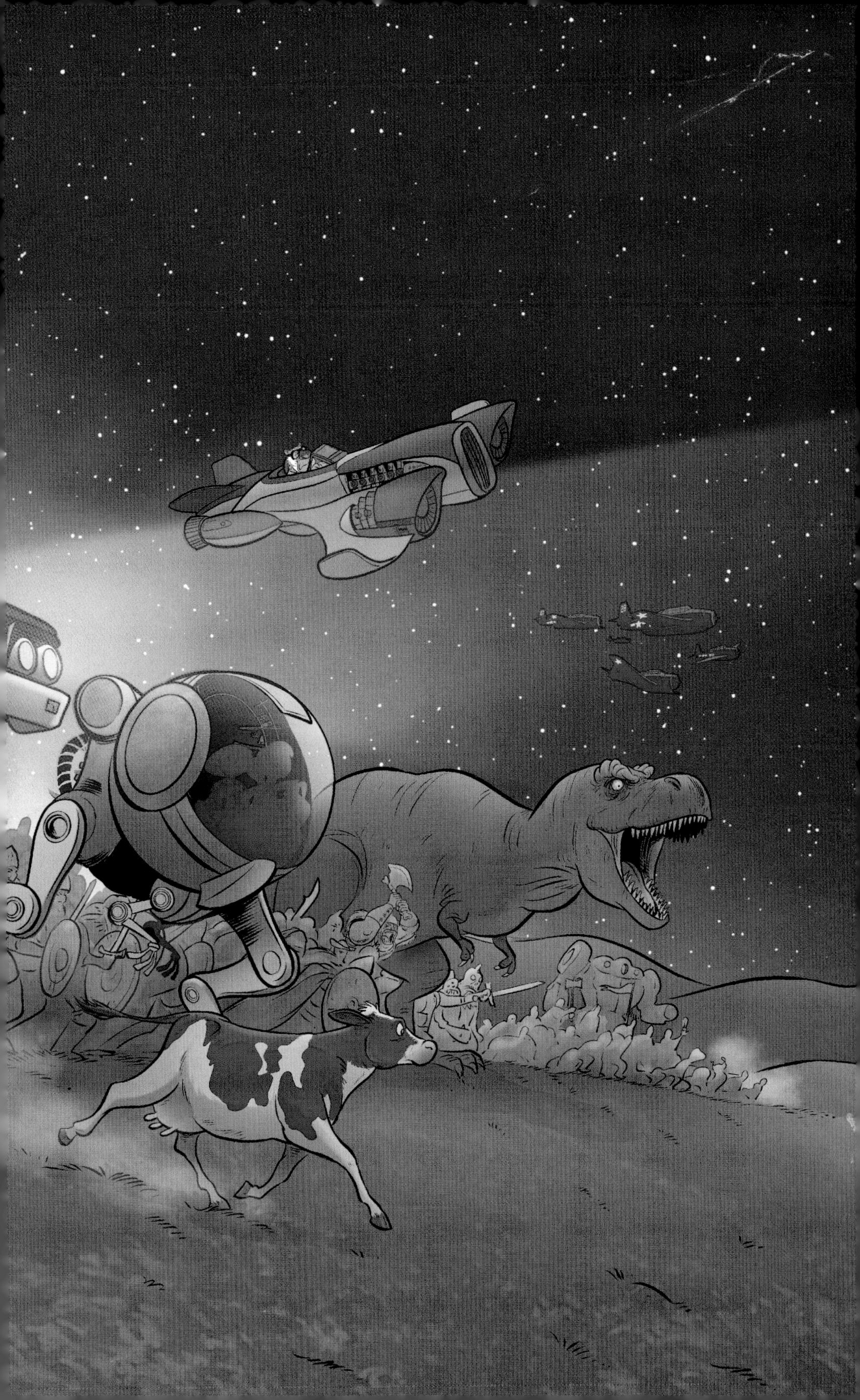

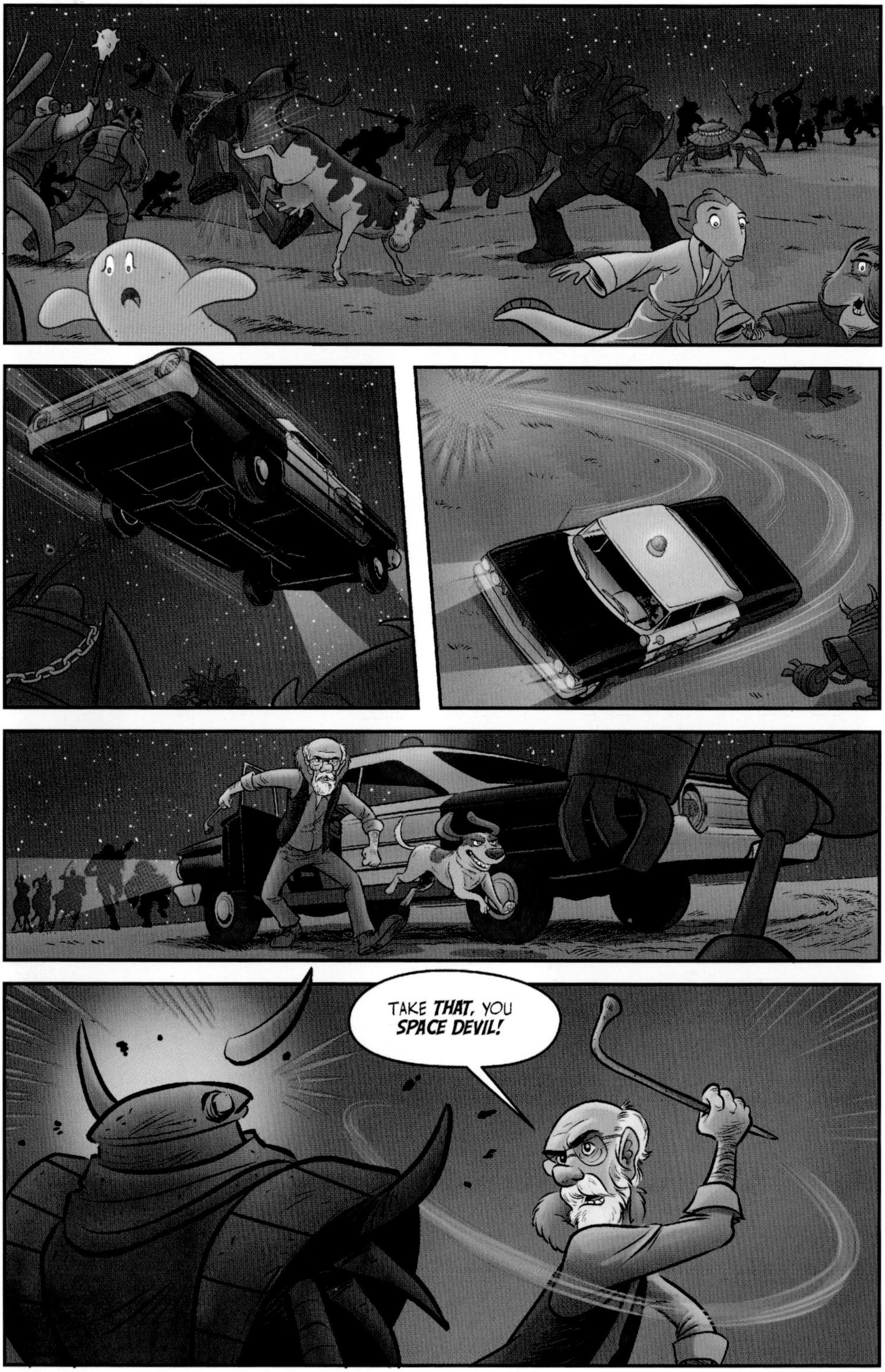
TAKE THAT, YOU SPACE DEVIL!

165

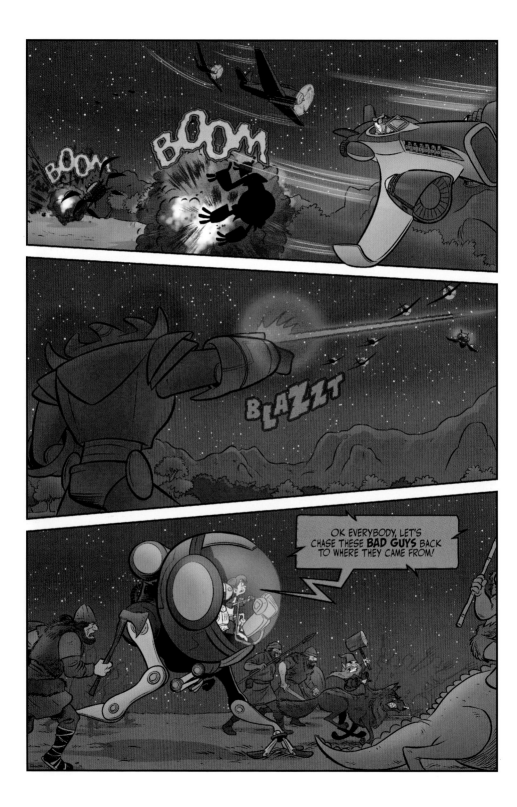

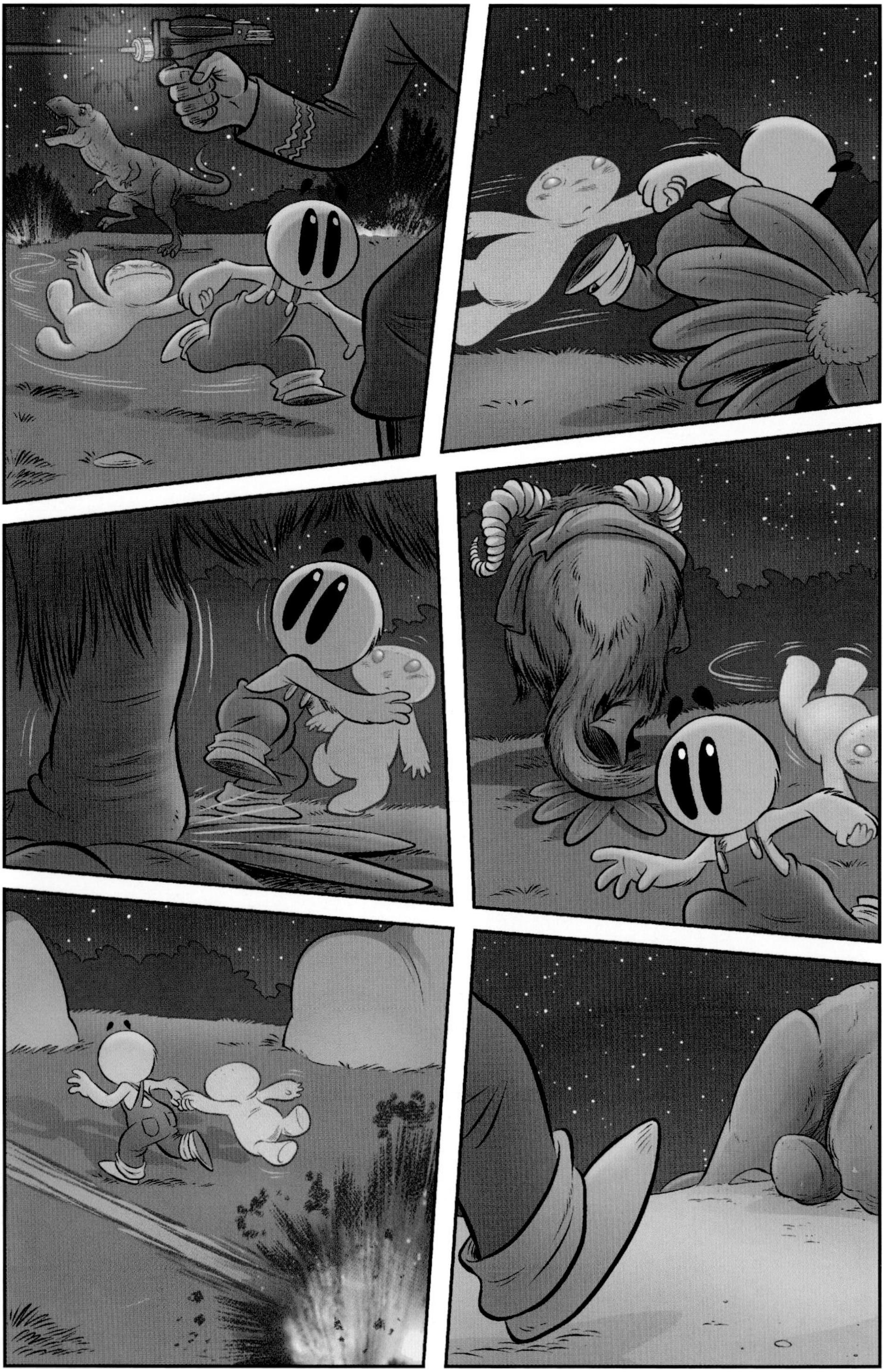

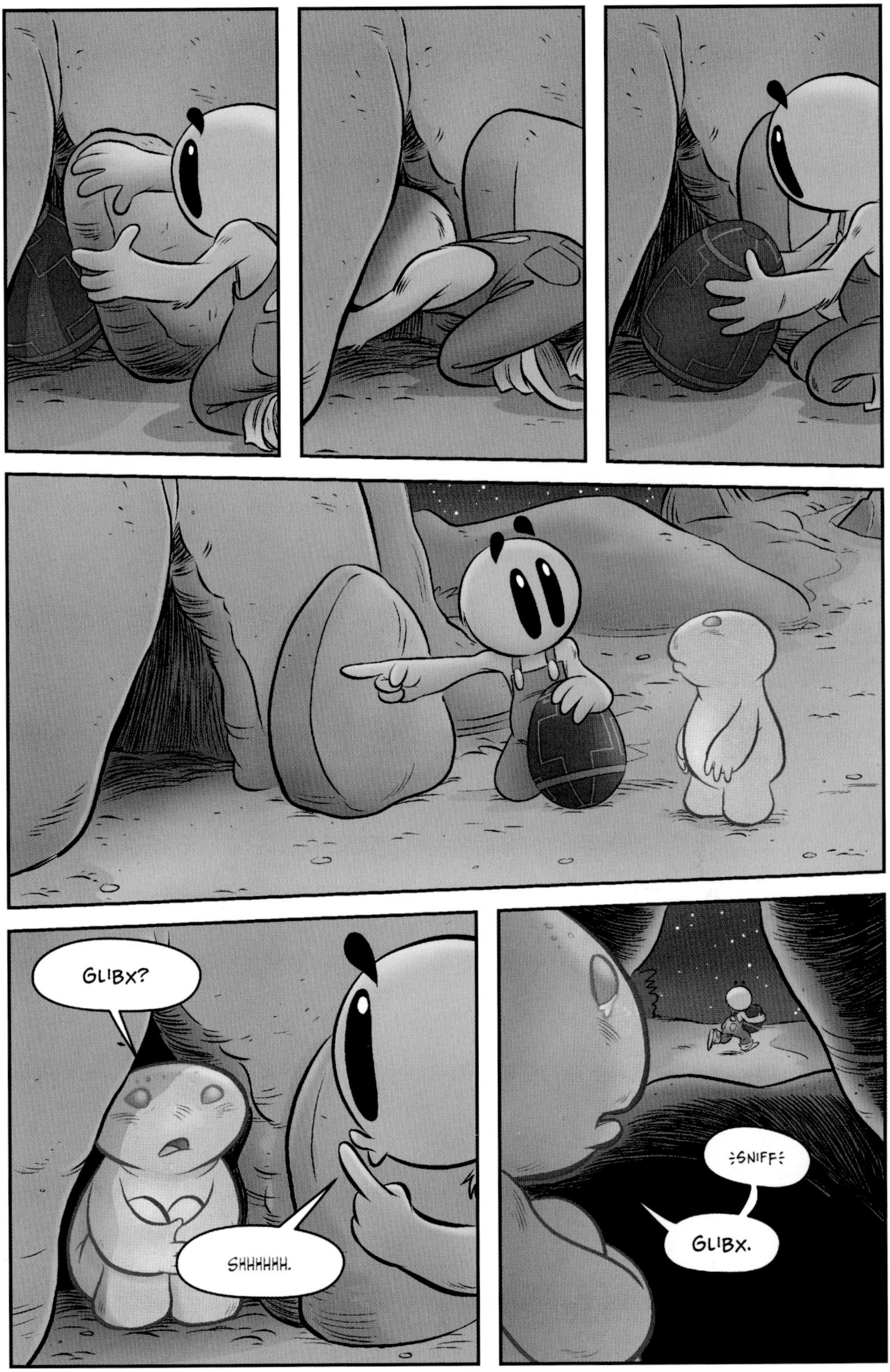
GLIBX?
SHHHHHH.
SNIFF
GLIBX.

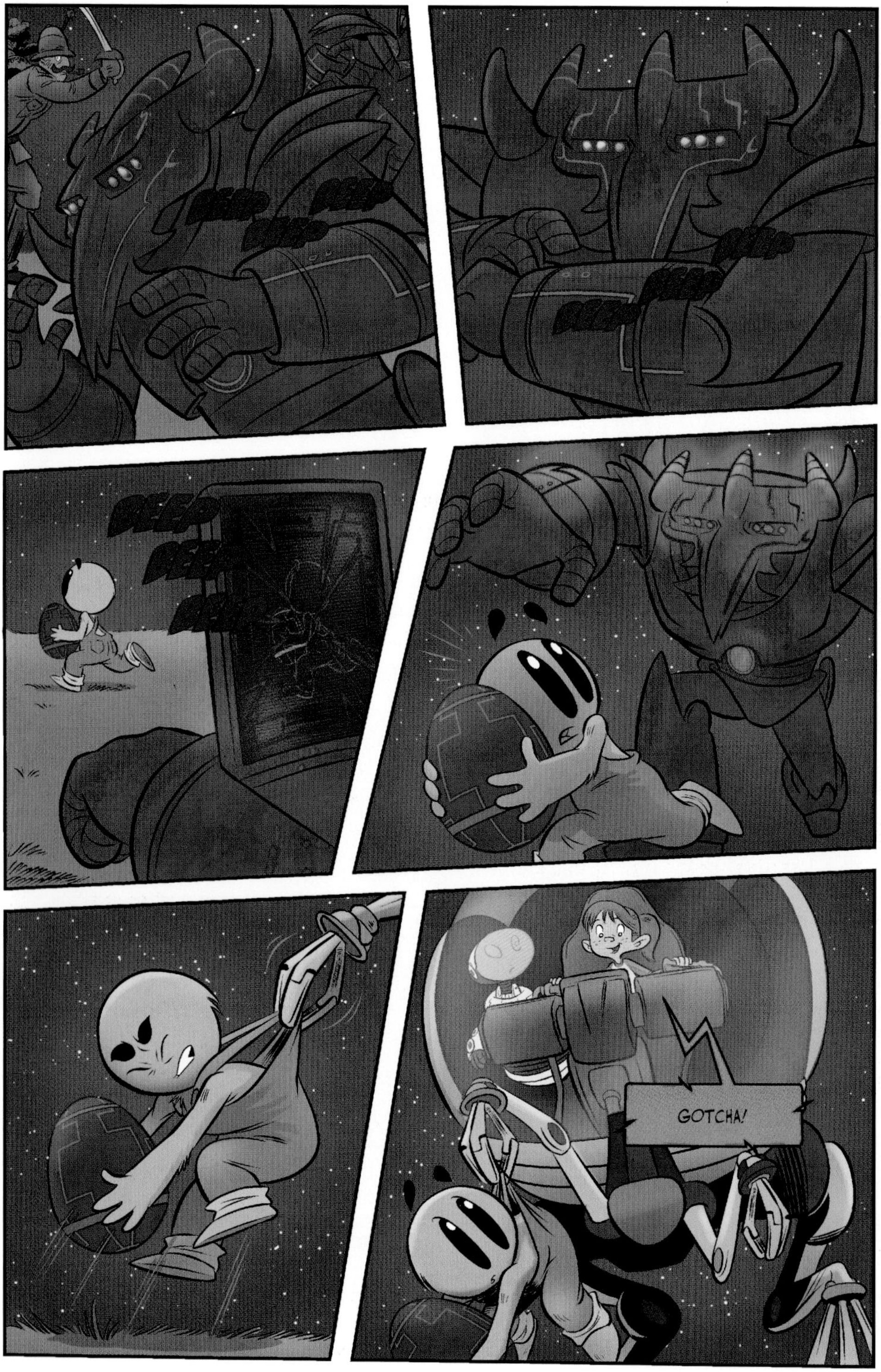
GOTCHA!

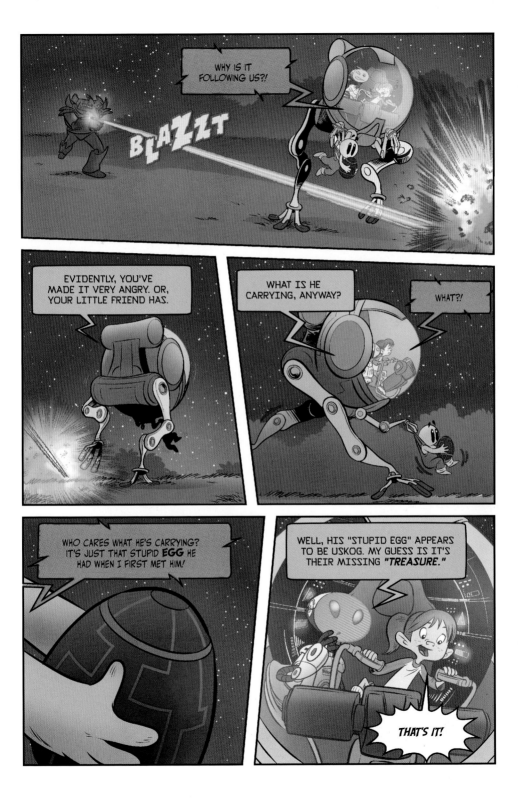

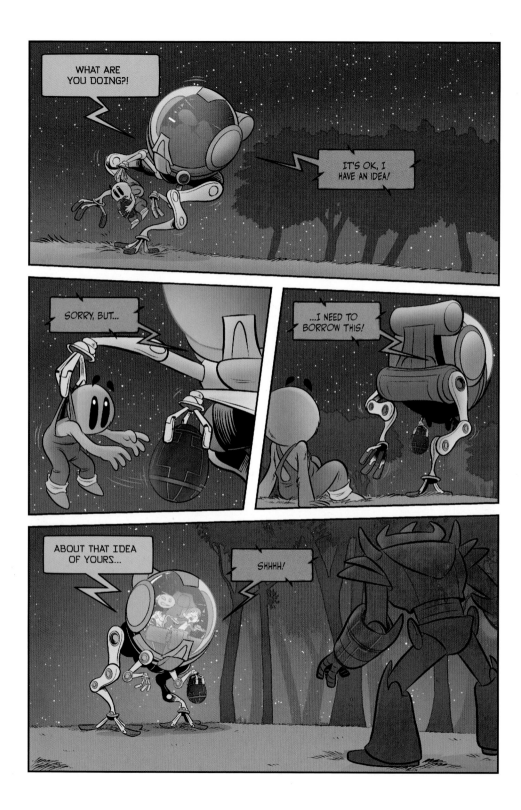

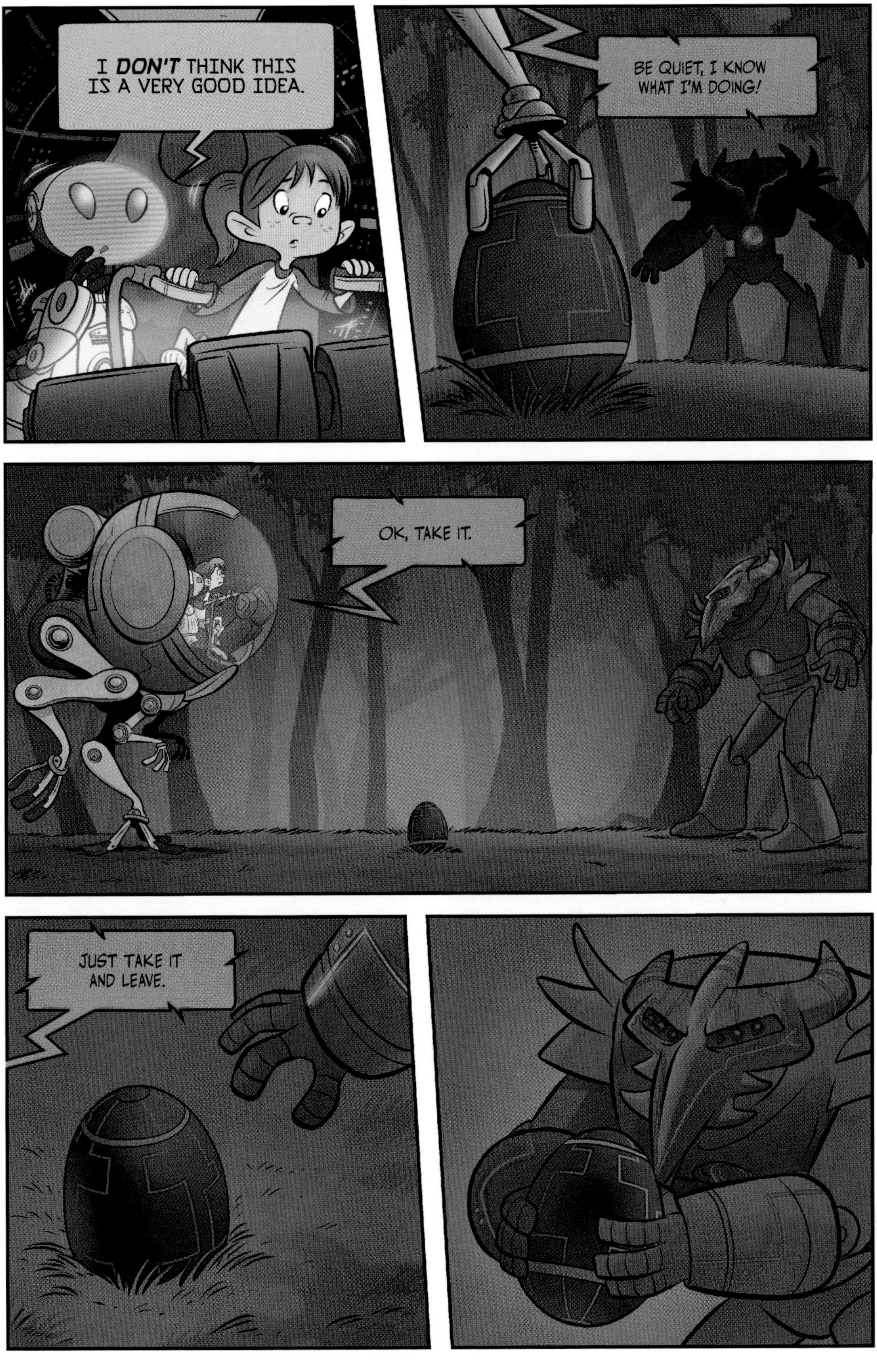
I DON'T THINK THIS IS A VERY GOOD IDEA.
BE QUIET, I KNOW WHAT I'M DOING!
OK, TAKE IT.
JUST TAKE IT AND LEAVE.

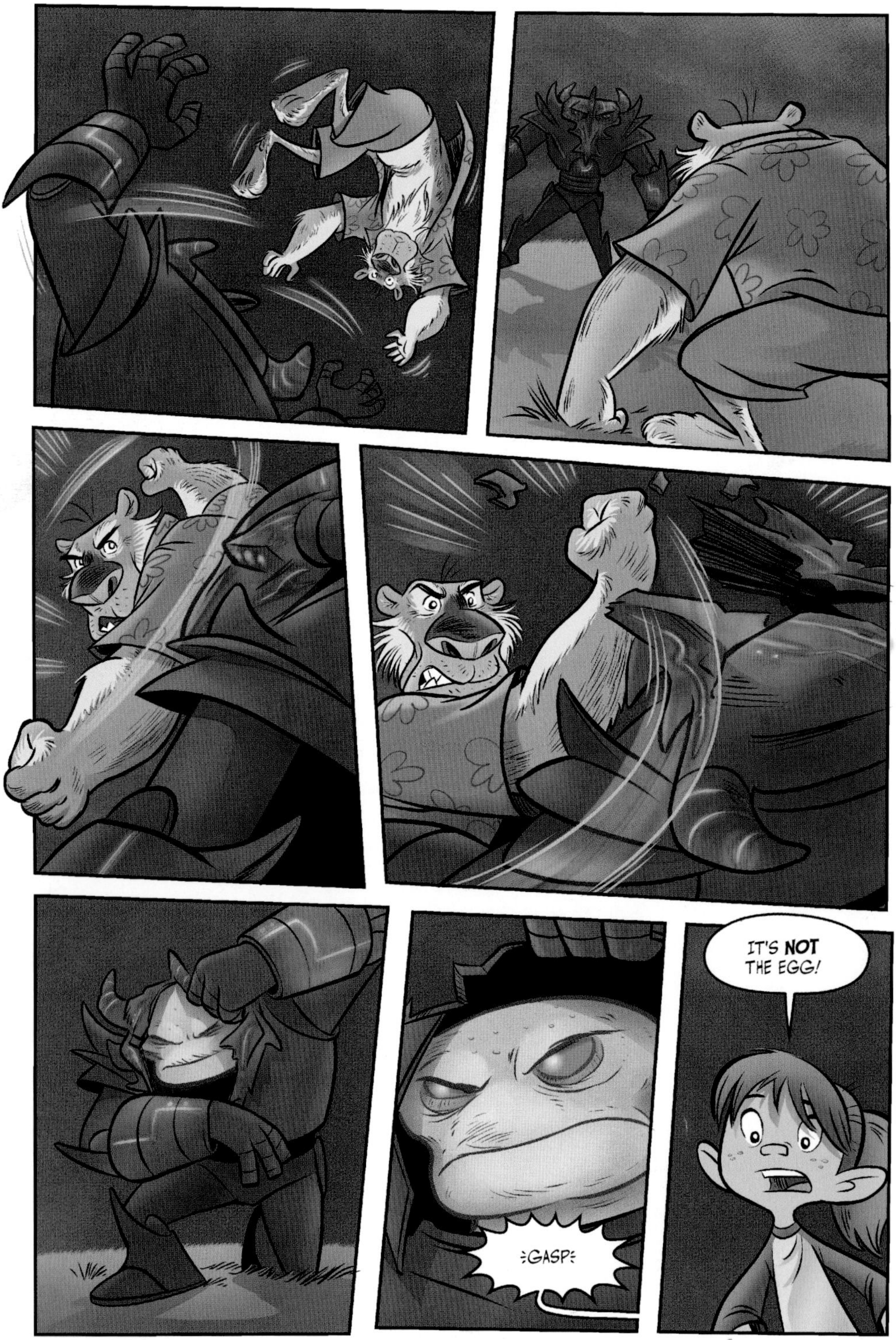
IT'S **NOT** THE EGG!
GASP

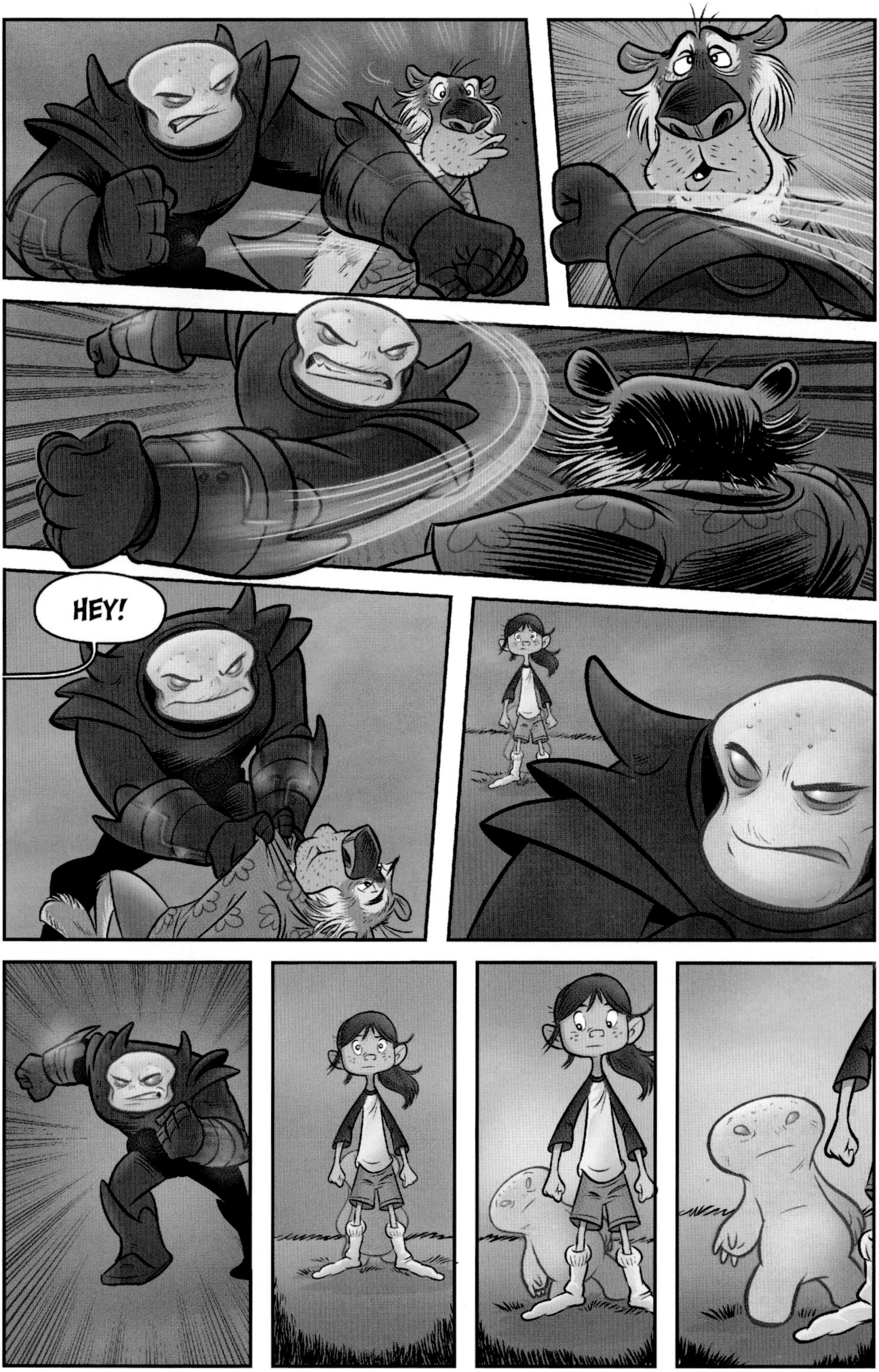
HEY!

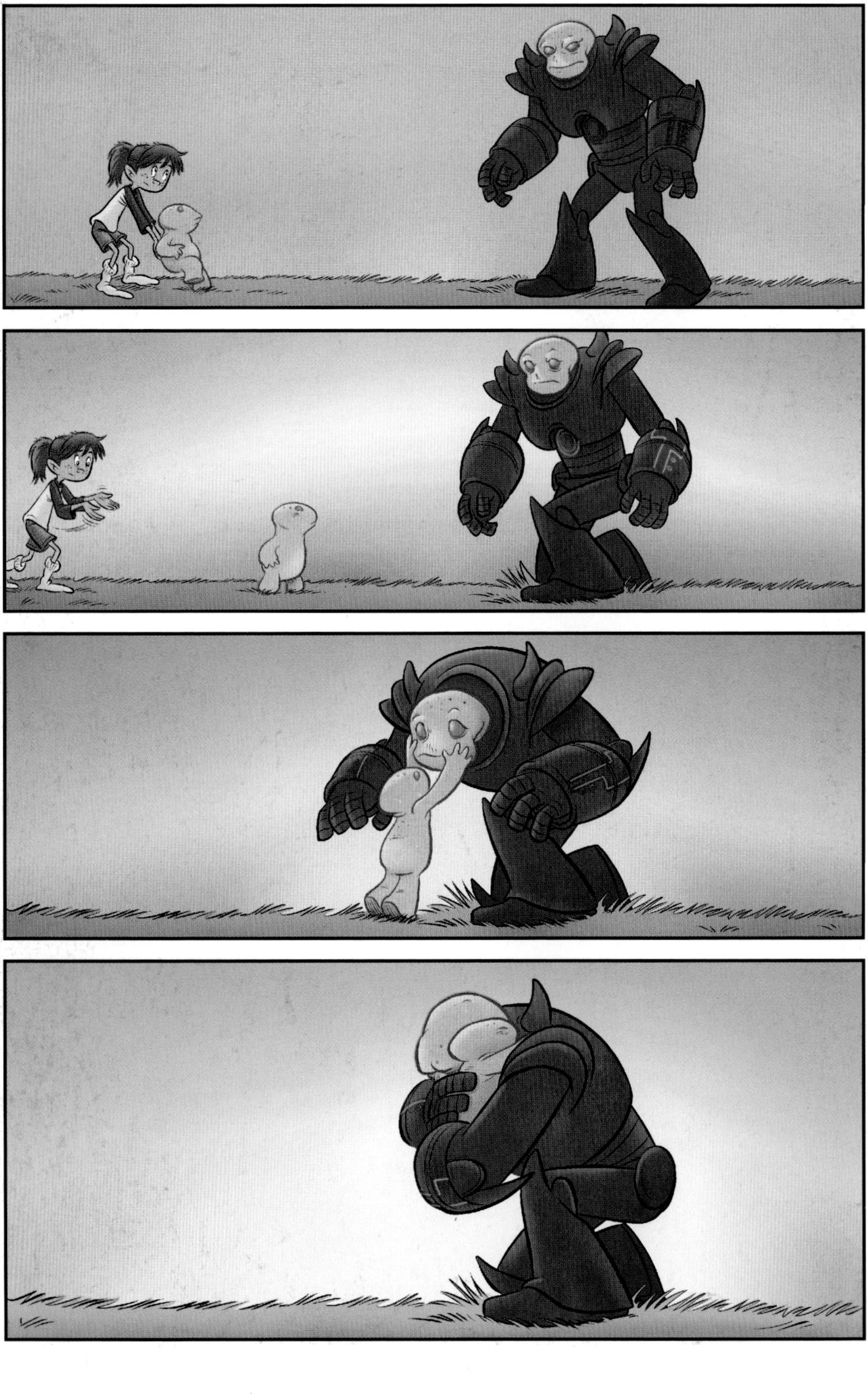

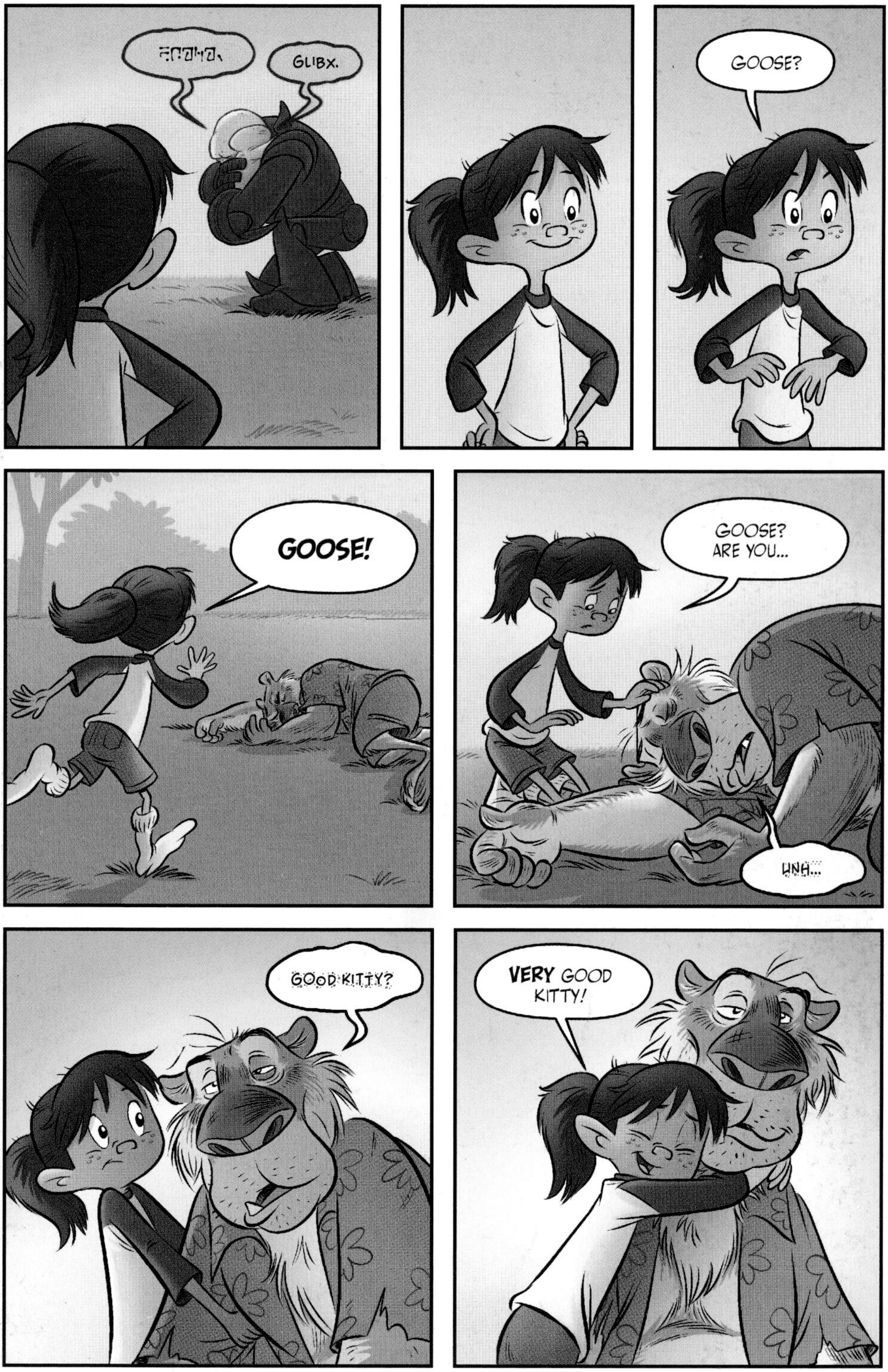
GLIBX.
GOOSE?
GOOSE!
GOOSE? ARE YOU...
UNH...
GOOD KITTY?
VERY GOOD KITTY!

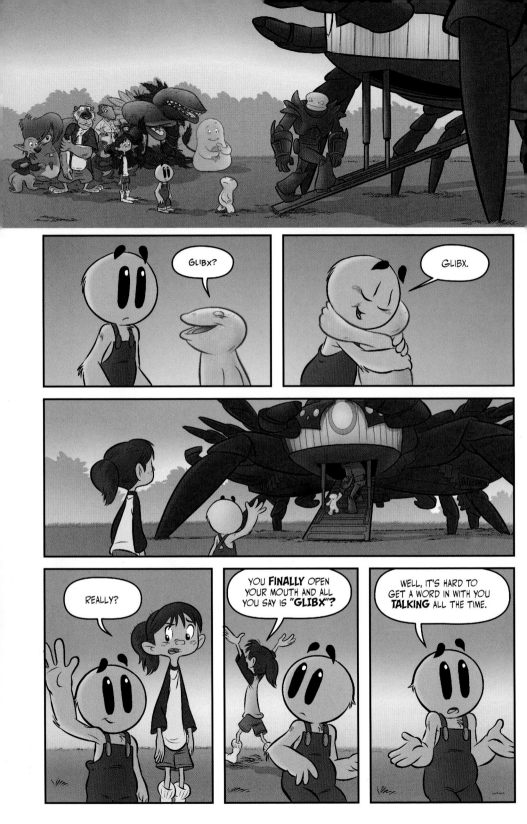

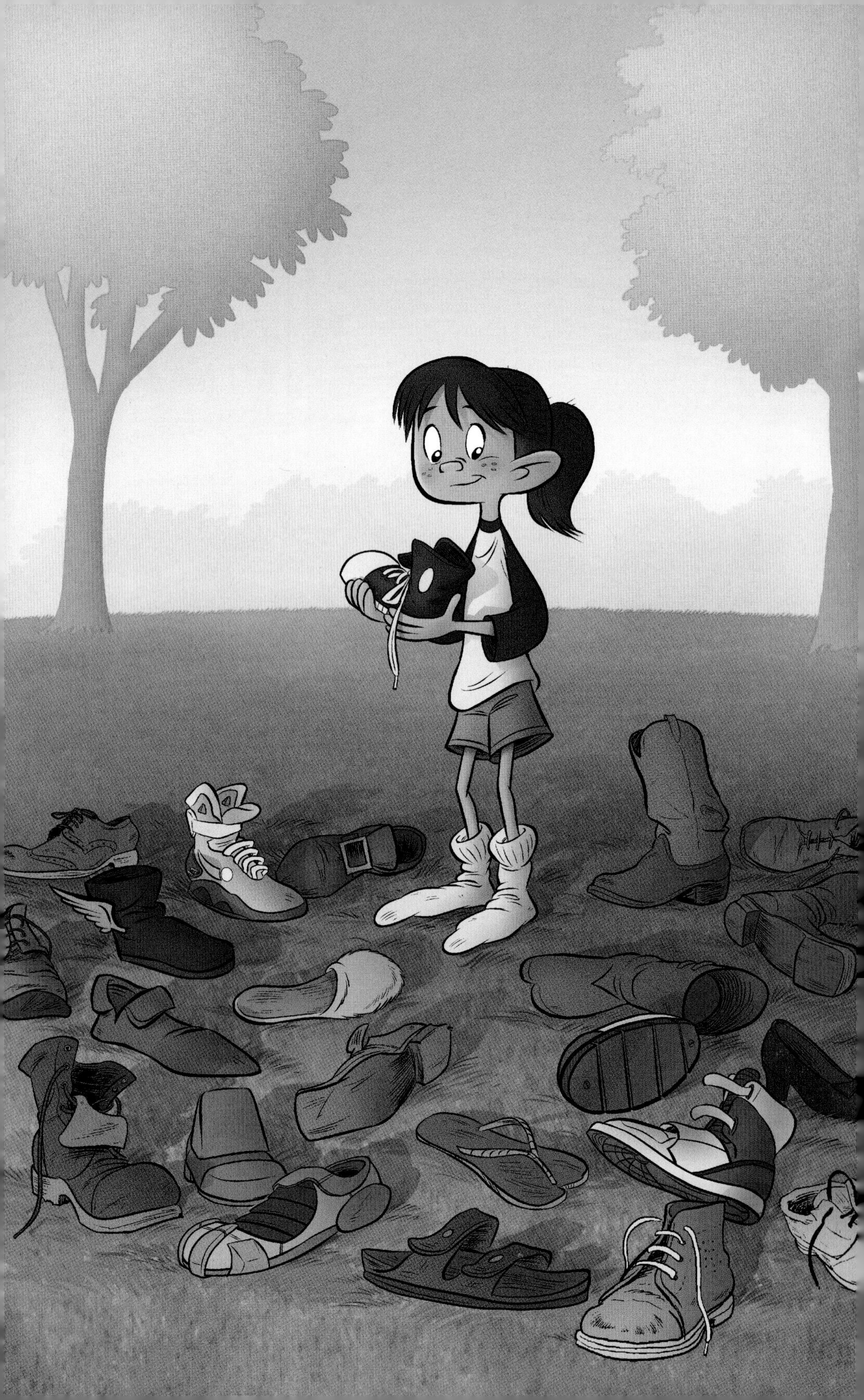

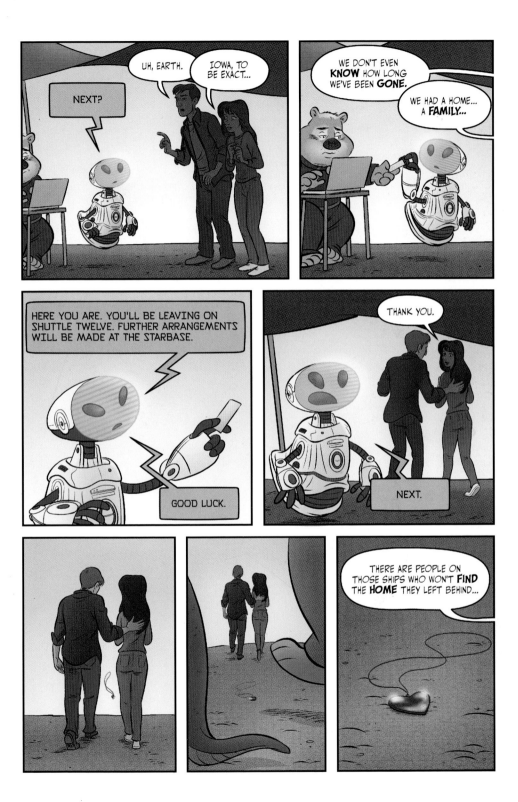

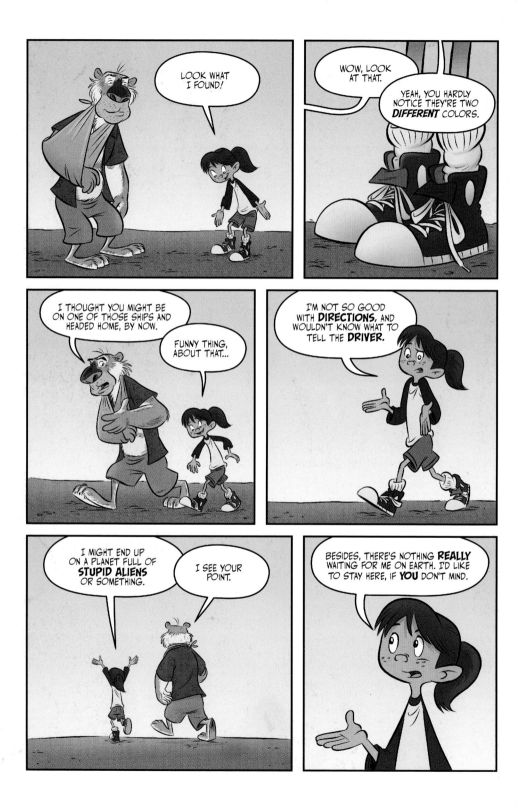

THE ADVENTURE CONTINUES IN *RED'S PLANET* BOOK THREE

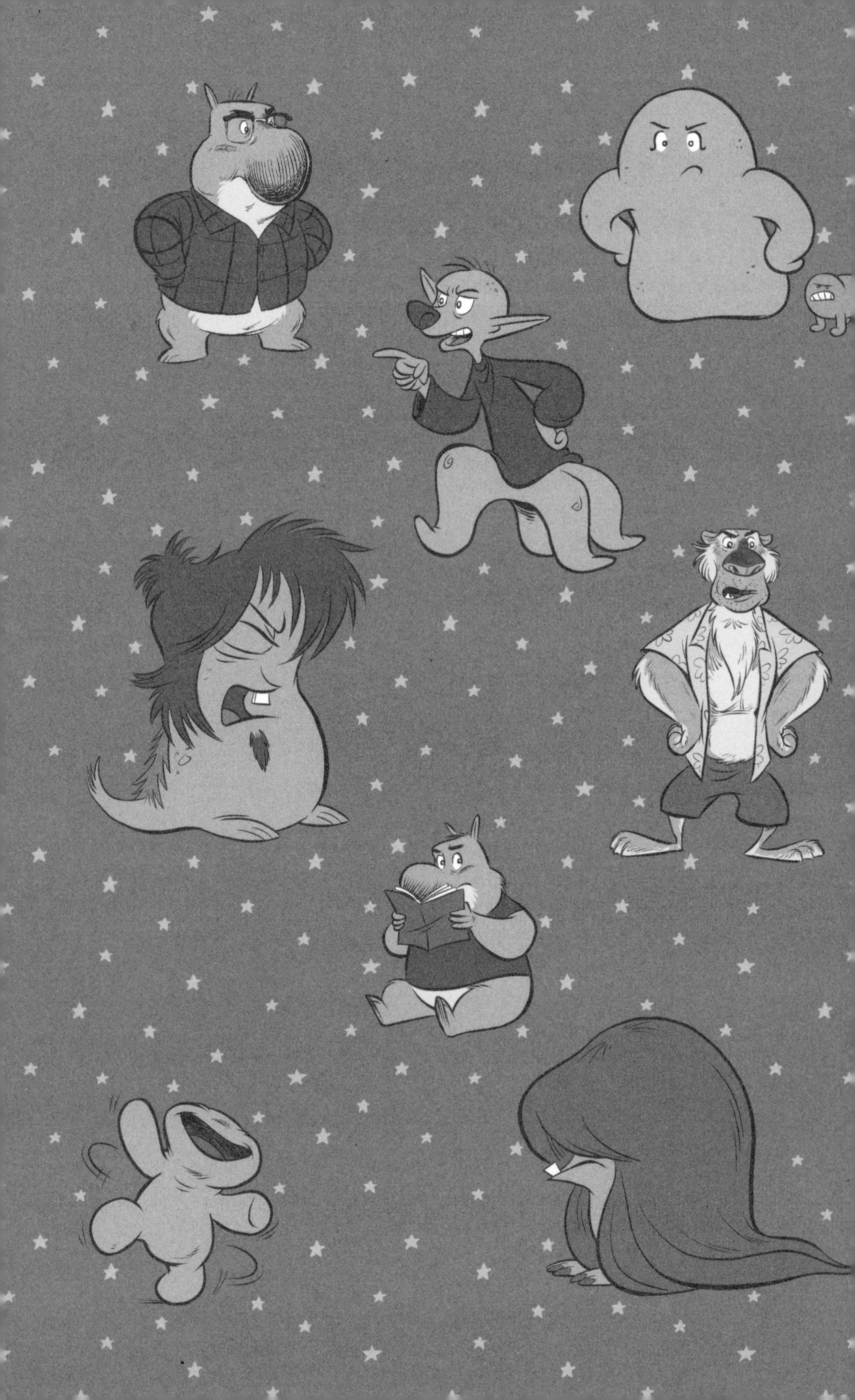